I0653688

BOILING POINT

JERRY HATCHETT

RED
HOUSE
PUBLISHING

This is a work of fiction. Names, characters, businesses, places, events, locales, and incidents are either the products of the author's imagination or used in a fictitious manner. Any resemblance to actual persons, living or dead, or actual events is purely coincidental.

ISBN for Generic Ebook (non-Amazon)

978-1-952088-00-1

ISBN for Print Edition

978-1-952088-01-8

© 2020 Jerry Hatchett, All Rights Reserved

FROM THE AUTHOR

THIS IS a re-titled and re-covered edition that was previously released under the name Fake News. The title caused a lot of confusion, with many assuming it was a non-fiction book instead of the novel it is. If you have already purchased Fake News, feel free to return this immediately for a refund.

(If you purchased Fake News in Kindle format, Amazon will soon be pushing out this new version as an update. Sync your reader to convert the old version to this one.)

With all that said, let's get started on this thrill ride!

JERRY

PROLOGUE

Produced

I READ THE DOCUMENT AGAIN. Tried to wrap my head around the ramifications. The "reliability indicator" of 100% left no doubt. I flipped to the next page, to the bottom where the dates were printed. Checked them against the calendar in my head. I couldn't do anything for ten days. After that, I'd have two days to act. I folded the papers and slipped them into the hip pocket of my jeans, then walked to the barn. Opened the door to Johnny's stall. He gave a happy snort and followed me out through the barn's breezeway and to the spot where he received his daily brushing.

Ten minutes later I watched a car make its way up my long gravel drive, dust puffing up from the rear of the sedan. The car parked, its engine shut off, and the driver's door opened. A man stepped out. What in the actual hell?

BARTHOLOMEW PITT WAS the last person on Earth I wanted to see, but here he stood, an unwelcome blast from the past. I finished brushing Johnny and gave him a pat on the haunch to signal we were done. He snuffled and headed for the flake of hay I'd laid out for him.

"Why are you here?"

"Need your help," Pitt said.

"Not interested."

"You will be." He handed me an iPad with a video paused on the screen. "Hit play."

I touched the play icon and a surveillance video began playing. It was night footage and the camera had been running in infrared mode, resulting in grainy black-and-white imagery showing the inside of a large garage, four cars wide, the stalls populated with three cars and one SUV. After a moment, a figure walked into view, coming from behind the camera, passing under it, then moving in front of it, back to the camera.

The figure was tall, obviously a man. Dressed in dark clothes head to toe, including a balaclava over his head. Slung over his shoulder in a fireman's carry was another man wearing only boxer shorts, his body limp. The man carrying him moved with ease, showing no signs of strain as he walked away from the camera. He walked to the SUV, opened the rear hatch, and placed the unconscious (or dead) man into the cargo area. He closed the hatch, then walked to the driver's door, opened it, got inside.

I dragged the play indicator back to where the man had first come into view and watched the footage again, this time paying particular attention to the man's gait. It was unique. Plodding. Almost mechanical.

I looked up at Pitt. "Oh, good hell, no. It can't be."

"It's him," Pitt said. "You know it is."

I looked at the screen. Watched the sequence again. Wanted to tell Pitt he was wrong. I could not.

IRAQ

Years Earlier

YOU COULD BARELY EVEN CALL it a village. More of a dusty pimple on Earth's ass. Sol and I approached under the cover of desert darkness, bringing us toward the cluster of dilapidated concrete buildings at a catty-corner angle.

Most of the guys called my partner Terminator because of his odd walk but that was too cheesy for me. I stuck with Sol, short for Solomon. We pulled our night-vision goggles down and studied the scene from thirty yards out, both of us crouched behind a burnt-out Toyota pickup.

Our intel said that Muhammed Al Wahari was in the building directly ahead of us, the one on the corner of the cluster. Al Wahari was an asshole in the first degree, a guy who made IEDs that had killed far too many American and allied soldiers. Our orders were to capture him alive and take him to a rendezvous point a few klicks away, where he would be transferred to a team of crack interrogators. Straightforward enough.

The sticky part was that we were to extract him as quietly as possible, hopefully without collateral damage, but in any case leaving no witnesses who could spread the word that he had been captured. And this is why I was partnered up with Sol on this mission: He was older than me, a seasoned player in this game. He was also known as the sneakiest, stealthiest guy in the BAM squad, a By Any Means black agency that existed nowhere on paper, its handful of operators deployed where needed by the agency's shady head, Bartholomew Pitt. If there was a way to do this without killing civilians, Sol would be the key and I was fine with playing second to his lead on this one, even though we'd never worked together in the field before.

Electricity to this area had been knocked out long ago, so the only lights in the buildings ahead came from candles and lanterns, or battery-powered lights. The target building was completely dark except for the faintest flicker in a second-floor glassless window. Too faint for the light source to be in the outer room with the window.

"What do you think?" I said.

"He's there," Sol said. "I feel it."

"Interior room?"

"Yeah."

"How you want to play it?"

"Right through the front door and up the stairs. Side by side. I'll use the trank gun on anybody we meet, but if they make so much as a whimper after I pop 'em, you end them. You're suppressed, right?"

I unholstered my Glock 19, pulled the suppressor from my vest, threaded it onto the barrel. "Yup."

"Let's do it."

We crouch-ran across the dusty street, backed up against the building on either side of the doorless opening that led into the building. Sol gave a 3-2-1 countdown with his fingers and we eased inside. A concrete stairway lay directly ahead, leading to a landing above and then a switchback flight on up to the second floor. Closed doors to our left and right.

We were two steps up the stairway when I caught a blur of movement on the landing above us. I heard the *phhhtt* sound of Sol's trank gun by the time I'd ID'd the movement as a cat. The dart hit it in the neck and it fell without a sound.

At the landing, we did a quick reconnoiter of the second flight of steps, then moved quietly up. Three steps from the top, we stopped. At the top were three openings. Apparently doors were in short supply since we had yet to encounter one. Straight ahead was the outer room. The left room was dark. The room on the right was flickering with what was obviously candlelight and we could hear quiet voices.

I looked over at Sol and he was looking at his watch. He held a hand up. We waited. After a couple minutes frozen in place, the conversation in the room stopped and we could hear soft scuffling and rustling. Some muted thuds. Then the unmistakable sound of Islamic prayers. I looked back to Sol. He winked and nodded, we flipped our goggles up, then crept up the last two steps.

With him on the left and me on the right, we entered the room, him with his trank gun, me with my Glock, both up and ready. We were looking at five asses, all men, as they bowed on prayer rugs, chanting, facing the other direction. At a speed that looked like something from a competition for The World's Fastest Gunman, Sol fired trank darts into the buttocks of all five. The darts were strong and quick, and we heard nothing from any of them other than soft grunts and moans as they sagged into unconsciousness.

Now we moved quickly, rolling the men over to expose their faces. Bingo. The one in the middle of the row was Al Wahari. Sol bent over, grabbed a handful of hair and ass, and threw him over his shoulder in a fireman's carry. He gestured with a nod to the others on the floor and whispered, "Take care of these?"

I nodded and put a quiet bullet into the forehead of each of the four, then dragged them to a corner of the room that wasn't visible from outside the room. After collecting and bagging everything from their pockets, including a couple cell phones, three handguns, and two knives, I piled them up and threw their prayer rugs on top of them. A quick look around for anything else of interest in the room came up empty.

On the way down, I led the way, Sol right behind me. We made it back to the ground floor without incident, checked the street outside, then hustled back across the open ground and ducked down behind the Toyota. Sol dumped Al Wahari on the ground.

"Good catch on the prayer timing," I said.

He nodded. "We have a problem."

"Yup. He wasn't supposed to have company. Now we have four bodies that somebody's gonna find."

Sol chewed his lip for a moment, then popped Al Wahari in the belly with another trank. "Cover me," he said and was headed back toward the building before I could answer. I un-shouldered my rifle and took position with it laid across the hood of the Toyota, watching and listening.

Over the next twenty minutes, I watched as he brought out the bodies one by one, jogging around the building and a good hundred yards into the desert behind the little settlement where he dumped them. It was like watching a machine. He never seemed to tire or slow, and I never heard so much as a footfall. Maybe I'd start calling him Terminator myself.

PRESENT DAY

I HANDED the iPad back to Pitt. "Who's the abductee?"

"You don't follow the news?"

"Very little."

"His name is Rob Acoma. Works for NBS News."

"Still doesn't ring a bell," I said. "Like I said, I don't really follow the news. Prefer my own peaceful world."

"He's a big deal there, anchors something or other on their nightly news."

I pointed at the iPad. "When did that happen?"

"Three days ago. Media's covering it nonstop, running that clip over and over."

"And you just happened to see this video on the news, thought to yourself, 'Hey, that's Sol Ringer!' Is that it?"

He grinned. "That's close enough."

"Right." This is what I hate about this clandestine crap. The people at the top are full of it, always bobbing and weaving, even with those of us they're asking to solve their problems. I said, "Why me, Bart?"

"One, you can handle yourself in a...physical sense. Two, you've worked with Sol. You understand how dangerous he is. Three, this hunt will involve utilization of a bunch of tech resources and that's your bucket. Besides, you know you miss it."

"Wrong."

"It's who you are, Sam. You'll have to admit that someday."

I shook my head. I didn't want to be back in the world of the BAM Squad, an agency so black it didn't officially exist. Operators who did the job and lived up to the acronym: By Any Means. I wanted to live my quiet life. Ride my horse. Work forensic cases where the biggest excitement was whether some guy used a flash drive to steal a client list from his employer. I wanted to spend time with my daughter who was starting her run as a high school senior. (I also wanted to win her mom back, but that's a long story.)

But there was no use pretending I could leave a rogue Sol Ringer in action. He was too dangerous, and he ran the risk of exposing the black agency I'd been a part of in my past life, which ran the risk of exposing my own past. I like my privacy. "I'll do it, but only as a contractor. That means you pay my rate, not the BS pay I got when I was active."

Pitt sighed as if he'd be paying the money out of his own pocket instead of the seemingly bottomless black budget he ran, but eventually said, "Fine."

"You handle all logistics and expenses."

"Naturally."

"I'll need an airplane on standby. Park it at Hooks Airport in Tomball."

"Not sure I ca—"

"A jet," I said.

"Sam, I—"

"Nice jet."

One more giant sigh, then a nod.

"So catch me up on what you know," I said. "Any leads on Sol?"

"No, but I'm already getting you set up with everything you'll need to run him down."

Swell.

BLUE DUCK TAVERN
WASHINGTON, DC

TUCKED into a rear corner of the restaurant with their backs positioned to the few other late-night patrons, Howard Hurd and Jack Dickey sat at their usual table and laughed over expensive liquor provided by the ever-generous American taxpayers. Hurd, an Alabama Republican who would turn eighty in a month, had been in the Senate for forty-seven years, preceded by eight years in the House. His pal Dickey, the senior senator from Nevada, was a spry seventy-one and a Democrat who had likewise spent most of his life on Capitol Hill.

Earlier that day, each had stood at the old podium on the floor of the U.S. Senate and lambasted the other, along with their respective parties, as the epitome of what was wrong with America. As the more seasoned political powers inside the Beltway liked to say, it was grand theater. Expected. Necessary. What the people wanted from their leaders.

Dickey threw back the rest of his drink and clunked the heavy glass back onto the tabletop as he looked around for the waiter. Within ten seconds, the waiter was there with a fresh drink, but Dickey looked at the young man as if he'd been waiting an hour.

"Can I get you gentlemen anything else?" the waiter said.

Dickey ignored him completely. Hurd shooed him away, flapping a liver-spotted hand without looking up.

"So let's talk turkey," Hurd said, forearms on the table, leaning forward. "I need that base. People back home expect it."

Dickey drew a long, showy breath. "Gonna be a tough sell to my colleagues, Howie. We just went through another round of closings, and now you want a brand new fifty-billion-dollar Air Force base in Alabama. Not sure I can pull that off."

"Cut the bullshit, Jack. Ain't no cameras, ain't no reporters up here in the Duck."

Lips drawn into a tight line, Dickey shook his head and stared down at his drink several seconds, then looked up and into the eyes of his old friend. "You prepared to move 642 out of committee?"

Hurd's eyes widened. "You have been to my state before, right? If I let that bill out, I might as well head back home with a noose around my neck."

"Time for you to cut the crap, Howie. You want me to rally my people for something as crazy as your base, it'll take something big. Like 642. Besides, what the hell do you care what a bunch of simple rednecks think? Your next election is five years away. "

Hurd flapped a hand in the air again. "I don't give a rat's ass what they think. But I'd prefer not to be lynched if it's all the same to you. And that's dang sure what'll happen if I have anything to do with shutting down Redstone."

"So keep Redstone."

"Damn you, Jack." Hurd took a long drink from his glass. "I've made promises on that base. Promises to people you don't disappoint. But I 'spect that ain't news to you."

Dickey shrugged, said nothing.

Hurd leaned forward and lowered his voice, his words in early slur: "So you know? That ten thousand acres outside Vegas? Been wondering why the hell anybody would buy that much desert that ain't worth a damn for nothin'. Think I'm seeing the picture now."

Dickey's eyes narrowed and his brow tightened for the slightest moment before his poker face returned. "I don't know about any land, but something near Las Vegas would be ideal for a research facility and Army base, don't you think?"

"You played me, Jack. This whole thing has been about you getting Redstone. Thought we were friends."

"For Christ's sake, Howie. You know how this game works. Do we have a deal?"

Hurd turned up his glass and drained it, set it back down. Looked for the waiter and flapped him over. The new drink was half gone before the waiter was safely out of earshot. He stared down at his drink, shaking his head. After a few moments, he raised his head and looked Dickey in the eye. "Yeah. We have a deal."

SOL RINGER WAITED until the two senators had left, then pulled the earbud from his ear. He pulled a digital audio recorder from his pocket and hit the stop button. He walked to the table just vacated by Hurd and Dickey, reached underneath the edge of the table and peeled loose a small electronic device. He dropped it into his pocket, left a twenty on his table to cover the appetizer he'd had, and made his exit.

DAY 1
11:53 Pm

WASHINGTON, DC

HOWARD HURD LAY in his Georgetown bed, staring up at a dark ceiling. The liquor in his system had faded his mood from pleasant, to numb, to miserable. The pleasant stage had allowed him to convince himself that everything would work out. The numbness had given him a break from the whole mess for a bit. And now, the misery. The pounding in his head, the churning in his gut, and the worry in his mind. He had no choice but to make the deal with Dickey. He had guaranteed the new base and billions in construction contracts to people you don't let down.

Sure, he had gotten a little something in return for the promise. His son-in-law had a fine new job, which meant Hurd's daughter and grandchildren lived in the comfort and style they deserved, and Howard had gotten the little yacht that let him get away from the Beltway grind now and then. He was due an occasional perk after giving his whole life to public service. But still, the loss of the Redstone facility, including Marshall Space Center, would be devastating to

Alabama. It was a fixture in the state, its largest employer, and a great point of pride.

He would never be re-elected, but that was fine. He was old, he had four years left on his term, and he had given enough already, hadn't he? Maybe it was all a blessing in disguise. In any event, he wouldn't have to spend the rest of his years worrying about the union mafia going after him or his family. And that's what mattered most when you got down to it, family. He had protected his, just like anyone would.

FOR NO PARTICULAR REASON, Sol Ringer stood over the old man while he slept. His job was done. Had been done nearly an hour before the senator got home. As was the case on most home-entry assignments, the homeowner had made it entirely too easy. For the past three days, every time Hurd had come or gone, Ringer had been concealed in a long stand of thick shrubbery that grew along the brick wall that served as the back wall of the garage. Hurd had a key-fob that he kept in the right front pocket of his trousers. Three of the device's six buttons armed or disarmed the house's alarm system in the standard way. Arm-Stay. Arm-Away. Disarm. Button number four toggled the deadbolt on the front door. Number five did the same for the back door that fed the home from the garage. Number six toggled the garage's overhead door.

Because all the power senators had their alarms installed, monitored, and serviced by the same outfit, all had the same manufacturer and model of key fob with the same layout. Cloning them was something a child could do, and once it was done, Ringer could come and go as he pleased when the residences were empty. The handful of senators all had the same alarm provider because the systems were furnished at no charge via the government contractor who knew all the right people to keep happy in order to keep the contract in place year after year after decade.

Sol Ringer knew the habits of each member of the senatorial gang as well as he knew his own. When they came home. When they left. Who they screwed. Which pills they took to make that possible with their geriatric penises. There were five of the old crooks right now, three from the majority, two from the minority. He had their house phones tapped, the video streams from their surveillance cameras broadcasting to his little DC server farm, and he'd even been able to clone three of their smartphones as they snored off their booze night after night.

All was in order, and the time was near.

DAY 2
02:12 Am

WASHINGTON, DC

SOL AWOKE and had the phone to his ear by the second ring. He checked the time on the alarm clock bolted to the hotel nightstand. 2:12 AM. "Yes?" After listening for ten seconds, he said, "Roger that."

He hung up the phone, got out of bed, and made his way to the bathroom. He showered, used the toothbrush and deodorant, then stowed those items in his go-bag. As always, he had already packed everything except those items and his work clothes before going to bed. It didn't matter that he had been living in this same room for the past two months. He prepped for a rapid departure every night.

After donning tactical pants, a form-fitting undershirt, his shoulder harnessed Kimber, and a combat vest, all black, he was ready. Six minutes had passed since the phone call. Sol had not expected an order to execute for another two weeks or so, but here it was. Time to work.

The white minivan with its 'MOBILE MECHANIC' signage was parked just outside his room. He unlocked it old-school, key in the door, no fob use now that the mission was underway because when you unlocked it with the fob, the lights flashed momentarily. Unstealthy. He didn't care that no one here knew him—even his hotel-registration persona James Williams had not interacted with a soul since he had been here—he cared only that he was now working in earnest. Maximum stealth was the way.

He pulled the door closed, locked it, and climbed between the two front seats into the little van's windowless cargo area. Working his way from one toolbox to another, he removed the trays of wrenches and other hand tools, then pressed the corners of what looked like the floor of each box, gathering his real tools. Flexicuffs. Black hoods. A lock-pick gun. Zero Tolerance combat knife. Several loaded mags for the Kimber model 1911 he already wore. Small rolls of duct tape. And finally, his night vision googles.

He closed the hidden compartment in the bottom of each toolbox, then quietly replaced the decoy tools before crouch-walking back to the front and into the driver's seat. He applied the brakes and pushed the button to start the engine. Backed out and made his way through the parking lot, then turned on the lights as he pulled onto the road in front of the motel. Time to ruin the evening of a couple geriatric assholes.

TWO U.S. SENATORS MISSING

WASHINGTON — At a joint press conference this morning, both the FBI and the Secret Service confirmed that U.S. senators Howard Hurd (R-Alabama) and Jack Dickey (D-Nevada) are missing and an intensive search for the men is underway. Citing the ongoing investigation, FBI Director Henrik Blass and Secret Service Director Jason Tudor declined to provide much detail beyond the fact that the two men were together last night in the Blue Duck Tavern, a local restaurant popular with officials on the Hill, and that both men arrived safely at their respective homes after departing the Blue Duck.

Sources close to the investigation, however, paint a grimmer picture. Speaking under the condition of anonymity, the sources say the bedrooms of both Hurd and Dickey contained significant amounts of blood. Quoting one source, "Hurd's bedroom looked like the scene of a vicious murder, not an abduction."

Both men have served for decades in the United States Senate and were known to be friends, despite the fact that Hurd is a Republican and Dickey a Democrat. We will provide continuing coverage of this situation.

DAY 2

5:21 Am Eastern

NEW YORK CITY

BRUCE BERRINGER LAY STILL and quiet, as he had for hours. He had made his nest on the rooftop of a mid-rise on East 49th, looking directly at the iconic New York building across the street that most famously housed MBC, one of the nation's largest TV networks.

His two views of the building's north entrance were picture perfect. The first, with his eyes, looking right down on it. The second look, far more interesting, came via the VR goggles he wore. A tiny cable snaked behind his left ear and routed down inside his tactical vest, where it connected to a computer no bigger than a pack of cigarettes. Two more cables left the computer and fed through the sleeves of his shirt. The left wire terminated in a simple push-button switch mounted on a ring on the tip of his index finger. The right one ended at what resembled a game controller half the size of his palm that he wore on all four fingers like a pair of brass knucks.

He pressed the button in his left hand and a small clock appeared in the upper left corner of his field of view. 5:23 AM. Another press, and the view changed completely. He was now looking at the same entrance to the building across the street, but from a rooftop perspective two buildings to his left, about 300 yards away. This camera view was highly magnified and could be made more so in an instant if needed. He thumbed the little joystick in his right hand and tweaked the view just a bit, then went back to his natural eye-view.

Four minutes later, the target finally appeared, turning the corner from Fifth Avenue onto 49th. A walking waste of humanity in a five-thousand-dollar suit. His name was Chad Scott, but it didn't really matter. He was one of a dozen just like him. Famous faces delivering propaganda and pretending it was news. Pushing agendas and creating news instead of reporting it. Corrupt to the core, they lied and steered the people of the country into believing the lies. If anyone questioned their lack of journalistic ethics, Chad Scott and his ilk mocked, ridiculed, and marginalized them. They knew what was best, not the ignorant peasants. The little people were just there to be led and to make their multimillion-dollar salaries possible. It had gone on long enough.

Berringer worked the button and selected the view he had been waiting for. A highly magnified view filled his eyes now, glowing red crosshairs and other reticle markings superimposed over Scott as he walked toward the camera. Working the joystick with the expertise of a twenty-hour-a-day gaming addict, he positioned the red circle in the center of the crosshairs so that Scott's face filled it. He pushed a button on the back of the controller with his index finger. A small beep sounded in his ear and the circle turned green as the tracking software took over, keeping the sights perfectly aligned on the target.

Three hundred yards to Berringer's left, the camera and the rest of the motorized rig moved with precision and silence. The camera was mounted in the position a scope would normally occupy, on top of a Knight's Armament M110 semiautomatic sniper rifle. The gun's stock was gone, replaced by a mounting system built to secure the rifle to the robotic shooter mechanism controlled by the pocket computer he wore. The mount was gyro-stabilized and nothing moved a millimeter that wasn't intended.

· · ·

IT WAS TIME. Scott was six feet from the entrance door, the laser rangefinder reporting a distance of 289 meters from gun to target. Berringer pushed the button and a mix of technology and old-fashioned ballistics went into action. First, to his right and across Fifth Avenue, another rooftop device activated. This one was simple, a black metal tube pointing through an ornamental opening in the three-foot-tall parapet that surrounded the flat roof. From the street, it looked every bit like a gun barrel, and it sounded like one as it began firing the first of its four small "shots," the illusion created by small serial charges built from black powder and simple electrical detonators. The shots would fire in an uneven sequence over twenty seconds, and numerous witnesses would swear the shots came from the top of the building at the northwest corner of Fifth and 49th.

Microseconds after the decoy unit fired its first shot, the suppressed M110 sniper rifle fired. A close shot like this required no exotic ammunition. The rifle was loaded with 7.62x51 NATO rounds, commonly known as .308, spitting lead hollow-point bullets jacketed in copper that weighed in at 168 grains. Millions of the cartridges were in circulation. With the suppressor in play, no one at street level would hear it at all as it competed with the booming and fire-spitting "barrel" down the street.

Through the goggles, Berringer watched. Less than a half-second after he pushed the button, a spray of blood, brain, and bone burst from a spot on Scott's forehead, an inch above the bridge of his nose. He stood stock still for a moment, his eyes bugged open by some involuntary reflex taking place in the dead man's body. Then his knees buckled and he toppled backward, the back of his head actually bouncing a tiny bit when it hit the concrete sidewalk. Berringer pushed the button again and waited. The crosshairs moved to Scott's unmoving throat as the computer waited for the next distraction report from the decoy unit. To his right, the boom sounded and a hole opened up in the target's throat. He pushed the button one more time. A few seconds later, a bloom of bright red appeared on the white shirt above Scott's heart, just to the left of the blue tie that lay skewed to the right. Berringer said, "Red, white, and blue, you sonofabitch."

MBC ANCHOR GUNNED DOWN AT 30 ROCK

NEW YORK CITY, NY — Respected MBC News anchor Chad Scott was killed this morning by apparent sniper fire as he approached the New York building where he worked. Scott, who has anchored the MBC News operation for more than six years, was on his way to host the morning newscast when he was gunned down mere feet from the north entrance of his building near Rockefeller Center. Multiple eyewitnesses at the scene state they heard the gunshots, then subsequently saw a gunman on a rooftop across Fifth Avenue. One witness described the scene as "pure chaos, people running around and freaking out when the shooting started."

Scott was pronounced dead on the scene and while the official cause of death will be determined in an upcoming autopsy, NYPD sources say he was shot multiple times and described "precision wounds to the head, neck, and chest." The NYPD also held a brief news conference in which the spokesman assured the public that the investigation is already in full swing and that the killer will be brought to justice.

"I and millions of others here in New York and around the country are mourning the death of a beloved journalist," Mayor William Ragsdale said. "but our real focus must be the prevention of such atrocities.

There is no excuse for this country to continue to allow members of the public to own weapons capable of such barbaric acts, and I am moving immediately to institute a complete and total ban of all civilian ownership of firearms in our city. It's time for heartbreak like this to come to an end and my administration is poised to make that happen."

DAY 2

Location Unknown

MORNING

SENATOR JACK DICKEY opened his eyes and shook his head, trying to clear the mental fog. Where was he? How long had he been here? He was lying flat on his back, looking up at an old ceiling with flaking pale green paint. His head felt like it had a freight train running through it and his back ached like a mother.

He rolled onto his side and managed to get his stiff legs moving enough to get his feet on the floor and push up into a sitting position. He was on a cot with an old mattress covered in ticking material he hadn't seen in fifty years. He took in his surroundings, unable to believe what he saw. He was in a by-damn jail cell! What the actual hell was going on here?

Forcing himself to his feet amid creaks and pops from his knees, Dickey shuffled over to an ancient metal toilet affixed to one wall. First things first. He had to piss like a race horse. When he got to the toilet he realized for the first time that he was dressed in a jumpsuit. A prisoner's jumpsuit. Black and white stripes! Whatever shit was going on here, there would be almighty hell to pay. That was a fact.

He undid buttons down the front of the jumpsuit and worked the thing down around his ass so he could get his johnson out and in position. He groaned as the flow finally began. With his business done, he got the damn jailbird outfit back up into position and refastened the buttons. He walked to the bars that formed the entire front wall of the cell. They were iron, painted pale green. Grabbed the door and checked to be sure it was locked. Solid. Beyond the bars was a room three or four times the size of the cell, no lights on. It contained a desk and filing cabinet, both of which looked like something from an old government surplus sale. Concrete floor, like the cell. Nothing on the desk. A wall of shelves, also empty. On the far wall was a closed door, wooden framed with textured glass in the upper half. He could see light coming through the glass but it was an odd bluish hue, impossible to tell if it was daylight or some artificial light from another room.

Craning his neck left and right, he tried to tell what was on either side of his cell but couldn't get an angle to see. He grabbed the bars and shook, but only managed to send pain shooting through his arthritic wrists and elbows.

"Hey!" he said. "Somebody better get their ass over here right now! Do you know who I am? I'll have your ass!"

To his left, someone said, "Jack? Jack, is that you?"

"Who's there?"

"It's Howard, you dumb bastard, who do you think?"

"Howard? What the hell's going on here?"

"Wish I knew. Woke up about an hour ago."

"You dressed like a nineteen-thirties jailbird, too?"

"Sure am."

"Seen anybody else?"

"Not a soul."

This time a voice came from Dickey's right. "Would you two codgers mind shutting up? I'm trying to sleep."

In near-perfect unison, Dickey and Hurd said, "Who is that?"

"Acoma. Rob Acoma."

Dickey scrunched his face up for a moment. "Acoma. The NBS news asshole?"

"Watch it, Senator," Acoma said. "This, whatever it is, will be over when the ransom is paid and I'll be back on the air."

"How do you know who I am?" Dickey said.

"I'd recognize your voices anywhere, but I saw them drag your asses in here a few hours ago."

"How long you been here?"

"Days. Three, four, not sure," Acoma said.

"Anybody else here?"

"Just us three. Some douchebag shows up a couple times a day with food, if you can call it that."

Hurd said, "You mentioned ransom. Why'd you say that?"

"What else would it be?" Acoma said.

Dickey grunted. Hurd said nothing.

"The network has insurance for this kind of thing," Acoma said. "Probably just taking a few days to work it all out. I assume the government will pony up for you boys, right?"

Neither senator answered.

HOUSTON, TX

PITT HAD SPUN up a BAM office suite for me on the fortieth floor of one of Houston's newest skyscrapers. I'd rather have officed in The Woodlands, the suburb near my farm, but he couldn't find a suite on short notice with the necessary connectivity, so downtown it was. In addition to a killer collection of computer workstations, the suite-with-a-view was outfitted with a hot fiber internet pipe and an array of VPN connections to helpful resources I might need. One wall was covered with a half-dozen flat panels running news feeds.

On the human side of things, a BAM Girl Friday named Sheila Vasquez had been flown down from DC to assist. On paper she worked for the Department of Health and Human Services in some obscure bureaucratic role. In reality, she coordinated operations that existed nowhere on paper. According to Pitt, she was brilliant and a showcase in competence. She would need to be. Pitt had emailed me in the early morning hours saying two high-power senators had been murdered or abducted and that he was certain Sol was the culprit.

Sheila was in the office when I arrived. She was tall enough to dunk and so thin she probably had to run around in the shower to get wet. No makeup on an attractive face. Black T-shirt and black jeans. We got acquainted over a cup of coffee and then got started.

"You wanna get me up to speed on the tools we have?" I said.

"You bet. For starters, we have a live mirror of the FBI's investigation. All their evidence, case notes. If they've entered it into a computer on this case, we have it. Plus the standard FBI databases, the 'people files' and such."

"Surprised the Bureau went along with that."

She winked and smiled. "Who said they did?"

"Gotcha."

"We can get direct access to any government-run video surveillance systems, traffic cams, stuff like that. These can take some time to set up, so I started with the DC metro area. If you want access to other cities, let me know and I'll get on it."

I nodded.

"And the real juice? NSA. We couldn't swing direct access to their systems, but we do have an operator there on standby who will run whatever searches we need."

"And this operator has full access? PRISM and the other systems?"

"Carte blanche. If they have it, we can get it."

"Damn."

"You like?"

"Love."

THE NEWS COVERAGE, in the odd moments it switched off **coverage of news** anchor Chad Scott's morning murder, pivoted to the missing anchorman and senators, playing heavily on the angle that Acoma and the senators were murdered, primarily because all three crime scenes were bloody. I didn't buy it. There was no reason for Sol to haul dead bodies away. He's a consummate operator and he could have killed them and never left a clue tying back to him. My gut said he took these people alive and left the scenes bloody as a ruse.

I dug into the FBI's case files, starting with the Acoma case since it was the oldest abduction. Acoma's photos showed a forty-something version of a guy you'd meet stumbling around at a frat party. He anchored everything his network did that was politically oriented, operating out of their DC studio. Divorced three times, currently unattached and living alone in a McMansion in a ritzy Washington neighborhood.

I downloaded the plans for his house and a detailed map of the neighborhood, along with a mashup of surveillance clips the FBI had collected from other nearby homes. They'd edited the clips into a video sequence that tracked a plumber's van entering the area an hour before the abduction. Notes accompanying the video identified the van as the likely means by which the culprit had arrived in the vicinity. The van was parked in the driveway of a vacant house in a cul-de-sac two blocks away from Acoma's place.

A figure I knew to be Sol got out of the van, walked around behind the house, and the next clip was obviously shot on Acoma's surveillance system. The Bureau undoubtedly searched every camera between the van and that house, but they came up empty because, well, Sol didn't want to be seen.

From the perspective of an outdoor camera aimed at Acoma's back-yard, Sol approached a back door. The source switched to an indoor camera looking at that door. Through its glass panes, Sol was obviously keying in a code. The door opened and he stepped inside. No alarm evident; he'd disarmed it by code. The view tracked Sol through the house and into what I'm sure was Acoma's bedroom, which obviously didn't have a camera inside. The timestamp overlay jumped seven minutes and Sol exited the bedroom with Acoma draped over his shoulder.

A couple of cameras caught clear shots of Acoma as Sol carried him through the house. Wearing only boxer shorts, Acoma's head and body appeared uninjured, leaving me to wonder what Sol had used to bloody up the bedroom while he was in there. It also made me ponder the media assumption of murder. Their "sources close to the investigation" were either nonexistent or feeding them false information. This footage was compiled by the FBI and they certainly didn't miss

Acoma's pristine-looking condition. The video sequence ended with the first clip I'd seen on Pitt's iPad, Sol putting Acoma in the back of his own SUV and backing out of the garage.

Knowing that the FBI would've tried and failed to follow Sol through traffic cams, I moved on to the case notes. The afternoon following the abduction, a toll booth registered Acoma's SUV passing through, complete with a decent photo as it passed through the gate. Police were alerted and state troopers stopped the vehicle with great fanfare and a massive show of force on the south side of the Beltway near Alexandria, snarling the area traffic for hours. The SUV had Acoma's license plate, Acoma's E-ZPass, and was identical in every way to the newsman's vehicle. But it wasn't his vehicle, and the sixty-six-year-old cardiologist driving it had come close to needing his own services. Sol had found an identical vehicle and switched both the license plate and the E-Z Pass. A day later, the process repeated. He'd done it again, leaving police exasperated.

I perused the case files for the two senators and found, as expected, a similar sequence: Sol ghosting in, nabbing his targets, ghosting out. *What are you doing, Sol? Why? For whom?* I thought back to the few times I'd worked with him. He said little aside from discussing missions. I couldn't recall him expressing an opinion on anything outside that. Ever. Give him an objective and he'd complete it because that was his job. That was Sol then, and I felt sure it was Sol now, dispassionately following orders. I was wrong.

DAY 2

9:42 Pm

WASHINGTON, DC

SOL WAS glad to be in action. The time for talking and voting and begging had run its course and it had failed. Miserably. The federal government was a self-feeding, self-perpetuating monster rolling over everything in its path, and enough was damn well enough. Sol had bled and killed for his country. He didn't give one rat's ass about left, right, Republicans, Democrats. He cared about right and wrong, and it was time to put an end to the corruptocrats' reign. He'd leave the politics to the general.

Security had been ramped up around DC since he took care of the two senators the night before, but true to form, the government had been reactionary. All the high-visibility politicians on the Hill had been wrapped in new phalanxes of protectors as the senators and congresspukes ran to every camera they saw and started yapping about how they were introducing legislation to make them and their colleagues more secure so they could safely continue their tireless work for the American people. The protectors should have directed their frenzy of attention elsewhere.

Sol lay still as the ground itself, positioned beneath a hedgerow in a small Georgetown park. Directly across the street was the home of Supreme Court Chief Justice Marcus Wilder. As expected, at 9:45 PM a black government Suburban pulled into the driveway of Wilder's posh pseudo-Victorian house. The left rear door of the SUV opened and Wilder emerged. Though he was seventy, Wilder was fit, with a lively bounce in his step as he went to his front door. Still dressed in a tee and shorts from his nightly workout, he keyed in the digits that would open his front door. Sol echoed them under his breath as he watched through binoculars: "Four, nine, three, eight." Same as all the other nights. The justice opened the door, stepped inside, then turned and waved to the driver in the SUV. Same as all the other nights.

The door closed and Sol checked his phone, watching the status of the judge's alarm system on its screen. It switched from AWAY to OFF, then rearmed in STAY mode. The SUV backed out of the driveway and drove away. Sol preferred to do this kind of work in the middle of the night, but that wasn't feasible this time. This was the natural window of opportunity, before the too-young and far-too-good-looking wife and former clerk of the Chief Justice arrived home. He waited five minutes to be sure the judge had made it into the shower, looked around, and shimmied from beneath the hedgerow. He stood, brushed bits of leaves and other detritus from his clothing, and made one more quick check of all his gear.

He pulled the thin black balaclava down over his face and neck, crossed the street, and used the phone to disarm the alarm system as he approached the front door. He imagined the judge in the shower, washing the exercise sweat from his body as the alarm panel in the master bedroom issued one tiny beep and switched its LED from red to green. If the judge heard it at all, he would assume it was his wife arriving home.

Sol keyed the code into the door lock—4-9-3-8—pushed the expensive door open and stepped inside, closing and locking the door behind him before two seconds had passed.

AT THE MOMENT the door closed behind Sol, another car turned onto the street less than a quarter-mile from the house. Less than a minute passed before the Lexus convertible made a right turn into the Wilder driveway.

SOL MOVED THROUGH THE FOYER, down the hallway to his left, and into the master bedroom suite. The water in the shower died when he was halfway across the bedroom on his way to the bathroom. Seconds later, he heard the shower door open, followed by the soft *fffft* of a towel being pulled from its bar. He increased his stride and stepped into the bathroom just as Wilder finished toweling his head and face. Sol was three feet away when Wilder dropped the towel enough to uncover his eyes. His eyes widened for a half-second before Sol drove a gloved fist into his gut. The judge doubled over and fought for breath, and Sol slapped a precut piece of duct tape over his mouth before slipping a black cloth bag over his head and cinching its drawstring loosely around the judge's neck.

"You have one option, Your Honor," Sol said. "Do exactly as I say. Nod if you understand."

Wilder shivered, his wet body throwing off tiny droplets of water. The black bag bobbed up and down.

"Good. Stand up and finish drying yourself. Then we—" Sol froze when the alarm panel on the wall sounded three quick beeps. Shit!

The judge tried to scream and it came out as muffled gibberish.

Sol leaned in and whispered into his ear. "Make another sound and whoever just arrived will pay dearly for it."

The noise stopped. Sol crossed to the door that led to the hallway, closed and locked it, returned to the bathroom. "Dry yourself. Quickly."

Wilder got to work with the towel.

Sol stepped into a huge closet off the bathroom, jerked a tee and pair of jeans off a shelf, then grabbed a pair of deck loafers. He returned to the judge and said, "Put these on."

Wilder had one leg in the jeans when the second door to the bathroom, the one that opened onto another hallway, opened. Sol looked and saw the wife. She was in yoga tights, her brunette hair pulled back in a ponytail, green eyes wide and mouth open. Before he could get to her, the scream erupted, a shriek worthy of any horror film. With his left hand, Sol reached around her head and grabbed the ponytail as he clamped his right hand over her mouth.

After securing her mouth with duct tape and covering her head with a sweatshirt from the closet, he said, "Folks, we're going to take a ride now."

DAY 2
6:40 Pm

ATLANTA, GEORGIA

BERRINGER HAD BEEN busy since dispatching the douchebag Chad Scott. While witnesses pointed to the decoy "gun" on Fifth Avenue and beat cops gawked up at it while speaking urgently into their shoulder mics, he had made his way quietly in the other direction. After breaking down the robotic sniper rifle and stowing it in its case, he made his exit from the scene.

Three hours later, he boarded a United Airlines flight out of JFK and tried to ignore the squalling child to his left and the snoring man on his right. It didn't work, but at least the flight to Atlanta wasn't a marathon. Once there, he took a cab to a hotel in Buckhead. He wasn't staying at that hotel, but it was only a thirty-minute walk from there to the low-rent motel in which he would hunker down the rest of the day.

The Mountain View Motor Court didn't have a mountain within ninety miles, and its views were uninspiring: a convenience store across the street, a small warehouse on one side, and a self-service storage unit complex on the other that was at least ten times the size of a football field. Berringer paid cash for four nights and more cash to avoid the hassle of providing an ID, then went to his room and took a shower.

With the sweat of the morning and the funk of air travel washed from his body, he lay down on the springy bed, closed his eyes, and fell asleep. When he awoke, it was dark outside. He checked the time on his watch, dressed, and walked over to the convenience store. He bought a six-pack of Red Bull, a loaf of bread, and a pack of Oscar Mayer bologna.

Back in his room, he ate and waited. At ten o'clock, he left the room and walked next door to the spread of rental storage units, where he entered the code he had been given into the keypad beside the front door. He opened the door, walked inside, and began the walk to his interior unit. The outside units were cheaper and larger, but without climate control. Unacceptable, especially in the humidity of the South that would turn precision metal components into a rust-pitted mess.

Keeping his jacket collar up and the brim of his Braves cap pulled low, he made his way through the camera-laden corridors until he reached unit #177C. Using the key that was the only object of any kind on his person other than clothes, Berringer unlocked the windowless door and stepped inside. He closed the door and flipped on the light switch. His unit appeared as he had left it months ago after his contact had trained him on the use of the gear inside, but he carefully made his way around the tarp-covered pile, checking to be sure the tiny threads he had glued to both tarp and floor were still intact. Satisfied that no one had prowled around, he checked the interior lock on the door and pulled the canvas away from the equipment.

Two hours later, all the batteries had been topped off to replenish the small amounts of energy they had lost while sitting here for months. Every tiny joint and servo had been checked, the circuits verified, and everything had been cleaned. He had checked pairing and connectivity between the devices, then finally shut everything down. On his way out, Berringer took one Pelican case with him.

After walking the camera gauntlet in reverse, he exited the front door of the complex and made his way to the street to watch for the Uber ride he had scheduled earlier in the day, using a burner phone and prepaid debit card, both purchased in a part of town that wasn't close to this location or tomorrow's target. Five minutes later he saw his ride turn into the parking lot of the convenience store and headed toward it.

HOUSTON, TX

AFTER SPENDING all day digging through the FBI's files on Acoma and the senators, I was exactly nowhere. My eyes were tired and I decided to walk across the street and have dinner in a peaceful steakhouse. The elevator doors were opening when Sheila came bounding down the corridor.

"Hey! Got something!"

I stepped back and let the elevator close up and move on without me. Gestured for her to spit it out.

"Our FBI stash just populated with a ton of material from the Chad Scott scene this morning."

The steak could wait.

THERE WERE about a hundred photos in the file now. Every conceivable angle of Scott's body, clearly showing the three hits. Head, throat, heart. Every one of them perfectly placed. Sniper? I moved on to the photos of the two rooftop sites.

One of them still had the device in place, an obvious decoy and distraction, as was annotated in a note with the photo. The antenna made clear it had been controlled remotely. The other rooftop site was empty but showed four clear indentations on the tar paper where something had been. I checked the accompanying note and saw that the FBI had confirmed that this placement jibed with the trajectory of the shots that had killed Scott and that they had deemed this the shooter's nest.

What the notes didn't mention was the oddity of *four* indentations. Not two like you'd see with a bipod. Not three for a tripod. Four. I'd never seen any kind of four-legged rifle support and tucked this away in the back of my mind. A smattering of footprints surrounded the area, vague bordering on nonexistent.

Aside from the left-behind decoy device, which was under forensic examination, there were no indicators of other tidbits of evidence left behind.

"Sheila, keep an eye out for any more info on this decoy device that turns up in the file. Photos, forensic reports, anything."

"Will do."

In addition to the photos, the file had been populated with more notes and reports, and I settled back to read through all of them. My stomach growled.

"How about grabbing us some dinner somewhere?" I said.

"Sure, got anything in mind?"

"Surprise me."

She would definitely end up doing that.

SUPREME COURT CHIEF JUSTICE WILDER MISSING

WASHINGTON, D.C. — At a joint press conference held by the FBI and the Metropolitan Police Department, authorities announced that Chief Justice of the United States Marcus Wilder is missing, along with his wife, Jamie Bigham-Wilder. Wilder's Secret Service driver dropped him off at his Georgetown home at 9:45 p.m. . Authorities said the GPS system of Jamie Wilder's car shows she arrived at the home four minutes later at 9:49 p.m.

Wilder's staff at the Supreme Court became concerned when the 70-year-old judge, known for always being the first person in the office, failed to show up for work today. When staff members contacted the Secret Service, they were told the matter was under investigation. The law enforcement press conference was called an hour later.

Authorities refused to speculate on whether they believe the Wilders' disappearance is related to a string of other missing high-profile people, but sources close to the investigation say they believe all the cases are related. One major difference between the Wilder case and those of news anchor Rob Acoma and senators Howard Hurd and Jack Dickey is that the Wilder home showed no signs of a struggle and no blood. The prior cases all featured bloody crime scenes that left many assuming murder and disposal of bodies, as opposed to abduction. The Wilder case is also the first of these incidents in which someone other than the "primary" was taken, although little can be inferred from this because all three prior victims lived alone.

Developing…

DAY 3

Houston, Texas

11:40 AM

SHEILA WAS at the office when I arrived. She said, "Batch came in on that device."

I brewed a cup of coffee and settled in at my workstation. The forensic file on the decoy device had dozens of photos and several pages of notes. As I'd expected, the device was fairly simple and definitely homemade. The pseudo-barrel of the pseudo-gun was a piece of standard half-inch iron pipe that had been spray-painted black. A common piece of plumbing material that could be purchased in any of tens of thousands of stores or, better yet, a used piece picked up from a countless number of places.

On the back end of the pipe, an adapter stepped up from the half-inch pipe to three-quarter-inch, then to a bright metal tee. The notes said it was a forged fitting made of #316 stainless. One two-inch female opening and two three-quarter-inch openings, all threaded NPT, for "national pipe thread," a threading specification widely used in North

America. At the bottom of the page discussing the pipe and fittings was a handwritten note:

6000 PSI fittings. Expensive. Limited suppliers.

I JUMPED on the web and found a similar fitting on Amazon. $463. The part was overkill for a one-use, leave-behind device like this. The guy was taking no chances. I tucked that tidbit away.

The fitting had a motorized apparatus on top that dumped a portion of black powder down into the fitting to be detonated by an electrical spark igniter on the bottom. Simple and efficient. The firing mechanism was controlled by a remotely activated relay. Aside from the pricey stainless fitting, the only other thing that piqued my interest was the wireless transceiver on the firing mechanism that communicated with the controller, obviously controlled by the shooter.

The FBI file identified the pinky-sized chip as a model NRF24L01+. I looked it up and saw that sellers commonly claimed it had a range of a kilometer or more. Further digging revealed that, in the real world, the range was considerably less than that. I pulled up an online satellite view of New York and bounced back and forth between that and the FBI notes until I was looking down on a view of the area where Scott was killed. I used the scale legend on the map to estimate the distance between the decoy device and the spot designated as the shooter's nest.

After chewing on it for a minute or two, I said, "Sheila, call the pilot and tell him we're going to New York this afternoon."

A news alert popped onto my screen: **EXPLOSION AT GNN'S ATLANTA HEADQUARTERS.** I clicked the link and my news aggregation page loaded. Every feed I followed had the same story top and center. I clicked into one of them and started reading.

DEVELOPING: At approximately 2 p.m. EST, an explosion rocked a GNN studio while a live show was in progress. The number of casualties is unknown at this time but multiple deaths have occurred. We can state that this was a deliberate attack, given the fact that someone has already claimed responsibility. Police had no comment other than to say they and other first responders were on the scene and that an evacuation of the building was underway. See video below. WARNING: GRAPHIC VIOLENCE. NOT APPROPRIATE FOR CHILDREN.

I CLICKED play on the video. Some panel discussion was underway, the kind that plays *ad nauseum* these days. Three people yammering at a news desk, wearing too much makeup and trying too hard for a look of serious intellectual discussion. The newsies had their backs to a window that looked out onto the city. Something came straight at the window, moving fast. The window broke, followed almost instantly by a wall of flame that rolled over the news desk and toward the camera, bright enough to wash out the whole picture. The sound went to crap. A crack appeared across the entire image, probably in the camera lens itself. The sound settled back to normal and the image faded back into view. Somehow the camera was still looking right where it had been. The news desk had split and flipped forward. Obviously dead bodies in the view. One of the newsies holding one of his arms in the other and screaming.

I'd seen scenes like this too many times in too many shitholes and was moving to click out of the video when the screen flashed and the image and sound cut to something entirely different. On the screen now was a closeup of someone wearing a clown mask, the cheap kind you'd see kids wearing on Halloween. Then he started talking:

"WE ARE FED UP. For decades, we have watched the news media in this country spread propaganda, promoting the degradation of everything that made this nation the most successful in history. They attack anyone who doesn't subscribe to their far-left agenda, and cover up the crimes and misdeeds of the most guilty among us. No more will this be tolerated. News

media, listen and listen well. Return to real journalism or we will kill you all."

THE IMAGE SHRANK to a bright dot in the middle of the screen, and then faded back to the carnage of the GNN studio. I killed the video feed, leaned back in my chair. Said "Wow" to no one but myself.

DAY 3

Location Unknown

LATE MORNING

HURD, Dickey, and Acoma all came to the front of their cells when the door at the front of the office opened. The same oafish man who had been bringing their food came through the door but this time he wasn't alone. He was guiding a man with his left hand and a woman with his right.

"Oh my Lord," Hurd said.

His jailmates stared without speaking at first, then Dickey said, "Someone has well and truly lost their damned minds. You!" He pointed at the oaf. "Do you know who that man is?" The oaf ignored him. "You kidnap United States senators, and now the chief justice of the Supreme Court? You get someone in here to talk to me, you Neanderthal buffoon! Do you hear me?"

"Don't forget me," Acoma said.

Hurd said, "Screw off, newsboy."

The oaf—he looked like something right out of backwoods 1975 in a silky floral-print shirt and gaudy jewelry—steered Marcus Wilder and his wife, Jamie, toward the right end of the room, beyond Acoma. The sound of a big key in a big lock followed, and after another twenty seconds or so, the sound of bars clanging shut reverberated through the room. The oaf left, leaving the office door open this time.

Dickey looked to see if he could make out anything on the other side of the door but it seemed to lead into a dark corridor.

"Marcus, Mrs. Wilder," Hurd said, "are y'all alright? Are you hurt?"

A new voice from the front of the room said, "No one's hurt."

The prisoners watched as the man behind that voice strode into the room with purpose and a ramrod sense of ownership. He wore blue Air Force BDUs, each side of the collar adorned with three stars. He looked to be in his mid-fifties, short military haircut, fatigues tucked into combat boots.

Dickey lit up. "General, thank God you're here. I knew the cavalry would arrive soon. These—" The general held up a hand, silencing the politician.

"My name, gentlemen, ma'am, is Lucian Harrow. As you can see, I'm United States Army. I'm not here to save you. I'm the one who had your sorry asses brought here." He nodded toward the left side of the room where the Wilders were. "You excluded, ma'am, and you have my apology. Your detention was unplanned and unfortunate but there's nothing to be done about that now. I—"

Hurd interrupted, wagging a long wrinkled finger toward Harrow. "General, I don't know what you think you're doing but it will not stand. You may rest assured of that. I will per—"

Harrow's voice thundered. "Shut. Your. Mouth. If you interrupt me again I'll have you bound and gagged. If that doesn't do it, I'll have you sedated."

Hurd drew a breath as if he were about to say something else but when the general locked eyes with him, Hurd just stood there like a statue, an orator frozen in time.

"Anthony," Harrow said back over his shoulder, voice directed at the door, "distribute the materials."

Moments later, the oaf returned. He was carrying four binders, each about two inches thick, each a different color. He passed one through the bars to each of the four men: Blue to Dickey. Red to Hurd. Yellow to Acoma. Black to Wilder.

As they looked down at the binders, Harrow continued, his voice large and in charge. "Each binder contains information prepared specifically for each of you. You are to study that material. You are to know that material. There will be no discussion among yourselves about the material. None. If you violate this rule, the consequences will be immediate and harsh. Do you understand?"

The men all stood there in their cells, looking down at their binders. Dickey looked angry. Hurd confused. Acoma nonchalant. Wilder's look was a bit harder to read. Dread?

"What's this about?" Acoma said. "We're, what, studying for a test? This is bullshit. Why don't you get on with the negotiations so we can all get back to our lives?"

Harrow laughed but it sounded more like a tight bark. Then he walked to Acoma's cell, right up to the bars, placed his hands on his hips and said, "There are no negotiations, Mr. Acoma. There will be no negotiations. You have been given your instructions and I almost, *almost*, hope you have the temerity to not follow them. If there's one person in this room I would enjoy bringing to heel, it's you, sir." He smiled at Acoma, eyes locked and twinkling. Acoma took a step back without even knowing it.

The general stood there a moment longer, then returned to the center of the room and faced the row of cells again. "Three days, gentlemen. I suggest you use them wisely. Remember the rule. That is all." He spun on his heel and left the room.

When he was gone, Hurd moved to the front of his cell and gripped the bars. Looking at the oaf, he said, "Anthony, you look like a reasonable man. Surely you know that whatever this is"—he flapped a hand around in the air—"there's no way it will succeed. The government will bring all its resources to bear to find us. Help us, and when this is over, we'll help you. *I* will help you. You have my word."

Anthony said, "I don't need your help, and there ain't a damn thing you could do for me if I did, Big Shot." Heavy Southern drawl. Then he left the room and closed the door behind him on the way out.

DAY 3
Atlanta, Georgia

1:58 PM

BERRINGER HAD SPENT the morning verifying the equipment in the city was in place and functional, then returned to the storage unit. Now he sat in the control chair fashioned for the operation. A joystick rose from the right armrest, a control pad with a half-dozen buttons and switches on the left one. He pulled on the VR goggles, the same type he had used in New York to give the media maggot what he had earned with his years of bullshit. Years of acting like people who believed in traditional Americanism were some kind of inbred freaks, tearing them down at every opportunity. Attacking every conservative who came before him, while coddling and covering for the leftist politicians and their minions who hated everything that had made America great. Bruce Berringer had had enough, so when the opportunity arose to join an operation that would send an unmistakable message, he took it.

He had tried all the conventional things: Protests at the headquarters of the media giants. Writing letters. Doing his part to expose them on social media. Emailing his congressman and senators. Nothing worked. The corrupt machine just kept rolling, shaping the weak minds of the sheep, dragging the country ever deeper into moral and financial decay. Now the time had come for an alternative approach. It was time to water the tree of liberty with the blood of those who were destroying it, and he would do his part.

A button press brought the system to life and data overlays populated his field of view in the goggles. Moments later, a live video image appeared from the quadcopter positioned on top of the building across the street from GNN headquarters. He was linked to it via an encrypted digital link with thirty miles of range, a link that would leave no trace, no Wi-Fi signatures or artifacts to trace back to him. The only public connection in use was via his phone, which he used to put a small view of the live GNN broadcast in the bottom left corner of his view.

Berringer positioned his hands on the controls, watching the GNN feed and the clock. A commercial advertising some new drug with one potential benefit and a laundry list of side effects was playing. He pressed another button and saw a slight vibration in his video feed as the drone powered up. Within seconds, the gyros in the camera gimbal spun up and the picture went rock steady again. On the thumbnail, the GNN blurb played, followed by the intro graphics for the upcoming show. He twisted the joystick and his view showed motion as the drone rose slowly into the air. Using a thumbwheel on the joystick, he adjusted the camera until it was looking directly at the target window across the street, then held a button on the control pad down for three seconds. Now the camera was locked onto the window and would stay that way for the duration. Satisfied with the targeting, a final three-second button press slaved the drone's navigation systems to the camera's target.

The show began in earnest on the GNN feed, a supposed news discussion by a panel of two men and one woman. The man in the middle of the trio launched into a diatribe about the latest "scandal" plaguing the Republican president. They had exhausted their supply of attack material for anything vaguely current, so their new scoop was focused on a speech the president had made twenty-some years earlier. He had cracked a joke about homosexuals and they were playing the video and wringing their hands over the horrors of homophobia. Middle Man turned to the woman on his left, his face contorted in grave concern. "Julia, can the president survive this episode, given the bigotry on display?"

She tilted her head and pursed her lips. "I don't know if he can. This is bad."

Berringer squeezed the trigger on the joystick. "Survive this, assholes."

DOWNTOWN: The drone was five feet across, its frame a lattice of titanium tubes. The landing struts extended a foot in front of the main body. The center of the craft cradled batteries, circuitry, and a kilo of Semtex, the charge shaped to direct the bulk of its force forward. It hovered two feet above the rooftop, its propellers in a high-pitched whine, the downdraft scattering dust and pebbles below.

Its antenna received a short data burst and it obeyed the command, initiating a "go" routine in its digital brain. The machine rose a few feet more, tilted forward, and increased prop speed to maximum. The overpowered drone sped toward the skyscraper, its destination locked to the center of the camera's view. Its speed was 78 MPH when the distance sensors on the front of the craft told the microprocessor brain that the building was fifty feet away. A "fire" routine executed and shot the blunt tips of the landing struts forward like bullets from a rifle. They struck the heavy glass separating GNN's Studio 4 from the world outside, each one knocking a fist-sized hole and spider-webbing the glass. A half-second later, the drone hit the weakened glass. An onboard accelerometer registered the impact and executed one last routine from its code, this one called "sendMessage." A relay closed and delivered a surge of electrical current from the batteries to the detonator buried in the Semtex. Then the drone was no more.

BERRINGER HOVERED a finger just above the last button he would push, watching as the building grew larger and larger in his goggles. The instant the drone's video feed disappeared, he hit the button. The GNN broadcast now filled his field of view. There would be the brief delay inherent in all modern satellite-based broadcasting, but he wouldn't have to wait long. Four seconds later, he heard a split second of breaking glass, then the view turned to hell. The studio set was designed so that the view outside the window was the backdrop for the news desk, the pretend newscasters with their backs to the window. They barely had time to register that anything was happening, much less time to understand that their time on Earth was done.

The screen filled with a fireball so bright it bloomed the image to pure white for several moments before fading back to the orange and black conflagration that had been the news desk area. The sound was so loud that it overpowered the microphones and came across as a crackling distortion. Then the sound levels dropped and the mics were working again. Screams and a wailing fire alarm filled his headphones. A crack appeared in the lens of the camera that was recording the melee. The news desk had split in half and toppled forward, its top surface now facing the camera. Berringer could make out blood and gore where slick wood had been moments before.

Middle Man was simply gone, but his side-mates were visible. Julia, who had sat on his left, lay sprawled in front of the desk, limbs akimbo, dead eyes in a half-burned face staring at the camera. The other one, whose name Berringer didn't recall, was on the far left side of the frame. He was covered in blood and char, holding his severed left forearm and hand in his right hand, screaming at the top of his lungs. The fire suppression system fired, water spraying from above in conical patterns. Other people started staggering into the frame, wandering, dazed, everyone in such a state of shock that no one thought to kill the broadcast. Berringer watched.

DAY 3

In Flight

4:15 PM EASTERN

THE GULFSTREAM HAD a clever satellite-based system I'd never encountered that enabled cellular communications at altitude, which made staying in touch a lot easier. No crappy VoIP calls over Wi-Fi. My phone simply worked as if it were on the ground. After takeoff, I called Pitt and told him what I needed to see in New York so he could pre-grease the wheels of access. He pushed back against my investigation of the media attacks instead of focusing exclusively on the abductions by Sol, but he eventually gave in and agreed to work the situation in New York. Not long after that my phone lit up with news alerts about a new media attack, this time in Atlanta. I booted my laptop and dug in. Thirty minutes later, I knew everything publicly known about the attack. Damn. Another attack using tech. Interesting.

I did some online research and called a New York electronic-goodies store called Tinkerplace and asked for the manager. She was exceptionally polite, especially for a New Yorker, and had a pleasant

Slavic accent. After a fifteen-minute discussion, she agreed to immediately build the device I needed. I closed my laptop.

"Hey, Sheila?" I said.

"Yeah?"

"You've been organizing the FBI data for me. Tell me something. Are the kidnapping-slash-murders and media attacks being handled by the same team or different?"

"Separate."

"You seen any rationale in the files to explain why?"

"Actually, yeah, there are minutes from a meeting in which that issue was debated and decided. Several agents argued for one task force to handle everything but the brass wasn't convinced, thought they were different problems with different bad actors."

"Hmmm."

"Disagree?"

"Yup. Why do you think I'm bothering with the media attacks when my goal is to locate Sol Ringer? This is all connected."

"What makes you say that?"

"My Spidey senses."

She chuckled.

"Laugh, but you'll see," I said. "My Spidey senses don't miss."

WE LANDED at Teterboro and a limo was waiting on the tarmac. Good job, Pitt. The driver handed me two bags, one from Harbor Freight and one from Tinkerplace, and we were on our way.

As the Manhattan skyline came into view I got that same sick feeling in my stomach I've gotten every time I've been there since 9/11, a sadness and anger over the missing twin towers. The skyline looks balanced again with the Freedom Tower in place and it's a beautiful building, but it's not the same and never will be.

I unpacked my goodies and tested everything while Sheila watched with a quizzical look on her face. Satisfied that I was good to go, I put everything back into a single bag and dropped it on the floorboard just as we came up out of the Lincoln Tunnel. I rolled my window down.

The driver immediately cut eyes at me in the rearview mirror and lowered the partition between us. "Everything okay back there, buddy?"

"All good," I said. "I like the smell and energy of this city. Taking it in."

"If you say so." The partition raised.

DAY 3

New York City

5:55 PM

PITT HAD COME THROUGH AGAIN. An NYPD detective in plainclothes with a badge on his belt stood waiting on the sidewalk when we exited the limo. I walked toward him, Sheila in tow. He was tall, at least six-four, dressed in khakis and a black leather jacket over a polo shirt.

He said, "You Sam Flatt?"

I stuck my hand out. "One and the same."

He had a great handshake. "Vince Mattoni. You wanna tell me what we're doing here?"

"Need to test a theory I'm working on about the shooting."

"Nobody explained much a' nothing to me, just said be here. You a cop?"

"It's complicated, Vince, but I'm a hundred percent authorized to be here. You ready?"

He locked eyes with me for ten seconds without saying anything, then shrugged. "What the hell. Come on."

After a few minutes and some badge-flashing by Mattoni, the three of us were standing on the rooftop exactly where the decoy device had been found. I pulled one of my gizmos from the bag, a simple box with an on/off switch and an LED. I switched it on, then tested it by pushing a button on my second gizmo. The LED glowed. I handed it to Sheila. "Stay here," I said. "And keep your phone handy."

I headed back to the stairway and Mattoni followed. We descended to the top floor of the building, then took the elevator to the ground floor.

"You working this case?" I said to Mattoni.

"Yeah, I'm on the task force. Supposed to be, anyway. Damn feds all but locking us out. Where we going now?"

"To the so-called shooter's nest."

"Why 'so-called'?"

"You'll see."

Once we were in place on the rooftop where the shots had come from, I called Sheila. When she answered, I said, "Ready?"

"And waiting."

I pushed the button on my trigger device. "Anything?"

"Nothing."

I moved all around the rooftop and tested it a dozen more times. The LED on Sheila's end never lit up. I pulled out my final gizmo, a laser rangefinder. "Sheila, face this way and be as still as you can, please."

Looking through the rangefinder at six-times magnification, I had a good view of her on the rooftop down the street. I keyed the laser and saved the distance it calculated. "Sheila, hang tight, I'll call you back in a few," I said into the phone and ended the call.

Mattoni scratched his head. "You gonna fill me in on what you're doing here or not?"

"Patience, grasshopper."

That drew a laugh from the big cop. "Man, I haven't seen that show in a thousand years."

We made our way back down to the street and crossed the street. I looked at the building down the street to my left where Sheila waited, then the one to my right we had just left. I studied the buildings between them. I pointed to one that was about halfway between the two locations, almost directly across the street from where we were standing. "That one."

We crossed back over and entered the lobby of the building I'd identified. More badging. A little pushback this time from building security. The guy at the front desk called in his supervisor. He got a little testy but when Mattoni went full-blown pissed-off NYPD on him, he backed down. The guy at the desk created keycards that would get us to the roof and we were on our way.

When we stepped out onto the roof I said, "Walk carefully up here." Watching every step, I eased my way to the parapet that looked down on the location across the street where Scott met his maker. After five minutes of studying the surface, I found it. An area about six feet square held numerous indentations, some of them clearly recognizable as footprints. Not detailed enough to capture shoe tread, but definitely footprints.

I backed up and shot a dozen photos of the area with my phone, then dialed Sheila. "Ready?"

"Go."

I pushed the button on the trigger device.

Before I could ask, Sheila said, "Light's on."

Damn skippy. "Okay, face this way and stand still again." I used the rangefinder again and saved the distance between us and Sheila.

"Alright," Mattoni said, "I've been patient. What the hell?"

"You familiar with the theory of the shooting?" I said.

"More or less. Guy shot from down there," he pointed to the building with the so-called shooter's nest. "And had a decoy over there." He pointed toward Sheila.

"Right. Except it didn't happen that way." I held up the trigger gizmo. "This has the exact electronic guts that the shooter used on the controller for the decoy device. And the little box Sheila's holding has the same guts that were on the decoy device itself. What happened when I tried to trigger Sheila's device from the other building?"

"Nothing."

"Exactly." I held up the trigger gizmo. "That's because this type of system doesn't have the range to reach from there"—I pointed to the other building—"to there." I pointed to Sheila.

"Ahhhh," Mattoni said. "So you think the guy was actually here?" He pointed to the area with the footprints.

"Right."

"But forensics clearly shows the shots came from the other building."

"They did."

"Then I don't get it."

I pointed at the footprints. "The guy was here." I pointed toward Sheila. "The decoy device was there." I pointed at the other building. "And the gun was there. He sat here and controlled both the gun and the decoy device remotely."

"Remote-control gun, huh?"

"Yeah. Some kind of robotic shooting platform that he controlled from here."

"Sounds crazy, like a movie."

I would later think back many times on that statement by Mattoni: *Like a movie.*

DAY 3

Location Unknown

EVENING

ACOMA SLAMMED his binder shut and dropped it on the floor. "I don't know about the rest of you, but I've had enough of this bullshit."

No one answered.

"I'm sitting over here with a bunch of transcripts of interviews I've done over the past few years. Fucking history. What's the point?"

Hurd, in a quiet voice, said, "Maybe you should shut up, Acoma. This place is probably bugged."

"Oh come on, you bunch of candy-assed boomers. Fuck this guy. He's probably some weekend warrior, a militia asshole or some shit."

"No, he's not," Wilder said.

Acoma said, "And how do you know that, 'your honor'?"

"You know him, Marcus?" Dickey said.

"Know him, no. But I've seen him in DC before, a couple times, in fact."

Hurd: "Where?"

Wilder: "Once at a formal affair at the White House, a dinner honoring some ambassador. The other time, some conference. He spoke. Been racking my brain to remember what about."

Dickey: "When?"

Wilder: "Hard to say. You know how it is, we do so many of these things."

Acoma: "I don't give a shit. He can—"

The door opened and Harrow strode through, went straight to Acoma's cell. Oaf Anthony showed up seconds later. Harrow looked at Acoma. "You were warned not to discuss the provided material."

"Go fuck yourself, General," Acoma said.

Harrow looked over his shoulder at Anthony and gave one tight nod.

Anthony pulled the big key ring from a desk drawer, walked to Acoma's cell, unlocked it. The door of bars creaked as he opened it.

Acoma said, "Stay the—"

Anthony hit him flush in the mouth with such force that the inside of Acoma's lips now had a series of cuts that were a perfect map of his teeth. Not that Acoma knew this. He fell straight back onto his back, his head making a slight *thock* sound when it hit the concrete floor, and never moved. His glassy eyes stared at the ceiling as he blinked.

Without a moment's hesitation, Anthony reached into his pocket and pulled out a heavy pair of wire-cutters. He knelt, picked up Acoma's left hand, then looked back at Harrow. The general nodded. Anthony cut off Acoma's thumb as if he were trimming a rose bush.

Blood poured from the stump and Acoma did a reflexive sit-up, shrieking like an animal. Anthony said, "Shut up."

Acoma shrieked again.

Still holding Acoma's hand with his own left hand, Anthony hit him in the mouth again with a right. Acoma fell back into a prone position and the shrieks turned into a mewling sound.

Anthony retrieved a cigar lighter from his pocket, flicked it, and a blue flame extended an inch in a pointed jet. He held the flame to the stump where Acoma's thumb had been. The blood boiled, then turned to black char as Acoma sprang back up with another shriek and tried to jerk away.

"Shut up and be still or I'll hit you again," Anthony said.

More mewling. Seconds later, Anthony released Acoma's hand. He stood, left the cell, and calmly closed the cell door. It clanked into the locked position. Harrow turned and left the room. Anthony followed and closed the office door as they left.

There was no more conversation, just the sound of a grown man bawling.

DAY 3

Location Unknown

EVENING

GENERAL LUCIAN HARROW sat behind an old metal office desk in an office with bare concrete walls, floor, and ceiling. The desk held a phone, a closed laptop, mouse pad, compact mouse, and a steaming cup of coffee. The windowless office's only light pushed its glow up at the ceiling from a floor lamp with a stainless shaft and a blue glass cone on top. The office door was closed.

Harrow sipped the coffee, closed his eyes, and inhaled the aroma of the blessed liquid that was keeping him going. At fifty-eight, he prided himself on his stamina, but stress and insane hours were draining it. For the thousandth time, he wondered if he was doing the right thing. For forty years he had served. No Air Force Academy. No ROTC. He had come in as a rawboned high school graduate looking to prove himself, looking to carry on a family tradition of patriotic service set by his grandfather in World War I and his father in World War II. And he had.

He had risen in the Reagan years, stalled somewhat in the nineties, then hit his real stride and rose through the ranks in the aftermath of 9/11, earning the first star for his collar in 2006. Adding the third just two years ago. Now here he was, already guilty of enough crimes to put him away for several lifetimes. Senators in his jail. A SCOTUS justice, for Christ's sake. And this was just the beginning. Had he been crazy to start this?

For the thousandth time, he came to the same conclusion: He was doing what had to be done. The United States had gone 150 years without major internal conflict, an extraordinary run, but things had started to unravel over the past decade or so and the fraying of the national fabric was accelerating by the day. Someone had to act. He would bear that burden. Besides, with the things already in motion and the number of people involved, trying to stop it would be nigh impossible and would probably turn out far worse in the end.

He took another sip of the coffee. Enough rumination. He pushed a button on the phone and said, "Wilson, report to my office."

"Be right there," a voice answered.

Three minutes later, Wilson Bradshaw arrived. Wilson was pure civilian but dedicated to the operation, dedicated to Harrow. He was twenty-eight, a baby-face who looked closer to fifteen. Dressed in baggy blue shorts and a Spiderman T-shirt, he was a far cry from the disciplined world Harrow had lived his entire adult life, but that was trivial. Wilson was a key element in the operation and he could dress in feathers for all Harrow cared.

Harrow gestured at the chair in front of his desk and Wilson sat.

"Update?" Harrow said.

"On target. The backdrop is up and wired. Carpet being laid right now. The rest of the pieces will be in place before we stop tonight. Tomorrow I'll start wiring all the tech. We'll be ready on time."

Harrow nodded. "Wilson, I need you to be my eyes and ears out there. If anyone looks shaky, you see any signs of cold feet, you bring it to me immediately."

Wilson practically beamed. "You got it, sir."

"Seen anything like that so far?"

Wilson shook his head. "Nope. Course, most of them don't know the details but they know what we're doing is important."

"Okay, keep me posted. That's all for now."

Wilson nodded and made his exit.

Harrow opened the laptop and a map of the United States painted the screen. He zoomed in and out, studying the status indicators at a dozen locations around the country. The three green markers and eight yellows were good news. The lone red symbol parked on top of Washington, DC, was not. Festering hellhole.

He pulled a simple cell phone from his pocket and punched in a number. Moments later, the call was answered.

UNKNOWN MALE: "Yes."

HARROW: "Problem?"

UNKNOWN MALE: "Town's crazy with all that's going on. Looks like every politician above rookie has a phalanx of security around them. Traffic's clogged up and that's clogging me up."

HARROW: "What's your plan?"

UNKNOWN MALE: "Flipping shifts, moving the bulk of the prep to night instead of day, after the pricks have been tucked in at home."

HARROW: "Can you do that without raising questions?"

UNKNOWN MALE: "We should be okay. Will advise if not."

HARROW: "Roger that. Standing by. Out."

Harrow ended the call and returned the phone to his pocket. Closed the lid on the laptop. Stood and walked to a calendar on the wall. Pulled the cap off the red Sharpie that hung on a string beside the calendar. He marked an X across the current day and said to himself, "Seven days. Everything changes in seven days."

DAY 3

New York City

AFTER WE FINISHED up at the crime scene I invited Mattoni to join us for a nice dinner at Keens Steakhouse in appreciation for his help. We filled up on glorious beef in the warm atmosphere of the old restaurant. I liked Mattoni. He was a no-nonsense New Yorker and a funny guy once he had imbibed a bit.

I'd hoped to be able to influence the investigation with what we learned on the rooftops but the more we talked, the more obvious it became that the FBI was running the show. Telling NYPD next to nothing. Listening to NYPD on exactly nothing. Calling the FBI guys working the case wasn't an option since they'd want details on who I was and how I knew what I knew. *Me? I'm just some black-ops guy working for an agency that doesn't exist. Oh, we hacked your systems and I have access to everything you're doing.* Yeah. No.

I decided I'd call Courtney Meyer, an FBI agent here in the city who worked RICO and other corruption cases. We'd butted heads a year earlier on a case I was working for a private party in Vegas, but things eventually smoothed out and we helped each other. This case probably wasn't in her wheelhouse but I thought she might be willing to ask a few questions and get my info to the right people. We'd see.

"Hey, Earth to Sammy! Come in, Sammy!" Mattoni said.

I jerked back into the moment. "Sorry." I looked and realized Sheila wasn't at the table. I'd really zoned out.

"Looking for your chick?" Mattoni said.

"Not my chick, but where'd she go?"

He shrugged. "Got a phone call and disappeared."

"I need to hit the head. If you see our waiter, get us a dessert menu?"

"You got it."

When I turned into the little corridor that held the restrooms I saw Sheila in a corner at the far end. She had her phone to her ear. Her eyes met mine and she quickly ended the call and walked toward me. She smiled and painted on a nonchalant look but it was too late. She'd tripped my hinky trigger with that instant hang-up.

"Hey," she said and held her phone up. "My mom."

"Everything okay?" I said.

"Yeah, yeah. Wanted to know when I'm coming for a visit." She let out a sad sigh. "Hard to tell her I don't know when. You know how it is in this line of work."

"Gotcha. See you in a minute." I entered the men's room. Took care of business. Washed my hands and face. Dragged wet fingers through my hair. Headed back to the table, sat down.

"Where does your mom live?" I said.

"Sandusky, Ohio."

"Sweet," Mattoni said. "Cedar Point. Love all those roller coasters. Took the family there on vacation a couple of years ago. You been, Sammy?"

I nodded. "Same as you, took my wife and daughter a few years ago. Flew in and out of Cleveland, checked out the Rock and Roll Hall of Fame while we were there."

We yakked about roller coasters and gorged ourselves on dessert, then called it a night. I offered to have our limo drop Mattoni somewhere but he declined and we said goodbye. Sheila was chatty as we headed back to Teterboro. Too chatty. Trying too hard. She finally quieted down when I pulled out my laptop.

I was about to email Courtney Meyer when I changed my mind. I pushed the intercom button for the driver and said, "Change of plans. Turn around and take me to the Four Seasons."

"Which one?" the driver said.

"The one near 26 Federal Plaza."

"Downtown."

"Right."

"What's the plan?" Sheila said.

"I need to see a friend at the FBI in the morning, and I need you to head back to Houston to work the computers for me tomorrow. Find a red-eye and have him drop you at the airport after you drop me off."

"Yes sir, boss." Catty.

"Problem?" I said.

"No, no. Sorry. Just tired."

I smiled. "No worries."

IN THE HOTEL, I found myself thinking of Abby. Missing her. Remembering how when we were married and I was on the road (here in the States on a forensic gig, not the BAM work earlier in the marriage), I'd always call her when I made it to my hotel. Tell her about my day. Listen to her about hers. Exchange 'I love yous.' Say good night. I missed that so much.

I did what I often do with my heartbreak and longing. I wrote a letter. One that will never be delivered but somehow provides catharsis.

DEAR ABB,

Sitting here in a lonely place on a job and found myself thinking about you. That happens a lot. Even after six years. I wish it didn't. I wish I'd been able to move on by now, but I have to be honest and say I haven't. You're the love of my life, I miss you, and suspect I always will. I miss your smile, your kisses, the smell of you. I even miss you using me as a heater for your freezing hands. (Ha!)

Would you believe that after all this time I've never had a dream about another woman? It's true. Not once. If I dream about a woman, it's you.

I know I didn't always express how I feel in words very well. It's a weakness of mine and even though it's no excuse, that's the truth. Whether I said it enough or not, I've loved you every moment since the first time I laid eyes on you. (While having a pepperoni pizza at Papa Pete's Perfect Pizza. Remember?)

You're the most beautiful woman I've ever known and on top of that, I have more respect for you than any woman I've ever known. Aside from Ally, which is a different kind of thing altogether, you are the only person in my entire adult life whose opinion of me mattered to me. Everyone else? I couldn't care less. You? Your praise warmed my soul, and your criticism, or me feeling I lessened myself in your eyes, always devastated me. That's the power of love, I think.

Well, I'll stop rambling now. I just want to say...I miss you. I love you. Please come home, baby.

Sam

I SAVED the file into a secure folder on my cloud, naming it AbbLetter14.doc.

ARLINGTON, VIRGINIA

FOR SOL RINGER, the other missions had been for duty to the general and the cause. This one would be satisfying on a more personal level. Robert Hecht was a DC fixture, but not a limelight figure like politicians and judges. He was a cockroach, scurrying around in the hidden game, lobbying and fixing and bribing at will in the sewer of power politics. All that was bad enough, but it paled in comparison to the cretin's personal perversions and exploits that preyed on children.

Sol crouched in the bushes beside Hecht's garage, watching the marker on his phone screen that tracked Hecht's approaching car. When he saw the sweep of headlights as the car made its final turn a block away, he killed the phone and stowed it. The ridiculous ten-bay garage was on the back side of the house, out of view from the street, facing acres of manicured lawn behind the home. *Thanks, asshole.*

The driveway lit up as the car turned into the property. The Tesla's approach was all but silent, just the faint sound of tires on concrete as it passed by Sol and made a looping turn to line up with the garage.

The door rose on the third bay and the car moved forward, making more left-right adjustments than should have been necessary as it pulled into the bay.

Sol pulled his tactical mask down, covering his face, and moved toward the open bay. The driver door opened just as he stepped inside, and from fifteen feet away he could smell the whiskey. Sol was six feet away when Hecht turned and saw him.

Hecht wobbled, placed a hand on the roof of the car to steady himself. Squinted and jutted his face forward. "What the fuck?"

Sol said nothing. He slipped the slapjack from his pocket and swung it hard. The crack of the leaded leather on the asshole's chin warmed Sol's soul. Hecht's eyes rolled back and he melted to the concrete floor like a popped balloon with a thin dribble of blood oozing from a cut left by the slapjack. Sol fished through the man's pockets until he found the Tesla's key fob. He popped the trunk, grabbed the unconscious drunk by the back of his belt, dragged him to the back of the car, then picked him up and literally tossed him into the trunk. Sol bound Hecht's ankles, knees, wrists, and mouth with duct tape, then closed the trunk.

SOL PULLED over and sent a text that said simply "10." He then removed the battery from the burner phone that had fulfilled its one-use purpose and tossed both into the woods that lined the road. He resumed the drive, the Tesla quiet and smooth on the curvy road. Six miles later, he turned off the county road and onto a narrow gravel lane that wound through the woods. Finding separate suitable locations for the week's exfiltrations hadn't been the easiest thing, but he'd done it and his operation was nearing its end. After a couple miles on the gravel and a sequence of NO TRESPASSING signs nailed to roadside trees, the woods gave way to a half-acre clearing with a rustic cabin on its back side, as expected. What he didn't expect were the lights in the cabin windows and a pickup parked over on the right side of the cabin. *Damn.*

He pulled a new burner phone from his pocket to send an abort message, then two things happened: The cabin's front door opened and a man wearing nothing but boxers and sandals, holding some variant of an AR-15 to his shoulder as he trotted toward the car, shouted something Sol couldn't hear from inside the car. Then a blinding light appeared overhead and a maelstrom of dirt and leaves kicked up as the helicopter descended toward the clearing. Boxer Shorts stopped, jerked his head toward the light and noise above.

Sol watched in disbelief as the man raised the gun to take aim at the helicopter. He hit the accelerator and the car shot forward, no spin, all go. He saw a muzzle flash just as the front of the car hit the man, knocking him ten feet forward. The rifle clattered onto the hood of the car and Sol hit the brakes. He exited the car and looked toward the helicopter. It bobbled momentarily, then stabilized. Its spotlight crossed the ground in front of Sol and stopped when it got to him. He held one finger high above his head, then jumped back into the car and backed it up out of the clearing.

He got out of the car and motioned the helicopter down, then went to the rear of the car, opened the trunk, hauled Hecht out and dropped him to the ground. The man was conscious now, writhing around like a fish out of water, trying to scream through the duct tape. Sol left him there and returned his attention to the helicopter as it settled onto the ground. He ran to it and opened the rear door, and shouted to the pilot, "Go get Hecht."

The pilot nodded, throttling the engine down. Sol crossed in front of the helicopter and ran to Boxer Shorts where he lay on the ground. He was auto-reaching to check for a pulse when he saw that there was no need. The man's back was broken, the upper half of his torso angled back at a twenty-degree angle. His eyes were open and empty, his mouth and neck stained with blood that no longer flowed. Sol grabbed him by the arms and dragged him behind the cabin, where he left him lying on a small crude patio. He headed back. Just as he was about to turn the corner of the cabin, an awful shriek sounded behind him. He turned toward the sound and pulled his balaclava up for a moment to uncover his ears. He heard a soft ruffle of feathers cross right to left. *Creepy-ass screech owl.* He pulled the balaclava back down.

When he got back to the helicopter, the pilot was trying to wrestle the struggling Hecht into the rear compartment. Sol hit him again with the slapstick and the struggle was over. He and the pilot shoved him in, and Sol strapped him to the floor of the compartment with a pair of ratcheting tie-down straps. The pilot returned to his seat and Sol was climbing into the copilot seat when he backed out of the helicopter and said, "Be right back."

He ran to the Tesla and grabbed a laptop bag he'd noticed on the front passenger seat, then returned to the helicopter and tossed the bag into the back. He mounted the copilot seat, buckled himself in, and spun a finger in the air. "Go!"

SOL RINGER

30 Years Earlier

JASPER, ALABAMA

"Time for bed, Solly."

"Can I stay up a little while longer, Daddy? Please?"

"No. You have school tomorrow. You go brush your teeth and get your pajamas on and I'll come tuck you in."

Eight-year-old Solly's insides drew into a tight little knot as he fought not to cry, not to beg. It wouldn't do any good. He went to the bathroom and brushed his teeth with bubblegum toothpaste on his Batman toothbrush. He peed and then his stomach got upset and he had to do number two. It was nasty and runny and so stinky. He cleaned his bottom, washed his hands, and put on his favorite pajamas, the ones with little Optimus Primes all over them. He turned off the lights and got into bed. Tucked himself in and pretended to be asleep.

He prayed his daddy wouldn't come. Or that if he did come and saw that he was asleep, he'd just leave. But the prayer didn't work. He heard the door creak open, then quietly close. Then he heard the lock turn. Solly lay perfectly still. He felt the mattress sink as Daddy sat down on the edge of the bed.

"Hey, Solly? You know Daddy loves you?"

Solly nodded, his eyes squinched shut now. He tried not to jerk when he felt Daddy's hand on his head, stroking his hair, but he couldn't help it.

"There there, special boy," Daddy said. "Scoot over so Daddy can lie beside you."

Solly's insides shook so much that they made his outside shake, too. "Daddy, please don't." Daddy didn't say anything, but Solly heard the worst sound in the whole world, Daddy undoing his belt, then the snap on his jeans, then the zipper going down. The rustle of the jeans as Daddy pulled them down and then off. The whisper of Daddy pulling his T-shirt over his head.

"Scoot over like I told you." His voice a little meaner sounding now.

Solly scooted as far as he could in the little bed, till he was against the wall. He wished he could roll right through that wall and never come back. But he couldn't. He felt the bed give as Daddy laid down beside him. Then Daddy's hand was rubbing his back. Then his bottom. Then the bad part, Daddy pulling Solly's Optimus Prime pajama bottoms down, then off. Then his underwear. Daddy rubbing his bare bottom.

"You remember what we talked about, how one day we would do something *really* special?"

Solly shrugged. Solly shook. Daddy kept rubbing his bottom, now running his finger through Solly's crack.

"I know you remember. Tonight is that special night. I need you to get up on your knees, like a dog."

———

THE NEXT MORNING, Solly could barely move. Mama came in and cooed at him, then helped him stand up. His sheets were bloody, just like his bottom and the backs of his legs. He tried to walk but something was wrong. It hurt too bad. He fell down on the floor and screamed.

"Shhhh, baby," Mama said. "Shhh." She had big tears on her face.

Then she picked him up and said, "I'm so sorry, baby. No more. You hear me? No more."

Solly hurt so bad he didn't remember a lot of that day, but he remembered the doctor talking about a "severe tear." He remembered the doctor telling Mama that he would walk funny for a long time, maybe forever. He remembered a lot of policemen. He remembered Mama apologizing over and over and over. Then he was in a hospital room and stayed there a long time, many days. Maybe even weeks.

Solly never saw Daddy again and he was glad.

RIGHT-WING EXTREMISTS BELIEVED BEHIND TERROR ATTACKS

NEW YORK — FBI investigators now believe the abduction of political VIPs and attacks on members of the press are part of a coordinated right-wing domestic terror campaign. United States senators Howard Hurd (R-AL) and Jack Dickey (D-NV), as well as Supreme Court justice Marcus Wilder, are missing and presumed dead, according to highly placed sources within the investigation. In addition to these abductions, popular MBC news anchor Chad Scott was gunned down on a New York street, and a day later, GNN's Atlanta headquarters was targeted in a drone explosion that killed three and injured a dozen more.

The president, himself a conservative considered extreme by many, has been remarkably quiet on this unprecedented series of attacks on the government and the American press. Lawmakers from both sides of the aisle are calling for immediate congressional investigations, and some have gone so far as to suggest that the president tacitly supports the murder and mayhem being unleashed against these institutions.

"It's becoming pretty obvious that the president is okay with what's going on," Democratic Representative Alexa Smith-Wellington said. "It's time for Congress to say we're not okay with him continuing as president."

Numerous high-profile members of the news media are speaking out and vowing to continue covering the news in the same fact-based way they always have. Despite the defiant stance, however, many of the most visible news personalities have hired personal security details or expanded the security they already had.

OPINION: TIME FOR THE PRESIDENT TO ACT, OR GO

WASHINGTON, DC — The deafening silence emanating from the White House as our most cherished institutions are under attack is unfathomable. In the span of three days, three high government officials and four members of the press have been murdered, while many others have been injured, some seriously. This cannot continue. Not the attacks themselves, and not the vacuum of criticism and leadership emanating from 1600 Pennsylvania Avenue. While it is widely believed that President Cartwright will address these issues at the annual State of the Union address next week, that is insufficient. The country needs to hear from its purported leader. Now. Yes, the stakes are personal for me. As a journalist in twenty-first century United States, I should not have to fear for my life for speaking truth. As a father, I should not have to console my daughter, who is afraid her daddy won't be coming home tonight.

At today's White House press briefing, the White House spokesperson refused to answer any questions about what's being done to protect government officials who don't enjoy a blanket of Secret Service protection, or members of the fourth estate, aside from meaningless platitudes about "staying out of the way of the investigation" and "not commenting while an investigation is ongoing."

This is unacceptable, Mr. President. We understand that you don't like the press because we hold you accountable to the American people, but we are supposed to be protected by the First Amendment to the Constitution, and all Americans should be able to walk safely down the street. That includes those who may not have voted for you, sir. For the love of country, for the love of humanity, if you have any left, do something, sir. If you won't, then perhaps it's time for the people to find someone who will.

TERROR IN THE SOUTHLAND

ATLANTA, GA — In a city where the air is hot and the tea runs sweet, a bitter pall has seized the day. Yesterday, during what should have been a routine televised discussion panel, three people met their deaths and ten more were injured. Four of those wounded remain hospitalized. The dead had no opportunity to call their loved ones, whether children or parents or life partners, and say goodbye. They were killed without warning when someone flew an explosives-laden drone into the studio where they were discussing the latest scandal to lay siege to embattled president John Cartwright. In addition to the loss of life, the attack occurred on live television, resulting in a video clip that has gone viral and is approaching one billion views on the internet.

While this morbid recording memorializes the last moments of life for the journalists who were killed, it also shows the level to which some are willing to go to silence those espousing views different from their own. Gone are the days when a different opinion was opposed but tolerated. Thanks to intolerance and hate, many journalists now fear for their very lives in this city that prides itself on congeniality and hospitality.

In a statement today from Director Henrik Blass, the FBI stated that leads were being followed and efforts were being made to track down the terrorists responsible with "great and decisive speed," but no details were forthcoming as to what the investigation looked like or what leads were being followed. Although the accounts differ somewhat, multiple eyewitnesses near the scene of the explosion report seeing a suspicious man holding what is believed to have been a remote control of the type used to fly drones. All witnesses agreed that he was a white man of average height and build, and at least one of the witnesses said he was wearing a jacket emblazoned with white supremacist language and symbology.

Those who saw anything or may know something about this man are encouraged to call the Atlanta Police Department at the number shown below. A reward of $50,000 is being offered for information that leads to the conviction of those responsible for this heinous crime.

DAY 4

9:40 Am

NEW YORK CITY

SPECIAL AGENT COURTNEY MEYER and I shook hands and sat down at a sidewalk table in front of a coffee shop near her office at 26 Federal Plaza.

After a couple minutes of small talk, Meyer said, "What's this about, Sam?"

A waiter showed up, took our orders, and left.

"You involved in the big kidnappings or the media attacks?"

She shook her head. "No, why?"

"I have some information the investigators would find helpful."

"Should I ask how you came by such information?"

I gave a mini-shrug. "An hour of investigation and experimentation at the crime scene."

She cocked her head and narrowed her eyes. "Why would you be at the crime scene doing anything?"

"Don't ask."

Meyer blew out a long breath. "Why am I not surprised you'd say that?"

"'Cause you're a smart lady."

She laughed. "Right. So you want the contact info for the investigators?"

"I'd prefer to remain officially uninvolved. Think you could pass it on to them for me? Discreetly?"

This drew a big sigh. "And where am I supposed to have gotten this information from, on a case I'm not remotely involved in?"

"Like I said, you're a—"

"Smart lady. I know. And you can be a manipulative S-O-B, Mr. Flatt."

"Not really, at least not on purpose. Unless it's really necessary, anyway."

"And this is one of those times?"

"It is."

She pulled her phone from her purse and opened a note-taking app. "Shoot. And you owe me."

"Agreed," I said. I pulled a hand-drawn sketch of the area where the shooting took place from my pocket and handed it to her. "The big X is where the shooter was. They have him at the spot marked A. They're wrong."

Meyer studied the sketch. "Your rationale is?"

"The decoy device was remote controlled. The type of gear the guy was using isn't capable of transmitting from A to B."

She looked at the sketch. "B is the decoy device?"

"Right. The shooter sat at X and controlled the decoy device at B and the shooting rig at A. It works. I verified it myself."

"Wait, you're saying the guy used what, a remote-controlled gun?"

"An 'advanced, remotely operated robotic shooting platform' is a better description."

She entered that on her phone. The waiter returned with our coffees. "Okay, I'll pass this on," she said. "Now tell me why and how you're involved in this case."

"I can't, Courtney. I really can't, but I only want to help."

She shook her head, took a sip of her coffee, then started blowing across the surface of the hot coffee to cool it. "Who the hell are you?"

"You know who I am. You checked me out nine ways from Sunday last year when the Vegas thing went down."

"Bullshit. In the system, you're just an expert witness in digital forensics. And that's a damned lie. You're something else...some*one* else."

I sipped my coffee and said nothing.

"I'll tell them this came from an unrelated CI but know this: If they lean on me—if they push—I'll give you up. I'm not about to screw my career in order to keep your name out of this."

"Of course," I said. "I wouldn't want you to. Just do your best, and I do owe you one."

"You owe me a big one."

"A big one," I said.

I dropped a ten on the table for the coffee and we said our goodbyes. I texted my driver and he was there three minutes later. "Head to the Lower East Side," I said. "Allen Street. One-hundred block."

"Place where I picked up your goodies the other day, huh?" he said.

"Yup."

I raised the partition and dialed Sheila. "Anything new come in this morning?" I said when she answered.

"Nada."

"Roger that. Need you to use that NSA resource we have on standby."

"What are we looking for?"

"When we hang up I'll send over a list of search terms. They'll be narrow, granular. Looking for any emails NSA has captured over the past year that are responsive to the search terms and conditions I'm sending you."

"I'll get on it."

"Thanks, Sheila." I ended the call and emailed her the search terms I'd put together the night before. It was a long shot, but one I wanted to explore.

I leaned back and eased the volume up on the radio. I wished I hadn't when one of the many songs I associate with Abby came rolling out. Six years later and still all it takes is a song to make my stomach flip and my heart sink. Damn. This eventually led my mind back to the document in my pocket. I imagined trying to explain that to Abby. To Ally. I had a week to go before I could deal with it and tried not to dwell on it but it kept creeping in. How was I going to handle it when the time came?

DAY 4

10:11 Am

NEW YORK CITY

TINKERPLACE WAS my kind of store, a compact NYC shop brimming with gadgets and tech trinkets of great variety. I walked to the counter and asked for Alla.

A woman a few feet away turned and walked toward me. She said, "I am Alla Repina. How may I help you?"

I instantly recognized her voice from the phone. Then I went momentarily stupid. She was perhaps—scratch that, she was—the most beautiful woman I'd ever seen. Thirtyish. Five-six, five-seven. Dressed in snug jeans and an orange Tinkerplace T-shirt. Silky brunette hair in a ponytail. Olive skin. And the eyes. Oh, the eyes. They were so blue they were almost violet. I couldn't stop looking at them. They had what looked like tiny flecks of silver in them.

She reached out and tapped me on the shoulder. "Hello? How can I help you?"

"I—I'm so sorry. I'm Sam Flatt." My mind raced. How had I gone from lovesick for my long-gone wife to struck stupid by a pretty girl within the space of fifteen minutes? But that wasn't fair. She wasn't a pretty girl. She was extraordinary.

"Okay, Sam Flatt. How can I help you?"

"We spoke on the phone yesterday. You built the custom test rig for me on short notice."

"Ahhhhh. Did it meet your needs?"

I nodded. "Worked perfectly."

"Good. Do you need me to build something else?"

"No, I was hoping to pick your brain a bit if you have a few minutes."

"About what?"

"Robotics. The controllers for them. High-grade gear like that."

She made a sweeping gesture around the shop with a beautifully feminine hand. "We specialize more in the affordable, the hobby level."

"I see that, but I could also tell from our conversation yesterday that you're brilliant and knowledgeable. I have no doubt that knowledge goes beyond"—I gave my own little sweeping gesture—"this."

That generated a little smile, the first I'd seen. Yes, it was exquisite. Cute. Lopsided. Heart-thumping.

"I'm not sure I can help but if you come back in"—she glanced at a retro nixie tube clock on the wall—"forty-five minutes, you can buy me lunch nearby and pick my brain. How's that?"

I executed a slight bow. "I'll be back."

———

WALKING THE BLOCK OUTSIDE, killing time, I felt as giddy as a school kid at the idea of having lunch with her. Then I pondered once more how I'd gone from pining for a lost love to this ridiculous state. Bought a cup of coffee from a street vendor. Decided I didn't care how I went from one state to the other. This one felt better.

———

AT TWO MINUTES TILL ELEVEN, I was back at Tinkerplace. Alla saw me and gave a little wave and held up a finger. I waited by the door. A couple minutes later, we were crossing the street at the corner. I followed her into a small grocery store, through the aisles, dodging other customers in the cramped space. We pushed through a curtain of clear vinyl strips to a back room that held a long buffet. With her leading the way, we got Styrofoam to-go boxes, picked what we wanted, and went to a cash register in the corner where I paid for our lunch by the ounce, adding a couple bottles of water.

"Come," she said, and we were on the move again. We crossed another street and after a half-block we arrived at a small park with a handful of picnic tables. The day was warm and sunny, a rarity in New York for the time of year. We picked one and sat.

"So pick my brain, Sam Flatt," she said around a little bite of bourbon chicken.

I pulled up a photo on my phone and handed the phone to her.

"Ahhh. Robotic turret. Lots of fun. Airsoft guys are building robotic guns on this platform." She handed the phone back.

"Where would I get a larger version of this, something more heavy-duty, professional grade?"

She took a drink of water and looked up into the tree above us while she thought. Her nose was sprinkled with tiny freckles. "I have some suppliers that deal in things like that but I'll have to look them up at the shop. We only do high-grade gear like that on special order."

"Have you by chance ordered a high-end platform like that for anyone lately?"

She shook her head. "No."

"Let's say I wanted to control something on that platform that's fairly heavy, around ten pounds. The control would need to be precise, stable, no vibration, no jerkiness, smooth all the way."

"You'd be talking a lot of money. Gyro mounts, gimbals. Certainly custom coding. Anti-backlash measures. It would be a complex project. Do you know anything about robotics?"

"Not really." That wasn't exactly true. I'd used them both for recon and ordnance delivery, but I wasn't going into that with Alla, and everything I ever used was pre-built and ready to go.

She squinted her eyes a wee bit. "What's the ten-pound object you want to put on this turret, Sam Flatt?"

"Oh, not me, no no. I'm investigating something that's already happened, trying to wrap my head around it, figure out what to look for."

"A gun?" she said.

My nature was to clam up and offer no confirmation on this point, but I had the feeling that if I pulled that with this girl, she'd be done with me. She was very bright and shrewdness exuded from her. So did pheromones. A cloud of them.

I said, "Yup, a gun. A sniper rifle. Remote."

"Ahhh. The news man in Midtown, yes?"

On this, I smiled and gave a little shrug.

"Yes," she said. "The news man, Scott."

'News man' struck me as an odd thing for a New Yorker to call a high-profile network anchor. And there was the little accent buried in her excellent English. "Where are you from, Alla?"

"Before New York, you mean?"

I nodded.

"Kiev."

"How long you been here?"

Her eyes roved up toward the tree again, went left and right as she counted in her head. "Twelve years. Where are you from, Sam Flatt?"

"Texas."

"Are you a cowboy?"

"I have a horse."

"What is name of horse?"

That awkward phrasing delighted my heart. She was getting comfortable talking to me, dropping the caution, easing back into familiar patterns.

"His name is Johnny."

"After lunch, I'll look up the information you want. For now, tell me about Johnny, Sam Flatt."

So I told her all about Johnny. And my daughter Ally. We had a chuckle over the Ally and Alla coincidence. I didn't mention Abby.

Two hours later, I was in the limo headed to Teterboro for the flight back to Houston. I called Sheila again. When she answered, I said, "I'm sending you a revised set of search terms and conditions. Get them in to the NSA contact as soon as you can. I'll see you later today."

DAY 3

Location Unknown

MIDDAY

GENERAL HARROW SAT in his spartan office and looked across his desk at Sol Ringer. "Excellent work, Sol. I wanted to say that first. To get all these targets in the time you did, unbelievable."

Sol nodded. "Sir."

"Are we exposed with the incident at the cabin?"

Sol said, "Don't think so, sir. No indication of anyone else at the cabin, and that guy won't be talking to anyone."

"What'd you do with him?"

"Stashed him behind the cabin. It's in the middle of nowhere. Actually, in the woods, in the middle of nowhere."

"Good. And I appreciate your bringing Hecht in unharmed except for the minor dings."

"That was the mission."

Harrow nodded slowly. "I know, but I also know about your history, and we've talked about your animosity for people like him."

"Animals like him. He doesn't qualify as human."

"I understand. Just wanted you to know I appreciate your restraint. You and I are a little outside the traditional military chain-of-command relationship but you've been a professional all the way. I notice and I'm grateful to have you on our team."

"Glad to be here, sir. Do remember our deal, though."

Harrow nodded again. "After he's served his purpose in the operation, he's yours to do with as you please."

Another nod from Sol. Another "sir."

SOL LEFT. Harrow stood, smoothed his BDUs, and left the office himself. After a short walk he unlocked a steel door and stepped inside another small jail, this one more bare-bones than the one that held the other prisoners. It had two cells and nothing else.

Robert Hecht sat on a cot in the cell on the right. He hadn't been put into a jumpsuit yet. He wore the same clothes he'd had on when he arrived home the night before to find Sol waiting for him. His white shirt, pushed out by a large soft belly, was untucked and splotched with grime and a couple spots of blood. His fat face had a good-sized welt above the left eye. Harrow thought he had the eyes of a rat, tiny, black, and beady.

Hecht didn't get up. He raised his huge head and sneered at Harrow. "Whoever you are, you've made the biggest mistake of your life, asshole. Do you know who I am?"

"Your tough talk doesn't bother me, Hecht. You're a fat slob and a parasite on humanity."

"You'll be bothered when you find out the kind of names I have on speed dial."

"You're boring me, Hecht." Harrow slipped a phone from a shirt pocket and waved it at him. "I know exactly who you have on speed dial. I also have access to your bank accounts from this phone."

"Not without me, you don't."

"Wrong again. The only protection you had on anything was face recognition. I used your face to unlock it and did away with all that. It's all as open and free as a Montana sky now."

Hecht lumbered to his feet. "You mother—"

"You should know, that while you have lots of bank accounts, that's all you have now. Accounts. Empty ones. But take heart, you blubber-assed cretin, it will go to good use."

Hecht scowled. "What do you want?"

"I'm glad you asked," Harrow said, then gave Hecht a cold smile.

DAY 4

In Flight

2:36 PM CENTRAL

AFTER TAKEOFF, I called Sheila and told her to go on home if she wanted, that I'd be late getting back to Houston and was probably going straight home myself. I told her to auto-forward anything that came in from the NSA to my computer and then said goodbye.

I called Ally, got her voicemail. Of course I would, school was in session and it was the middle of the day in Las Vegas, where she lived with her mom. I left a message asking how school was going. How life was going. How her mom was doing. Told her I loved her and to call me.

The jet's fridge had a nice stash of ice-cold Coors, as requested. I popped a top on one, kicked off my shoes, and reclined my seat. Halfway through the beer I was nodding off, the white noise of the engines combining with not enough sleep the night before. My phone rang. I looked at the screen: ABBY.

"Hey," I said.

"Hey back."

"What's going on?"

"I actually just landed in Houston, here for a meeting. Thought I'd see if you want to get together for dinner tonight."

Now I was wide awake.

"Yeah, sounds good, Ab. Where you staying?"

"I haven't picked a place yet. I'll text you when I have a handle on when I'll be done with the meeting. That work?"

"Yup. I'll watch for it."

"Bye-bye," she said and the call ended.

After that I did fall asleep and didn't wake up until the landing gear bumped me awake when it hit Texas pavement.

I DROVE from Hooks Airport to the office downtown. I was glad to see Sheila had taken me up on my offer and left early. I checked my computer for anything from the NSA or anything new from the FBI mirror. Nothing. I moved over to Sheila's workstation and went to work on what I'd really come here for. I pulled out some of the goodies I'd bought from Alla at Tinkerplace earlier in the day. Thirty minutes later, I had full control of Sheila's computer anytime I wanted it, as well as the ability to see everything she was doing, either in real-time or via recording for delayed playback. As a final step, I installed a fake smoke detector on the ceiling that contained a hidden camera.

Back on my own computer, I double-checked my access to all the gear. Prime. I was done. My phone chirped. The text from Abby said, "Meeting over in 15. I'm downtown, will get an Uber up to your place and we can figure out dinner. K?"

I texted her back: "I'm downtown, too. Tell me where you are and I'll pick you up."

DAY 4

Montgomery County, Texas

10:51 PM CENTRAL

THE RIDE from downtown to my suburb had been pleasant. Dinner at Perry's was delicious and more fun than anything Abby and I had done together in many years. Now we were back at my farm. The temperature and humidity had both dropped into pleasantness and a beautiful moon bathed my dozen acres in a glow that was almost ethereal. I spotted Johnny grazing way back near the back of the property.

Abby gave a little whistle and said, "Hey, where's my Johnny-boyyyyyy?"

I saw him raise his head and start casually walking our way from three hundred yards back. She called again and he broke into a run. That beautiful run, the mini-thunder picking up amplitude and speed as he got closer, properly thumping my chest for the last fifty yards. He braked ten yards out and went straight for Abby. He nuzzled and snuffled her as she cooed and stroked. A proper reunion of two old friends, it melted my heart.

After a while we headed back toward the house. Time to find out where this night was headed.

"You need a ride to a hotel?" I said.

She stopped walking, turned to me, put her arms around my neck. After a moment of looking into my eyes, she kissed me. Sweetly at first, then with hunger. I responded accordingly to both. Then she backed up to arm's length and said, "No, I don't want a ride to a hotel."

WE LAID IN BED AFTERWARD, Abby's head on my chest, my arm around her. We stayed that way a long time. No words. I tried to wrap my head around it. This was something I'd longed for for years. Dreamed about. Fantasized about. Tried several times, unsuccessfully, to make happen. Then she'd popped up out of nowhere, and on the very day I'd had my man triggers tripped by someone else for the first time since we split.

After at least a half-hour, she said, "Sam?" Raised up on an elbow so she could look me in the eye.

"Hmm?"

"Do you still love me?"

I smiled. It was the exact question I'd dreamed so many times of her asking and me answering. I gave the answer I'd long wanted to give, word for word. "You know I do. You're the one. You've always been the one." The moment the words rolled off my tongue, I had a panicked thought: *Did I still mean them?* Of course I did. Dream question. Dream answer.

She laid back down into snuggle position. Traced a finger down the center of my chest, past a pair of scars on my stomach, and stopped at my belly button. "Tell me how you got these two scars. The truth. No more fiction. No more excuses about nondisclosure agreements."

The proper answer, the one I'd given her so many times when we were married, was *Babe, you know I can't talk about it.* But that's not what I said. "Sit up so I can see you."

She raised back up on an elbow.

I touched the first scar, a six-inch jag. "An asshole got me with a knife called a *janbiya*. Curved, wicked looking."

"Where were you?"

I shook my head. "I'll answer your questions as far as I can. You deserve that. But there are still limits to what I can say. If you want to have this talk, I need you to respect that."

She drew in a sharp Abby breath, ready to do verbal battle, but then she let it out and said, "Okay."

I guess there's a first time for everything.

"Why did he cut you?"

"You sure you want to know?"

"I need to know."

"I'd just killed his son and he was pissed."

She flinched a bit. "His son? How old was he?"

"Twenty-three."

Her eyes were wide now, her lips a little parted. "Why'd you do that?"

"He was raping an eleven-year-old girl. His new wife."

Abby's mouth dropped wide open.

"Yeah," I said. "The girl was screaming, begging. His friends and father and uncles were in the next room laughing, making jokes about Amir finally 'becoming a man.'"

"And you what, just walked in there and did, what exactly?"

"Went in through a window. Pulled him off her. He started bellowing and charged me. So I killed him."

"How?"

"Shot him."

"Then the father came?"

I nodded. "He saw his son on the floor and flew into a rage, started slashing at me with his knife." I touched the scar again. "One of those slashes got me."

"What'd you do to him, the father?"

"I defended myself." I thought about that statement, then added, "And then some."

"What happened to the girl?"

"I took her to a US base, left her with them."

"And this one?" She touched the other scar on my belly. It was only an inch long but was half that wide.

"Piece of shrapnel from an IED."

She had tears in her eyes now. "How could you live a life like that and then come home and act like a, like a—"

"Normal person?" I said.

"A normal husband. A normal father."

I shrugged. "When I was there, that was my job. When I was home, loving and taking care of my family was my job. I'm pretty good at compartmentalizing."

"That's an understatement."

"Explain."

"You were basically living two completely different lives, Sam. I knew you were keeping secrets. Tried to understand that you had to, but in the end I couldn't take it. I need to know who I'm with. All of who I'm with."

I kissed her on the forehead. "Understood. Any more questions?"

"I think I've heard enough for tonight." She wiped her eyes and gave a sad little smile.

"You still love me?" I said.

She kissed me very gently. "I love you. I miss you."

After that, she drifted off to sleep. I got up, walked to the bathroom. Along the way, I stepped on my jeans on the floor. Felt that document in the right hip pocket crinkle under my foot.

DAY 5
8:35 Am

THE WOODLANDS, TEXAS

I woke to the smell of coffee brewing and breakfast cooking. Bacon. Eggs. Buttered toast. It was delicious.

Abby took a bite of bacon. "I have an event downtown for the next couple days. Mind if I crash here with you?"

"It'll cost you," I said.

She bit her bottom lip and batted her eyes, a look that always got me. Still did. "What's the price, mister?"

I wiggled my eyebrows and used my best German accent. "You vill see."

9:52 AM

Downtown Houston

"You have some updates," Sheila said as soon as I walked into the office. "NSA hits and some new info in the FBI files. Sent it all to your workstation."

"Thanks." I woke my workstation and started with the FBI files. Courtney had come through. Once the Bureau focused on the middle building as the real 'shooter's nest,' things had started to come together. Unlike the building that had the decoy and the one that had the robotic gun, a couple different surveillance cameras provided a great look at the exterior of the middle building and its lobby camera had a solid view of the entrance. I watched the clips.

At 1:40 AM, three-plus hours before the shooting, a camera across the street showed a man dressed in dark clothes and a baseball cap carrying a briefcase-sized case walking to the entrance and then entering the building *with a key card.* I paused the footage and looked through the notes. A subpoena had already been served for the building's entry/exit logs, which meant that info should populate in the file soon. I returned to the video.

The lobby camera picked up where the exterior camera's footage ended. The man walked through the lobby and passed out of sight, presumably heading to the elevators. The notes said they had no record of the guy leaving the building. I backed the clip up and froze it on the best view of the guy. Without any kind of reference it was hard to be sure, but he looked to be of average height, stocky. To my surprise, he was a black guy. I guess I'd bought into the media theory of a right-wing extremist being behind the attacks, and right-wing extremists typically come equipped with white skin.

Of course, the only thing driving the right-wing-extremist theory seemed to be a lot of assumption on the part of the news media. If the FBI had right-wing extremism on its mind, it wasn't evident in the files. The investigation I was following was focused on evidence, with little conjecture or theorizing. Maybe there was some other profiling group in the Bureau with that on its mind but I hadn't seen it.

I brewed a cup of coffee and drank it while standing at the wall of glass that looked out over the pancake-flat landscape south of downtown. Thinking. Given the leftward tilt of the media, their right-wing theory had been reasonable on its face. Conservatives ranted long and loud about the bias, so it was no stretch to imagine some zealot getting fed up. With a black shooter, however, that theory lost a lot of steam. Still possible, but not likely. So if not political, what was his motive?

You couldn't collect ransom on dead bodies so that angle was out. A stock market play? Shorting media companies? Too far-fetched, too much of a paper trail. So, not money. That left the old standards to consider: love, sex, revenge. The first two didn't fit here. That left one option.

I went back to my workstation and pulled up the NSA search results. There were hundreds of hits on the first set of search terms and conditions I'd given Sheila, but the narrowed set I'd sent her after researching the issue with Alla was much more manageable. With Alla's help, I knew the item I was looking for was a Talon Universal Weapons Mount, a gyro-equipped robotic platform made specifically for guns. Its footprint perfectly matched the four indentations on the rooftop where the shot had come from. It was made by a company called Paradigm RSP, right here in Houston, and it was tailor-made for attaching a variety of rifles and controlling them remotely with fantastic precision.

The NSA results were fourteen invoices issued from Paradigm to its buyers over the past year. Thirteen of the invoices were directly to the US military, with the quantities of the mounts sold varying from invoice to invoice. The lone outlier was a single Talon that had been sold to a robotics research firm in Portland called Oregon Robotics. The skittery tendrils out on the edge of my psyche were tingling now. I was on the trail.

I did a web search on the company and found a boilerplate website that told me little beyond an address and phone number. When I looked through the other results, my psyche went from tingling to electrified. Bingo, baby. Bingo.

DAY 5
8:15 Am

HALFWAY, OREGON

IN ANOTHER CABIN deep in the woods, Bruce Berringer sat in a recliner and flipped from channel to channel, checking the news, soaking up the commentary, gauging the effectiveness of what he'd done. The current show was playing video footage of a fire burning in the head-quarters of one of LA's biggest newspapers. The dumbasses behind it had already been identified and arrested. He knew his movement would attract the impulse actors at the beginning. The thinkers and planners, the smart ones, would join the fight later. The fire had taken out two floors of their operation but no one had been hurt. That was unfortunate. Not because he enjoyed hurting people—he did not—but because this was war. They were the ones who had made them-selves enemies of the people, not him. The injury and death was therefore on them, not him. Fear of that injury and death was what would eventually bring change. There was no appealing to journal-istic ethics that they had abandoned long ago in favor of pushing their agenda. They were elitists without conscience, assholes who viewed anyone who hampered their list of pet causes with disdain and condescension.

He flipped the channel and caught a story on the protests ramping up in the major cities. A few misfits marched and chanted idiotic things like "DON'T MESS...WITH OUR PRESS" and similar banalities. The real movement, however, was *against* the media, exactly as he had hoped. The numbers were growing by the hour as others seized the momentum he had created and took to the streets.

A BLONDE BOBBLEHEAD of a reporter was interviewing a man who had stepped out of the crowd of marchers in Times Square. "Sir, why are you here?"

The man responded in a Brooklyn accent. "I'm out here to demand that you people start telling the truth. We're sick of it, sick of you!"

"Aren't you concerned about the message you're sending, a message that many consider to be in poor taste given the heinous murders of members of the press?"

His face reddened and the volume of his voice ticked up as he pointed a finger in her face. "See, that's exactly what I'm talking about. You didn't care one bit when a bunch of thugs in black masks were beating people like me and setting fire to businesses. When you weren't ignoring it altogether, you were defending that scum, acting like they were some kind of 'noble warriors.' Gimme a damn break, lady."

"But sir, surely you see th—"

"Here's what I see," he said, sweeping an arm toward the crowd filing by. "Peaceful protesters, not one person bothering anyone, not one store on fire, unlike we saw with the cockroaches you love so much, a bunch of punks living in their mamas' basements."

"But aren't you worried that some in your ranks, the extremists, might actually do harm to people simply doing their jobs, people like me who just want to inform the public?"

He laughed in her face, a thin spigot of spittle catching her on the chin. "Give it up, honey. What you're selling, we ain't buying no more! You had your run for a long time, one so-called conservative after another smiling at you and your buddies while you were angling to take them down, reporting every bit of dirt you could dig up, while you ignored liberal crimes that really hurt people. I'm not hurting anybody out here, and if you're that worried about it, try this: Tell! The! Truth!"

BERRINGER SWITCHED THE CHANNEL. A couple guys in three-thousand-dollar suits were going back and forth, serious looks on their faces: "David, do the protesters have a point? Is there a bias in our coverage?"

His companion was shaking his head. "I'm proud of the work we're doing here. We serve—"

SWITCH.

THIS ONE WAS MORE INTERESTING. An angry-looking bunch had one of the frauds backed up against a building. The title bar rolled its message across the bottom of the screen: BOSTON RESIDENTS THREATENING REPORTERS ON STREET. One of the protesters was in the reporter's face, nose to nose. "You need to be worried, asshole!" The reporter looked terrified.

BEAUTIFUL. *Switch.*

MORE TALKING heads at a news desk, blathering about some trade alliance on the other side of the world.

SWITCH.

AND JUST AS he switched back to the most slanted bunch in the land,

GNN, a BREAKING NEWS graphic filled the screen, then slid away to show one of their newsies looking like he was about to cry.

"Good evening, America. The bad news, the sad news, at GNN continues. Blaine Bartomo, one of our beloved colleagues, has been gunned town in cold blood outside his home in an Atlanta suburb. We go live now, to the scene of this latest attack..."

BERRINGER TURNED UP THE VOLUME.

TWO YEARS EARLIER
Portland, Oregon

THE BERRINGER FAMILY made their way through the park toward a large shade tree Bruce had picked as the perfect spot. He had the picnic basket, Alicia the blanket, and ten-year-old Ty handled the leash. Nitwit was surely the dumbest dog ever born, a mix of Jack Russell and space alien. No matter. The pint-sized dog and Ty shared a fanatic love. Not one cloud marred the blue sky. Mid-seventies and a Sunday afternoon with his family. It didn't get better than this. They reached the tree and set up their little headquarters for the day.

Ty and Nitwit ran and played, the leash extending and retracting as the two took turns chasing each other, a game Nitwit won every time. She was no intellectual canine, but she was athletic and sizzled with speed. When they ventured too far, Alicia yelled, "Tyrone Berringer, get yourself back over here!" He made a U-turn and headed back at a run, his American flag T-shirt that was two sizes too big flapping in the breeze as he tried to keep up with his companion.

After a half-hour of watching them play, Bruce and Alicia readied the food, the paper plates, and the plastic tableware. Bruce caught Ty's eye and motioned him in. "Time to eat, boy! Come and get—" Bruce's voice trailed off and he stood, looking toward where Ty and Nitwit were playing, about thirty yards out. What the hell? Fifty yards past them, a black mass approached. Some kind of protest, but they were all dressed in black. Wearing masks and hoodies and helmets. They were carrying signs: FUCK NAZIS. KILL CAPITALISM. WHITE SUPREMA-CISTS GO HOME. FASCISTS DIE. One of them waved a huge black flag with some kind of symbol on it and the word ANTIFA.

Bruce started out walking, then trotting as the mob closed the distance between them and Ty. He heard Alicia behind him, running and screaming, "Ty, get back here! Now!"

When he reached Ty, he took the leash and said, "Come on, let's get out of here." Ty turned to see what his dad was looking at, his eyes growing wide as he saw the crowd coming toward them.

Alicia was there now, taking Ty by the hand and heading back toward the tree. Nitwit tried to charge back toward the crowd, straining at her leash, barking as ferociously as she could at the approaching mob. Bruce pulled her back and they all took off toward the tree at a run. When they got there, Bruce began stuffing their things into the basket and the backpack. Then he said, "Forget it, let's go." They started out of the park, a reverse course of their arrival.

Then the mob was there, circling around them. Bruce guessed the number at about fifty, half of them holding crude shields, nearly all of them holding a variety of clubs, from baseball bats to two-by-fours to pieces of iron pipe. One of them stepped forward and said, "What in the *fuck*, man?" It was obvious from the accent that he was a black male. He was wearing black cargo pants, a black shirt emblazoned in yellow with MARX, a black ski mask, and some kind of crazy goggles. Bruce also noticed a can of pepper spray in a holster on his hip.

"What are you talking about?" Bruce said.

MARX pointed at Ty. "You let your fucking kid wear shit like that?"

"Are you serious? It's an American flag. We're in America." Bruce's heart was pounding now. This whole thing was starting to feel seri-ously dangerous and his family was right in the middle of it. He could sort out the insanity of it later, from a safe distance. "C'mon, baby. Ty. Let's go."

He checked to be sure Nitwit's leash was fully retracted and locked it in the short position; she was at a constant growl, her little teeth bared, hair standing up in a line on her back. He took Ty's hand in his left hand, and Alicia's in his right, handing the leash off to her. They started back toward the way they had come. The mob not only didn't part to let them pass. It tightened.

MARX walked around and got between them and the part of the mob that blocked their exit. He said, "What I don't get is how the fuck you, a black man, let your son wear that fucking symbol of oppression."

Someone in the crowd said, "Fucking right, man!" Another, this one female, said, "Asshole!"

"Look," Bruce said, "We just wanna be on our way, alright? We're not political. We're just a family enjoying the park."

MARX pointed at Ty again. "Take it off."

Bruce said, "Just step aside and let us pass, brother."

"*Brother?* Your skin may be black but I can see you ain't no real black man. What are you, some kind of fucking *nigger Nazi*?"

The mob started chanting: NIGGER NAZI! NIGGER NAZI!

Nitwit went nuts, barking and snapping and straining at her leash. In one movement, MARX yanked the pepper spray out of the holster and shot a stream directly into Nitwit's face. The poor dog yelped and flipped and rolled, hopelessly tangling herself in the leash. The yelps turned into a pitiful howl of pain. Ty jerked loose from Bruce's hand and dropped to the dog, trying to comfort her.

MARX grabbed at Ty's shirt, trying to tear it off him and lifting the boy off the ground in the process. Bruce reacted to the assault on his son, thought no longer a factor. His first swing caught MARX square on the chin and he dropped like a bag of sand. Bruce yanked the pepper spray away from him and turned in a circle, aiming it at the lunatics with one hand and gathering his family to him with the other. "Back up!" he said.

But they didn't. They attacked, like piranhas on some hapless beast that wandered into the wrong water. Bruce tried to shield his family and fight at the same time. He took blow after blow from clubs and shields and fists. He managed to wrest a two-by-four from a screaming black-clad girl and swung it for all he was worth, but then there was blackness. And nothingness.

. . .

WHEN HE REGAINED CONSCIOUSNESS, the mob was gone. Paramedics were working on Ty, his little head covered in blood. He looked around, shaking his head, trying to clear it. Where was Alicia? Then he saw it, a shape on the ground, covered in a white sheet. Including the head. He struggled to his feet and went to it, yanked the sheet off. He tilted his head to the sky and wailed. "Nooooo!"

"Sir? Sir?" A policeman, tugging at his arm. "Your son, he's in bad shape. We're taking him to the hospital. You need to go with him. We'll take care of her, okay?"

Bruce just looked at him, his mouth open. He tilted his head toward the sky again, and saw Nitwit hanging from a branch about ten feet off the ground, eyes dead, tongue swollen and hanging out. He turned back to the cop. "Why?"

"I don't know, sir. I'm sorry. Now go be with your boy."

HE SAT in the ICU waiting room, his mind numb, his *soul* numb. Time passed. Doctors with serious faces came and went. Friends sat beside him, trying to get him to talk but eventually giving up and just sitting with him. Church members started showing up. They held him and prayed. His pastor was there, praying, his hands holding Bruce's head and pleading with God. And then one of the doctors approached. Not a serious face this time. A sad face.

AN ENDLESS PROCESSION of "I'm so sorry" filed by at the joint funeral. Bruce remained in a stupor. Days before, life was wonderful. Now life was nothing. He had nothing. He was surrounded by people, yet utterly alone in a void so dark and empty that he wondered if he too was dead.

THREE MONTHS LATER, he visited the cemetery for the first time. He stood at the foot of the graves and looked at the headstones. ALICIA MARIE Berringer, WIFE, MOTHER, FRIEND OF GOD. TYRONE WILSON Berringer, A LIGHT TO ALL WHO KNEW HIM. And at the foot of Ty's grave, just as she had always slept at the foot of his bed, a small flat stone that said NITWIT, LOYAL FRIEND.

DAY 5

10:27 Am

HOUSTON

MY SEARCH FOR "OREGON ROBOTICS" yielded the company's boilerplate website and a string of links to various robotics-related curricula and research programs at Oregon universities that consumed the first couple pages of results. The third page was investigative treasure. Two years earlier, an employee of Oregon Robotics named Bruce Berringer, along with his family, had been attacked in a Portland park. His wife and son had been killed. A photo of Berringer coming out of the hospital showed a black man of average height and stocky build. Damn skippy.

It took two hours of reading and diving into and climbing out of web rabbit holes, but a picture coalesced and everything about the media attacks fell into place. Berringer's family had been killed by a gang of Antifa asswipes, but that hadn't fit the media's narrative of a white-supremacist rally being the real cause of the attack on the family. Berringer had begged and pleaded for them to tell the story he experienced firsthand, but aside from a handful of minor outlets he had been ignored. He waged a social media battle but got nowhere. And it was now obvious that the guy had snapped.

The good news was that I knew I had identified the media attacker. (Being the good citizen I am, I immediately emailed his name and a brief summary of my findings to Courtney Meyer, and also texted it to a still-email-free Bartholomew Pitt so he could pass it on to whomever he saw fit.) The bad news was that it sort of blew up my theory that the media attacks were related to Sol Ringer's reign of terror by abduction. Everything about the Berringer story sounded like a lone wolf, one brokenhearted man who turned into a very pissed-off man, and eventually a violent one. He was the FBI's problem now, even if I'd had to find him for their slow asses. Where did that leave me in looking for Sol? And why the hell had my Spidey senses failed? I didn't have long to dwell on whether or not my investigative hunchery was on the decline.

Sheila said, "Incoming from FBI."

"What is it?"

"New abduction last night. This time they got lucky. Video of the perp."

"No crap?"

"None. Just sent it to you."

ANOTHER MISSING POLITICO

WASHINGTON — Metropolitan Police Department sources announced this morning that Robert Hecht, a well-known Washington lobbyist and dealmaker, is missing and presumed to be the latest victim in a string of missing high-profile figures.

The 58-year-old Hecht has been a fixture in the capital for more than 20 years and has extensive connections to both Democrats and Republicans. When Hecht failed to show up for a meeting in his office with three congressmen this morning and didn't answer telephone calls, an employee feared the worst and contacted the police. Those fears turned out to be well founded when police investigated at Hecht's Arlington home. His car was missing and police recovered "a small amount of blood from the victim's garage," according to the police report.

Earlier victims in the perplexing string of disappearances include NBS Washington anchor Rob Acoma, senators Howard Hurd (R-AL) and Jack Dickey (D-NV), and the chief justice of the United States, Marcus Wilder. The investigation is ongoing and remains a joint operation with the FBI and Secret Service.

DAY 5

1:01 Pm

HOUSTON

I READ the FBI's investigative notes on last night's abduction of Robert Hecht, some DC swamp dweller. He'd gone missing from his home in Arlington, Virginia, along with his Tesla. The FBI had pressured Tesla into coughing up the location of the car through its telematics without waiting for a subpoena. It was outside a cabin in the woods a few miles from Arlington and when the FBI showed up at the cabin, things got interesting.

The file was loaded with photos from the scene. The cabin was a ramshackle mess that looked uninhabited from the outside, overrun with weeds and vines. The interior wasn't much better, but it had definitely been in use. Photos showed one big open room inside the cabin, filled with tables full of lab glassware and the other accoutrements of a meth lab.

Another series of photos showed a body on the ground. Male, bearded, forties, wearing nothing but boxer shorts and a ragged pair of sandals. Eyes open and dead. Dried blood from the corner of his mouth down onto his neck. Annotations identified him as Jason Butler, followed by a list of drug convictions that could've filled a small book. Then came the sweet photo, a close-up of the inside of a cabinet in the back of the lab. It showed a surveillance DVR and a monitor that still displayed feeds from four cameras.

I clicked through the folder of files until I found the video and double-clicked it. First up was a night-vision shot from a camera on the front of the cabin. It looked out at the overgrown yard and a narrow gravel drive that disappeared into the woods. The clock overlay in the corner showed 4:36:14 AM and counting. The yard was surprisingly clear in the video; the drug dealer had installed infrared lights somewhere to illuminate the area for the camera. A flash of light in the woods was followed by headlights that bloomed out the video.

As the car came into view and the headlights lit the yard with visible light, the camera auto-switched from its grayscale night mode to grainy color and dimmed the glow of the headlights with some sort of auto-compensation. There was the Tesla. Now a man—the drug dealer in his boxer shorts—appeared on screen, his back to the camera as he descended the steps from the porch into the yard. He raised an AR-style rifle and aimed at the Tesla. Suddenly a big circle of the yard, including the man and the Tesla, was brightly lit by something overhead. I saw leaves and dirt swirling in the air. Chopper.

The drug dealer spun to his right and raised his AR to the sky. The muzzle flashed just as the Tesla shot forward. The grill of the car hit the man in his lower back and knocked him forward into the gravel. He lost his grip on the AR and it clattered off the hood of the Tesla and the car stopped. The circle of light wobbled, then steadied and eventually centered on the man getting out of the Tesla. I said, "Hello, Sol."

The FBI had edited the video into a sequence that switched from camera to camera to follow the action that unfolded. I watched as Sol got someone who was obviously Hecht out of the trunk of the car and took him to a blacked-out helicopter. My old partner then dragged the drug dealer from the front yard to the rear of the cabin and left him there. Sol's head swiveled as if he'd heard something and then he did something most un-Sol-like. He screwed up. He pulled up his balaclava for a moment, looked off toward the side of the cabin, and then pulled the balaclava back down. The camera got a clear shot of his face. I finished watching as Sol boarded the helicopter and it lifted off. I saved a frame that best showed the profile of the helicopter and sent it to Sheila's workstation. "Find out what kind of helicopter that is, Sheila."

"Mind if I grab lunch first?"

My first instinct was to tell her she could damn well eat later, but after a few seconds I said, "Sure, go ahead."

"Thanks, I'll be back in thirty. Want me to bring you anything?"

"No, but thanks."

She left and I pulled up a recording of her computer activity for the day. She'd gotten here around seven AM, checked email and found nothing interesting (to her or me), checked for population of new material on the FBI mirror and found that the FBI had repositioned the shooter's location, and then logged into a private cloud our NSA contact had set up for us. That bucket contained the search hits I had already gone through and nothing else. I fast-forwarded through the playback of her screen, stopping whenever she used the computer. Nothing interesting until about twenty minutes ago when the FBI mirror populated with the new info and video on Hecht's abduction that I was looking through right now.

I made a Wi-Fi connection to the hidden camera in the smoke detector and watched the motion-triggered events it had recorded since I'd installed it the night before. She zipped around the office as I watched the footage at five times normal speed. She'd brewed and drunk an impressive six cups of coffee, done the computer work I'd already seen, left and come back with two envelopes that she shredded without opening, and received no phone calls on either her mobile or the office's landline.

That covered her entire day. Nothing suspicious. Maybe I was being paranoid. I closed out my surveillance and returned to the FBI file on the Hecht matter. Time to call Pitt and give him the bad news: The FBI would soon know who was abducting people, if it didn't already.

DAY 5

Noon

HALFWAY, OREGON

BERRINGER SAT HUNCHED over a laptop on a rustic table. He read through his manifesto one last time. He'd never been much of a writer, but he thought he'd covered all the points he needed to. Next he tidied up the folder with the hundreds of documents, links, photos, and other material he'd compiled on the news media. He had gone through every article or broadcast he could find on what happened to his family. To the written articles, he added annotations explaining the truth that corrected each faulty passage. To every video, he'd added a recording of himself in the corner, explaining what the newscasters got right and what they got wrong. There were far more instances of the latter.

He moved on to the section containing a spreadsheet of national reporters and on-air personalities at large, each with a LIAR SCORE that ranked from 50 to 100; he had left off everyone with a score under 50. The spreadsheet was sorted with the worst at the top and least despicable at the bottom. Each name had a photo thumbnail beside it, as well as links for MORE INFO (a history of articles and appearances during which that person had butchered the truth), CONTACT (email addresses and phone numbers), and LOCATION (maps to their home, work, and any other addresses Berringer had been able to find).

In addition to his own research, he included links to a plethora of books and videos documenting the longstanding bias of the media. Some were written or produced by honest insiders who had gotten their fill of the rigged game and bolted. Some by researchers who had meticulously documented the bias using empirical data and repeatable methodologies. A smattering of material that theorized a heavy CIA influence in the news narrative; Berringer wasn't so sure about that one but included it out of thoroughness since the Smith-Mundt Modernization Act of 2012 had indeed made it legal once more for the government to propagandize Americans.

Satisfied with the package of information he'd put together, he went to work writing the code to distribute the information. When the time was right, activation of one script would post the package to hundreds of different sites within minutes. Every social media site. Every major forum, from mainstream venues like Reddit to esoteric, heavily-trafficked sites that specialized in conspiracy theories. Not just WWW, but the dark web, too. It would spread too widely and too quickly for Big Tech to shut down. The truth would reach the masses. Once that happened, Bruce Berringer's work would be well and truly done.

DAY 5

2:10 Pm

HOUSTON

SHEILA SAID, "The helicopter is an AAS-72XY-plus, a variant of the Eurocopter UH-72 Lacota."

"That's a pure transport helicopter, right? Medical evac, stuff like that?"

"Most of them are. This version is armed. Come look."

I walked over to her workstation. She pointed to a frozen frame of the video that showed Sol approaching the open rear bay of the helicopter. "And here's the image inverted," she said, clicking her mouse. The image transformed into what looked like an old photo negative. I leaned closer for a better look.

She made a circle on the screen with her mouse cursor. "See that?" The inverted colors made it possible to make out a mounted gun with its barrel protruding from the rear bay and pointing at the ground. She pointed again, this time at the tail of the aircraft. "This style shroud on the tail rotor is used only on this model. It's a positive match."

"How many in service?" I said.

"That's the good part. This model is new, and I mean *brand new*. It's made in Columbus, Mississippi, and to date they've only delivered four of them."

Four. My heart beat a little faster, the investigative juices flowing. "Where?"

"Three to Fort Rucker in Alabama. One to Peterson AFB in Colorado."

"Interesting. Next door to Cheyenne Mountain, NORAD. Been able to track any of them?"

She closed the video and pulled up a photo of three helicopters parked in a row on a tarmac. "This is all three of them assigned to Fort Rucker. Pulled it from their surveillance system minutes ago."

All three were tied down, engine covers in place on the turbine inputs. And all three were painted flat Army green. There was enough light on the cabin video to show that our helicopter of interest was black. I stuck out my fist and Sheila bumped it.

"Any info from the Air Force on the status of that helicopter?" I said.

She shook her head. "I have no access to anything at Cheyenne Mountain and they're ignoring my emails and calls."

"Call the pilot. Tell him to get the plane ready."

"Where're we going?"

"Just me this time. Keep monitoring everything and give me a shout if anything new comes in."

After a fat pause, she said, "Will do."

IN FLIGHT

As SOON AS we were airborne I called Pitt and brought him up to speed. He said, "Does this mean you're done pursuing the irrelevant media case and sticking to the mission? I've really had enough of that. I asked you to find Sol, and this rabbit-hold excursion of yours has gone on long enough."

I stared at the phone a moment before answering. "Already told you, I'm convinced this is all connected."

"I'm not, and I'm paying the bills. Leave that angle alone."

I shook my head. "No problem, Bart. Already figured out who the media attacker was, already told you, and already passed it on to the FBI. I'm done." I then laid out the actual reason for my call: "Do you have someone at Peterson we can trust? The military is obviously involved in this, or rather, someone *in* the military is involved. We need to track that helicopter."

"I'm on it," he said. "Call you back soon. Bye."

"Roger that." I looked at the phone, dreading the next call. Steeled my nerves. Opened my contacts and touched the icon to call Abby.

She answered on the second ring. "Hey, you."

"Hey, listen, I still want you to hang out at the house but I had to make a quick business trip. Should be back tomorrow. Hopefully."

Silence on the phone. Ten seconds. Fifteen. She said, "Where are you going?"

"Colorado."

"Forensic case?"

I hesitated a beat too long.

She said, "You're back in the government thing, aren't you? The thing that put scars all over your body. The thing that created ten years of secrets and lies and distance and a missing husband. Aren't you?"

"Abby, this is a one-time affair. An emergency that I'd—"

"—explain if you could?" she said. "You really want to, but can't?"

What was I to say to that other than that she was right? I said nothing.

"Six years you've been telling me how you want me back, how things are different now. I resist and resist, and then on a foolish impulse, I decide to at least explore the idea, spend time with you for a few days and see if things really have changed. I put my heart out there just a little bit, and look what happens." Her voice was breaking.

"I love you, Abby."

"I love you too, Sam. It's not enough."

"Don't say that."

"It's the truth. Love is great, babe, but people have to live together, have to trust, have to be there for each other. You can't do that."

"But I can!"

"I won't be here when you get back. Bye, Sam." She hung up.

I stared at the phone. Wiped my eyes. The phone rang, vibrated in my hand. Pitt. I answered. "Hey."

"Got you an in, a general."

"That works. What's the plan?"

"I'm on my way there, too. We'll all meet this evening. I'll text you the details as soon as I have them. Sit tight. Bye."

"Roger roger." I ended the call and laid the phone on the little table beside my seat. Walked to the bar. Poured a hefty glass of vodka. Killed it. Poured another.

DAY 5

7:51 Pm

COLORADO SPRINGS, COLORADO

BARTHOLOMEW PITT and I sat in the back corner of a greasy little diner a few blocks from the sprawl of Peterson Air Force Base. He drank iced tea. I swigged coffee to erase the vodka. A bell jangled and a man in civilian clothes, but of obvious military bearing, stepped through the front door.

Pitt said, "That's our man." Pitt stood and extended his hand as the man approached our booth.

"Marshall, great to see you. This is Sam Flatt."

I stood and shook his hand.

"Marshall Harbuck." His handshake was strong, the skin rough. No pencil-pusher here. He eased into the booth on Pitt's side and I sat back down, studying him. Sixtyish, short gray hair freshly buzzed, clear green eyes that darted left and right, taking in his surroundings. This was a man who gave many orders and took few. Harbuck looked around, placed his elbows on the table, and leaned in toward me. "Bart tells me you can be trusted. I'd like to hear that straight from you."

"General, I don't want to be here. I want to be on my horse. But I am here, because a dangerous man is up to dangerous things and he needs to be stopped. As for trust, I didn't betray my country when I was waterboarded, or when I was beaten unconscious, or when I had a spark plug wire hooked to my nuts. I won't betray it now. With that out of the way, Bart says you're up to speed. Can you track that helicopter?"

"Not directly. I command the 721st Mission Support Group. When it comes to the physical facility and anything that connects to it, we run the mountain. We don't run the aircraft. That's Peterson."

Red tape. My head hurt. I blew out a long sigh.

Harbuck said, "I have a call in to my counterpart over there. We'll get the info on the aircraft. In the meantime, let me run something else by you."

I raised my eyebrows.

"Several months ago, I was notified of unusual attempts to hack into our primary network."

"Unusual?" I said.

"We get hit with intrusion attempts all the time, as I'm sure you know."

I nodded. "Sure."

"Most of this activity tracks back to China, Iran, Russia, some other Eastern European countries. And a few domestic idiots trying to make a name for themselves."

I nodded again. "And this activity is different how?"

"My people tell me it's coming from inside the mountain. But that's about all they've been able to tell me, and I've run out of patience."

"No suspects?"

"I have one, but it's a hunch and not much else."

"Who?" I said.

"A technical sergeant named Sadie Grossman. Transferred in just before the attempted intrusions began."

"And what are Sergeant Grossman's duties?"

"For me, she works in a Client Services role, a lot like a senior level IT position in the private sector. I had put in a request for a Client

Services resource, and she's who they sent. She seems competent in the role, so I didn't object."

"Why would you have objected? Are you saying she did something else before transferring into your group?"

"She spent the past six years in SIGINT. Specifically, communication signals intelligence."

"Okay. So your hunch is built on timing and perhaps her skillset?" I said.

Harbuck pursed his lips, looked at me a moment. "And my intuition."

I nodded, chewed my bottom lip, thinking. "Our helicopter came from here. You have hinky intrusion attempts. I don't much believe in coincidences like that. You?"

Harbuck shook his head. "I do not."

I felt an inexorable tug, being pulled into something deeper than the original mission of finding and stopping Sol. Then again, hadn't I believed all along that the abductions and the media attacks were connected, part of a larger whole? Wasn't it natural to pursue all angles at least until I *had* found and stopped Sol?

My mind jumped to Abby. This damned thing had cost me the chance I'd waited years for. I was suddenly angry at being involved in it at all. Angry at Pitt. Angry at myself for agreeing to help him. But the damage was done. To quit now would mean it was all for nothing. Right?

I looked at Pitt, then Harbuck. "Why do I suspect you guys already have a plan?"

Pitt grinned. "Because you're a brilliant S-O-B, Sammy Boy."

"We've put together a fictitious forensic case for you to investigate," Harbuck said. "You'll go in as a civilian contractor, which isn't uncommon, and I'm setting you up close to Grossman in case I'm right."

"Alright," I said. "Let's get something to eat and put this plan together."

DAY 6
Twitter

GLOBAL

BREAKING: Hostage situation at Houston bank robbery. #HoustonHostages

Hostages taken in Houston bank. Robbery gone bad. Police on scene. Developing... #HoustonHostages

Shots fired. Active shooter on scene. #HoustonHostages

Chaos at Houston bank. Multiple injuries reported. Active shooter. #HoustonHostages

Gunfire exchanged between police and suspects at Houston bank scene. #HoustonHostages

i'm across street from action. cops shooting reporters! #holyshit #houstonhostages

Seriously? WTF!

no lie! i work across street, just saw two cops open up on a bunch of reporters! #houstonhostages

Record it, dude! #ViralVideo

Asshole. People being shot!

Fuck you. #ViralVideo

Prayers for all @ #HoustonHostages!

total chaos now. shooter cops running. i count six people down. blood everywhere! #houstonhostages

Payback for media getting cops killed? #KillThemAll

Damn.

What about hostages?

no clue. recording now. will post. #houstonhostages

DAY 6
8:44 Am

CHEYENNE MOUNTAIN, COLORADO

I'D STARTED the morning by spending an hour and a half in the Air Force's administration building located outside the mountain. I was photographed, furnished with an ID, had my fingerprints taken, and sat through an orientation video for non-military contractors that would have put a meth-addicted insomniac to sleep. I was apparently expected inside the various systems because I faced no resistance as I worked through the process of being cleared and credentialed to enter the mountain. Bureaucratic maze complete, I hung my spiffy new access badge around my neck and stepped back into the sunshine of a perfect Colorado morning.

A few minutes later, an old Air Force-blue school bus pulled to a stop and I climbed aboard with a dozen or so others and found a seat a few rows from the front. The door closed and we were rolling, past the guard shack and into the tunnel.

I liked the plan. I was going in as myself. I'd never used social media, never done anything outside my work field to generate awareness, and my pre-private sector background was already cloaked in cover. I'd be exactly who I appeared to be, making a slip-up in character far less likely.

The bus came to a stop at an intersection, complete with a traffic light hung from the granite overhead. I blended into the crowd and followed the herd as the others made their way across the intersection to a large bank of lockers mounted in the rough-hewn wall of rock. The air was cool and damp, the entire space dim and echoey. The walls were streaked everywhere with seeping water that glistened in occasional pools on the concrete floor. About half the herd fanned out to various lockers along the wall, unlocked them, and began stowing personal items like mobile phones, e-readers, and the like. I guess the others had left those things in their cars or at home.

Harbuck had briefed me well on what to expect, but hadn't mentioned how I was supposed to bring my electronics inside when it was obvious that even the employees weren't allowed to do so. The general had said he'd see me there and get me settled, but thus far that hadn't happened.

Now the others were entering the mountain proper through the huge blast door that stood open, its beefy gears and locking pistons on display through a glass panel. I followed, half-expecting my backpack full of laptops and other gear to trigger alarms, but nothing happened. After a short walk, I saw the entrance to the main body of the complex. The entrance was essentially a steel box with a door in it that happened to lead inside a rock wall. As I approached the entrance, I heard a heavy whine behind us, followed by a muted thud. The blast door had just closed.

"Don't see many of those," a male voice to my right said.

I turned and saw an airman in his early twenties. While most of the others in their group wore Air Force blues, this guy was in ABU cammies. He had blond hair, short but not buzzed, his eyebrows so light they almost disappeared against his skin. His stripes identified him as an Airman First Class.

"What's that?" I said.

"That." The airman tapped my access badge.

I looked down at it, then looked at the one worn by the airman.

Aside from the fact that mine had CONTRACTOR across the bottom in bold black letters, I saw no real difference, and I'm pretty good at subtle details. "Looks about like yours."

The airman laughed and I looked at his name patch for the first time. BOZEMAN.

"Vick Bozeman," the airman said, extending his hand.

I returned the handshake. "Sam Flatt."

Bozeman pointed to an ID number on his own badge. "You have this too, an ID number that ends in M-E. A 'me' badge. Rare to see that on contractor badges."

"What does it mean?"

"Mission Essential. If shit gets real outside, 'me' badges get to stay inside, safe side of the blast doors. Everybody else gets their ass tossed in a big hurry."

"Let's hope that never happens," I said.

"Just a matter of time," Bozeman said with a wink, then stepped through the door and disappeared.

CHEYENNE MOUNTAIN

MY INSIDES TIGHTENED when I stepped through the door behind Airman Bozeman and entered the main body of the Cheyenne Mountain complex. The path from the outside world to here had been spacious enough for comfort. Inside, that changed to steel corridors, narrow with low ceilings. The doors were hatches. I could tolerate it, had endured far worse, but I don't like being closed in.

I had drawn a breath to ask Bozeman for directions to Client Services when a voice behind me said, "Flatt."

I turned and saw Harbuck approaching. "General."

We shook, and Harbuck said, "Follow me," as he stepped past me and kept walking.

We snaked through a maze of corridors and tubular walkways between buildings. Harbuck looked sharp and crisp in his Air Force blues as he led the way with a quick step and purpose. Eventually we arrived in a space outside any of the steel buildings, a giant cavern, the buildings of the complex around us. In front of us, in the center of the cavern, a domed concrete structure dominated the view.

"Command and control center," Harbuck said, nodding toward the structure but not slowing down. "The heart and brain of the mountain."

"Impressive," I said. "Where are we going?"

"You'll see."

After another couple minutes, we arrived at a doorway that Harbuck keyed open with his badge. We stepped through the door and immediately headed down metal steps reminiscent of a basement stairway. At the bottom, I figured out that we were in the crawlspace beneath the numerous buildings we'd just navigated. The ceiling was low but the area was large and fairly open.

I had done a bit of research on Cheyenne Mountain the night before and knew what I was looking at, but the engineering around us was amazing. We were walking past the foundations of the buildings above, each one built on top of an array of massive coil springs.

Harbuck noticed me looking at the spring beds. He pointed at them without slowing down. "A nuclear detonation anywhere nearby would give the mountain a pretty good shake. We don't want buildings collapsing in here, so all major structures are built on these shock absorption bases." Harbuck turned right into the equivalent of an alley between the bases of two buildings, then right again at the end of the alley. Finally, he stopped and knelt.

I watched as Harbuck opened a metal panel on the ground just under the edge of a building. The panel was about a foot square. Beneath it was a metal junction box perhaps six inches deep, with a silver-colored conduit passing through it. Harbuck reached into the box and pulled out a pistol. After racking the slide and verifying an empty chamber, he handed it to me. "Not a lot I can do for you on weaponry without attracting attention, but I don't like deploying soldiers into any kind of operation defenseless."

"I'm not a soldier, but the gesture's appreciated anyway, General."

Harbuck grunted and reached back into the box. This time he came out with a plastic grocery sack and handed it over, as well. I looked inside and saw a half-dozen magazines. Judging by the weight of the bag, the mags were at least close to full. I racked the slide on the pistol myself and checked the chamber. It was a Beretta PT92, 9mm, and cosmetically it had been beat to hell and back. Mechanically, it still felt solid.

"Your badge will let you go most places in the complex without examination, but my suggestion is to leave the weapon here until the operation is a bit more advanced or you feel a likely need for it. Some of the areas have hidden X-ray sensors that are monitored twenty-four/seven, and it will raise eyebrows for a computer contractor to have a sidearm and a crapload of ammo on him in here, no matter what kind of credentials you have."

"Agreed." I handed the gun and the bag back to Harbuck, who stowed them in the box and closed the lid.

He stood, dusted his hands on each other. "Let's get out of here." We headed back the way we'd come.

"You have some details for me on my cover?" I said.

"In my office," Harbuck said and looked at his watch. "You can look it over while we get some chow. After that, I'll introduce you to our mole and you can get to work. And Flatt?"

"Yes?"

"Watch your ass. This whole affair has my hackles up."

"Care to elaborate?"

Harbuck stopped and turned to face me. "After thirty-four years of doing this, this whole thing just doesn't feel right. I don't like it, Flatt. Something seriously strange is going on and I don't like it one damned little bit." His eyes were intense, locked on.

I held the eye contact. "I can appreciate that, and General, I strongly suggest you watch your back, as well."

Harbuck cocked his head. "You care to elaborate?"

I raised a hand, palm out. "I have no elaboration to give. A week ago, my old job was the farthest thing from my mind. Then Bartholomew Pitt walked back into my life. I'm just saying be careful, that's all."

Harbuck gave a curt nod and resumed walking. We covered our route back through the crawlspace quickly, and climbed the metal stairway back to the main level, our steps echoing through the strange space. Just before Harbuck grabbed the handle to the door out, he stopped and said, "I can read men, Flatt. I trust you."

"I appreciate that, sir."

"You know you're not required to call me 'sir' since you're not in my military."

"Consider it a show of respect."

Harbuck nodded again and said, "I'll tell you one more thing."

"What's that?"

"I don't trust your boss as far as I can throw his ass."

I didn't answer, but I gave him a wink and a little smile.

Harbuck pulled open the door.

DAY 6
9:01 Am

CHEYENNE MOUNTAIN

"YOU READY?" Harbuck said.

I nodded. He opened an unmarked door and we stepped into the Cyber Systems Operations Sector, which is a snazzy piece of Air Force jargon for 'IT department.' Not that long ago, I had entered IT at SPACE, the world's largest and most futuristic structure. It blew me away. So did this one, but for completely different reasons.

This one looked more like a computer museum than a twenty-first century data operation. With Harbuck leading the way, we wound through racks and racks of components that qualified as antiques in the tech world. Big clunky servers ten times the size of modern units, with ten percent of the power, their fans screaming and hard drives grinding. So much for my vision of a high-tech wonderland from which steely-eyed missile men scoured the heavens to keep us safe. I half expected to find a punchcard reader around the next corner.

Instead, we turned the next corner and the racks ended, giving way to a cluster of about twenty cubicles. I followed Harbuck through the little maze, noticing that a lot of the cubicles were unoccupied, bare of any equipment or supplies. I didn't see a single person even in the cubes that looked to be active. Given the time of day, they were probably in the mess hall.

Harbuck said, "The stronger the tech, the fewer people we need to run it. We had people packed in here a few years ago."

I wondered where that strong tech might be hiding, but said nothing and kept following the general.

We reached the end of the row and Harbuck said, "Grossman."

And there she was, springing from her seat like a jack-in-the-box, pulling earbuds from her ears while she rose, her eyes wide when she realized it was Harbuck. She snapped to attention so quickly it reminded me of a mousetrap snapping shut. She gave a smart salute and said, "General Harbuck, sir."

"At ease, Grossman."

She relaxed her stance, slightly.

"Grossman, this is Sam Flatt, the contractor I mentioned earlier. He'll be doing some work here for a while and I want you to see that he gets whatever he needs."

"Yes, sir."

I extended my hand and she shook it, one firm pump. "Nice to meet you," I said.

She nodded, but kept her eyes on Harbuck.

The general pointed to a cubicle just this side of Grossman's. "You'll work there, Mr. Flatt." Then he spun around on his gleaming shoes and headed back the way we had come, leaving me alone with Grossman as his quick steps faded.

For some reason, the name Sadie Grossman had conjured up a mental image of a frumpy girl with thick glasses and hair in a bun. Not so. The young woman before me was slender, her uniform crisp, and her bearing taut and straight. Her eyes—there were no glasses—were bright and sharp, an unusual hazel color that had little specks of what looked almost like gold. Her nose was sprinkled with pale freckles that gave her a girlish look. Brunette hair, not quite shoulder length, that flipped out on the ends. She wasn't particularly pretty, at least not in a classic sense, but somehow it all came together in a very attractive package. She sparkled like a new penny.

She cleared her throat and I realized I'd drifted off, already strategizing on how to deal with her. "Sorry," I said.

The tiniest hint of a smile tugged at one side of her mouth. "No problem. I better get back to work. Let me know if you need anything." Her accent was neutral, no real hint as to where she was from.

"Will do," I said.

She sat down, started to put the earbuds back in, then stowed them in her desk drawer instead. Then she returned to work on her computer. I went about the business of unpacking my laptop and getting it connected to power and network in my cubicle. Within a couple minutes, I had my computer booted up, my chair adjusted to my liking, and it was time to get to work. I eased up out of my seat just enough to see over the wall between Grossman and me. "What should I call you?"

"How about Sadie? And you?"

"Sam, please."

With a little nod, she said, "Deal," and turned her attention back to something on her screen.

"Hate to interrupt, but I need network access. That something you can arrange?"

"Sure. Can I see your contractor badge?"

I stood, removed the lanyard from around my neck, looked at the badge-card, and handed it across the wall to her.

"Your contractor number will be your username on the network. The badge also has a chip in it that you can use to log in."

I looked around and saw a "dip" reader on my desk. "Gotcha." She dropped it into her reader and started working her way through a series of setup screens.

"What kind of chip is it?" I said. "It's not visible like the chips on modern credit cards."

I picked up a beat of hesitation, a tiny pause in the rhythm of her mousing and typing, but she answered the question. "R-S-A cryptochip, made just for us, the military. We've only had them a few weeks. Pretty slick tech. It's embedded behind the photo."

It was already obvious that this girl was sharp, alert, even wary, and I was only five minutes into this thing, making idle conversation. Not good. Earning her trust would require a slow, subtle approach. Slow wasn't ideal with Sol Ringer out there snatching people, and I'm not so good at subtle.

MEDIA TERROR STRIKES HOUSTON

HOUSTON — 9:20 a.m. CT — The latest terror attack against the news media has killed at least six and wounded several more, according to early reports from Houston, Texas. Details are sketchy, but it is believed that about an hour ago, a hostage situation was reported to be in progress inside Blue National Bank in downtown Houston, for the purpose of luring reporters to the scene for a terror ambush.

According to eyewitnesses, police arrived at the scene at about 8:15 AM. After cordoning off the area, officers used a megaphone to try to establish contact with the suspects inside the bank but were unsuccessful. A SWAT unit arrived approximately ten minutes later and shortly thereafter reporters began to gather. Police presence was heavy by this point and media members were restricted to a small section of sidewalk across the street from the bank. The media staging area grew congested and two men wearing Houston Police Department uniforms walked up to the group and opened fire. The shooters then walked away. When legitimate police realized what had happened, they began a search of the area but the suspects are believed to still be at large.

As for the purported hostages, there were none. The bank branch opens at 9:00 AM, which was discovered when bewildered bank employees began showing up for work in the middle of the chaos.

UPDATE: DEATH TOLL RISES IN HOUSTON PRESS ATTACK

HOUSTON — 11:30 AM CT — Nine people are confirmed dead and another four are seriously injured following a brutal attack this morning on a group of reporters and media crew in downtown Houston. The media personnel were gathered at a branch of Blue National Bank to report on what was then believed to be a robbery in which hostages had been taken. The hostage situation turned out to be a hoax perpetrated for the apparent purpose of drawing the press to the scene for the attack.

Two men disguised as Houston Police Department officers approached the crowd of reporters, camera operators, and assistants, then opened fire at point-blank range with semiautomatic handguns. The shooters fled the scene on foot and have not yet been apprehended. They are described as Caucasian, early to mid-thirties, one approximately 5'9" and the other approximately 6'2" or taller. HPD has stated that sketch artists are currently working with eyewitnesses to generate composites that will be publicly released as soon as they are complete. They also warn in advance that the suspects are considered armed and extremely dangerous.

18 MONTHS EARLIER
Portland, Oregon

BERRINGER HAD SPENT the past six months in a growing state of disbelief. After weeks of ignoring everyone and everything, he summoned the will to read the news coverage of what had happened to his family. He was dumbfounded by what he saw. Every major article, every major newscast talked about how an African-American family was killed at a white supremacist rally. Many of them went further, claiming outright that neo-Nazis had killed his family because they were black.

The problem was that he had never seen anything resembling a white supremacist that day. Hell, he had no idea there *was* any rally going on, since he'd seen no evidence of it at all in the park, just the mob that attacked him and killed his family. The leader of the mob had himself been a black man, for heaven's sake. He researched and discovered that the masked lunatics called themselves *Antifa*, which supposedly stood for "anti-fascist." They were anything but white supremacists; they were left-wing radicals who openly advocated for violence, Marxism, and anarchy. YouTube was full of videos of them attacking people, rioting, looting, and generally creating violent mayhem wherever they went. And he well remembered what had triggered the whole thing in the park: his son's American flag shirt. Nothing more.

Most of the thugs involved in the attack had been arrested, but the coverage always just talked names. No photos. No mention that they were a bunch of communist extremists. Instead, the implication of white supremacists as the culprits was always left hanging in the air. They had all been denied bail, and after that, any mention of them faded away.

He called the main local newspaper, identified himself, and eventually got through to the reporter who had written most of the articles about the affair. He told her he'd like to speak with her and clear up what really happened. She was ecstatic and they met. As he told her what had really happened, her enthusiasm faded and her demeanor cooled.

"What the hell is wrong with you?" Berringer had said. "You seem disappointed in the truth."

"Oh no, Mr. Berringer. It's just, well, I really appreciate your time."

"When will the article run, the one telling the truth about what happened?

"Our cycles are pretty jammed right now, but I'll be in touch."

No article ran. Subsequent attempts to clear the record with other major news outlets met with a similar lack of interest. He'd tried everything: Letters to editors. Calls to reporters. He even led a couple small protests around local media outlets. A handful of smaller online conservative news sites ran with the truth, but that was it. The big outfits had their narrative on what happened and they didn't give one damn about his corrections, no matter how hard he tried to communicate it to them.

Berringer was patriotic, but he had never been a political junkie. His interests, in addition to his family, had been tech and movies and books and football. Mouthy politicians and the bickering that surrounded them? Not so much. On that front, he tended to be a headline skimmer. So when he started digging into the issues surrounding the Antifa assholes, he was shocked to see politicians defending them. Oh, sure, they condemned "their tactics" with a wink and a nod, but then followed up with praise for their "fight against fascism." The more he read, the angrier he became, and the more obsessed he became with the way the news media coddled and covered for these barbarians, making a mockery of his family.

These liars needed to be exposed, and Bruce Berringer vowed to do that. For Alicia. For Ty. Even for little Nitwit. He thought about how he would go about doing that. Thought about it a lot. And the more he watched the news and saw how they lied, how they skewed everything, the angrier he became.

Then one day a man sat down beside him on a park bench. A man he hadn't seen in a long time. Berringer looked over at him, turned his head back to facing forward. "What are you doing here?"

The man scratched at his ear. "Chasing the same thing you are, Bruce."

"Such as?"

"What if I said 'truth and justice'?"

Berringer snorted at that.

The man put a hand on Berringer's knee, leaned forward and looked him in the eye. "Vengeance. I believe in vengeance. Do you?"

DAY 6

2:20 Pm Pacific Time

PORTLAND, OREGON

WITH SERENITY and purpose Bruce Berringer walked the rain-drenched streets of Portland until he reached his target, the headquarters of the major newspaper in town, the first media outlet that had turned the story of his family's murder into an agenda-driven narrative. The one whose reporter had said, "Our cycles are jammed right now" when he asked when they planned to print his story, *the* story." More than their "cycles" were about to be jammed.

Berringer entered the building, a fairly new mid-rise upon which some architect had tried to impose an aura of stateliness and failed. Just through the revolving door, he closed his umbrella, gave it a shake, and deposited it in a brass can with a dozen others. Across the lobby he walked, past a guard at a reception desk who never even looked up. Smart on his part. Perhaps he'd live.

At the bank of four elevators, he pushed the up button and waited. Twenty seconds later, an elevator cooed a melodic electronic sound as its doors opened and a white upward arrow lit up on its frame. He stepped inside, pushed the button for the sixteenth floor, and dropped his hand back into the pocket of his rain jacket as he moved to the back of the car. The heels of two women clacked in the corridor outside as they hurried toward the doors that had just begun to close. One stuck a hand in the gap when it was six inches wide and the doors parted to admit them, then closed once they had stepped inside.

Both women were young, in their twenties. One reached out and pushed the 15 button, then turned to the other and started chattering. Berringer tuned them out and watched the digits climb through their sequence. When the digits read "15," the elevator slowed and stopped. The doors parted and the chatterers made their exit. The doors closed and the elevator rose for a few seconds, then braked to a stop as the indicator read "16."

The doors parted and Berringer stepped out into the nerve center of the newsroom. It occupied the entire sixteenth floor and there were no corridors or entryways, just a wide open space filled with what had to be a hundred cubicles. There would be another hundred behind him, on the other side of the elevator shafts that occupied the central core of the building.

A small reception desk was positioned between the elevators and the main aisle that stretched out before him and into the cube farm. Behind the desk, a frumpy woman in her fifties looked up at Berringer as he walked toward her.

At the desk, he stopped. The woman looked annoyed and said, "Can I help you?"

Berringer took off his jacket and the woman gasped at what was underneath.

"Shut up," he said.

Her mouth hung open, her eyes wide. Berringer removed a palm-sized gadget with a lens and a small display screen on one side from the left pocket of the jacket, then folded the jacket and placed it on the desk. Small rivulets of rainwater dripped down from the edges of the garment and onto the faux-wood surface of the desk.

Elsewhere in the newsroom, no one paid the slightest attention to what was going on at the desk. Keyboards rattled, people huddled and yammered. The business of lying to people carried on. Berringer took four steps backward and was at the bank of elevators again. With his left hand, he reached up and placed the gadget on the metal frame of one of the elevators, where it stuck with an audible *snap* as its magnetic mounts found steel.

He pressed a button on top of the device and its little screen came to life. INITIALIZING. Seconds later, three vertical bars appeared. Below the bars, text said CONNECTING, then CONNECTED, then STREAMING.

Berringer strode forward to the desk, then turned and faced the lens of the gadget. In a clear voice that showed no sign of nerves, he said, "My name is Bruce Berringer. I killed Chad Scott. I blew up GNN. I started the campaign to rid the media of liars. I call on patriots across the country to carry on this vital work until the rot has been completely purged from the fourth estate. You can read my manifesto at the website now showing on your screens. You will also find helpful material there. Mirror the site everywhere you can. Spread the word. Defend the truth. Kill them all."

Then Berringer spread his arms wide. In his right hand was a small black cylinder with a red button on top. It was connected to the vest that circled his torso by a pair of wires, one red, one black. He closed his eyes, pictured his family, and pushed the button.

MANIFESTO OF BRUCE BERRINGER

Please Share And Mirror

MY NAME IS BRUCE BERRINGER. This is my story. I am 32 years old, African American. Until 2 years ago I was married with a family. On a sunny day in Portland, Oregon my wife Alicia, my son Ty, our dog Nitwit, and I were having a picnic in the park. A gang of people dressed in black and wearing masks attacked us because my 10-year-old son was wearing a shirt with an American flag on it. (Ty loved the flag. We bought him a flag on a pole for his room so he could start every morning with the pledge of allegiance.)

These criminals killed my entire family, leaving me alone in the world. I was not a political man. I worked in robotics and was a regular guy. I usually voted but really did not pay much attention to politics. I focused on my family. After they were killed I could not believe what I saw on the news and what I read in the newspapers. Every one of them talked about how my wife and son and dog were killed at a white supremacist rally. They implied that white supremacists attacked us.

This was not true. We never saw anyone except the masked criminals who attacked us. There was no rally that I could tell. I now know much more about the outfit that attacked us. They call themselves ANTIFA which supposedly means antifascist. I can tell you there were no fascists in the park that day. They attacked because Ty wore a United States flag, period. They called me a Nazi. (A NIGGER NAZI to be exact.)

They beat Ty and my wife to death and hung my little dog from a tree. They left me beaten and unconscious. I told newspaper and TV reporters exactly what happened many times. They ignored me. I could not believe it but they didn't care anything about the truth. Their story was white supremacists and that was that. I all but begged them to tell the truth. Nothing worked.

The police arrested the criminals and they were all convicted for what they did but the newspapers and TV news ignored it. In a trial that lasted 41 days I saw reporters in the courtroom maybe 3 times. They just did not care. I kept trying to get them to tell the truth. Nothing worked. I wrote letters to my congressmen. Nothing happened. I told my story on social media. Some conservative websites and bloggers wrote articles and told the truth but the big ones like the networks and the big papers still ignored it. I protested outside their buildings and studios. Sometimes as many as a hundred other people protested with me. Nothing happened.

I got angry. The more I watched the news and read news articles the angrier I got. Since I had not been political and not paid attention to much news besides big headline stories I was shocked to see how these people told the news. They have a story they want to tell and that is what they tell, no matter what the truth is. It's not right. They gripe and whine when people criticize them but they are nothing but liars.

I still do not care much about politics but I have found myself more drawn to conservative people because they at least listen to me and believe what I say. The others laugh at me, curse me, threaten me, call me names, and try to get me kicked off whatever online place I go to tell my story. I started to say these people (the liberals and progressives, both regular people and the news people) hate conservatives but it is much more than that. They hate anyone who disagrees with them on anything. The news people are liars and filled with hatred but they call the others haters.

The people in this country don't know what is really going on because the news people only ever tell them one side of the story. Any story. The crazier and further to the left side of politics and culture and just life in general, the more they push it down everybody's throat. I could no longer sit by and do nothing. It is not right that the people are lied to and the truth hidden from them by these evil people. Yes, they are evil. They attack anyone from "the right" and they protect some of the worst people you could imagine just because they are liberal or progressive or whatever you want to call them.

I got sick of it and decided to do something. THE LIES MUST STOP. This is why I killed Chad Scott. This is why I killed the people at GNN and the people here in Portland at the newspaper. Because enough is enough. They have no right to lie and brainwash hundreds of millions of people to think like they want them to. Their job is to just tell people what happened. They do not do that. They lie and cover up and destroy anyone who disagrees with them.

That is not what America is supposed to be. Sometimes blood is required. I decided to bring that blood, including my own. By the time anyone reads this I will be dead. I encourage all people who want to know the truth to continue the fight I began. Our nation cannot survive if this little group of hateful people are allowed to continue doing what they do. YOU MUST STOP THEM NOW.

Please follow the links in the sidebar of this document for a lot more detail on how crooked the news people are. Proof. You will find a detailed list of major news figures, what they are guilty of, where they live, and much more. You will find all the information I have gathered on ANTIFA, including many of their leaders, where they live, how they operate. I am not an evil man. I do not like hurting people but this is war and now you must carry on the fight that I have started. Godspeed and God bless the United States of America.

DAY 6

5:06 Pm

LOCATION UNKNOWN

GENERAL LUCIAN HARROW paced his small office, cell phone to his ear. "Sonofa*bitch*! Who is this guy? ... Berringer? Never heard of him. ... Right. ... Right. ... Yeah, I hate he killed all those people but I'm glad *he's* gone. We need this distraction out of the way before showtime. ... Bullshit. He damn well hurt us, not helped us. ... Okay, keep me posted."

Harrow punched off the call and put the phone back in his pocket. He sat down at his desk and ran a hand across his short hair, thinking. The seeming coincidence of this Berringer character doing all this, at this exact time, gnawed at his gut. Somebody helped this guy and Harrow needed to find out who that somebody was. Quickly.

DAY 6
5:45 Pm Central

CHEYENNE MOUNTAIN

I WAS EXPLORING the mountain's network when my phone vibrated. 212 area code. New York. I answered. "Sam Flatt."

"Sam, Courtney Meyer."

"Hey, what's up?"

"I wanted to give you a heads-up. I passed along your info on Bruce Berringer. After what happened today, my superiors demanded I reveal my source, and I complied."

So much for flying under the radar. "What do you mean, 'after what happened today'?"

"You haven't heard the news?"

"No, been buried in a new case. Tell me."

"Berringer blew himself up with a suicide vest a little over an hour ago. Took out a couple floors of a newspaper building in Portland."

I digested that for a few seconds, then said, "How many killed?"

"No reliable count yet but well over a hundred."

"Good grief."

"Yeah, anyway, I suspect you'll be hearing from the task force running the investigation, and probably sooner rather than later."

"I appreciate the heads-up, Courtney."

"No problem. Good luck and goodbye."

"Bye." I ended the call.

Sadie had obviously been eavesdropping. Hard not to from five feet away. She said, "How many killed in what?"

"Suicide bombing in Portland. The guy who's been attacking media figures."

"No shit?"

"I shit you not." My phone vibrated again. I glanced at the screen. Sheila. I answered. "Hey, Sheila."

"We have a big problem here," she said, her voice low.

I stood and walked to the other end of the room and found an empty cubicle. I too spoke quietly. "What?"

"FBI showed up here about five minutes ago with a search warrant."

"For what?"

"Sam, they're taking everything. All the files. All the computers. I had no warning, no time to clean up anything. They're gonna find our mirror of their investigative files."

I massaged my temples, trying to wrap my head around this catastrophe. How did they even know about the office? Having been set up by Pitt, it should've been invisible.

Sheila continued. "That's not all. They're looking for you hot and heavy. I told them I didn't know where you were but they're not buying it. I wouldn't be surprised if they take me into custody."

"Where are you now?" I said.

"In the hallway outside the office," she said, almost whispering now. "Gung-ho-looking guy guarding the elevator, staring at me."

"Damn. Nothing you can do but cooperate. I'll call Pitt now. Sit tight."

I hung up and called Pitt. It went to voicemail. I couldn't recall a single time that had happened before. I left him a three-word message: "Call. Me. Now."

DAY 6
6:04 Pm Central

CHEYENNE MOUNTAIN

HARBUCK and I met for dinner in a small private dining room near his office. We chatted for a moment about the Portland bombing and how I'd identified Berringer, then got down to business.

"Progress on the helicopter?" I said.

"Peterson claims it hasn't left the base in a week."

"That's an error or a lie, unless Airbus Helicopters has sold more of that model than we know about."

"The latter's unlikely," Harbuck said. "Like I said earlier, I don't believe in coincidences like this. Somebody over at Peterson has doctored the logs for that chopper."

"Got any ideas on proving it?"

"I have a call in to my counterpart over there," he said, and took a bite of macaroni.

"And?"

"I'll request that he provide you access to the systems that log aircraft usage."

"That works," I said. "You catch the news today?"

He pursed his lips and nodded slowly. "Country's going to hell before our eyes. You read that guy's manifesto?"

"I did. Disturbing."

"If he's right about how the media handled his story, he had a right to be pissed, but sounds like his mind snapped."

"He's right," I said. "The media totally screwed it." I regretted saying it the moment it rolled off my tongue.

"You know this how?" Harbuck said.

What the hell. Harbuck was trusting me. I'd trust him. To a degree. "I initially thought these media attacks were connected to the abductions so I was investigating everything I came across on both fronts. I stumbled across the guy's story, Berringer's, and dug in. I actually identified him and fed that to the FBI."

"Impressive. Dare I ask how you 'stumbled' onto something the FBI had missed?"

I wasn't about to get into FBI mirrors and NSA searches. "Best not to," I said.

"Fine by me," Harbuck said. "Sometimes ignorance truly is bliss. So back to business, what do you think of our girl Grossman?"

"Smart. Wary. If she's the culprit, I'm guessing she went about things very carefully, but I'm on it. If it's her, I'll nail her."

DAY 6

8:45 Pm Central

HOUSTON

SHEILA VASQUEZ PAID cash at the counter of the seediest motel she'd ever seen, parked her car at the back, and entered the room. It had a full-sized bed with a threadbare multicolored bedspread, rickety furniture, and accessories bolted to that furniture.

She sat on the bed and dialed Pitt for what had to be the tenth time since she'd given the FBI the slip at the office downtown. It went to voicemail. Again. Damn him! In the bathroom, she leaned over a chipped sink that had a mineral stain from years of a leaky faucet dripping onto it and washed her face. What to do, what to do?

She didn't want to call Sam. He was occupied in Colorado and besides, what could he do? She was on the run and on her own. She needed Pitt, with his magic power to put the FBI in line, to make them understand that what they were doing was authorized at the highest levels. Why wasn't he answering?

DAY 6

9:20 Pm Central

CHEYENNE MOUNTAIN

MY LITTLE ROOM was on the bleak side with its gray metal walls and built-in accoutrements. A small desk. A shower in the corner, separated from the rest of the room only by a white plastic curtain. A toilet behind a short partition made of odd little cinderblocks that had been painted so many times their rough texture had become smooth.

I thought about what I'd learned that day. Not much. Sadie Grossman sure didn't look like a traitor or spymaster. Of course, who does? Sleep was a long way off so I decided to go for a walk with my spiffy ID badge that was supposed to unlock all the doors. I pulled on jeans and a tee, then stepped into a pair of Wallabees that would let me be stealthy if the need arose. Outside my door, I reversed the course I'd taken to get to the officers' barracks earlier. Two minutes later, the metal corridor opened up into a larger room that served as a hub of sorts, five corridors leading off in various directions. I knew what lay down the next two to my left, so I headed right and started down the first one I hit. Unlike most other areas I'd seen, this one was narrow, no more than four feet wide, with a ceiling inches above my head. The metal surfaces of the walls and ceiling were different, too. Bare galvanized metal instead of the baked-on pale green that dominated this complex. It felt like walking through an air-conditioning duct.

After walking at least ten minutes, the passageway ended at a wall of rough rock. To my left was a door made of the same bare metal. No handle. No window. Nothing but a smooth door with a card reader on the left side. I swiped my ID. No beep, no LED to announce success or failure. Instead, the door pivoted in about an inch, with a slight hiss like you might hear when opening a tightly sealed door on a freezer. I pushed the door open and a gentle but steady breeze washed over me. What the hell was a positive-pressure section doing inside a mountain that's all about radar and missiles? This kind of thing wasn't usually seen outside biohazard facilities. I stepped inside and closed the door behind me. Whatever this area was, it appeared cave-dark and dead. I stood as still as the granite of the mountain, waiting for my eyes to adjust, listening for any sound at all. After three minutes, I could still see absolutely nothing, which meant there wasn't any light in this space. None. The only sound was the palest hint of moving air, the system that maintained the positive pressure that had washed over me when I opened the door. I waited a couple minutes more, then pulled my phone from my hip pocket and turned on its flashlight.

This was some spooky crap, and I'm hardly a stranger to dark places. The light from my phone revealed...nothing. The LED was bright but all I could see was a smooth, bare concrete floor that reached to the limit of the little light. I held the phone up and slowly turned in place, looking for anything the light might hit. Aside from the inside of the corridor wall behind me, nothing. I walked forward, taking full strides and counting them. The only thing I encountered were concrete support columns every eighty feet, each one a good six feet in diameter. Their condition was pristine but I could tell they were old. These columns had been poured not into the strong cardboard tubes that serve as pour forms today, but into wooden forms lined with plastic sheeting, the textures of both clearly visible in the hardened concrete. After walking almost exactly a quarter-mile, the cavern finally ended at another rough rock face.

I put my back against that rock face, pivoted ninety degrees to my left, and walked a hundred feet, dragging my hand on the wall to be sure I stayed on course. Then I turned right and started walking again, heading back toward the corridor and the door. The light from the phone had dimmed a bit, so I picked up the pace. I'd come back and explore this place with proper lighting. The metal of the corridor wall had just become visible ahead when I picked up a tiny glint on the floor to my left. I shone the light toward it but it was small and I couldn't tell what it was. I walked maybe fifty feet and there it was. I reached down and picked it up, turning it over in the weakening glow of the phone's light. What in good hell was something like this doing here?

DAY 6

9:53 Pm Central

CHEYENNE MOUNTAIN

AFTER LEAVING the cavern and retracing my steps back to the central hub of the building, I went to my workstation in the cube farm. After walking the entire area and verifying I was alone, I went to Sadie's workstation. Her computer was a mid-size tower, nestled vertically under her desk. I set up the same gear on her computer I'd used on Sheila's a couple days earlier, giving me access to everything she did.

With my data-spy in place, I pulled the second part of my surveillance setup from my pocket, a tiny video camera concealed in a thumb drive. The best placement I could come up with was a USB port built into the end of the keyboard on my desk. The device drew its power from the USB port and recorded video to its internal storage anytime the camera sensed motion within its field of view. The fish-eye camera lens was on top of the thumb drive, which meant I'd be recording a view that was chiefly of the ceiling, but after some repositioning of the keyboard, I eventually got it lined up so that it also caught the top edge of the short wall that separated my cubicle from

Sadie's. Not ideal but better than nothing. I checked to be sure every-thing was in its original place at her desk, then headed out.

It was after one when I got back to my quarters. I thought about going back out, finding a proper flashlight, going back to the cavern. But a guy no one knew, asking for a flashlight in the middle of the night, wasn't exactly the invisible approach I needed. I lay down on the cot and stared at the ceiling. There wasn't the slightest logical reason to think the cavern intersected with my mission. But it did. I know this because when I'd seen it, I'd felt the skittering. The featherlight dancing out at the edges of my psyche. My Spidey senses. I may've missed on my initial theory of one big operation but there was no way I'd miss twice in a row. Right?

I reached into my pocket and pulled out the object I'd found on the floor of the cavern. It was a button, the kind used in political campaigns. Its condition was pristine, but the construction left no doubt that it was old, original. Today's version would have been thinner and lighter. This one had heft, the built-in safety pin on the back thick and heavy. Then there was its content: The face of the button was inset with finely ridged plastic, with content that appeared to change as you tilted it back and forth. At one angle, a photo of JFK nearly filled the face, a label underneath his smiling profile that said JOHN F. KENNEDY. As I tilted it, a fat font that was plain and dated read THE 60s.

As Harbuck promised, a computer had been set up on the little desk. No telling what penetration or detection capabilities existed in this facility, and I wasn't ready to jack my own laptop into this network. Not yet. So I instead used the antique Dell with its 15" flat panel that was a good two inches thick. Unbelievable. It had exactly one browser installed, a vintage of Internet Explorer that probably dated back to the previous millennium. Given much of the tech I'd seen since my arrival, I counted myself lucky that I didn't have to use a 1996 version of Netscape to surf the web. My first instinct was to install Tor and bury myself in a proxy chain, but I backed off that for the same reason I'd hesitated to use my own computer. I'd get invisible soon enough. For now, all I needed was the quintessential embodiment of the evil corporation: Google.

On a site selling vintage political memorabilia, I found a picture of the exact button. The price was $30, the product photo showing the same button, albeit one that was old and faded, obviously from years of handling or poor storage. It was listed as "JFK flasher button." I dug around some more, hoping to find more details but struck out. I'd definitely be spending more time on this oddity, but for now I wanted to see if I could learn anything about the cavern.

After looking at a dozen sites about Cheyenne Mountain, my eyes were tired and I'd learned nothing new. I clicked back to the home page, which was set to an intranet page that said WELCOME TO CHEYENNE MOUNTAIN. I didn't expect to learn much from what looked to be the equivalent of the welcome page you get when you connect to the Wi-Fi network at a hotel. I was wrong. An ordinary guest account would not have gotten far, but my CM credentials clicked right through all the links in bold red with the parenthetical "WARNING! RESTRICTED ACCESS!" suffixes. Sweet.

Within five minutes I'd found what I was looking for, a diagram of the entire facility's layout. Not terribly detailed, more like a mall map with generic labels like PHYSICAL PLANT and ADMINISTRATION. The graphic was about five times the width and three times the height of the browser window, so it took a bunch of scrolling back and forth. I spotted my area, OFFICERS' BARRACKS, then worked my way through the route I'd taken that led me to the cavern. Or I tried to, anyway. Not only was the cavern not on the map; neither was the long corridor that had taken me to it. Maybe this diagram was old.

I scrolled to the bottom and found the copyright tag. It was current, so it wasn't a matter of an obsolete chart. The hub was clearly pictured, but instead of five corridors shooting off in different directions, there were only four. The skittering in my mind grew more animated.

DAY 7
8:10 Am Central

CHEYENNE MOUNTAIN

I TOOK a sip of very good coffee as General Harbuck sat down in the chair across from me. We shook hands across the table.

He took a sip of the coffee that had quickly appeared before him. "You making any progress?"

"Still getting the lay of the land." I powered up the screen on my tablet and pushed it across the table to Harbuck. "That's a map of the complex I pulled from the intranet last night."

He glanced at the screen and nodded.

I said, "That map is missing a corridor and a big empty cavern I wandered into last night. Know anything about it?"

"Not sure what this has to do with hackers, but yes, I know a great deal about it."

"Might have nothing to do with it," I said, "but I guess you could call my investigative approach holistic. I look at everything."

"Fine by me."

The steward reappeared at the table and we placed our breakfast orders. When he left, Harbuck said, "That cavern was hollowed out decades ago, in the sixties. The plan was to build a continuity-of-government facility, a place for a skeleton government to safely operate in the event of a cataclysm."

"Why didn't they finish it?"

"Before my time but hell, I'm sure it was the same reason so many things get started and abandoned. Politicians. Somebody thinks it's a great idea and gets it started, then someone else takes charge and kills it. In this case, you end up with a big hole in the mountain that's good for nothing."

I pointed to the tablet. "Why wouldn't it be on the map, though?"

"The map is active areas only. There are other unused areas in the mountain that aren't diagrammed, but nothing on the scale of that cavern."

"Any way I can get a list of those areas?"

Harbuck shrugged. "Not sure, but I'll find out. You'd probably be looking at old-school blueprints."

"Not a problem," I said. "Might be a hacker hideaway stashed in some nook or cranny."

"I'll get someone on it."

DAY 7
8:40 Am Central

CHEYENNE MOUNTAIN

AFTER BREAKFAST, I went to my cube and settled in. Sadie had her earbuds in and was hunched over her keyboard with busy fingers. She looked up and gave a quick wave, but said nothing.

I set up a hotkey I could use to instantly switch my screen to something innocuous, glanced over to be sure Sadie had no view of my screen without standing up to look over the little wall, then loaded the spy mirror of her screen. She was typing a personal email. It started, "Hey Dad!" and then jumped into typical family e-banter about missing him and her sister, planning to see them soon, blah blah. I killed the mirror and loaded up a batch of network traffic captures that one of Harbuck's tech minions had sent me.

They were right: Within a few hours I had confirmed their claim that the attacks had come from within Cheyenne Mountain, but that was an oversimplification. The mountain had countless separate networks servicing the myriad operations going on inside. The more accurate description was that the attacks had come from a computer on the main facility's network, the network that handled all the logistics for the mountain. The network that Harbuck's direct reports managed, including Sadie. From that network, the attacks had gone after a number of subnets that were dedicated to specific operations. Power, heat, media and internet feeds, access control, things like that. What was immediately odd to me is that the information I was looking at showed no efforts to hit the *really* juicy targets, like NORAD and its support nets. All the attacks came from a single computer on the facility network, and every one of those attacks was trying to gain entry to a direct subnet.

Time to engage Sadie. I said, "Hey," and rapped on the wall between us.

A few seconds later she stood and looked over into my space. "Yes?"

"Got any lunch plans? I need to pick your brain a bit."

"Uh, yeah. Sure. Give me fifteen minutes to wrap something up?"

"Perfect."

CHEYENNE MOUNTAIN

"So what are you looking for exactly?" Sadie said between bites of salad.

"I'm not really supposed to talk about it."

"No problem. Just thought I might be able to help you more if I had a little more info."

I looked her in the eye for ten seconds or so and leaned across the table. "What's your clearance level?"

"Top secret."

After a few more seconds to set the hook, I quietly said, "It stays between us?"

"Believe me, they trained me well on keeping secrets. You and me, no further." She crunched on a piece of lettuce and leaned a little closer herself.

"The Air Force is concerned that someone may have exfiltrated the code that runs access control for the facility."

"A hack?"

I shook my head. "No. They think it was an inside job."

Her chewing glitched. Just a bit, but it was there. "The suspected event was about a year ago, but for some reason they only discovered it recently."

This time her tell was definite. She visibly relaxed, her shoulders dropping and the little creases in her forehead disappearing. "I can believe that," she said. "In some ways, the military is rapid response. Others? Not so much. Lot of red tape."

I nodded. "How familiar are you with the access control systems?"

"Very. One of my primary areas of responsibility, along with climate control. If a door or card reader or furnace goes wonky on the software side, I fix it."

"That keeps you busy?"

She laughed. "You wouldn't believe it. The people in admin are always screwing up something on a badge, or an officer wants his office three degrees cooler than his thermostat allows, crap like that."

I smiled. "Good old operator error. So pretend you wanted to tinker around, tweak some of these apps that you support. How would you go about it?"

DAY 7
1:01 Pm Central

CHEYENNE MOUNTAIN

THE LUNCH WAS PRODUCTIVE. I got a little useful techno-info on how the mountain works, and the process opened Sadie up a bit, nudged her toward early friendship. On return to my cube, I found a pleasant surprise in my inbox: an email with the mountain's blueprints and much more attached. I opened the first file and started digging.

It was a geek's treasure trove. Not just for my investigation, but for any geek. One of the files was a network map from the eighties that had numerous labels for ARPANET components, a military data network that would eventually mature into the internet. Very cool stuff. After a bit of self-indulgence with that nostalgia file, I moved on and eventually found the two files of most current interest. The first was a dynamically generated network map that had been created a week earlier. The other had nothing to do with tech *per se*, but was an old-school blueprint that showed a before and after of the cavern area. The "after" revealed something interesting.

The drawing of the cavern on the old blueprint, which had a date in the corner of 01SEP1961, featured the typical views from different perspectives. The overhead view revealed a space that was generally rectangular with rough, uneven walls. The front view showed the height of the space to be likewise uneven, but generally speaking it was about two hundred feet from concrete floor to hewn rock ceiling. The most interesting feature, however, was a smaller illustration that depicted a pair of six-inch tubular conduits mounted to the ceiling. One was labeled UTILITY, the other DATA.

As expected, the two pipes fed from the hub where the five corridors met, through the rock, and into the cavern. What excited me was the fact that the UTILITY conduit fanned out to a vast array of lights that hung from the ceiling. If they had actually been installed, it sure would make my exploration easier. During my discovery wandering in the space, I hadn't seen anything to suggest any features at all. It had looked and felt like a giant empty cave with rock walls, a concrete floor, and nothing else. But given the staggering height of the ceiling that I now knew, there's no way the LED flashlight on my phone would have revealed anything that far overhead. Time for another look.

DAY 7

2:20 Pm Central

CHEYENNE MOUNTAIN

WITH HER OFFICIAL work caught up for the time being and her new cubicle neighbor away from his desk, Sadie got to work on her real mission, the reason she had been maneuvered into this facility months ago. It had been tough going, as she'd known it would be. Pulling off the re-routes and taps was easy enough since maintaining the relevant systems was part of her official duties. Doing it without leaving a trace was another matter. It was painstaking and required great patience, a trait of which she had none to spare.

She minimized all the windows on her screen and opened a Power-Shell prompt. It was hard to avoid leaving breadcrumbs in the normal Windows environment, but here in the realm of the command line, staying invisible was a cinch. It was also a lot more fun. Within a minute, she had *ssh* connections opened to all the relevant facility servers. Water and climate were done. Now it was time for the big push, power and media. She really wanted her hacking music, but the earbuds would make it impossible to hear her neighbor approaching, so silent was the game today.

Her fingers flew across the keyboard. Multicolored text scrolled. And in the heart of the Cheyenne Mountain server farm, things were happening.

DAY 7
2:23 Pm Central

CHEYENNE MOUNTAIN

HARBUCK MET me in the hub and handed me what I'd asked him for in an email. He raised an eyebrow but asked no questions, just handed me the biggest flashlight I'd ever seen and said "Good luck" before doing one of his efficient spin-and-depart moves.

No one was around so I headed down the corridor and into the cavern. I stepped through the door and closed it behind me, this time paying attention to the echo created by the huge space when the steel door hit home in its frame. I switched on the flashlight and it threw a wide beam that lit the swath before me like daylight. I played the light back and forth, checking out the area that last night had been so daunting as I worked with nothing but a tiny LED.

According to the blueprint, the electrical panel should be on the wall to my left, beneath the point where the conduits exited the rock and fed the room. And it was. I headed that way, and after a few minutes of walking I stood before the biggest panel of breakers I'd ever seen. There were more than a hundred of them and they looked simultaneously old and brand new. Unlike the modern breakers I was used to, these were huge, each one about eight inches tall and six inches wide, all with vertically oriented switches fitted with six-inch levers.

Unfortunately, there were no labels and there was no legend on the blueprint to indicate which breakers controlled what. Only one way to find out. I picked one and threw the lever up. Holy hell! On the other side of the cavern, some big electric motor spun up and within a few seconds I felt the air move. In this enormous underground space, the noise and the thought of equipment coming to life for probably the first time in decades was spooky as hell for some reason. I pulled the lever back down and listened to the motor's spin taper down to a stop.

The creepy sensation didn't get any better as I worked my way through groups of breakers. Some did nothing that I could tell. Some launched a hum that seemed to jack right into my nervous system. Some turned on more ventilation equipment. And finally, I threw a lever and a spot toward the rear of the cavern lit up in the yellow light of old incandescence. I looked up and saw the source of the light. It was hard to judge size from this far away, but the fixture had to be four feet in diameter, a metal cage enclosing a bulb that looked as big around as a basketball. I kept switching breakers and more of the lights came to life, although several of them flashed on momentarily, popped with the sound of a vintage camera flashbulb, then faded back to darkness.

I turned and surveyed the cavern. If I had expected it to be less spooky in the light, I would have been sorely disappointed. There was nothing on the floors, walls, or ceiling that I could see. Just a massive unnatural cave, sitting dead, its floor bathed in countless pools of amber light. I looked up from the electrical panel and studied the spot where the conduits entered the room. Smaller conduits dropped from one of the main tubes, the one, which had been stencil-painted in yellow with the word UTILITY.

The other main conduit was similarly labeled DATA, this time in green. Nothing dropped from this one at the wall. The six-inch pipe continued straight across the ceiling. I walked, my head craned up and following its route. At about a hundred feet, a two-inch conduit dropped from the main and ran down the side of one of the concrete support columns. At about three feet off the ground, it terminated in a coverless metal box that looked to be a standard electrical box built to accommodate a pair of dual-outlet receptacles. A couple feet of thick black cable protruded from the box, its end cut clean with no conductors exposed. I dropped to a knee and made a closer inspection. The cable was about a half-inch in diameter. Inside the outer sheathing, I could see a number of discrete bundles of smaller wires. My guess was that these internal bundles of wires had been intended to connect dumb terminals to a mainframe somewhere. I stood and resumed my trek across the room.

After a while it became evident that these terminal cables dropped from the main data conduit every hundred feet. No sub-conduits fed toward the front or rear of the room. All the drops came straight down from the main, which was positioned roughly halfway between the front of the cavern where the entry door was and the rear wall. I walked all the way across the cavern, still following the data conduit. It was at the far wall that I saw something that set my investigative psyche alight: According to the blueprints, both the utility and data conduits terminated at that wall, but my eyes told a different story. Both continued into the wall. So where the hell did they go?

DAY 7

2:55 Pm Central

CHEYENNE MOUNTAIN

"I'LL BE DAMNED," Harbuck said, looking up at the conduits continuing into the rock wall. I had tracked him down and brought him here as soon as I made the discovery.

I pulled a folded sheet of paper from my pocket, spread it out, and pointed to an enlarged view of the conduits that clearly showed them terminating at this wall, not routing into it. "Not on the plans."

Harbuck shook his head. "According to the plans, *and* according to everything I've ever been told, there's nothing beyond this wall but solid rock, all the way to the other side of the mountain."

"Any ideas on how we could find out what's really in there?"

"I'll work on that. Any progress on the electronic end of things?"

"Still probing. Also working the social engineering angle," I said.

"Social engineering?"

"Sorry. Getting close to Grossman, see if I can get anything out of her."

He nodded. "Need anything else from me?"
"Not now."

DAY 7

7:10 Pm Central

CHEYENNE MOUNTAIN

AFTER DINNER I went to my cube. As I'd hoped, Sadie was gone for the day. I woke my computer and pulled up the spy app, then set it to give me a playback of her activities for the day. A picture of her computer screen rolled in fast motion as a clock at the bottom of the screen told me what time the current activity had occurred. Her morning work looked routine. Same for the first part of the afternoon.

I hit the good stuff at 14:20 on the playback clock. That was about the time I had left for the cavern. To confirm that, I opened a folder for the *camera cum thumb drive*, keyed in the password, and checked for recordings around that time. Bingo. I had left my desk at 14:18. At 14:19, the top of Sadie's head appeared on the edge of the picture, peering over the wall into my cubicle. I killed the video and returned to the playback of her computer activity.

She opened a PowerShell window and made a number of *ssh* connections to various servers that ran the mountain's facilities. During our lunch conversation that day, we had made tech talk about her job. She had told me how the systems worked, what she did, and the software interfaces she used to do it. All standard Windows environment, she had said. So why was she connecting to the servers with PowerShell, a command-line approach that had its roots way back in the geeky days of MS-DOS? There were a couple obvious reasons. PowerShell could be configured to remember nothing of what had transpired within its environment. Not so easy to do that in Windows, with its convenience-based features that tried to remember all it could about what a user did and how they did it. In addition to that, Power-Shell got the first half of its name from the fact that it gave a sophisticated user great power to manipulate systems at a fine, granular level.

As I replayed her work, it became obvious that, yes, Sadie Grossman was a sophisticated user. Very. It was also apparent she wasn't carrying out her Air Force duties. I'd have to do some more research to understand exactly what she was doing, but the big picture was obvious: She was creating scripts to interact with those servers, scripts that would provide access to the servers from the suspect computer that was the source of all the attacks on the mountain's nets. That computer was digitally sitting at an IP address of 10.0.0.224, the same IP address Harbuck's geeks had identified as the source of their troubles, and that I had verified while looking through the captures of network traffic.

Even more damning, she had gone to great pains to cover her tracks. The connections she was setting up to the servers would be all but invisible. And once she got a script working just the way she wanted, she changed it to a hidden file and then protected it with encryption. Sadie, you bad, bad girl.

DAY 8

8:33 Am Central

CHEYENNE MOUNTAIN

AT BREAKFAST I asked Harbuck if he could do something to get Sadie out of her cubicle for the morning. He nodded and bit off half a sausage link. After chewing it to what must have been just short of liquid, he said, "Progress?"

"She's your girl."

"Positive?"

I nodded. "Nailed that down last night. Need to dig some more this morning."

"Good."

A couple hours later I was back at work, replaying the recording of her actions from the day before, studying them in detail. It took a couple hours, but it all started to come together. She wasn't trying to steal data. She wasn't attacking the mountain's systems to bring them down or to disrupt operations. Little Miss Sadie, the girl who shines like a new penny, was *sharing* the mountain's resources. Specifically, she was doing two things. First, she was providing access to power, heating, cooling, water, and some communications lines. Second—this was really clever work on her part—she was covering her tracks by tweaking the reporting of the resources used by the legitimate mountain systems. By adding electrical usage to the amount reported by numerous facilities in the mountain, the power she was routing elsewhere appeared accounted for. I knew now without checking that if we ran a detailed report of the amount of electricity consumed by every bona fide operation in the complex, it would tally perfectly with the consumption metered at the mains that fed the entire mountain. Same for water. Ditto for climate control.

It made no sense. Why would anyone risk prison to pilfer some water and lights and heat? And what was the deal with the comms? They didn't consume resources in a way that could be easily measured. The tinkering she had done on comms wasn't like the other elements. She wasn't intercepting anything going on inside the mountain. What she had set up there was access, the ability to communicate with the outside world. Why? And who was the beneficiary of her chicanery?

I moved to her cubicle and logged into her computer using the login credentials that I had captured with the keylogger. Two minutes later, I had her computer set to allow me to log into it and take full control from my computer. I wanted to do some direct digging, but I sure didn't want to be sitting at her desk if she happened to walk in.

Two hours later, as a screen filled in before me, I got that wonderful skitter out on the edge of my psyche, a subconscious process turning tiny bits of information into puzzle pieces that could be slid into place on the game board. A physiological and psychological reaction that told me I was moving toward the core of the mystery. On my monitor was a map of sorts, a diagram of the facility onto which were overlaid not just symbols for data and water and power connections, but actual routes for each of those elements. Routes animated to depict usage and volume of usage.

The map wasn't a big deal in and of itself, just another graphical representation of digital and physical elements. What made it special was the fact that it was different from the earlier maps and diagrams I'd seen of Cheyenne Mountain, the official ones. On those, places were missing. I knew this because I'd found one of those places, walked

around in its enormous darkness, heard the echoes of its vast empti-
ness. On Sadie's map, that big space where I'd found the old JFK
button had walls and pipes and conduits. On her map, it had a *name*:
AMPHITHEATER 1980.

I spun the wheel on my mouse, zooming in to be sure I was right,
comparing the electrical, plumbing, and data pathways shown on the
screen to those I'd seen with my eyes the day before. They matched. I
dragged the image so I could see the right side of the space in more
detail. Got to its righthand wall. Zoomed in some more. Tweaked until
I had just the spot I was looking for, the spot where I had seen iron
pipes and galvanized conduits the day before, not terminating on that
wall, but passing through it into some other space beyond the rock
wall, a space that didn't exist on the official maps.

My heart thumped in my chest as I moved the map to the left side
of my screen, exposing the area beyond the cavern's righthand wall.
The big cavern I had explored was dwarfed by the space I saw
depicted before me. The "amphitheater" covered an area of perhaps a
dozen football fields. What I saw now was a space that would have to
be measured in *acres*, acres of space inside a mountain. What the hell
could it be? Whatever it was, I instantly knew it held the answers I was
looking for, the key to the riddle that had brought me here.

On my screen, blue digital water moved through the wall and into
the space, along with yellow electricity and pulsing green data bursts.
Rolling the mouse wheel backward, I zoomed out so I could see the
entire space on the screen. It had a roughly rectangular shape, but
offshoots of irregular shapes branched off from the right half of the
rectangle. The digital resources branched out, leaving a stylized junction box where they entered the space and feeding various locations
within the borders of the space. It looked like some of the areas used
water, power, and data. Others just power. Some with water and
power but no data.

I didn't know exactly what I was looking at, but I knew something
big, something important to the puzzle, was on the other side of that
rock wall in the big cavern.

UNREST SPREADING IN NATION

VIOLENCE AND CHAOS continue to spread across the country in the wake of widespread publication of media-killer Bruce Berringer's manifesto. While the national mood has been on edge since several high-profile personalities went missing and attacks on members of the news media began, the distribution of Berringer's document has significantly exacerbated tensions. Conservatives have for years alleged, without evidence, liberal bias in much of the national news media. Berringer's attacks, which have killed more than a hundred members of the press, have fueled new levels of hostility against journalists, with many reporters and other personnel around the country not showing up for work due to fear of being attacked. Most are still on the job but major figures are routinely surrounded by heavy security as they go to and from work.

Berringer's screed, which experts have said indicates serious mental illness on the part of the Portland roboticist who killed himself and scores of innocents in a suicide bombing the day before yesterday, included not only an outright call for violence against the media, but accompanying material that falsely purports to document the bias he claims. NBS anchor Charles Barkham, who is filling in for the missing lead anchor Rob Acoma, said, "We've had to deal with these baseless claims of bias for years. Now these lies and the rhetoric of the right have turned deadly. We do our job with integrity and transparency." When asked if he intended to change his reporting style, Barkham said, "Hell, no. I'll keep doing my job as I always have. I will not cave to terrorism." Some other news figures are taking a softer approach. An independent journalist who wished to remain anonymous said, "It never hurts to reevaluate one's work and seek to always improve. That's what I'm doing."

Most major cities are experiencing mass protests in the streets, with angry crowds surrounding network headquarters, local television stations, and newspaper offices. More than a dozen instances of arson, fourteen assaults, and numerous reports of vandalism and threats have been reported over the past 24 hours.

DAY 8

Noon Pacific

PORTLAND, OREGON

REGINA WEBB WALKED through the bar and into the back room the owner allowed them to use as a meeting and staging area. The room was packed with comrades gearing up, at least forty. Her phone vibrated and she glanced at the screen. Text from Mom about dinner. Whatever. Who had time to worry about dinner when there were Nazis on the street to fuck up?

She shucked off her backpack, dropped it on a table. Opened it up and emptied the contents. Three minutes later she was ready. Black hoodie on. Logo bandana covering her face. Big dark glasses. Pepper spray, the kind made for bears, stowed in a right-side pocket of her black cargo pants. Ice pick in a left pocket. She extended the special umbrella Cody had made for her. It had a spring sectioned into the shaft and a big-ass weight tucked in right under the apex of its canopy.

"Listen up!" Cody said, holding up a hand. While the group had no formal structure, everybody yielded to what Cody said. The room went quiet. "This is the day we've been waiting for. These streets belong to us. Am I right?"

"Damn right!"

"Hell yes!"

Cody said again, "Am. I. Right?"

The room lit up with cheers. Regina got goose bumps. She'd done a few protests before but hadn't seen a lot of action. Not real action, anyway. Yeah, she'd punched a few Nazis but that did no real damage. Today would be different. Today these motherfuckers would bleed.

"Alright," Cody said. "Watch for the cops. They usually leave us alone but keep an eye out. This is war. Today we do real damage and when the blood starts to flow the cops might move in. Stick together, watch each other's backs, and let's go fuck up some fascists." Another round of cheers broke out and their black-clad army filed out through the bar and onto the street. She saw Cody talking on a handheld radio.

Grouped into a tight knot, they made their way toward the TV station where most of the fascists were gathered. A block later, additional groups joined theirs from the left and right. Now they had well over a hundred warriors, maybe a hundred-fifty. She could see the fascists ahead now. A few dozen? Waving fucking American flags and chanting some bullshit toward the TV station's building she couldn't make out.

She hustled and drew up beside Cody. He looked over at her, pulled his sunglasses down just a bit, and gave her a wink. Her stomach fluttered. They drew closer to the fascists, a half-block ahead now. One of them had a megaphone leading a chant and now she could tell what they were saying: "USA! Tell the truth! USA! Tell the truth!" Fucking assholes.

Twenty yards out now. Cody at the front of their pack, Regina right beside him. He looked back over his shoulder at their black mass and screamed, "Now!"

They broke into a run and dove right into the motherfuckers before they knew what hit them. She swung her umbrella and felt the *thock* as the weighted end connected with the side of a Nazi boomer's head. God, that felt so fucking good. The old bastard crumpled to the ground. She pulled the ice pick from her pocket, squatted down, started poking the fucker over and over, wherever she could get him. Blood spread across his white T-shirt, drowning out the writing on the front that said AMERICA, LOVE IT OR LEAVE IT. He was gasping now, blood running out of his mouth. She hocked up the biggest wad of spit she could and put it right in the racist motherfucker's face.

She stood and moved on, adrenaline flooding her body and mind. This was living. This was making a fucking difference. This was righting wrongs and putting assholes in their place. These fuckers were the ones who had oppressed and enslaved the poor, the people of color, the helpless. Pride and righteousness filled her heart.

Dead ahead of her, another target. This was one of the assholes who had been waving one of those fucking offensive-ass flags. Now he was running like a pussy, dragging a miniature fascist alongside him, a girl in pigtails who looked to be maybe ten years old. Fuck him and his little bitch of a Nazi-in-training. She charged and drew back her umbrella for the swing.

Something was wrong. What the hell? She opened her eyes and was looking straight up at the sky. Loud pops were going off all around her. Now people were running, screaming. She thought some of them were running over her, but how could that be? She realized she was lying on her back on the pavement. She shook her head. She needed to think. Something was wrong, really wrong.

Yes, people were running right over her, trampling her. Her own people. What the fuck? She turned her head to the left and managed to raise it up enough to look around. It was madness. She wasn't the only one on the ground. It was littered with her comrades, everywhere she looked. And that loud popping kept on going.

Then she saw him, a guy in some kind of camouflage outfit, holding one of those fucking assault rifles that should've been banned, collected, and destroyed years ago. This asshole was standing in the street, calm as you please, aiming and firing. Aiming and firing. A weird burning smell filled the air. She pushed up on her elbows, then pressed her palms to the pavement and pushed up into a sitting position. Her hands were sticky.

She looked around and saw blood all around her. It dawned on her that it was her blood. She tucked her chin to her chest and looked down. She couldn't see anything on her hoodie. It was black, though. Then she noticed that it had two holes in it, maybe a foot below her breasts. She grabbed the bottom of the hoodie and pulled it up so she could see herself.

Oh God, oh God, oh God. Her stomach had two holes in it. Both pouring blood, bright red from the top hole, almost black from the bottom one. She tried to scream but her throat felt stopped up, wet, gurgly. How could this have happened? Now she was having trouble seeing, like the edges of her vision were closing in, color fading. For some reason, she thought of the text she'd gotten from her mom. She wondered what they were having for dinner. Then Regina wondered no more.

MASSACRE IN THE CITY OF ROSES

PORTLAND, OR — Thirty-nine people are confirmed dead with dozens more injured, following an attack by right-wing extremists in Portland today.

A group of far-right agitators had gathered around a Portland television studio and were screaming and threatening those inside when a collection of counter-protesters arrived on the scene. When the counter-protesters confronted the extremists, several men dressed in military garb and carrying AR-15 assault rifles appeared and opened fire on the unarmed counter-protesters.

Police responded within minutes but were too late to prevent the carnage. The suspects fled the scene and are still at large. Portland mayor, Harvey Pickford, declared a city-wide emergency and ordered residents to shelter in place. Police are gathering surveillance footage from the surrounding area and are expected to release photos of the suspects shortly.

Meanwhile, Oregon governor, Penn Hempstead, has ordered the National Guard to deploy to Portland to provide assistance and enforce a strict curfew that goes into effect at sundown. First responders and hospitals are overwhelmed and are asking for blood donations, but it is unknown at this time how donors can reach the blood banks given the state of emergency. We will update this site with more information as it becomes available.

OPINION: IT NEEDS TO BE SAID

ANONYMOUS: As the nation grows more chaotic by the hour, it is past time for those of us in the news media to accept a measure of responsibility for the state of affairs in which we find ourselves. No, there is no excuse for the violence. Not now, not ever. But the truth is this: We in the news media have been biased, horribly so, for decades, and in recent years much of our profession has completely abandoned any legitimate semblance of objectivity or journalistic integrity.

This reporter wants to come clean. Not out of fear, although I confess that I am afraid. I am speaking out now because, as I look around and see the self-righteous manner in which the press writ large has responded to this crisis, I know that there is no chance whatsoever for this situation to be resolved unless we dismount our high horses and clean up our own house. The mainstream media, of which I am a part, has long put personal political preferences above truth. We have figuratively hammered conservatives at every opportunity while coddling and protecting our friends on the left.

Even today, the bias—scratch that, it's not bias, but outright lying—continues largely unabated. I just read an article entitled "Massacre in the City of Roses." That article, with blood literally still drenching the street on a block of downtown, is a farce. I know this because I was there. While there has been plenty of real violence directed at the media over the past week, that was not the case in Portland this afternoon. The people gathered around the television studio were peaceful. Angry, yes, but peaceful. I saw men, women, and children, waving American flags and voicing their opinions. I saw not one instance of violence, vandalism, or threatening behavior.

As for the "counter-protesters," they were nothing of the kind. This was Antifa, a deranged collective of anarchist thugs who have been allowed to wreak havoc in the streets of the nation in general and Portland in particular for far too long. If we in the press had told the truth about these dangerous people years ago, perhaps something would have been done. We did not. We painted them as noble warriors resisting fascists, fighting "Nazis," when in reality this **gaggle** of criminals are nothing more than a **gaggle** of misfits intent on shutting down any speech that doesn't perfectly attune to their own twisted idea of "social justice."

Today I saw this group of more than a hundred masked thugs charge violently into the group of protesters at the television station. They were not provoked in any way. Without warning, they punched, kicked, stabbed, and beat innocent people for absolutely no reason. This is the simple truth and this is how news is supposed to be reported.

The status quo cannot continue, and this reporter will no longer be a part of the old way. If we are to heal, it must begin with truth. If I am able to remain in this profession, I will from this point forward do my best to tell that truth. To those whom I have unfairly maligned over the years while safeguarding far worse figures simply because I agreed with their politics, I can only say this: I am sorry.

DAY 8

5:07 Pm Central

CHEYENNE MOUNTAIN

We were in Harbuck's office, sitting at a small conference table. On the wall, a muted TV played endless coverage of the media attacks and how the fourth estate was a vital part of American democracy and blah yada puke. After giving Harbuck a summary of where I was in the investigation, I got to the real business at hand. I pulled up the facility map I had found earlier in the day and pointed to the screen. "This is the big cavern." I scrolled the image to the right. "And this is the really interesting part."

Harbuck stared at the screen.

"Know anything about it?"

He shook his head. "To my knowledge, the only thing beyond that cavern wall is solid rock. Maybe this is something that was planned but never built."

"I don't think so." I opened a recording I'd made of Sadie's screen, showing the animated flow of resources into the huge open area on the diagram. "There's no reason to think this isn't reflective of reality."

"Except for the fact that nothing's there," Harbuck said.

"Nothing's *supposed* to be there. She's routing your resources to someone, somewhere, General, and this is the logical place. She thinks no one knows about this, so why would she create a falsified control system?"

"I'll see what I can find on this nonexistent location. In the meantime, I think it's time to arrest and interrogate her."

Now I shook my head. "Not yet."

His head snapped up and his eyes met mine. Generals aren't accustomed to such challenges, even with people who aren't technically under their command.

"Hear me out."

He looked at me, saying nothing for a few seconds, then nodded.

"She thinks she's in the clear, no one onto her. Give me a few days to see what else I can find."

"I'm not in the habit of allowing spies or thieves to continue plying their trade, Flatt. Whatever she's doing, we can shut her down now, get her to give up the big picture."

I said, "And if she won't?" Harbuck said nothing, so I continued. "If she goes dark, her accomplices will probably bolt. Give me three days."

Harbuck stood, hands flat on the table. "Forty-eight hours, Sam." He glanced up at a clock on the wall. "Starting now."

WHEN I GOT BACK to my workspace, Sadie was in her cubicle. She pulled her earbuds out. "Hey. What's up?"

"About to grab dinner," I said. "Care to join me?"

She gave me a crooked smile and bit her bottom lip. "You asking me on a date?"

This caught me off guard. Flirty Sadie? I decided to roll with it. "Maybe."

"Make up your mind." Head tilted a bit, still biting her bottom lip, eyes twinkling with a bit of mischief.

"Sure. Let's make it a date." I gave her a wink. What could go wrong?

. . .

HOURS LATER, I lay in bed, wondering what the hell had come over me. Except that was a lie of a question. I knew exactly what had come over me. A song playing in the restaurant had reminded me of Abby. That was what had come over me. Sadness. Then anger. At her, for getting my hopes up. At me, for killing them. Now this, which had been a monumental mistake.

Sadie awoke and propped herself up on an elbow, wedged tightly between me and the wall on the right side of her bed that had been intended for one service-member, not two. She smiled.

At this point, why not? I smiled back.

She hopped over me and walked toward the little bathroom, turning back toward me before she passed through the door. "I'm thirsty. You?"

I nodded.

She closed the door. A few minutes later, she was back, glass of water in hand. She took a drink and licked her lips like a vixen. The alcohol had left me dehydrated and I took it and gulped it down. The sooner I could flush the alcohol, the better. She crawled over me and resumed her earlier position, propped up, still smiling. "Feel okay?"

I nodded again.

"Good." She snuggled in beside me, her skin warm against mine. We lay like that a few minutes, neither saying anything. Then my vision blurred and my mind wobbled. *Sadie Sadie, you ba—*

DAY 9

5:15 Am

LOCATION UNKNOWN

I OPENED my eyes and saw a ceiling far above, old paint flaking away from the surface and hanging down. I blinked a few times, shook my head, tried to clear the mental haze. Pushed up and swung my legs over the edge of the old cot on which I lay. Sat there, looking around, trying to make sense of what I saw. I was in a jail cell. The walls matched the ceiling, aged, paint crumbling. The whole space was maybe twelve feet square. A sink and toilet combination was mounted to the rear wall at the head of the cot. The room was bare, lit by a dirty incandescent bulb in a ceiling fixture.

After sitting a couple minutes more to let my head clear, I stood and walked to the bars that formed the entire front wall of the cell. They were iron, painted pale green. I looked through the bars and reconstructed the events that preceded this. Dinner with Sadie. A little too much to drink. Going back to the mountain and to her quarters. Frenzied sex. A rest for me and a nap for her. A glass of water. *The bitch drugged me.* I shook the cell door. Yelled. Shook it some more. Yelled some more.

A thick, gravelly voice to my left said, "Save your energy."

I said, "Who are you?"

"Bob Hecht. You?"

"Uncle Sam."

"Smartass."

I yelled some more. After three or four rounds of this, the door in the outer room opened and a man walked in. Mid-thirties, about six feet, dressed in jeans and a silk shirt out of a bad movie. He closed the door. "Might want to pipe down, Hoss," he said, and flashed a stupid-looking grin. "Folks are trying to sleep." Heavy Southern accent.

"Why, what time is it?"

He checked a blingy wristwatch. "Twenty till five."

"AM?"

"You think folks are in bed at five in the evening?"

"I see your point," I said. "I'm Sam."

He laughed. "Like I don't know that?"

"Who are you?"

"Nunya. Nunya damn business."

"Gee, that's original. You learn that one in junior high last week?"

He reddened. "Watch yourself, Hoss."

"Shove it up your ass. Better yet, come on in and I'll shove it up your ass for you."

He stomped over to the desk, yanked open a drawer, and pulled out a large keyring. *Very good.*

"Gonna fix that mouth for you, Hoss." He headed toward the cell.

The door opened again and a woman about the same age as him walked in, sized up the situation in a flash. "Anthony, what in Hades do you think you're doing?" Also heavy Southern.

"This one has a smart mouth on him, Pammy. Gonna teach him a little respect."

"You'll do no such thing. You put those keys back where they belong and get." *Git.*

He froze and turned toward her. "Don't boss me around, Pammy. You know I don't like it."

"I don't give a dadgum what you like right now. Put the keys back and get out of here or I'll call Daddy." She placed her hand on a two-way radio clipped to her waistband.

The transformation was instant. The bravado melted and he looked like a child as he plodded to the desk, put the keys back in the drawer, and sulked out.

With the galoot gone, she turned her attention to me. "Mr. Sam Flatt, you've caused us a lot of trouble."

"And who might 'us' be?"

"All in due time. For now, just know that you have a debt to pay."

"Sorry?" I said. "You drug me, kidnap me, lock me up, and I owe *you*?"

"Like I said, you caused a lot of trouble, but it's all gonna work out okay in the end. Turns out you're a smart man with useful skills."

I didn't say anything, but my face no doubt betrayed my bewilderment over this bizarre conversation.

She said, "Don't worry about it for now. Get some sleep. You'll need it." She flipped a switch I couldn't see and my cell went dark. "Later, Mr. Flatt."

LOCATION UNKNOWN

I HAD GONE to sleep after my visitors left, hoping to shake the remnants of Sadie's chemical treachery. It worked. I awoke when the door in the outer room opened and my brain was back at full power. I stood and walked to the cell door. This man was new, tall, mid-fifties, neat gray hair. He wore civilian clothes but there was no hiding the military bearing and presence as he approached.

He stopped a foot from the bars of my cell and placed his hands on his hips. "Mr. Flatt, my name is Lucian Harrow." He had strong hazel eyes, focused and piercing. A touch of Southern drawl, but not pronounced like Pamela and the idiot I presumed to be her husband or boyfriend.

"Can't say I'm pleased to meet you," I said.

"Understood, but it is what it is."

"Which is what?"

"I know who you are, at least as much as anyone knows who you guys are. I know your reputation, I know your skills, and I know why you were at Cheyenne Mountain."

Maybe he did. Maybe he didn't. I said nothing, let the silence hang, no intention of falling for his interrogation tricks. A full two minutes passed, our eyes locked.

"Sorry," he said. "I see I'm insulting your intelligence. I'll be more specific. I know you're part of that snake Bartholomew Pitt's outfit, but I don't judge people by their superiors and will assume you're an honorable man until you prove me different."

Again, I said nothing. He did seem to have a handle on Pitt, a tidbit worth remembering.

"I know you've served this country. I know you're a stone cold killer when need be. I know you're one of the top tech guys in the country, and I know General Harbuck brought you in to find a mole. My mole, Sadie Grossman. Is that better?"

"It's a start. Why am I here? Getting too close?"

He cracked a lopsided smile, one I'd seen before.

I said, "You put your own daughter at risk of prison?"

The smile turned into drawn lips and his eyes narrowed, just a bit, just for a moment. "I'll be straight with you if you'll do likewise."

"You go first," I said.

"Yes, Mr. Flatt. You got too close and you had to be removed before you became a real problem, but now that you're here, you should be thanking me."

"For what?"

"The FBI is in Cheyenne Mountain, raising all amounts of hell demanding that Marshall—General Harbuck—produce you. If I'd left you there, you'd be in custody by now."

"In that case," I said, "thanks so much for the favor."

"They have a warrant for your arrest."

"Bull."

Harrow raised a hand, palm toward me. "On my honor. They want to arrest you for conspiracy to commit murder, conspiracy to bomb a public building, and a laundry list of other charges. They want to try you as a terrorist, Mr. Flatt."

That notched my heart rate up. "How would you know this?" I said.

"I have contacts in the mountain."

"Other than Sadie?"

"My daughter is no longer there. I pulled her when we got you."

"You called Harbuck by his first name. I assume he's one of your contacts."

"Observant. Yes, I know Marshall Harbuck well, but he's not my source on this. It doesn't matter who told me. The information is real and reliable."

"So you're aiding and abetting a fugitive by hiding me here, although I'm guessing that's the least of your legal troubles."

Harrow smiled. Not a sarcastic smile. It looked real. "I'm unconcerned. And I'd like to make you an offer that might interest you, given your predicament. Quid pro quo."

My mind raced. Why would the FBI think I was involved in the ongoing mayhem around the country? I thought about the computers they'd pulled out of the office in Houston, its mirror of the FBI investigation. Crap. I needed to talk to Pitt.

"Sam?" Harrow said. I jerked out of my preoccupation. "Mind if I call you Sam?"

"Fine. What do I call you?"

"Lucian is good. Do you want to hear my offer?"

"I'm listening."

"We have an operation in progress, something of vital importance to this nation, and we have some tech issues I believe you could help us solve."

"Such as?"

"Communication issues, mainly."

"Despite what you think you know," I said, "that's not really a specialty of mine."

"Maybe not, but it is something I suspect you're sharp enough to figure out."

"What's this operation?"

"We'll get to that in due time. Help me out and you'll have a front row seat to the show of the century. And you'll be safe from the long arm of the law."

Time for the big question, though there was no reason to think I'd get an honest answer. "And if I won't?"

He blew a long sigh. "Despite circumstances that may suggest otherwise, I'm an honorable man, Mr. Flatt. I take no pleasure in coercion of a fellow soldier and—"

"I'm not a soldier."

He waved a hand, dismissing my claim. "Maybe not in name, but I've been looking at soldiers a very long time and I know what they look like. Now back to your question. If you refuse to help, then you'll stay locked in this cell until my operation is complete. I'm not going to threaten you, torture you, or anything of the sort. You'll be fed, get occasional showers, and when I'm done you'll be free to go."

"Right," I said. "I know who you are, know who your daughter is, and that knowledge could put both of you away for life, but you'll just let me walk away." I was of course going to play along eventually, so I could find a way out of wherever the hell I was, but my resistance needed to be believable.

"You have my word on what I just said."

"And if I did help you, when do I get to walk away?"

"The timing is the same either way, when my op is complete. It's just a matter of whether you'd rather spend that time in this cell, or outside with me, doing something great for your country."

"I take it personally when people break their word."

"As do I, Mr. Flatt, and do know I'll be asking for yours before this door is unlocked. Take some time to think about it, and I'll be back in a few hours. I'll have Pamela bring you something to eat." He turned and made his exit.

DAY 9

4:55 Pm

LOCATION UNKNOWN

I HAD SPENT the hours since Harrow's visit examining every facet of the cell for weaknesses to exploit. There were none. The place was well designed, meant to keep its occupant in place. There was something strange about it, though; despite the yellowed and peeling paint that confirmed age, I could find no evidence that it had ever been used before. No graffiti or memorial marks on the walls. No scratches on the toilet-sink combo. No scratches on the bars. No stains on the thin mattress. It was as if it was decades old and brand new at the same time. Who would build a jail and not use it for all that time? Something very odd was going on, or I was in the most crime-free location of the modern world.

The door opened and Harrow strode in, now in Air Force BDUs, one star on each shoulder. A general. He came to the bars and said, "What's your decision, Mr. Flatt?"

"You really didn't leave me a lot of choice, General."

"I did not. May I assume the answer is yes?"

I shrugged. "What's the gig?"

Harrow waved a hand. "We'll get to that later. For now, I'll send someone to get you out of here. One thing, Sam."

"What's that?"

"I know how resourceful you are, how dangerous you are. I also know you're going along with this as a pretense to attempt an escape. Understand this. You will not leave town until my mission is complete. I've covered every contingency, including the ones you think I haven't. Accept the situation for what it is." He did a military pivot and headed for the exit. He turned the knob, then looked back over his shoulder and said, "I'm dangerous too, son." He left and I was alone again.

One sentence was replaying in my mind by the time the door had closed: "You will not leave *town* until my mission is complete." It wasn't much of a clue, but it beat what I'd had five minutes earlier. I tried to think of any small towns near enough to the mountain to be feasible, but I didn't know the area well enough. Maybe I was in some old ghost town? Abandoned mining village? I supposed I'd find out soon enough.

My mind shifted to other questions. What the hell was going on here? What was his operation? How could Harbuck not know that his mole was the daughter of a fellow general? One thing was certain, though. With the FBI looking to arrest me, I had to talk to Bartholomew Pitt and get that squared away.

A HALF HOUR LATER, the door opened again and in walked Sadie, all sparkly in her Air Force uniform, lopsided girlish grin in place. She retrieved the cell keys from the desk, walked up to the bars, and said, "Hey, handsome."

DAY 9
5:37 Pm

LOCATION UNKNOWN

I LOOKED Sadie in the eye, saying nothing. The smart move was to get closer to her, but I have my limits.

"Don't be pouty," she said. "It doesn't become you."

"So tell me," I said, "how often do you play the whore for your dad?"

She didn't take the bait at all, instead burst out laughing. "Daddy would die. My instructions were to somehow drug you and call the haulers. I took you to bed because I wanted to."

Daddy, not *Dad*. Just like her older sister Pamela. Close relationship with their father. I filed that tidbit away. "How gratifying," I said. "Was it good for you?"

"Damn right."

"Glad one of us enjoyed it. You were a little over the top for my tastes."

She jerked her head toward me. "Excuse me?"

There's the reaction I wanted. Put her off balance. "I generally prefer lovemaking over the slut act you put on last night."

Her lips pursed and the playful bad girl vanished.

"Anyway," I said, "tell me what this is all about and get me out of here."

"Maybe I'll just leave your smart ass where you are."

"No. You won't. Because Daddy won't like that. So get on with it and tell me why I'm here."

"The main reason you're here? You stuck your nose where it didn't belong and apparently thought I was too stupid to detect what you were doing. You think I didn't have my own camera watching my workstation once you showed up?"

"Whatever, Sadie. You caught me. What now?"

She bit her bottom lip, stared at me for a few seconds, and blew out a dramatic sigh. "Since you're here, we need some tech help."

"Such as?"

"We're having some trouble with new video gear talking to some really old systems."

"Not my area," I said.

"I think your background qualifies you to help with this issue." She inserted the key into the cell door, then paused. "Attack me, and my father will kill you. Just so you know."

"I don't hit girls unless they pose a direct threat to my life."

"Ah, such the gentleman." She turned the key, the lock clanked, and she pulled the door open and gestured me out of the cell with a maitre d' flourish.

I left the cell and watched as she re-closed the door, locked it, and returned the keys to the desk drawer.

"After you," she said.

I walked to the exit door, opened it, and stepped out. Then I froze. *Oh. My. Gosh.*

DAY 9

5:40 Pm Central

COG CITY

I EXPECTED to step out onto a street of some small town lit by late afternoon sun. I *was* in a small town, standing on the sidewalk of what
looked like the main drag. I looked around, trying to take it all in.
Across the street was a small row of typical storefronts, each with a
simple sign on its facade, no branding, just utilitarian identification:
DINER. LIBRARY. LAUNDRY. GENERAL SUPPLY. Every storefront
was similar, but with design and color differences that gave the place a
classic Americana flavor. Quaint and cozy. I turned around and looked
at the building I'd exited. Its sign said JUSTICE CENTER. On the right,
ADMINISTRATION OFFICE. To the left, POST OFFICE.

Everything was squeaky clean. Not a piece of litter to be seen. Side-
walks that looked like they'd been poured a week ago. No grit or
grime. I walked and gazed. A closer look at the storefronts nearby
revealed the same thing I'd seen in the jail cell: peeling paint, yellowed
or faded with age but no evidence of use. Aside from me and Sadie,

who stood leaning against a wall while I gawked, not a soul was to be seen. Nor were there any cars.

I was standing in a place that looked like it had been beamed in from another era. And not to some parcel of rural land. We were *underground*, inside Cheyenne Mountain, I was sure. This was the weird space I had found on the map, had to be. Someone had hollowed out an enormous cavern and built a *town* inside it.

I looked up and saw the source of the strange light. The top of the cavern had to be 150 feet above where we stood. Suspended from the rough rock were dozens of floodlights, pointing up at the rock and bouncing an indirect amber glow down onto the town.

Sadie said, "Different lights come on at different times to simulate the time of day. In a little while, the gold lights will turn off and the blue ones will turn on. Then when it's sundown outside, all those up there will turn off and the streetlights will power up." She pointed to what looked like normal old streetlights on wooden poles.

She walked out into the street, gave me that lopsided grin, and said, "Let's declare a truce and I'll give you the grand tour."

I followed her down the street. At the end of the block, she turned right into a narrow alley. A modern golf cart was parked there. She unplugged a charging cord, took the driver's seat, and I sat beside her. She steered the cart onto the main street, its electric motor near silent as we rode.

"What is this place?" I said, as we drove onto a block that looked slightly industrial, storefronts giving way to windowless brick buildings and metal structures that looked vaguely like garages and small warehouses.

"An old continuity-of-government facility, built in the early sixties."

The place went momentarily dark except for the occasional light in or on one of the buildings. I heard the sound of big relays overhead, their *snap* echoing in the massive chamber, then a bluish glow lit everything around us.

"Twilight," Sadie said.

"How could something like this be built and no one know anything about it? Aside from the diagram in your app, there's no record that this exists."

"Which made it perfect for our needs."

"But how is something like this kept secret?"

"Daddy says Eisenhower commissioned it on the hush-hush in '58. It was about half finished when JFK took over, and they kept knowledge of it confined to Kennedy and a couple of his top people. Just about the time construction was complete, he was killed and Johnson took over. Kennedy's people hated LBJ, thought he was involved in the assassination, and they walked away without telling him anything."

"And 'Daddy' knows all this how?"

She shrugged, said, "Don't know." We passed a Quonset hut with a sign that said COMMAND.

I said, "How do you get in and out of here?"

She laughed. "Nice try." She pointed straight ahead. "Check that out."

I looked and saw that we were nearing the wall of the cavern, rough rock tapering down in somewhat of a dome shape. In places, the rock glinted with a metallic reflection of the blue light that bathed the area. As we got closer, I could see that the reflective areas looked like ribbons in the rock. "What is it?"

"Sheer luck," Sadie said. "They happened to build this place in a chunk of mountain loaded with veins of gold."

"Good hell."

"Pretty cool, huh?"

"So this is all about money, just like every other criminal operation on Earth."

"Oh no," she said. "Like I said, the gold is plain dumb luck and it's not feasible to mine it anyway. Not yet." She made a tight turn and headed back toward the main part of town. I saw a sign on the right side of the road, typical city-limits style, that said COG CITY, UNITED STATES, POPULATION VARIES.

"If it's not money, exactly what is the point of your 'operation'?" I said.

"To save the country and change the world, handsome."

"Swell."

DAY 9

6:15 Pm

COG CITY

WITH MY LITTLE tour of the town wrapped up, I found myself in the COG CITY COMMUNICATIONS CENTER. To get there, we had gone inside the COMMAND Quonset hut, then down a switchback stairway that by my count covered the equivalent of three stories, then opened up into a bunker-style room about the same size as the Quonset hut on the surface. Panels of ancient electronic controls filled the walls and work surfaces. One wall held an array of four televisions, tilted so that their clicky knobs and curved glass screens looked down upon what was obviously the main control console.

A guy who looked early twenties stood from the console, glanced briefly at me, then turned to Sadie. Before he could speak, Sadie said, "Wilson, Sam. Sam, Wilson."

Wilson stuck a hand out and I shook it. He said, "You're not old enough to have worked with equipment like this. You tinker with gear like this as a hobby or something?"

"Uh...no," I said. "I've never touched tech like this."

Wilson turned back to Sadie. "Thought you said he could help with this?"

Sadie grabbed the sleeve of my T-shirt and gave it a tug, then walked to a corner of the room. I followed.

She said, "Your freedom is contingent upon helping, so cut the shit, okay?"

I started to question her definition of freedom, but there was no point. "I *don't* know anything about equipment like this."

"Your uncle ran FLATT GOOD TV REPAIR for decades, and as a kid you hung out there all the time."

I rolled my eyes, but filed away the fact that they obviously had my full BAM file, the dangerous one. *Pitt.* "You think hanging out and watching my uncle work on TVs and VCRs gave me expertise in broadcast systems designed decades before I was born? Are you mad?"

She returned the eyeroll. "I think that's where you learned to love technology and I think you're resourceful enough to put it all together and make yourself useful. Be good and maybe I'll take you to bed again."

I smiled and leaned in toward her, used my most seductive whisper. "Sadie?"

"Yeah?" she said quietly, biting her lip, eyes dancing.

I said, "If we were on a desert island, the last two people on Earth?"

She nodded, waiting for the rest.

I gave it to her. "The human race would go extinct, you backstabbing skank."

Her face flushed and her eyes fired. I caught her open hand a foot before it got to my face. "Our truce is over," I said. "Get away from me and I'll do what I can here."

She stomped out of the room and up the stairs, her footfalls echoing around the concrete until they faded away. I went to Wilson. "Seriously, I have no expertise on this gear, but maybe two heads brainstorming is better than one. What are you trying to do, and what's stopping you?"

Wilson touched a modern laptop sitting on the console. "This is my video source." He laid his hand on the console of big buttons and switches. "This is my conduit." He pointed to a flat panel hanging on the wall beneath the old TVs. It showed a test pattern that said EMER-GENCY ALERT SYSTEM. "That's my target."

"Are you generating that pattern locally?"

"No, that's a live feed off the EAS satellite."

"And how is this antique contraption supposed to get a signal to the EAS satellite?" I said.

Wilson said, "This facility was set up for the president to be able to broadcast to the nation at any time." He tapped the console. "This feeds directly to a camouflaged antenna array up on the mountain."

"That was more than fifty years ago," I said. "Had to be analog, and surely EAS has gone digital by now."

He grinned. "Sure, but here's the thing. We're talking about the government here. They built a new digital system with all the bells and whistles, but what they didn't do was—"

"Turn off the old system," I said.

He snapped his fingers. "Roger roger."

"Still, it's hard to believe that this," I said with a gesture sweeping the room, "could possibly still work, much less be able to tap into the new system."

"But it does," Wilson said. "They had to keep an analog component in play for AM and FM radio. Rather than separate it out, they piggy-backed the old onto the new. Like I said, we're talking about the government, so don't expect everything to make sense."

"Have you actually tried this?"

"Affirmative. I generated an old test pattern straight from this console, then activated the system for one second. It worked."

"Unbelievable. So what's the problem? They told me you needed help with satellite comms."

"Nah, solved that already. The issue now is that I need to get a digital audio-video signal from this laptop, into this clunker of a system."

"Should be a simple matter of a digital-to-analog adapter, which I assume you have?"

"Lots of them, but nothing's working."

"Why are you broadcasting at all? Why not just stream it everywhere?"

"We're doing that but the general wants the broadcast, too. FedGov has an internet kill switch and he's afraid they'll use it when we go live."

"Okay, show me what you have. And by the way, what exactly are you trying to broadcast?"

He shrugged. "Wish I knew. The general is a real need-to-know stickler on things like this. My job is to have the capability ready to go. I'll find out what the show is when it happens."

"That's...interesting," I said.

Wilson's face brightened. "Hey, I don't know what we're broadcasting, but I do know where. It's badass. Wanna see?"

Indeed I did.

DAY 9

6:37 Pm Central

COG CITY

I FOLLOWED Wilson up the stairs and onto the street. With the upper lights off and the streetlights on, the place almost felt like a normal town. The streetlights were the mercury-vapor type that preceded today's yellow-glow sodiums, lighting the street in pools of cool white. A few minutes later we were back in the center of town where I had emerged from jail. He entered the nearby storefront-style building that said ADMINISTRA-TION OFFICE. In a back room, we descended a switchback stairway that was reminiscent of the one that led to Wilson's control room beneath the COMMAND hut. This one, however, took us far below the surface, the equivalent of about ten floors. At the bottom we stepped into a dark space.

Wilson said, "Hang on a sec," and vanished into the darkness. Moments later, I heard him throw a big switch and the space lit up with a glow of overhead fluorescents, their ballasts humming and about half the tubes dark or flickering.

The room was about sixty feet square. At the far end, an elevated stage faced us. It was backdropped with a blue curtain and flanked by an American flag with gold fringe, on a floor pole on the left. On the right, an easel held a large world map. Dead center of the stage, a podium with the seal of the president of the United States. Its wood construction looked antique compared to the streamlined versions of today, but it still projected a sense of awe and power with that seal. Wilson walked to the right side of the stage and flipped another switch. A rack of Fresnel lights above the stage illuminated, bathing the stage in warm white.

The area on our end of the room was filled with spectator seating, a half-dozen rows of pews. An aisle up the middle of the room split the seating area into left and right sections. I walked up the aisle, taking it all in.

"So this is it," Wilson said.

I was lost in the ambience of the place. "Sorry, this is what?"

"This is where the show will happen, whatever it is." He pointed to the back of the room, where we had entered.

I looked and saw three modern cameras on tripods arrayed across the width of the room. "And you have no idea what it is?" I said.

He shook his head.

"Question, Wilson. If you have no idea what this is about, why are you here, risking prison? I guarantee you this whole affair is illegal as hell."

"Have you taken a good look at our country lately?" His voice and body language were now energized.

"What do you mean?"

"It's broken, man. The politicians, bureaucrats, and fat cats have run it into the ground and they're never going to fix it because they don't give a damn about us. They care about themselves, getting richer, grabbing more power. Something has to change."

"I don't necessarily disagree with that, but you think whatever you're doing here is really going to change the country? That's mighty ambitious, and I hate to say, naive."

"The general believes it will, and I believe in him."

"How do you know him?"

He looked suddenly leery of me. "Maybe you need to save the rest of the questions. Ask him."

I held my hands up in surrender. "Just making conversation, Wilson."

He nodded. "Wanna see the rest of the place?"

"Sure," I said.

He walked to the stage, stepped up onto it, then pulled the right side of the curtain back and stepped through an opening. I followed and waited in the opening while he found and threw another switch. I looked around, trying to take it all in. Everything I'd seen until now had been utilitarian in style, almost austere. Not this.

"Welcome to the presidential quarters," Wilson said.

We were standing in a large open living area, dotted with leather sofas and chairs. The walls were finished, painted an ivory color. I stepped farther into the space and my feet sank into deep blue carpet. I walked and looked, admiring paintings of scenes from American history that adorned the walls. Only the absence of windows differentiated the area from a lavish suite one would expect to find in a mansion. In the center of the room, between a pair of red sofas facing each other, an ornate coffee table held a variety of magazines. I picked one up. LIFE, January 25, 1963. A headline at the top of the cover said HOW JOE KENNEDY AMASSED HIS FORTUNE. Interesting reading choice for this place and that time. I put it back and continued my exploration.

I went through a door on the right side of the room and found myself in the most lavish bathroom I'd ever seen. Marble galore, gold-colored plumbing fixtures. A shower the size of a large walk-in closet and a tub that could hold three or four people. I continued through the bathroom and passed through a door at the far end. A bedroom fit for a king lay before me. The king-sized bed was perfectly made, covered in a white comforter dulled with age, the presidential seal embroidered in its center. The furniture, while dusty, was exquisite, huge and made of burled walnut. A sitting area off to the side had a love seat facing an antique console TV.

Going from room to room, I guessed the apartment to be about three thousand square feet. Three bedrooms total, each with its own bathroom. A kitchen worthy of any restaurant, the stove and other fixtures brand new yet more than fifty years old. I laughed out loud when I saw the gym. In addition to barbells, dumbbells, weight bench, and exercise bike, it had a stand-up massager with a wide belt that you leaned back against while it shook your soul apart and accomplished nothing.

After seeing everything, I found Wilson stretched out on one of the sofas in the living room. "What you think?" he said.

"Impressive. And kind of spooky, like we've stepped back in time."

"Funny you should say that," he said. "Come on, I have one more thing to show you. You're gonna like it."

DAY 9
6:52 Pm Central

COG CITY

I FOLLOWED Wilson into a walk-in closet in the master bedroom. He pulled a hook on the wall and a section of shelving clicked open a few inches. He pulled the hidden door open and lights flickered on in the space beyond. We stepped through into a concrete corridor that led left. After about fifty feet, the corridor opened up into a huge room. At the threshold, an American flag was painted on the concrete floor, with two lines of text painted above the flag: UNITED STATES CULTURAL ARCHIVE. COG CITY, COLORADO, USA. The center of the room was filled with row after row of floor-to-ceiling shelves, while the outer walls were lined with large glass showcases.

Wilson went left, pointed at the first showcase. "Start here. Each row is a type of item and the items on each row are arranged in chronological order. It's cool stuff."

That was an understatement. Inside the first glass showcase were three individually glassed versions of the Declaration of Independence. Each one had a small placard to the side that explained the document. The top document was a parchment filled with handwriting, replete with numerous markups, strikeouts, corrections. The placard said EARLIEST KNOWN COMPOSITION DRAFT OF THE DECLARATION, HANDWRITTEN BY THOMAS JEFFERSON. The second placard said DUNLAP BROADSIDE, ONE OF TWENTY-SEVEN KNOWN COPIES. The final one was the stunner: ONE OF TWO ORIGINAL DOCUMENTS SIGNED BY FOUNDERS.

I said, "I can't believe these are sitting down here in unregulated conditions. These are invaluable."

Wilson shrugged.

I moved on, blown away again and again by the artifacts I encountered. The entire first aisle was an array of priceless historical documents. The Constitution. The Emancipation Proclamation. Handwritten copies of landmark Supreme Court decisions. Just this aisle of treasures was worth tens of millions, more likely hundreds of millions. Then I got to the end of the document collection and started my browse of the next aisle, weaponry. Then flags. Household items. Industrial tech. You name it, it was here. This was the greatest museum on the planet, beneath a mountain, unseen and unknown.

"Hey," I heard Wilson say from somewhere near the front of the room. "Gotta go take care of something. Know your way out?"

"I'm good," I said. His footsteps receded and I was alone in this surreal place. Alone and free for the first time since I got to town, which meant it was time to end the recreational exploration and start scouting.

DAY 9

7:09 Pm Central

COG CITY

SOMEONE HAD TAKEN my phone but my watch was still on my wrist. It was a smart model and I'd turned it off to preserve battery when I first woke up in the jail cell. I knew I wouldn't get a signal of any kind; I couldn't even get one inside the facility proper. That didn't mean the watch was useless. It booted up and I switched to the compass app. It worked.

I thought back to my time examining the diagram on Sadie's computer. Now certain that COG CITY was the huge open space on that diagram, I at least had crude bearings to work with. The space, COG CITY, was up on the northwest corner of the facility. That meant if I trekked generally southeast inside COG CITY, when I found the end of town, I should be close to that cavern. I worked my way out of the archives maze, back into the presidential living quarters, then up and eventually into the administration building. Before walking outside the office where I would be visible to anyone else on the street, I checked the compass.

Main Street—I'd seen a street sign during my little Sadie-guided tour—ran pretty much north and south. North to my right. South to my left. Back outside, I headed south, casually strolling, stopping on occasion to look around, examining the layout of the place as if I were a tourist. The "downtown" section of Main Street was only two blocks long. When I got to the end of it, the retail-style storefronts ended and a variety of plain metal buildings began. I checked the street sign and took a left on Camelot Avenue. That had to be a nod to JFK. The next intersection was East Street. How creative. Government brainpower at work there. Camelot continued another block and dead-ended at Washington Street. It only went to my right, south. Its left terminus was the side of a metal building that reached back to the rock wall that should mark the easternmost boundary of COG CITY.

Mentally recording the layout, I headed right on Washington. The silence of the place was eerie. No traffic. No planes overhead. No insects of the night. Just my footsteps on the sidewalk. The area now looked industrial. Metal buildings one after the other, some square, some rectangular, some Quonset huts. I walked and watched my shadow play in and out of the pools of light cast by the streetlights. Washington continued for four blocks, crossing only one street—Excalibur Avenue—and then ended at a rock wall. I ducked left between a pair of buildings and checked to see if there was more space behind them. Nope. I went back to Washington and went to the wall. I laid my hand on the cool granite with the occasional metallic sparkles. If my calculations were correct, the big empty cavern called AMPHITHE-ATER 1980 was somewhere beyond.

I looked up and scanned the rock as far as I could see left and right, looking for the gang of pipe and conduit that fed COG CITY from the would-be amphitheater. Seeing nothing, I reversed course on Washington, then took a left on Excalibur and another left on East Street. I followed it to its end and again scanned the wall in search of the pipes and conduits. Nothing. I worked my way back to Main Street and explored the area to its west until I had covered every bit of the southeast rock boundary of the town that was visible. Still no joy on the pipes, which meant their entry point was inside a building. Swell.

Deciding there was no time like the present, especially since I had no idea how much free exploration I'd be able to pull off, I started making my way back to the first boundary terminus I'd found, where Washington Street met the rock. I turned the corner off a side street onto Main Street.

"Hey, Hoss," a voice said from the shadows between two Quonset huts on my left.

I stopped, trying to remember the asshole's name. When it clicked, I said, "Anthony, it's not nice to sneak up on people in the dark. You could get hurt that way."

He stepped onto the sidewalk, grinning like a fool, reflection from the streetlight bouncing off a ridiculous gold chain hanging outside his shirt. A shirt with the top four buttons undone, exposing enough chest hair to weave a rug. "You didn't seem so bothered by it. You're a cool one, ain't you?" He still had that stupid grin on his face.

I said, "What do you want?"

"Seem to recall you said something about whipping my ass."

I exhaled, already bored with this idiot. "Actually, Anthony, I told you I'd shove your bullshit up your ass. But since you're married to important 'townspeople,' I'd rather not do that. So let's say good night."

The smile faded. "You gonna say good night alright, big shot." He stepped closer, now about six feet away.

Why do I always encounter assholes like this?

He closed another couple feet, on the verge of entering my personal space. I don't like assholes in my personal space. "Last warning, Anthony. Walk away."

Then he charged, drawing back his right fist and growling like a dog in the process. The night went into slow motion. I stepped into his advance, caught his bicep with my right hand and his wrist with my left. I yanked his wrist back and pulled down on his bicep with my right. He went down hard, his back hitting the concrete sidewalk with an audible slap a half-second before all the air blew out of his lungs and left him gasping for breath.

I released his arm and hit him three times square on the nose. Not hard. Quick love taps, *pop-pop-pop*. I didn't want to complicate matters by hurting him, but I did want to make an impression. The nose gushed blood. I stood. "You have a good night, Anthony."

He glared up at me with fury in his eyes, but said nothing. I walked away.

DAY 9

10:11 Pm Central

COG CITY

AFTER A LATE DINNER in the diner and picking up a couple changes of clothes (Army BDUs) from the commissary, Harrow set me up in a room that made me feel like I'd taken a time machine back to a 1960s motel. The only thing missing was a slot for quarters on the night-stand. He warned me again that there was no escape and bid me good night. I'd asked to use a phone to call Pitt about the FBI mess but he'd flatly denied that request.

I took a shower and put on fresh clothes, feeling like an imposter dressed in the soldier outfit. I was deciding whether or not to go exploring again when a knock sounded on the door. I opened it, stared for a moment, and said, "Hello, Sol."

"Sam."

He looked the same as he had twentyish years earlier except for a few more and deeper creases around his eyes and across his forehead. I stepped back and gestured him into the room. We sat down in chairs at a little round table.

"How's life as a low-life mercenary?" I said.

His eyes flared and his mouth tightened. "Don't insult me, partner."

"Well gee whiz, Sol, pardon the absolute hell out of me. I didn't realize kidnapping senators and judges had become a respectable profession. Quite a gig you've got going."

"It's for a good cause."

"Right. Save the country? Save the world? Stuff like that?"

"Exactly like that, and I'm hoping you'll help. You're the best operator I ever worked with."

"C'mon, man. Cut the crap and tell me what this is all about. I got drugged over in the other part of the mountain by Harrow's daughter and woke up in a jail cell in an underground city."

"You were too close. Timing too critical to risk leaving you over there."

"Timing for what?"

He put his elbows on the table and leaned forward, his eyes intense, passionate even. "Do you know how far off the rails our country, our government, has gone?"

"What's new about politicians being politicians? Bureaucrats being bureaucrats?"

"It's way worse than that now," he said.

I started wondering if I'd missed something big that had happened while withdrawn into my own little world on my farm. I guess it was possible. Up until a week ago, I hadn't watched a newscast or paid any significant attention to the news in a number of years. Aside from the travel I did for forensic cases, I'd become something of a hermit, content to trade the noise of the world for the smell of grass and hay and horse.

"How so?" I said. "What specifically is going on that justifies what you've been doing, Sol?"

"You serious? You that out of touch?"

"Apparently. Educate me."

"I understand you were in a cell beside Robert Hecht."

"Yeah, that's the name he gave me, except I think he called himself Bob instead of Robert. I never even looked at the guy. Never heard the name before, either. Who is he?"

"He's a DC power player. Lobbyist. Fixer. Crook. Makes tens of millions of dollars a year helping politicians screw the taxpayers."

"Again, nothing new about that game. I don't like it, but I'm also smart enough to know there's nothing I can do about it except vote, which I do."

"He's also a pervert. He rapes children, Sam. Five, six years old."

I said, "How do you know this?"

"You'll see proof soon enough. Irrefutable proof. But it's worse than that. He doesn't just do it himself. This animal buys, sells, trades kids the same way he does political favors. He supplies them to other perverts, including a *lot* of politicians in Washington. Hell, not just Washington. He's international."

I looked Sol in the eye, wondering if this was true, or some ploy to suck me into whatever this was. My own daughter had been abducted and taken into this hideous world a year earlier. I do not condone or tolerate or allow such to go on if it's within my power to stop it. Did Sol know about what had gone down in Vegas? Did Harrow? Were they playing me? "If you really have proof, you'll have my attention on that."

"You'll see," he said. "Tomorrow. You'll see just how rotten, how evil, our government has become. Other governments, too. A whole lot of evil is about to be exposed, Sam."

"Okay. Tomorrow. Whatever it is, I'll keep an open mind. Good enough?"

He nodded, stood, shook my hand, and plodded out of the room, his gait as stiff and awkward as ever.

I decided to call it a night. Stripped down to my underwear. Got in bed. Lay there wondering how I got drawn into such things. Felt almost stupid for admitting to myself that, despite being held prisoner in a cave town while being hunted as a terrorist in the outside world, I was growing most curious about what I would see the next day. Whatever scenarios I imagined while lying there and tossing and turning, they would be dwarfed by the reality that was about to unfold.

DAY 10

7:45 Am Central

COG CITY

I ORDERED BACON, eggs, toast, and grits in the diner, all cooked to perfection by a giant of a short-order cook. He was a black man in his thirties who had to be six-eight or six-nine and looked as solid as a lead pipe.

"I'm Sam," I said, extending my hand when he put the plates down before me.

My hand was like a child's in his. I couldn't begin to reach around it for a proper shake. "Willie," he said.

"Appreciate the food, Willie."

He nodded. "Happy to oblige. General told me take good care of you."

"You known him long?" I said.

"Twenty-some years, since I was fifteen."

"Long time."

"Yup. Man's like a daddy to me. Got me off the streets. Set me straight."

"How so?"

"I'd done went and got mixed up with some gangbangers. The general, course he weren't no general back then, just a major, he was walking down the street in Birmingham one night. We seen him struttin' in his uniform acting like he owned the place and we thought we'd rob him. 'Fore we knew what was happening, he'd done pulled a gun and backed us all up against a wall with it. He said 'git' and everybody took off but he held on to me, told me to stay. Said I wasn't like the rest of them. Said I had kind eyes. You believe that?"

"I'd agree with that, Willie. You do have a kind look about you."

"Took me to a store, bought me some respectable clothes, told me he better not see me again with my pants hanging off my butt. And he looked out for me ever since then."

I mulled that over, trying to square this affectionate account of Harrow with the fact that he had Sol Ringer kidnapping people and his daughter working as a mole, not to mention the fact that he was holding yours truly prisoner. I said, "Glad he did that for you. How long you been here, inside this mountain?"

Willie grinned. "Sorry. Done been told not to talk about all that."

"Gotcha," I said, and dug into my food.

With a full belly, I told Willie goodbye and made my way to the comms room in the belly of the COMMAND Quonset hut down the street.

Wilson looked up from his computer. "Hey."

"Let's see if we can square your problem," I said.

It took an hour but I eventually got the new digital gear to talk to the antique analog console in the room. We ran a one-second test of the emergency broadcast system. It worked. Whatever Harrow planned to broadcast, the gear was ready for it.

COG CITY

I LEFT Wilson and made my way back up to street level and out into the town. Time to explore some more, find a way out of this cave. Behind me, someone said, "Sam." I turned and saw Harrow approaching, carrying a laptop bag and a backpack. My backpack that I'd brought into Cheyenne Mountain with me.

Harrow said, "I have a request, one I hope you'll oblige."

"I'm listening."

"Did you meet your neighbor during your time in our pokey?"

"He told me his name, which I didn't recognize. That's about it. Why?"

Harrow raised the laptop bag. "This is his. Sol forgot to mention it until this morning. I'd like you to take a look, see what's on it."

While I had no desire to help Harrow and his "operation," whatever it was, I had nothing to gain by saying no to him. I also remembered the things Sol had accused the man of the night before. I was always willing to take down someone hurting children. I pointed at my backpack. "All my gear still in there?"

Harrow handed it to me. "Everything that was in it, plus whatever you'd unpacked in your cubicle."

I reached for the laptop bag and Harrow gave it over. "You looking for anything in particular on this?"

"Communications with politicians. Any bank account information. Dirt in general. Anything that might give us a better picture of this animal's activity. But especially anything related to child pornography, abuse, things like that."

I nodded. "When do you need the results?"

"The sooner the better. Couple hours?"

"Whoa," I said. "Forensic analysis takes time. It's not unusual for me to spend two or three days examining a computer."

"We don't have that kind of time," Harrow said. "Don't worry about any of your normal protocols and such. Admissibility doesn't matter. Finding out what's on it is the only thing that does."

Just like the old days overseas. Rapid exploitation of electronic assets. I'd done exactly this kind of work for years on laptops and cell phones yanked from the dead hands of jihadi assholes. "I'll check it out," I said.

DAY 10

10:03 Am Central

COG CITY

IN MY ROOM, I set up my computer and other gear and slipped back into my old electronic-exploitation mode with surprising ease. Hecht's laptop had been suspended, not shut down after its last use. It came to life when I raised the lid. Good battery charge. Best of all, it opened up to where he had been last working, no prompt for a password. After taking a quick glance through the myriad apps he'd had open, I acquired the contents of the laptop's RAM, then pulled its battery and cracked the case open. Removed the hard drive, hooked it up to my laptop via a write-blocker, and went to work.

I used passwords I extracted from RAM to get access to everything he'd had open when he'd last closed the lid. The browser had twenty-three tabs open, including two that were displaying bank accounts. His email store had nearly a half-million emails. He had two different encrypted volumes in use, one named PLAY and the other named WORK. The laptop was a treasure trove of evidence and it didn't take long to realize Sol's animosity toward Hecht was well founded, as was Harrow's labeling him as an animal.

The PLAY volume was filled with photos and videos that made my blood boil. Children. With adults, a number of whom were recognizable politicians and other public figures. Lots with Hecht himself. I was tempted, sorely, to go right then and pull him through the bars of his cell a piece at a time. I resisted.

The WORK volume contained copies of a lot of those same photos and videos in a folder named INSURANCE. A better name would have been BLACKMAIL. Not that a one of these wastes of human flesh were worthy of a milligram of pity or mercy, blackmail victims or not. Another folder named DOCS contained dozens and dozens of handwritten contracts between Hecht and various power players. Not the type of contracts that get filed anywhere. Agreements that laid out bald-faced corruption, fraud, you name it.

I plugged in a flash drive and started building categorized collections of material I exported from the scum's laptop. A search of his email for exchanges with *.gov* addresses yielded enough doubledealing and bribery right there in plain text to put Hecht and a significant percentage of DC's big shots in prison for life, without even touching the material he'd hidden in the encrypted volumes. The brazenness was astounding.

By 4:30 PM, my head was pounding and my stomach was queasy. I alternated between fury and sad disgust as I worked my way through the material, assembling and refining the exports and writing a series of mini-reports to accompany the various categories of data, summaries of what the collections contained. I shut all my gear down, pocketed the flash drive I'd prepared, and went in search of Harrow.

I found him in his office and handed him the flash drive. "There's enough on here to lock him up for a few hundred years. Not just him. It's like a Who's Who in the federal government."

Harrow opened his own laptop and plugged the flash drive in. After a few clicks, his screen appeared on a flat panel on the wall to the left of his desk.

I said, "If you'll let me drive, I can give you a rundown of this in about fifteen minutes."

He pushed back from his desk, stood, and gestured for me to take his seat.

COG CITY

PAM STRAIGHTENED SENATOR Howard Hurd's tie. "There, that's better. Now put your suit coat on."

Hurd put the coat on. "Listen, young lady, I'll do you the favor of warning you one last time to end this nonsense. If you do, I'll help you. I have powerful friends."

She smiled and worked the umbilical cable up his back between shirt and coat, then fished it neatly out at the top and let it hang down. "Senator, after tonight, you won't have a powerful friend in the country who'll claim you. Now clap your trap and listen carefully to what I'm about to tell you."

Hurd shook his head. "You're making a big mistake."

"Here's how this is gonna work. My daddy is gonna ask you questions. You're gonna answer them—"

"I'm not answering a damned thing."

"Don't interrupt. This is important. When he asks you a question, you'll get fifteen seconds to think about your answer. If you don't answer within that time, those electrodes we strapped all over your saggy self are gonna give you a jolt."

Hurd's mouth dropped open.

"Right," she said. "So don't think you're gonna get out there and stonewall or—what do you call it—filibuster. Won't work."

"I have a heart condition! You can't do this to me."

"You'll do it to yourself. Like I said, fifteen seconds, then a jolt. Fifteen more, and the juice gets doubled. Understand the program?"

The color was draining from Hurd's face. "You're barbarians."

"Save your name-calling. Nobody here cares. Now here's the rest of the plan. You'll be hooked up to a lie detector. If you lie, you get a jolt. If you lie a second time on the same question, the jolt doubles. Lie again, it doubles again. Got it?"

Hurd grew paler by the moment, causing his liver spots to stand out like blight. "Why are you doing this? What do you hope to accomplish?"

"Oh," Pam said, "This will all be on TV, so unless you wanna be flopping and jerking like a fish out of water in front of the whole country, just do right. Okay?"

DAY 10
6:48 Pm Central

COG CITY

WITH MY WORK done and turned in, I'd spent the last hour wandering the town, looking in futility for a way out. All I found around the perimeter of Cog City were rock walls. The only possibility was a tunnel that somehow connected back to the main area of Cheyenne Mountain. The *AHA!* moment hit me and I knew exactly where that tunnel originated. I turned to head that way and heard a voice behind me.

"Hey, handsome!" Sadie said. "Come on, it's showtime."

As bad as I wanted to escape, my curiosity about "the show of the century," as Harrow had described it, was hard to resist. I said nothing but turned and followed Sadie. We went to the ADMINISTRATION building, descended into the bowels of the facility via the stairs, and wound up in the "courtroom" Wilson had shown me earlier.

The room had been transformed. Gone were the dated-looking furnishings at the front of the room, replaced by a modern production set that looked like the love child of a news studio and a game show stage. A single chair sat in the middle of the stage. More than a chair. It reminded me of the captain's seat on a starship. To the left a dais sat at an angle that half-faced the audience section and half-faced the captain seat. A huge video screen backdropped the entire set, glowing a soothing blue. On the left edge of the stage, an American flag faced the audience from an easel. On the right, a Gadsden flag with its famous DON'T TREAD ON ME rattlesnake.

Three camera rigs were set up. Wilson on one at the back of the room. I caught his eye and he gave a little wave. The other cameras were positioned on each side of the room, in front of the audience and near the stage. I didn't recognize the operators of the two side cameras, just like I didn't recognize most of the people in the spectator area. The only people in the room I did recognize other than Sadie and Wilson were Willie the cook, Anthony the galoot, and his wife, Pam.

Sadie grabbed my sleeve and pulled me to the front row on the right side. I resisted the urge to break my honor by slapping her into next week. It was hard. We sat down. She said, "Get ready to witness history in the making, handsome."

DAY 10
7:00 Pm Central

COG CITY

As LIGHTS ILLUMINATING the stage ramped up in brightness, every other light in the room dimmed. Harrow walked onto the stage in his dress uniform and took a seat at the dais. I saw the camera operator on the right side of the room looking at Harrow and counting down with upstretched fingers. 3–2–1. A red light glowed on top of the camera. A tight image of Harrow appeared on the video wall that backdropped the stage. I glanced over at Sadie. She was wide-eyed, beaming.

I noticed several angled teleprompters in front of the stage. Harrow spoke. "Ladies and gentlemen, my fellow Americans. My name is Lucian Harrow. I am a general in the United States Army. What you are about to witness is something that is long overdue in our nation: Truth. Truth about the way this nation is being run by those elected to serve. Truth about those who work behind the scenes in the halls of power. Truth about how this information is presented to you, the people, by the news media whose duty it is to keep you informed.

"I realize the idea of truth and politicians is a difficult one to imagine, but this evening we will deliver exactly that to you."

Harrow stood, stepped down from the dais, walked to the captain seat, and laid a hand on the backrest of the chair. "This seat is special. We call it the Seat of Honesty, and it is where you will soon see a series of important witnesses sit as they are questioned. The chair is connected to systems developed by some of the brightest minds in our military and in our civilian sectors. These systems comprise the most advanced, the most accurate, and the most reliable detection of truth-telling, and lying, the world has ever known. They use a combination of technologies to monitor more than two dozen physiological measurements of the witness. They monitor the speaker's voice for minute tells of deception. They monitor involuntary reactions and movements in the speaker's eyes. This is not the polygraph of old. This is a scientific marvel that will, at long last, provide you, the people, with truth."

I imagine my mouth was hanging open at this point, although I can't say for sure. What I can say is that, at this early point in the program, knowing who the "witnesses" were, I instantly believed Harrow's earlier description of this as the Show of the Century. The audience, which probably amounted to a couple dozen people, was utterly silent, every eye on Harrow as he continued to speak.

"All of these sophisticated systems are interconnected. They feed a software program whose algorithms combine all of these measurements into a single metric."

Harrow stepped back toward the dais and the video wall changed. It now had a hollow rectangular graph bar that was centered just above the captain seat. On the left end of the bar was the word LIE. On the right end, TRUTH.

Harrow pointed at the screen. "You at home will see in real time whether the witness is telling the truth or lying, along with the degree of truth or lie being spoken by the witness at any moment. It's simple to follow. A lie will show up to the left."

The left side of the graph bar filled in red, starting at the center and progressing all the way to the left end.

General Harrow said, "Truth will be indicated on the right."

The red disappeared and green crawled from the center to the right edge of the bar.

I have to be honest. This was cool. I was excited, ready for the "trial" to begin.

Harrow went on, walking slowly back and forth on the stage now, using his hands as he spoke. "The indicator of truth or lie is only one part of this system." He stopped at the captain seat and laid a hand on its backrest again. "Each witness has been wired with an extensive array of measurement devices attached to their bodies to feed their bodies' data to the detection systems. We've applied these devices backstage, beneath each witness's clothing, so that a single connection to the chair is all that's needed for each witness.

"In addition to the measurement sensors, each witness has been fitted with a series of electrodes. While the other devices are all passive sensors, the electrodes work in the opposite direction. We call these electrodes 'motivators' and their function is simple: If a witness lies, they get shocked. The degree of shock is determined by the severity of the lie, as determined by the detection systems."

My excitement was now morphing into something else. This whole thing was surreal but it had just taken a turn from entertaining to dangerous. I knew full well that the witnesses were going to be the people Sol had been abducting on his little spree. Both senators were old and the judge was up in years, too. What kind of shock did Harrow plan to administer to these guys? He answered my question in short order.

"I realize," Harrow said, "that this may seem excessive, even cruel, to some of you. I take no pleasure in inflicting pain on people. But you, we, deserve truth. We've gone without it for too long. Each witness will have an opportunity to tell the truth, in which case these systems will inflict no harm whatsoever upon them. The comfort or pain levels they experience will be entirely up to them."

Harrow stopped and looked directly into the camera Wilson was manning at the rear of the room. "Because our time is limited, however, if a witness does lie, the punishment administered will be progressive. The shocks will at first be mild. Each subsequent lie will double the intensity of the shock. The highest levels of shock, those that will be triggered only by repeatedly telling blatant lies, may be fatal. Each witness has been warned of this fact. They have also been clearly notified that refusal to answer a question will result in punishment."

I couldn't believe my ears. The captain seat had the potential to become Mr. Sparky. It was literally a Hot Seat. This provoked no squeamishness on my part. I had done infinitely worse to countless jihadis and some other bad actors. I'd been subjected to the most brutal torture imaginable myself. What I couldn't believe was that this was taking place not in some God-forsaken cave in the middle of nowhere in a country that qualifies as a boil on the ass of humanity. This was here, in the US of A. Home. Had these politicians and the others done things to deserve this? Hecht certainly had, but the others?

Harrow said, "This is being streamed on every major internet platform in the nation, as well as on the national emergency broadcast system. The latter is firmly in our control, so in the event the authorities make the unwise decision to thwart our output by implementing their little-known kill switch for the internet, know that you can continue watching on any television in the nation that is within reach of a local television station.

"The time has come," Harrow said, looking offstage. "Bring in the first witness."

DAY 10

8:05 Pm Eastern

FBI HEADQUARTERS, DC

FBI DIRECTOR HENRIK BLASS stood behind his desk, glaring down at the visitor seated in a chair in front of the desk. Blass's face was as red as a black man's face could get. He pounded the desk with every word, spittle flying from his lips.

"How is this possible, Agent Alvarez?"

Elizabeth Alvarez, the head of the bureau's task force charged with solving the case of the abductees, shook her head. "I don't have answers for you, sir. All three divisions of the ITB are working it, but so far they don't have an explanation, either."

Blass collapsed into his chair and ran his hand across the close-cut hair on his head. "Perhaps you can answer this one: Why is it that I'm only hearing about this now? It's been, what? Twenty-four hours since you found out that some private-sector guy in Houston had a mirror to our entire investigation?"

"More like three or four days," Alvarez said. "And I passed it up to the assistant director IMD. I didn't know what else to do."

"Okay okay, you're right on that. Not on you. How about you give me the details of this disaster? Succinctly."

Alvarez nodded. "A New York agent named Courtney Meyer passed along a tip from a CI identifying Bruce Berringer as the Media Killer. After he killed himself while taking out a whole floor of people in Portland, I demanded that Agent Meyer provide me the name of her CI."

"Go on."

"She identified him as a digital forensic expert named Sam Flatt, said she'd interacted with him on that trafficking case in Vegas last year."

"Interacted how?"

"She didn't elaborate on that. We sent agents from the Houston field office to Flatt's home but no one was home. We then tracked his car using toll passes and traffic cameras, and found that he'd been going to the parking garage at a Houston high-rise office building for several days. Through a process of elimination we found the office he was operating out of. We got a warrant and raided the office.

"When the agents arrived, the only person there was a Sheila Vasquez, supposedly some kind of assistant or secretary to Flatt. Then the agents noticed that her computer had a bureau file on its screen. They called in our digital forensic people from the Houston RCFL. They were able to capture the passwords from her computer's memory. Then they pulled the plug and seized it, along with everything else in the office."

"Where's this secretary?"

Alvarez hesitated.

"What?" Blass said.

"She supposedly went to the restroom, then slipped down a stairway. Houston agents are looking for her."

Blass rolled his eyes. Shook his head. "And Flatt?"

She nodded. "We don't have him but we're making progress on that. We tracked his car again to a small airport north of Houston and found that he boarded a private plane to Colorado Springs five days ago."

"Any idea what he was doing there?"

She nodded again. We eventually tracked him to Cheyenne Mountain."

"NORAD? Are you kidding me, Agent?"

"No, sir. You know how the military can be, but we finally found out that he was there working some kind of angle on these abductions, and that wasn't all. The general in charge of Cheyenne Mountain was helping him. Guy named Marshall Harbuck."

"How do you know this?"

"Again, surveillance cameras. We tracked Flatt from the airport in Colorado Springs to a diner. He was there at the same time as General Harbuck. We matched Harbuck by facial recognition."

"And what did the general have to say about all this?"

"He said Flatt was in the mountain on a classified matter. Then he clammed up, wouldn't tell the agents anything."

"And Flatt?"

"Here's the thing. While Harbuck wouldn't tell us what Flatt was doing there, he said Flatt went missing yesterday and that he has no idea where he is."

"This is—"

A light knock sounded on the door and it opened. A thirtysomething man said, "Sorry, sir, but something's unfolding that you need to see."

"Can it wait?" Blass said.

"No, sir. You'll want to see this right now. The man started tapping a tablet in his hand, then walked to a flat panel on the wall and switched it on. After a few more taps, the signal from the tablet was on the flat panel.

Blass looked at it. His eyes bugged and his mouth dropped open. "Holy shit."

DAY 10
7:05 Pm Central

COG CITY

I WATCHED as Harrow's daughter Pamela walked Senator Howard Hurd onto the stage from the right. She guided him to the Hot Seat, aka the Seat of Honesty, and eased him into it. She walked behind the chair, fiddled with what I assume was the umbilical that connected Hurd to the apparatus, then left the stage the way she had entered.

Hurd looked shell-shocked. Pale. A sheen of sweat visible.

From the dais, General Harrow said, "Good evening, Senator."

Hurd looked toward him but didn't say anything. The video wall backdrop was close on Hurd's face, which looked splotchy and ancient.

Harrow continued. "I know the rules have been explained to you backstage, and I've explained them to our audience, so let us begin. Senator, state your name for the record, please."

"Howard Hurd."

The "truth meter" at the top of the video wall pinged all the way to the right in a strong green.

"Your party affiliation?" Harrow said.

"Republican."

"How long have you served in the United States Senate?"

After a few seconds, Hurd said, "Forty-seven years."

"What's the largest employer in the state of Alabama, sir?"

"Redstone Arsenal in Huntsville."

"And what is Redstone Arsenal?" Harrow said.

"It's an Army base. There's an important missile facility, and Marshall Space Flight Center."

Harrow nodded. "Would you say Redstone is important to the state of Alabama?"

Hurd took a breath, his eyes darting back and forth. "Why, uh, yes yes, of course."

The meter had pinged strong truth-greens for every one of Hurd's answers.

Harrow said, "You've been working behind the scenes to bring a new Air Force base to Alabama, is that correct?"

The high-res video screen now clearly revealed a twitchiness taking hold in Hurd's face. The seconds ticked by, the meter at neutral center, waiting for Hurd to speak. He looked down, then back at Harrow. "I have."

Green.

"How many jobs would that new base bring to your state, Senator?"

"Around eight thousand."

Hurd's face now visibly drooped. *Surrendered* might have been a better descriptor.

General Harrow said, "How many employees are at Redstone now?"

Hurd said, "Sixty thousand, give or take."

Green.

Harrow scrunched his brow, tilted his head, his lips silently moving for a few seconds. Then he raised his left hand, palm up, roughly even with his chest, and said, "Eight thousand jobs for the new base." He raised his right hand as high as he could, its palm up. "Sixty thousand at the current base. He put his hands down and turned back toward Hurd. "Senator, can you explain why you would trade Redstone and its sixty thousand jobs, for a new base with only eight thousand jobs?"

Now Hurd looked defiant, a classic politician putting on a face of righteous indignation. "I did no such th—"

The meter maxed out to the left, blood red, the word LIE appearing at the left. In the chair, Hurd grunted as his body gave one violent jerk.

Harrow's voice was low now, but his words were clear and well articulated: "Senator, the rules of testimony were made clear to you, and they were made clear to the people watching from around the country, probably even around the world. Correct?"

Hurd looked at him, drew a ragged breath, and nodded.

"Good. Now everyone understands what those rules look like in action. At this point, I'll give you a chance to catch your breath before I ask any more questions." Harrow looked offstage-left and gave a little nod.

Clear audio began playing through the sound system in the courtroom, an ambient sound that brought to mind a restaurant. Although Hurd wasn't speaking, his voice said, "So let's talk turkey."

I watched the video screen as captions scrolled across it in sync with Hurd's recorded voice. SO LET'S TALK TURKEY. A couple seconds passed.

Hurd's voice again: "I need that base. People back home expect it."

The captions scrolled. I looked at Hurd. He looked like a pale corpse propped up in the chair now.

A new voice now, accompanied by captions: "Gonna be a tough sell to my colleagues, Howie. We just went through another round of closings, and now you want a brand new fifty-billion-dollar Air Force base in Alabama. Not sure I can pull that off."

Harrow held up a finger and the audio went silent. He said, "Senator Hurd, please identify that second voice for us."

On stage, Hurd murmured something. The truth meter bobbled around in the center and went back to idle.

"Please repeat that, Senator," Harrow said. "Clearly, so the systems can hear you."

Hurd looked at Harrow with pure hatred now, liver spots glowing on his pale face. "Jack. Dickey."

The meter went strong green. TRUTH.

"The senator from Nevada?" Harrow said.

Hurd nodded.

"You have to speak your answers, sir."

"Yes, the senator from Nevada."

"Thank you." Harrow nodded offstage again and the audio recording began playing again.

.

HURD: Cut the bullshit, Jack. Ain't no cameras, ain't no reporters up here in The Duck.

DICKEY: You prepared to move 642 out of committee?

HURD: You have been to my state before, right? if I let that bill out, I might as well head back home with a noose around my neck.

DICKEY: Time for you to cut the crap, Howie. You want me to rally my people for something as crazy as your base, it'll take something big. Like 642. Besides, what the hell do you care what a bunch of simple rednecks think? Your next election is five years away.

HURD: I don't give a rat's ass what they think. But I'd prefer not to be lynched if it's all the same to you. And that's dang sure what'll happen if I have anything to do with shutting down Redstone.

DICKEY: So keep Redstone.

HURD: Damn you, Jack. I've made promises on that base. Promises to people you don't disappoint. But I spec that ain't news to you.

A few seconds went by, nothing but faint background sound coming from the speakers.

HURD: So you know? That ten thousand acres outside Vegas? Been wondering why the hell anybody would buy that much desert that ain't worth a damn for nothin'. Think I'm seeing the picture now.

DICKEY: I don't know about any land, but something near Las Vegas would be ideal for a base and a brand new space research facility, don't you think?

HURD: You played me, Jack. this whole thing has been about you getting my base. Thought we were friends.

DICKEY: For Christ's sake, Howie. You know how this game works. Do we have a deal?

HURD: Yeah. We have a deal.

THE SOUND SYSTEM went quiet again. Harrow walked to within three feet of Hurd and said, "Senator, please explain why you would trade Redstone and its sixty thousand jobs to Senator Dickey for Nevada, when you and Alabama would only get a new base with eight thousand jobs in return."

Hurd raised his head and looked at Harrow. "Please," he said, tears now pooling in his eyes, then spilling down his cheeks, "please."

"You only have a few seconds more to answer," Harrow said.

The tears poured. Hurd said nothing. After a few seconds, his body jerked violently, harder than before. Hurd's teeth clenched and something like a growl came out.

Harrow said, "Senator, why did you make the trade with Dickey?"

Hurd sniffed. "You have to understand. They threatened my kids! My grandchildren, for God's sake!" His voice was pleading now.

"Who threatened them?" Harrow said.

"Have you no shame?"

"WHO?!" Harrow shouted.

Hurd flinched. "The union."

Green. TRUTH.

"A labor union?" Harrow said.

Hurd shook his head. "No, no. That's just what they call themselves. Bunch of 'lobbyists.' That's what they call themselves, anyway. More like gangsters. Big outfit of them."

The meter remained green.

"Where are they based?" Harrow said.

"Everywhere."

"Do you know the names of individuals in this organization?"

Hurd nodded.

"Good, we'll get to that in a moment. For now, tell us why this organization wants an Air Force base in Alabama."

"They're into everything. Construction. Logistics. Weapons. Oh

God, how they're into weapons. They make billions off anything military."

Green.

"Explain what you mean by that, Senator. 'How they're into weapons.'"

"Researching them," Hurd said. "Making them. Selling them. Hell, *using* them. Private contractors."

Harrow said, "Are you saying this 'union' is affiliated with private military contractors? What most people would call mercenaries?"

Hurd nodded and said, "Yes."

Now Harrow walked right up to Hurd and laid a hand on his shoulder, leaned forward, said, "Thank you, Senator. You're being very helpful." He looked like a man talking to a venerated grandfather. "And why would these people threaten you and your family? Had you given them assurances on—what—contracts?"

Hurd nodded. "Yes."

"What prompted you to do that?"

"They gave me things."

"Things?" Harrow said.

"Houses. Apartments. Trips. Hell, a damned yacht that I've been on two times. And money, of course. It takes money to stay in office, you know?"

Harrow nodded, now cutting a sympathetic figure. "So you took bribes from an organization that profits from military activity?"

"Yes," Hurd said. "I did."

"And made promises to them?"

"I did."

"Then Senator Dickey, would you say he extorted you because he knew of your predicament?"

"Damn right he did, the sonofabitch."

All green. No deception in sight, according to the whiz-bang lie meter.

"I see," Harrow said. "How long have you been taking bribes from the union, Senator Hurd?"

Hurd shrugged. "Forty years?"

The meter was green.

DAY 10

8:45 Pm Eastern

FBI HEADQUARTERS, DC

DEEP in the bowels of the J. Edgar Hoover building, every workstation, every laptop, and every console was manned in the FBI's Criminal Justice Information Services Division (CJIS) Virtual Command Center (VCC). Massive screens covered the walls of the large room and provided the bulk of the lighting in the dimly lit environment.

On those screens, routes drew themselves between locations on a giant map of the world, then disappeared, only to appear somewhere else a tenth of a second later.

A woman standing at a slightly raised podium on the side of the room said, "Tell me we're getting somewhere, people! Report!"

"Proxies," a scruffy guy who looked to be in his late teens said. "Never seen such a chain of them. Fuck me!"

"Lose the language or get out of my room, Zack," Podium said.

"Sorry," Zack said. "Russia, Iran, China, all the 'Stans. The proxies are bouncing faster than we can track them. If I didn't know better I'd say...oh, never mind."

"No," Podium said. "Say it."

"If I didn't know better, I'd say this is a government operation."

"Russia?"

"No."

"Then who? China? NoKo? Talk to me."

Zack still looked hesitant to speak.

"Zack! Who?"

"Either us or the Israelis. No one else could pull this off."

A dark-haired, dark-complexioned man at a desk just to the right of the podium said, "Don't start blaming this on us. Israel has nothing to do with this. Why would we?"

Podium ran both hands through her short hair. "Mary and Joseph on a piece of cheese toast. We know it's not us, not the Bureau. Someone at NSA?"

A thirtyish woman with lime-green hair spoke up from a large console. "No. Wrong protocols. Not NSA."

"We're running out of options, Candace," Podium said.

"This is military, ma'am. US military. I'd bet Fritz's life on it."

"Who the hell is Fritz?"

"My ferret. I love him. He—"

Podium held up a hand. "Okay. I better call the president."

DAY 10
8:45 Pm Eastern

TIMES SQUARE
NEW YORK CITY

MIDTOWN TRAFFIC HAD GROUND to a halt as people near Times Square stopped their cars and got out to watch the show unfolding on every screen in sight. NYPD had tried to get things moving again but gave up after fifteen minutes. Nobody was going anywhere.

Chatter had rippled through the throngs when the old senator from Alabama was led from the stage looking like he'd been run through a washing machine. Now it quieted again as the next witness in what everyone was calling "The Show" was guided to the Hot Seat and plugged in.

The general running things—Harrow was his name—started off by getting the new guy, also an old fart, to identify himself as Senator Jack Dickey, Democrat, from the state of Nevada. Weren't he and the other one the two who'd been missing for a week? Yeah, that was them.

Then before asking Dickey any real questions, the general played a recording of the interesting part of Hurd's "testimony," the part where he'd laid out the deal between him and Dickey. When that was done, the wall behind the little stage reverted to a closeup of Dickey's face, the "TruthOMeter" (trooth-AH-muh-ter was how everybody was saying it) sitting at its middle spot.

The only sounds were the audio from The Show bouncing and echoing its way around the skyscrapers. The normal sounds of the city, the sirens and honking horns, were distant, forgotten. Harrow got the next segment of THE SHOW rolling in earnest.

HARROW: Senator Dickey, would you say your colleague Senator Hurd gave an accurate account of the "deal" you two made regarding Redstone Arsenal, a new Air Force base in Alabama, and a massive new facility to replace Redstone in Nevada?

    DICKEY: Go fuck yourself and the horse you rode in on.

THE TRUTHOMETER FLASHED NON-RESPONSIVE at the top of the screen and Dickey jerked.

HARROW: Let's try again, Senator. Did Senator Hurd—

    DICKEY: Same answer, asshole. Shove it up your ass.

THIS TIME DICKEY'S body jerked even harder. He gritted his teeth. Threw back his head and laughed.

HARROW: One more time, sir.

    DICKEY: Give it your best shot, you arrogant prick. When this is done, I'll have your ass.

THE CROWD GASPED at the violence of the next shock that hit Dickey. His whole body seized and arched, his head jerking forward and backward. Two seconds into it, Dickey said through clenched teeth, "Stop! Stop it!" His body relaxed and he gasped, gulping in air, his eyes bugged out on giant screens all around Times Square.

HARROW: Was Senator Hurd's account of the deal he made with you accurate?

DICKEY: Yes.

HARROW: Were you aware that he was under threat from an organization that calls itself "the union"?

DICKEY: Of course. Why else would he be stupid enough to give up something like Redstone? I had his old ass by the short-and-curlies and I yanked 'em.

HARROW: Why were you so desperate to move Redstone to Nevada?

DICKEY: Seriously? I wanted to bring those sixty thousand jobs to my state.

THE TRUTHOMETER SHOT to the right in red, LIE blinking. Dickey's body spasmed and his eyes rolled back in his head. Spit drooled from the corner of his mouth and tears poured from his eyes. When the shock ended, Dickey was wild-eyed and grasping at his heart. Harrow gave him two minutes to recover, then resumed the questioning.

HARROW: You're approaching the danger zone, Senator. I urge you in the strongest possible way to answer these questions carefully from here on out. Can you do that?

DICKEY NODDED.

HARROW: Answer verbally, please.

DICKEY: Yes, yes, yes.

HARROW: Thank you. Why were you so desperate to move Redstone to Nevada?

DICKEY: I own thousands of acres that would be leased to the military for the base.

HARROW: Do you own this land openly, in your name?

DICKEY: I'm not an idiot. The land is owned by shells I set up.

HARROW: How much money would you stand to make off the deal?

DICKEY: Tens of millions, maybe hundreds.

HARROW: Thank you for your honesty, Senator. Do you know a man named Robert Hecht?

DICKEY: Yes.

HARROW: What is Mr. Hecht's occupation?

DICKEY: Lobbyist. Fixer. Dealmaker. Broker.

THE TRUTHOMETER WAS PULSING to the right but only slightly and its green color was muted, not the vibrant shade it had been displaying.

HARROW: Is Mr. Hecht known around Washington for any other services, something outside the conventional political realm?

DICKEY DROPPED HIS HEAD, chin on chest, then raised his head and shook it slowly back and forth a couple of times before speaking.

DICKEY: He...procures things...people to meet certain sexual needs.

HARROW: What kind of people does Mr. Hecht "procure"?

DICKEY: Minors.

HARROW: Minors of what typical age range?

DICKEY: May I have a glass of water?

HARROW LOOKED OFFSTAGE AND NODDED. A woman walked to Dickey

and handed him a bottle of water. Dickey cracked the top and drained the entire bottle in one extended gulp.

HARROW: Minors of what typical age range?

DICKEY: Whatever you want. I'd say most are in the five- to fifteen-year ballpark.

THE TRUTHOMETER WAS GREEN, pinging to the truth side at about 90%. The bravado and arrogance with which Dickey had begun his session was long gone. A thick sheen of sweat was visible on his forehead and upper lip.

HARROW: Are you saying that Mr. Hecht somehow provides children as young as five years old to be used for sexual activity?

DICKEY: He does.

HARROW: Are you a client of Mr. Hecht's "procurement services," Senator?

DICKEY: Please don't do this, I'm begging you.

HARROW: You have seconds remaining in which to begin answering the question truthfully.

DICKEY: Yes, I'm a client.

HARROW: And what is your preference, Senator? What "special needs" does Mr. Hecht meet for you?

DICKEY BEGAN TO CRY, sniffing and wiping his eyes.

HARROW: Answer the question.

DICKEY: I prefer boys, at least eight, no older than ten.

GREEN. TRUTH.

The crowd watching the screens remained quiet, aghast in a monolithic block. Then a low murmur began. Facial expressions began to morph, anger supplanting shock and bewilderment.

Someone shouted, "String that bastard up!"

"Yeah!"

"Damn right!"

"Fucking-a!"

DAY 10

8:20 Pm Central

COG CITY

HURD'S SESSION had left me shaking my head at the corruption that had just been uncovered. Dickey's blew my mind. By the time Harrow finished with the Nevada octogenarian, he had uncovered a ring of pedophilia, abduction, and trafficking that defied belief. How could something like this have gone on right under the authorities' noses for so long? Right in the heart of our government? I had uncovered plenty of the filth on Hecht's laptop and already knew what he was, already knew what his "clients" were from the photos and videos. But if Dickey had been telling the truth, and that likelihood was near certain, the scale of it was breathtaking. How?

I heard and felt my heart pounding in my ears. My mind was shifting into a hazy veneer of anger. It took every iota of restraint I could muster to not walk backstage and rip these creatures apart with my bare hands. Maybe later. Yes, later.

Pamela walked Hecht onto the stage. He was a short man with a small gut that flabbed and jiggled behind his unbuttoned suit jacket as he walked. He looked early fifties to late sixties. Wiry gray hair that stuck up on his head in little tufts. Once he was seated in the Hot Seat and plugged up, Pamela left the stage and Harrow approached Hecht. He said, "Mr. Hecht, to save time I'm going to play some highlights of the session that preceded yours, one in which Senator Dickey enlightened us as to the nature of your 'special business.' Please pay attention."

The video backdrop replayed key clips of Dickey describing how Hecht provided children to him and other power players to abuse and discard. Hecht's face went as gray as his hair. When the video sequence ended, Harrow began.

HARROW: Mr. Hecht, was Senator Dickey telling the truth in the video you just saw?

HECHT: I'm not talking to you. You have no authority over me.

THE METER STAYED CENTERED and added NON-RESPONSIVE to the display. Harrow sighed.

HARROW: The rules have been explained. You have a few more seconds to answer.

HECHT TIPPED his head up and stuck his chin out in a show of defiance. Until the chair lit him up. After the spasm, he spoke.

HECHT: You can't be serious! You're really doing this? Do you know who I am?

HARROW: Was Senator Dickey telling the truth? You have fifteen seconds in which to begin a truthful answer. After that, the voltage and duration of the shock double. Your choice.

· · ·

HECHT LOOKED side to side as if he expected the Child-Abuse Cavalry to show up at any moment and free him from a nightmare. The countdown on the video screens was down to two seconds...

HECHT: Yes!

HARROW: Thank you. What is your preference for children to have sex with, gender and age?

HECHT: I don't personally par—

THE JUICE HIT him and he spasmed, much harder this time, his belly jiggling like a glob of JELL-O in a dress shirt.

HECHT: You will pay for this, I promise you that.

HARROW: Perhaps. You'll pay first, by telling the truth here tonight, or I swear before all that is holy, sir, I will watch you fry in that chair until your black heart stops beating. Am I clear?

I SUDDENLY WANTED TO APPLAUD, to cheer the man who'd had me kidnapped and was holding me prisoner at this moment. Unusual? Yes. But it's how I felt right then.

HECHT: I understand.

HARROW: Your preference?

HECHT: Girls. I like them just when their tits are starting to sprout. That what you want to know?

HARROW FLINCHED JUST A BIT. I could see his jaw working, color spreading into his face. I thought for a moment he might order the chair cranked up to max right then and there, but he didn't. He took a few breaths and resumed.

. . .

HARROW: Where do you get these children?

HECHT: (laughing) I have a variety of suppliers. More than half pass right through the checkpoints at the southern border, courtesy of their "Uncle Hector" or "Papa Pedro." Some of my clients are "ethnically" particular, though. Don't want the brown-skins. They want white. Black. Yellow. There's always someone out there willing to part with them for the right price. The Chinks are easy to deal with, especially girls since they don't value them much over there.

HARROW: What kind of price do you typically pay for a child?

HECHT: Depends. Age. Color. How pretty they are. Oh, and how long they've been on the job.

THE METER WAS green throughout this horrid exchange. TRUTH.

HARROW: Give me a range.

HECHT: Three hundred bucks for a used-up fifteen-year-old Mexican with track marks up and down their arms. Thousands for clean ones, young ones, first-timers.

HARROW: And you, what, resell them to your clients?

HECHT: Oh, hell no. More like rent them out for a weekend or something. Occasional longer-term leases. (laughing)

HARROW: What's the going price to rape a ten-year-old over a weekend, Mr. Hecht?

HECHT: (shrugging) Two thousand to ten thousand. Lots of variables.

HARROW: What happens to these children in the end, when they're no longer of any use to you and your clients?

HECHT: Again, it depends. I unload some of them to pimps around the country who put them to work full-time. Some of them require a more "permanent" solution.

HARROW: Clarify what you mean by "permanent solution."

HECHT: They're killed, you dumb fuck. Sent through a wood-chip-

per. Dissolve in acid. Different contractors have different methodologies.

HARROW: What does that cost you?

HECHT: Twenty-five hundred bucks. That's what I pay. No more.
All my contractors know it.

HARROW: I'm sure everyone watching this is impressed with your
keen business acumen.

HECHT: (laughing) Watching, my ass. There's no way in hell the
government is allowing this bullshit to be seen. Mark my word on that.

HARROW: I want to know the names of your clients. We'll debrief
you off the air for a complete list, but for now give me five names.
Names people might recognize. And their "preferences."

HECHT: No can do. I have a reputation to uphold, not to mention
the fact that my clients are powerful people who count on my discre-
tion. I mean, they *really* count on it.

HARROW GAVE HIM NO WARNING. The clock expired and Hecht flopped
around in the Hot Seat like a fish on a hot lakeside rock. When the
jerking stopped, Harrow told someone offstage to restart the fifteen-
second countdown. Hecht obviously feared his clients more than he
did the juice because he still said nothing. The next round of "motivation" was violent. Hecht flopped and jiggled, drool running out of the
corners of his mouth, his eyes bugged out like something in a cartoon.
At the end of it he held up a hand, panting.

HECHT: No more. No.

HARROW: Five names. Now.

HECHT: (nodding) President Cigar, you know who I'm talking
about. Preference: Anything with a cunt.

HARROW: Go on.

HECHT: Jack Dickey, you know about him.

HARROW: He doesn't count. Four more.

HECHT: Betsy Higgins.

. . .

HARROW LOOKED SURPRISED. Not sure why. Did he think this kind of demonic behavior was limited to men? Higgins was a former Secretary of State with a long history of criminal accusations that always seemed to fizzle in the so-called halls of justice.

HARROW: Her preference?

HECHT: Girls. Teenagers. Skinny and pretty. A special affinity for true blondes.

HARROW: True blondes?

HECHT: Blonde hair. Everywhere.

HARROW: I see. Go on. Three more.

HECHT: David Harcourt. Boys just out of puberty. They have to be well-endowed. Needless to say, his needs are expensive.

HARCOURT WAS the Speaker of the House, an All-American-looking fortysomething Democrat from Iowa who had an absolute knockout for a wife. Not to mention five kids. He positioned himself as the quintessential family man. I'd run out of the ability to be surprised by this point.

HARROW: Down to two. Keep going.

HECHT: Henry Blass.

HARROW: The FBI director?

HECHT: Yeah. You getting the picture now as to what you've gotten yourself into with this clown show? *Dumb fuck.*

HARROW: Mr. Blass's preferences?

HECHT: Young. Pre-puberty. Always wants a boy and a girl, makes them do stuff to each other in front of him.

HARROW: One more.

HECHT: Joshua Henson.

HARROW: The tech billionaire?

HECHT: That's the one. Little black boys. Key word, *little*. The younger the better.

. . .

THESE PEOPLE HAD TO PAY. No way around it. If the system didn't hold
them accountable, and the system had a piss-poor record of holding
power to account, then I would.

HARROW: What kind of dealings have you had with the president,
John Cartwright?
    HECHT: (laughing) Are you kidding? None. Guy's a Boy Scout. It's
why the town hates his guts.

GREEN. TRUTH.

DAY 10
9:45 Pm Central

FBI HEADQUARTERS, DC

HENRIK BLASS WISHED he had stayed in his office and watched this nightmare alone. Instead, he had joined a half-dozen of his high-level deputies and staff in a presentation room to watch it. Now he was trapped. That cretin Hecht had just named him. *Him*, Henrik Fennington Blass, director of the Federal Bureau of Investigation. This couldn't be happening. He felt detached from his body, like he was a third party just looking on.

"Sir?" It was Elizabeth Alvarez, the agent in charge of the task force. The one he'd been chewing out less than two hours ago.

Blass didn't answer. His mind cycled like a tornado. His wife. His kids. His *life*.

"Sir?"

He jerked himself back into the reality of the room. "Yes, agent?"

"Is this"—she pointed at the flat panel on the wall—"is this true?"

He looked around the room. Every eye was on him, awaiting his answer. Men and women he'd supervised for years. People he'd lectured on ethics, on doing the right thing, on being above reproach as members of the most powerful law enforcement agency the world had ever known. Christ.

"Who all is seeing this?" he said, his mind spinning again. "Just us, right? Our people intercepted and isolated it, right? We can contain this. Yes, we'll contain it. Get the tech—"

"Henry," a voice said quietly from several seats away. It was his deputy director. They'd come up through the rank-and-file together.

Blass stared at him, his eyes wide and his mouth open. The man looked like a stranger to him. He felt like a stranger to himself, out of body.

"What?" Blass finally said.

"Is it true?"

He decided on a course of action. "Hell no, it's not true. I can't believe you'd even ask me such a thing." Yes, this was the course. Deny. Forcefully, by God. He looked around the room, into eyes, gathering himself back together, looking offended. How dare they even ask him such a ridiculous thing!

The faces looked back at him. He expected to see relief on those faces, relief at hearing that he was innocent. That's not what he saw. He saw skepticism. One of them lowered his head. Another turned away. Alvarez stared at him, a look of judgment on her smug little face. How was that for loyalty?

DAY 10

9:10 Pm Central

COG CITY

ROB ACOMA HAD SAT in a room by himself for the past two hours and watched this shit-show of degenerates. Now the hillbilly woman was steering him onto the stage. He still didn't know what this bunch of backward-ass criminals wanted with him, but he had nothing to hide. He didn't fuck kids. He didn't trade military bases like baseball cards. They had jack-shit on him.

He walked with his head high and proud, his walk straight and confident. Before the bitch eased him into the chair, he unbuttoned his suit jacket and smoothed it. Straightened his tie. He didn't like his situation at the moment—who liked being kidnapped?—but he was an innocent man and when this theatrical production was done, he'd return to DC as the *king* of political coverage. Maybe he'd stay with NBS. Maybe not. They'd all probably be in a bidding war for him, the man who'd been here to witness the story of all stories.

Hell, he'd get that new legacy rolling right here, right now. If these asshats were telling the truth about distribution, he'd be playing to the biggest audience of his life. May as well make good use of that.

The general he'd seen a few times was seated at a little raised platform a few feet away. He said, "Mr. Acoma, you've been watching this evening's event since it began, is that correct?"

Showtime, baby. "Correct, General. It's been difficult to watch, disheartening, but I've paid attention. I have to say, I would have been happy to interview these men and get to the truth for you without all the barbarism. You only had to ask, but you didn't." He found the active camera by its tally light and looked directly into it with a confident nod.

The general stared at him for a moment, one side of his mouth almost up in a tiny smile. "Did you review the binder of material that was provided to you?"

"I skimmed it." Acoma noticed a monitor of what he presumed to be the program output facing back toward the stage. On the screen, the meter behind him pegged green and read, "TRUTH."

The general—something Harrow—stood from his pissy little throne and walked to Acoma, handing him a document. "Do you recognize this?"

Acoma looked at the document and his heart rate quickened. Being an old pro at dodging, he reflexively said, "I can't say that I do."

Electricity shot through his body and his head snapped back. When it ended and his body relaxed, Acoma licked his lips and tasted blood. He had bitten his tongue. *Fuck! Get it back together, stay strong.*

Harrow said, "Do you recognize the document?"

Acoma almost denied it again—old habits die hard—but caught himself. "Yes, I believe I do." He noticed that the program monitor now showed the document, a document he was intimately familiar with. *Shit shit shit.* It was an email that had been sent to him a couple years ago:

FROM: KirstenDShattuck@rhyta.com
To: racoma@nbsnews.com

Subject: Urgent information that the public should know

Mr. Acoma,

My name is Kirsten Shattuck and I am sharing this with you under the condition that you never involve my name in any way. If you do not agree to this condition, I expressly forbid the use of this information in any way.

I have worked for Senator Jack Dickey for 31 years. I have always been loyal but I have seen something that my conscience will not allow me to ignore. I routinely handle the Senator's e-mail correspondence because he has so much of it and he is not good with computers. Last week I was in his office answering a lot of e-mails for him and I accidentally clicked on a tab in his internet browser that contained a secret e-mail-box I was unaware of. I would normally not have given this any thought but there was a video on the screen, in an e-mail to what I presume to be the Senator's secret e-mail address. To my horror, the video showed the Senator raping a child, a boy who could not have been more than ten years old.

That video was sitting there playing over and over again. I cannot get it out of my mind. I cannot sleep. I am afraid to go to the police because the Senator is so powerful that I fear he will be able to make the whole thing vanish without a trace. I have attached this awful video and the whole e-mail that the video was attached to. You will find it attached here as ENJOY, JACKY-BOY.eml.

I am sending this to you so that this atrocity can be exposed. There are obviously others involved in this. I do not know how many. Please do your part to see that this information is publicized so it can be stopped.

. . .

THANK YOU,

Kirsten

COG CITY

I WATCHED the news guy strut onto the stage like the cock of the walk and had a distinct urge to walk onto the stage and knock him into next week before he'd uttered a word. I refrained. It took effort.

He started off the session as if he were the star of the night. Hell, maybe he was. He settled down a little bit when the Hot Seat popped him, and when that email hit the screen, hubris and smarm drained from the pompous ass like a balloon shot with a BB gun. Even from twenty feet back I saw the film of sweat erupting on him. His handsome, tanned face sagged and the color washed from it. He ran a hand through his primped hair, leaving it in a disheveled heap. Harrow continued.

HARROW: Did you know Ms. Shattuck?

ACOMA: Not really, but I had exchanged a number of emails with her in the past.

HARROW: About what?

ACOMA: Questions for Senator Dickey, offers for him to comment on stories we were running, things of that nature.

HARROW: Would you say you found her credible in your past interactions, generally speaking?

ACOMA: (shrugging) I suppose so.

HARROW: Did you respond to this email when you received it?

ACOMA: No.

GREEN. TRUTH. Harrow drew his head back a bit and cocked it to the side at this answer. That conflict inside me was growing. I was driven to bring down this operation. It was my mission. Find Sol. Stop him. At the moment, though, all I wanted to do was watch these jackasses squirm while they told the truth and jerk around in pain when they didn't.

HARROW: No?

ACOMA: No.

HARROW: What did you do after you received the email?

ACOMA: You have to understand, I receive so many crazy stories that I can't possibly take them seriously.

HARROW: Answer the question.

ACOMA: Look, these things require context. This isn't f—

NON-RESPONSIVE, the meter said. Having already been juiced once, the doubled-up current hit him hard when the fifteen seconds expired. Poor Robby.

HARROW: What did you do after you received the email?

ACOMA: I watched the video.

HARROW: What did the video show?

ACOMA: Like she'd said, it appeared to show the senator raping a kid.

HARROW: Elaborate.

ACOMA: It was in what looked to be a cheap motel room. The kid, a boy, was bent over the foot of a bed, buttocks out. The senator was behind him, having...intercourse with him.

HARROW: Where was the camera placed in relation to this activity?

ACOMA: To the side, uh, on the left, I think. Yeah, to the left of what was happening, at first. Then it moved to the other side.

HARROW: The camera seemed to be manned by someone?

ACOMA: Yes.

HARROW: Did the video have sound?

ACOMA: (nodding)

HARROW: Answer verbally.

ACOMA: Yes, there was sound.

HARROW: What did you hear?

ACOMA: Dickey—the senator—was grunting. Someone else was saying, "Oh yeah, Jacky-Boy. Hit it." He kept saying that.

HARROW: And the child, the victim, was he saying anything?

ACOMA: No. He, uh, had—his mouth was duct-taped.

HARROW: You seem to have quite a vivid recall of details from this video, Mr. Acoma, especially since this email was sent to you nearly two years ago.

ACOMA: Who could forget something like that? Christ!

HARROW: So you found it disturbing?

ACOMA: Of course I found it *disturbing!*

HARROW: So you watched the video, which was so disturbing that you vividly remember it even today. What did you do after that?

ACOMA DREW a breath to say something, then stopped. The sweat had grown from a light film to fat droplets beaded up all over his face, some dripping down onto his jacket, some onto his lap.

· · ·

HARROW: What did you do after you watched the video?

ACOMA: I showed all of it, the email, the video, to my producer.

HARROW: Who was that?

ACOMA: Bish. Bish Fogleman.

HARROW: And what did Fogleman say?

ACOMA: He asked if I thought it was real or some kind of effects, a deep fake.

HARROW: How did you answer that?

ACOMA: I thought it was real. I told him that.

HARROW: And after that?

ACOMA: Bish said it was my call whether to run with it or not.

HARROW: Did you "run with it"?

ACOMA: No.

HARROW: Neither you nor anyone else at your network covered the story at all?

ACOMA: No.

HARROW: Why not?

AT THIS POINT, Acoma's head drooped, chin on chest, head shaking slowly from side to side. Harrow didn't prompt him, only waited. The time ran out and Acoma's body jerked like someone shaking a rag doll for at least five seconds, maybe more. When it stopped, Acoma raised his head. His eyes were bloodshot, tears streaming. I didn't give one shit about his tears.

HARROW: Let's try a different question. Did you do any further investigation of the issue?

ACOMA: (shaking head)

HARROW: Verbal answers, unless you want the motivators to move to level four.

ACOMA: No, I didn't.

HARROW: Did you do anything at all?

ACOMA: I, I, sent it to the senator's chief of staff. Forwarded it to him.

HARROW: Why?

ACOMA HELD his hands up in front of his face. They shook like someone with a neurological disease. He stared at them.

HARROW: Why?

ACOMA: I wanted him to know this information was...out of the office.

HARROW: I want to be very sure I understand everything clearly. You received a video, which you believed to be real, of a United States senator raping a child. You had the option to expose this to the public, but you chose not to. Instead, you betrayed your source and warned the office of the rapist. Is all that correct, Mr. Acoma?

ACOMA SOBBED NOW.

HARROW: Choose your next answer carefully, sir. Why did you do this?

ACOMA: Dickey, the senator, was in a tough reelection fight. This would have ruined him. I didn't want that to happen.

HARROW: Was that because of some personal relationship or fondness that you hold for Senator Dickey?

ACOMA: No.

HARROW: Then what was your motivation for protecting him?

ACOMA: You have to understand, if Dickey lost, the Democrats would have lost the Senate. I couldn't have that on my conscience.

HARROW, who had to this point been a picture of professionalism and composure for the most part, looked like he might blow a gasket then and there. His face flushed crimson, his jaw muscles working, fists clenched.

· · ·

HARROW: Your <u>conscience?</u> You ignored a child being raped so the political party of your choosing would maintain power?

ACOMA: Yes.

HARROW: What else do you do to protect those in power who share your political views?

ACOMA LOOKED WILDLY from side to side, then blew out a long sigh.

ACOMA: Fuck it, fuck it, fuck it. I do whatever the hell I can, okay? I ignore stories harmful to Democrats. I run with anything I can to hurt a fucking Republican. Is that what you want to hear?

GREEN. TRUTH.

HARROW: I only want to hear the truth.

ACOMA: Well, there you have it, you backward piece of shit. Damn right I do. You realize what's at stake here? Do you expect us to sit back and let a bunch of racist, homophobic, xenophobic Bible-thumpers continue to rise in this country? Fuck no! We'll stop that any way we fucking can. It's our job.

HARROW: Is that what you learned in journalism school, that it's your "job" to hide the truth, to manipulate people?

ACOMA: J-school is bullshit. Too much is on the line. We're in it to set things right.

HARROW: If you are so convicted of your positions, why not simply report the facts and let the people of the country decide how they feel about them?

ACOMA BROKE out in a bizarre hybrid of sobbing and laughing like a hyena.

· · ·

ACOMA: Are you serious? Leave the fate of the country up to the kind of people who put Donald Fucking Trump in office? Or this latest fuckwad, Cartwright? We're supposed to trust these Neanderthals to understand and process facts?

HARROW: I notice that during your past few answers, you have shifted from "I" to "us" and "we." Are you saying that others in your profession hold similar views to yourself?

ACOMA: No shit, Sherlock. We *own* the media.

HARROW: You don't believe in "diversity" of opinion within your industry?

ACOMA: Are you not listening to me? It's too. Fucking. Important.

HARROW: I'm listening, Mr. Acoma. The nation is listening.

THE ASSHOLE GAVE A START, as if he'd forgotten that this wasn't limited to the local audience. He wiped his face on the sleeve of his jacket, ran his fingers through his hair, straightened his tie. The idiot was *primping*.

HARROW: One more question. After you warned Senator Dickey's office, what happened to Ms. Shattuck?

ACOMA: I believe she was terminated from her job.

HARROW: Do you know what happened to her after she was fired?

ACOMA: I read that she was killed in a car accident.

HARROW: Do you believe her death was accidental?

ACOMA: How should I know?

RED. LIE. When the level-four shock hit him, it looked like an electro-cution scene from a movie, sans the theatrical arcs and flames. His body went rigid, then shook and jerked, his eyes bugged out. I heard his teeth chattering. His stiff body began to slide down out of the chair. When it finally stopped, his head flopped to the side, eyes closed, and his body went limp, half in and half out of the chair. I could see that he was breathing, but aside from that he looked dead.

Harrow looked offstage and touched his nose. Pam came onto the stage, walked to the Hot Seat, broke an ammonia inhaler that I could smell all too well, and stuck it under Acoma's nose. After a moment he spasmed once and his eyes shot open.

"Get back up in your seat there, Mr. Acoma," Pam said. He looked at her like she was speaking a foreign language. "Come on, now." She grabbed an upper arm and eventually coaxed him back into a sitting position.

Harrow nodded at her and she left the stage.

HARROW: Do you believe Ms. Shattuck's death was accidental?
   ACOMA: No.
   HARROW: Do you care?
   ACOMA: Not one fuck.

GREEN. TRUTH.

DAY 10
9:40 Pm Central

COG CITY

ONCE PAM LED A BEDRAGGLED Acoma from the stage, Harrow left the dais and stood to the side of the Hot Seat, his hand resting on the top of its backrest. He looked directly over our heads. I turned and saw the tally light glowing atop the camera at the back of the room. He began to speak.

"Ladies and gentlemen, I know this evening has not been pleasant to watch. I hope you agree that getting to the truth was worth the discomfort. I want to point out that these men were chosen merely as examples of the rot that has infested our nation. Men, and women, like these are now legion within the power structures that govern and influence everything that happens in the United States. Our government is infested with these people, both elected and unelected, and this is true for every branch of government.

"To my mind, it's even worse that the news media upon whom we should be able to rely for objective reporting of facts, is a corrupt, nearly monolithic propaganda machine. As Mr. Acoma just boasted, he and his ilk control the press apparatus in this nation now. They long ago abandoned the mission of telling truth in favor of promoting an agenda that matches their personal politics.

"If you go to the web address that will appear on your screen shortly, you will find a massive tranche of information we have collected that documents many, many more examples of behavior like you've heard described here tonight. You will find detailed statistics on the bias of the media. Not *alleged* bias, which is a term that gets thrown around a lot, but horrific bias like you heard Mr. Acoma brag about, bias that we have meticulously and empirically documented for your examination.

"We undertook this endeavor for one reason: To cut through the veil of secrecy and obfuscation that surrounds us, to show you the *truth* of what is happening. I ask you to absorb and evaluate this truth. Please visit the website. Share it. For those of you who are technical enough to do so, mirror it. Distribute it. Spread the word. Spread the truth.

"Good night, and God bless the United States of America."

From his camera perch, Wilson said, "That's a wrap and we're offline."

On the stage, Harrow looked out toward the little audience and made eye contact with me. He motioned for me to join him. I did so.

He said, "Thoughts?"

I chewed my bottom lip and pondered how to answer that, then decided to go with unvarnished truth. "Enlightening. Infuriating. Fascinating in a macabre way."

"It had to be done."

"Now that you're done, am I free to go?"

"Who said I'm done?"

"You turning this into a series?"

Harrow actually laughed. "It would have ratings through the roof, but no. This ends this phase."

"I need to leave here," I said.

"Sorry, Sam, I can't allow that."

"General—"

"Call me Lucian, remember?"

"Lucian, I'll put this as plainly as possible. I came to this mountain to find Sol and to stop him. I found him. After what I saw tonight, I have no interest in stopping him, or stopping you, for that matter. These assholes had this coming and if it were up to me, their punishment would be far more dramatic than what happened tonight.

"My one problem with you at the moment is that you're holding me prisoner. Let me leave here and I will not pursue you or Sol further. Nor will I assist anyone in pursuing you."

"And I'm supposed to, what, simply take your word on that?" Harrow said.

"I do not break my word, period. That said, no, you don't have to take my word for it."

Harrow cocked his head.

I pointed at the Hot Seat. "Hook me up."

NATIONWIDE PROTESTS ERUPT FOLLOWING BROADCAST

WASHINGTON, DC — Large protests, some violent, have broken out in cities across the nation in the aftermath of a bizarre broadcast of a "torture trial" featuring four of the five missing Washington figures. U.S. Senators Howard Hurd and Jack Dickey, lobbyist Robert Hecht, and NBS News anchor Rob Acoma were subjected to questioning by an Army general named Lucian Harrow. Notably absent from the show was Supreme Court Chief Justice Marcus Wilder, whose disappearance was earlier believed to be connected. The men were connected to a torture mechanism that shocked them if a purportedly sophisticated polygraph system detected deception.

General Harrow conducted the questioning, which he claimed was designed to "reveal truth." Under torture, which experts have long determined to yield unreliable information, the men admitted to a wide range of nefarious behavior, including corruption and child trafficking involving powerful Washington personalities ranging from senators to FBI Director Henrik Blass.

The broadcast was streamed on numerous online platforms, as well as the Emergency Broadcast System. Early estimates are that the event was watched by as many as four billion people in the United States and around the world, which would make it the most-watched live event in history, topping the 1969 broadcast of the Apollo 11 moon landing. The location of the event is unknown at this time, according to FBI officials.

NBS STUDIO UNDER SIEGE

NEW YORK — The New York headquarters of NBS News has been surrounded by thousands of angry protesters following the broadcast of an event during which the network's lead political anchor, Rob Acoma, admitted to a wide range of bias by the network, including his own decision to ignore a video in his possession that showed U.S. Senator Jack Dickey raping a young child.

Midtown Manhattan was in a state of traffic gridlock that sprang from large numbers of people exiting their vehicles near Times Square to watch the broadcast on the area's video screens. Once the broadcast ended, thousands walked from Times Square to the NBS headquarters. People from other areas of the city appear to be converging on the scene, as well. NYPD officials admit they were caught unprepared, since there was no forewarning about the broadcast.

Developing...

CROWD STORMS SENATOR'S HOME

WASHINGTON, D.C. — An angry mob has attacked the Barnaby Woods home of U.S. Senator Jack Dickey. Dickey, who featured heavily in an unprecedented broadcast this evening (See LIVE "TRIAL" CAPTIVATES WORLD), is alleged to have been videotaped raping a young boy. Metro PD sources say they are on the scene and attempting to restore order but are currently outmanned.

UPDATE: Sources on the scene report that the mob has broken into the senator's home. It is unknown at this time if anyone was home at the time of the intrusion.

CARTWRIGHT FIRES FBI DIRECTOR BLASS

PRESIDENT JOHN CARTWRIGHT has fired FBI Director Henrik Blass following an allegation of pedophilia aired during a heavily viewed broadcast that featured interrogations of previously missing Washington power players. Long-time DC power broker Robert Hecht admitted to running an operation of providing underage children to various politicians and other major figures, and claimed that he has furnished children to Blass.

A White House statement said, "While Mr. Blass is innocent until proven guilty, allegations of such heinous behavior render him incapable of effectively leading the FBI."

WHERE IS JUSTICE WILDER?

THIS EVENING'S surreal broadcast of a U.S. Army general conducting interrogations has brought into question the theory that Chief Justice Marcus Wilder's disappearance is connected to those of Jack Dickey, Howard Hurd, Rob Acoma, and Robert Hecht. The latter four were all questioned under threat of electrocution by General Lucian Harrow, but Wilder was nowhere to be seen.

Developing...

DAY 10

10:38 Pm Central

COG CITY

I PASSED my Hot Seat session without incident because I was telling the plain truth: I no longer had any interest whatsoever in stopping whatever Harrow (and Sol) were up to. As far as I was concerned, they had done the nation a service this evening. One of my main concerns about Sol had been the idea of a former BAM man running wild around the country, but that really wasn't the case, was it?

Harrow and I were walking down Main Street now. The mood was amiable, bordering on friendly. I said, "You care to fill me in on what comes next?"

"Not if you want to leave."

"I do. Are you saying that choice is mine?"

"What if I offered you a position in my operation? I could use your skills, your intellect. Your country could use them."

"Lucian, I don't see how this ends well. They're going to move heaven and Earth to find you and lock you away in a deep hole. Hell, after what you exposed tonight, you should probably worry more about staying alive than going to jail."

"I'll be fine," Harrow said. "If you'll stay, I'll fill you in on everything. If you want to go, you can, but remember that the FBI is right on the other side of the rock, gnashing their teeth for you."

"That's why I have to go. I have to find Pitt and make this right. Everything I did was authorized by him. I don't want to live as a fugitive. Don't want my name ruined, don't want that for my daughter, don't want it for me."

"Very well. Go get your gear from your quarters. Meet me back here and I'll get you blindfolded and take you out," he said.

"Oh, come on. I know the ingress-egress has to be a tunnel, and common sense says it connects to those antique presidential quarters."

"Like I said, I could use your intellect," Harrow said with a smile. "Still have to blindfold you. Knowing there's a tunnel won't do you any good without seeing how to access it, and believe me, that's tricky. On both ends."

I headed to my little room to grab my backpack. With this fiasco drawing to a close, I dropped my mental wall and allowed the outside world back into my mind and soul for a moment. The outside world where I'd had a chance with Abby and blew it. That old sinking-heart sensation hit me. It was like a miniature version of the heartbreak I felt when she divorced me. I'd allowed my hopes to surge and now I was paying the price for that.

Then something new hit me: Anger. At myself. And at her. She'd ripped my soul apart years before. Now she'd shown back up, uninvited, gotten my hopes up, and bailed again? Over the same old crap? She might have had a legitimate beef the first time. I was young, brash, gone a lot, distant, and kept a ton of secrets. They were necessary, but I could still see where they'd be hard for her to take.

But now? She knew who I was when she came bopping back into my life, didn't she? And what, expected me to become someone else? To hell with that. No more apologies. No more guilt. I am who I am. Unclavius Samuel Flatt.

DAY 10

11:40 Pm Eastern

THE WHITE HOUSE

PRESIDENT JOHN CARTWRIGHT sat at the head of the conference table in the Situation Room, a half-dozen officials scattered among the side seats. Cartwright was dressed in running shorts and a baggy gray T-shirt showing heavy sweat. Flat panels on the walls silently played a variety of newscasts, most of them running footage of what was going on in the streets of the nation.

Cartwright said, "Realistic alternatives at this point?"

Bart Chatham, the National Security Adviser, said, "If you don't do it now, we may lose the streets."

"Retta?" the president said.

SecDef Loretta Pennington, dressed in a sharp blue suit, said, "Mr. President, it's an extraordinary step."

"It's an extraordinary evening," Chatham said. "New York is esti-mating their crowd at a half-million and growing. Granted, they had a head start because so many were already in the streets watching that shit show, but you can expect other cities to catch up. We're on the brink of devolving into anarchy out there."

A woman in a golf shirt and a pound of makeup who was seated not at the table but in one of the chairs against the wall, said, "Mr. President, the Speaker objects to this course of actions."

"Why isn't she here to voice those objections herself?" the president said.

"She had prior commitments, sir."

Chatham said, "You mean she's out whipping the opposition into a frenzy, ready to blame the administration no matter which way it goes."

"I resent that insinuation," the woman said.

"And I *resent* your boss being an opportunistic snake in the grass who—"

President Cartwright held up a hand and the room went silent, as if a switch had been thrown. "We don't have time for this," he said, looking at Chatham. Then he turned his attention to the staffer the Speaker of the House had sent in her stead. Cartwright knew Chatham was right. His chief of staff had been fielding calls from Republicans in the House for an hour, confirming the accusation. Speaker Janice McMann was mobilizing her caucus. Even worse, she was mobilizing her squad of media goons. He said, "Tell the Speaker her concerns are appreciated and noted. You're dismissed."

The woman looked shocked. "I have a right to be here."

Cartwright looked over his shoulder and gave a tiny gesture to the suited man behind him. The man took three efficient steps to the woman and said, "Ma'am, I'll show you out."

She said, "I'm not—"

Suit Man took her by the upper arm. "*Now,* ma'am."

She stared daggers at the man but stood and walked to the door, which Suit Man opened, then closed behind her.

Cartwright looked back to his SecDef. "Retta, how long? Before you have the streets in all the major cities?"

Pennington, the first female Secretary of Defense, said, "Four hours, sir."

Cartwright looked down at his hands on the table. Pondered a full minute. "Do it. Declare martial law. Notify the military immediately. Curfew until dawn, and it resumes at six PM tomorrow in every time zone."

Pennington nodded. "Yes, sir."

COG CITY

I FOLLOWED Harrow down into the presidential quarters. When we entered the apartment, he blindfolded me, took me by the elbow, and started walking. Out of old habit, I counted every step, memorized every turn, paid attention to every sound. Comparing the steps and path to the mental picture I had from exploring this place with Wilson, I knew we were in the bedroom.

"Hold there," Harrow said, and let go of me.

I listened and heard a door open. Closet. A switch. Wood on wood. Six faint *clanks*. An electric motor, followed by a low rumble.

Harrow was back, had my elbow again. Steered me forward. Down steps. Sixty-two of them. The air grew chilly, slightly damp. I smelled metal, dust, age.

He left me again. One *clank*. The rumble again. Then he was pulling the blindfold off.

A tunnel stretched straight ahead, no discernible end in sight. I turned and saw that it also continued in the other direction. It was generally arch shaped, vertical rock walls roughly hewn out with the ceiling likewise rough but rounded. Conduits stretched along the ceiling, sprouting old metal-caged electric bulbs every twenty feet or so. On the floor of the tunnel, a pair of steel tracks, about the size of what you'd see on a roller coaster.

On the tracks right in front of us was a vehicle that reminded me of an overgrown golf cart. It had four rows of bench seats enclosed in a fiberglass body that was faded with age. I could tell its original color had been the same shade of blue that still graces Air Force One. A license plate on the back of it said LANCER. The rounded cowling on the front was emblazoned with the presidential seal.

Harrow said, "All aboard!" and got into the driver's seat. I sat beside him. He flipped a switch on the little dashboard and a weak glow shone from the front of the vehicle. He pressed the accelerator and we zipped forward with an electric whine. Three or four minutes later, we eased to a stop before a set of stairs that looked like the twin to the one on the other end. We got out and Harrow pushed a fat green button on the wall. I heard a whirring sound, looked down, and saw that the cart had stopped on a little turntable. It was rotating to point the cart back in the other direction.

Harrow pulled the blindfold from his pocket and reapplied it. *Clank.* Rumble. He grabbed my elbow and soon we were climbing steps. Sixty-two, just like on the other end. The air was still cool, but not as chilly as in the tunnel. I quietly sniffed, recognized the smell. We were in the giant cavern I'd discovered on my first night in the mountain. He walked me forward. Thirty steps. Left me there. "Be right back," he said.

I waited and heard one faint *clank*. Rumble. Then nothing. And more nothing. I counted off about three minutes in my head and pulled the blindfold off. Pure darkness. I said, "Lucian?"

No answer.

FBI HEADQUARTERS, DC

THE ATMOSPHERE in the Virtual Command Center was manic as the FBI's premier cybersleuths homed in on the source of the broadcast. The woman in charge still stood at her podium, watching the video wall, querying operators, issuing commands and demands.

"Got it!" the girl with lime-green hair said.

Podium said, "Talk to me, Candace."

Candace pushed back from her workstation. "Cheyenne Mountain."

"NORAD? Are you serious?"

"I don't know that it's NORAD," Candace said. "Whole lot of separate things going on over there. But it is coming from the Cheyenne Mountain complex."

"You're sure?"

Candace bobbed her head, green hair bouncing. "Oh yeah."

DAY 10

11:02 Pm Central

CHEYENNE MOUNTAIN

I DUG THROUGH MY BACKPACK, found my phone, powered it up. It had 16% power and three bars of service. Finally, I could communicate with the world, but first I wanted out of this mountain. I switched on the phone's flashlight and eventually made my way to the exit door for the cavern. What had this place been called on those diagrams I saw? The *Amphitheater*. I pulled the heavy door open and looked outside. Empty corridor. I pinned my contractor's badge to the front of my BDU shirt and stepped through the door, made a right, and started walking toward the hub that I knew would connect me back to the main body of the facility and eventually out.

Ten minutes later I stepped through the huge door that delineated the complex proper from the outside world. I had only to walk through the tunnel, the one I'd ridden a bus through when I arrived here, and I'd be out.

When I'd taken fifteen or twenty steps, two things happened simultaneously. Directly ahead of me, maybe fifty yards out, I saw someone looking straight my way through a pair of binoculars. All around me, a klaxon came to life that sounded like the signal for the end of the world. Red lights mounted in the tunnel's ceiling flashed, bathing the entire area in a bloody-looking wash with every flash. The person looking at me through the binoculars lowered them, then pivoted to say something to someone behind them. I saw F-B-I in huge yellow letters across the person's back.

I looked back the way I'd come. The giant door that would seal the facility was moving. Slowly, but definitely coming down. I looked forward again and FBI Jacket was pointing at me and shouting. *Sono-fabitch.* I turned around and ran toward the closing door. Soldiers—airmen, actually—were quickly forming a perimeter just inside that door. I ran faster.

Looked back over my shoulder. Jacket and his friends were running now. Toward me. Shouting, although I couldn't make out what they were saying over the screaming Klaxon of Doom.

Looking forward again. The gap in the door was at about six feet now and I was ten feet away. I ducked under it and was instantly met by three airmen wielding rifles. I grabbed my badge and held it out, remembering what an airman—Bozeman?—had said about it on my first day here. It was special, privileged.

The airmen looked at it, and one of them held up a handheld device and scanned my badge. The scanning device glowed green and beeped. The airmen parted.

"Come on, sir."

I moved through their cordon and trotted ten yards ahead. Looking back. The gap in the door was three feet now and Jacket was trying to come under it, screaming, "FBI! FBI!"

I heard an airman say, "No entry, sir! No entry!"

Now Jacket was trying to push his way under the door. Gap now at two feet. The airman who'd been saying "No entry" put his boot on Jacket's shoulder and pushed him back outside the door. The airman drew his foot back through. One-foot gap. Jacket was still screaming as the gap closed completely.

I'd lost Jacket and his buddies, but now I was sealed inside the mountain. Swell.

DAY 10

11:13 Pm Central

CHEYENNE MOUNTAIN

I MADE my way through the beehive atmosphere of the facility to General Harbuck's office and rapped my knuckles on the frame of the open door.

Harbuck looked up from his computer screen. "Sam! Where in hell have you been?"

"Drugged and abducted by our girl Sadie."

"Close the door," Harbuck said.

I pushed it shut and sat in the chair in front of his desk.

"I knew she was involved when she went AWOL at the same time you disappeared. Where'd they take you? How'd you get out?"

"General, did you watch the show tonight?"

"I saw pieces of it."

"That's where I was. Front-row seat. Do you know Lucian Harrow?"

"I do, for years. Can't believe he's doing this."

"After what he exposed tonight, what are your thoughts on what he's doing?"

"Thoughts?" Harbuck said. "My *thoughts* are that he's lost his damned mind."

I gave a little shrug.

"What? You disagree?"

"He's as sane as you or me, General."

Harbuck stared at me, his mouth open, eyes narrowed. "Did you play me? Have you been a part of this bullshit all along?"

I held up a hand. "I didn't play you, and I had nothing to do with it."

"But what, you've had a change of heart?"

"I think the country has a right to the information that was exposed tonight."

"Kidnapping? Shock treatments? You can't be serious."

"It's not a plan I would've come up with, but...well, it worked."

"We're a nation of laws, Sam. Not vigilante game shows."

I nodded. "True. But the chance that this information would've ever gotten to the public via our conventional system is nonexistent."

"Where is Harrow, this operation?"

"Sorry. In exchange for my release, I gave my word that I wouldn't be involved in pursuing him. By the way, Sadie is his daughter."

Harbuck stared at me, confusion on his face. "Didn't see that coming, but back to the issue." He dropped his head, slowly shook it side to side. "I trusted you, brought you in here to get to the bottom of this. Now you've betrayed my trust."

"Sorry you see it that way. I don't. Mind telling me why the mountain is scaled up?"

"Yes, I do mind. When the situation clears, I'll be turning you over to the FBI. Until then, I'm confining you to our little brig." He picked up the telephone receiver and pushed a button.

Well, hell. If it's not one thing, it's another. The thought of sitting in another jail cell, this time waiting to be railroaded as a terrorist, was unacceptable. I had to get in touch with Pitt and have him pull the levers of power to switch off this insanity. Instinct took over. I shot my hand out, yanked the receiver from him, put it back in its cradle. His eyes went wide. "I'm not going to be locked up, General."

"Tread carefully, Sam. You're about ten seconds from spending the next twenty years in Leavenworth." His hand was moving slowly toward a drawer on the right side of his desk.

I wagged a finger at him. "You're about three seconds from forcing me to hurt you. Put your hands on top of the desk where I can see them."

I WAS BACK in the cavern, the Amphitheater. It was a spot unlikely to draw visitors, at least until someone found Harbuck tied up and gagged in his office. I briefly considered retrieving the gun Harbuck had hidden for me when I first arrived at the mountain, but dismissed that idea. It's not like I was going to shoot my way out of a sealed mountain, or shoot American servicemembers at all except as a last resort. I instead went on a quick scavenger hunt. Thanks to my BDUs and my spiffy super-contractor badge that still worked, no one gave me a second glance as they scurried about. After striking out in a handful of offices, closets, and utility rooms, I found the items I needed and headed back to my giant lair. I switched on the little LED flashlight I'd found and walked to the right-hand wall that I knew to be the divider between this part of the mountain and COG CITY. Located the pipes and conduits that passed through the wall. Folded out the stepladder I'd commandeered and climbed up within reach of the pipes. Pulled my final piece of scavenger booty from my pocket, a pair of Vise-Grips. Started tapping on the largest of the pipes.

NEW INFORMATION ADDED TO BODY OF "EVIDENCE"

WASHINGTON, D.C. — Tonight's unprecedented broadcast that featured a "trial by electricity" implicated Washington power-players from senators, to a lobbyist, to the director of the FBI in schemes of corruption and sexual abuse of children. At the end of the broadcast a website was shared that contains what purports to be "evidence" of media bias and other alleged malfeasances.

Now that site has been updated with a list of additional people allegedly involved in sexual trafficking of children. According to the site, these additional names were provided by long-time Washington lobbyist Robert Hecht after his appearance in the broadcast. The new list includes 23 members of Congress, four upper-level members of the intelligence community, two governors, and numerous members of local, state, and federal law enforcement agencies.

Developing...

COG CITY

Lucian Harrow stood on the stage where the show had taken place and looked out at his in-house team, all thirty-six of whom he'd called to the meeting. "We knew it was only a matter of time before the FBI tracked us, and our sources there have just confirmed that they know we're in the mountain. We still have some time, since everyone who knows about COG CITY is in this room."

His lummox of a son-in-law, Anthony, said, "Except that asshole you let go."

Harrow saw Pam elbow him and shush him. What his daughter had ever seen in that loser was a mystery, but he did his best to tolerate the idiot for her sake, for family's sake. This was not a moment for tolerance, not a moment in which such dissent could be tolerated. He motioned to a pair of soldiers standing at the entrance to the room and said, "Put him in a cell."

Anthony jumped up. "Oh, hell no!"

The soldiers walked quickly toward him. Harrow said, "If he says another word or even looks like he might resist, Tase him."

Anthony stared at Harrow with his mouth hanging open, drew a breath to say something, then thought better of it. The soldiers reached him. Each took an arm and led him out of the room.

Harrow looked at Pam to see how she was taking it. She didn't seem surprised or flustered, even gave him a tight little smile. His girls made him proud. Back on track, he said, "We're now less than twenty-four hours away from the moment we've worked so hard to prepare for. Everything outside is proceeding according to plan. I know this sounds cryptic, and I appreciate all of you putting your trust in me. Compartmentalization has been necessary, but by this time tomorrow I will have brought everyone here up to speed with all the details. For now, I need all of you to stay focused. Do your jobs. Not for me. For your country. Let's get to work."

The crowd began filing out of the room. Harrow caught Pam's eye and gestured for her to join him. When she reached him, he pulled her into a hug. "I'm sorry, baby."

"I understand, Daddy. Really."

"Thank you." He kissed her on the forehead. "Why don't you grab Sadie and meet me in the diner for a quick bite?"

Pam nodded and left. Harrow sat down, placed his head in his hands, and began to pray. After several minutes, he left the room and made his way up the stairs and exited onto Main Street. He was halfway to the diner when one of the soldiers who had taken Anthony away came jogging up to him.

"Sir," the soldier said, "I need you to see—rather, *hear*—something."

"Lead the way."

Harrow followed the soldier down the street and into a Quonset hut with a sign that said UTILITIES. The interior was a maze of conduits, pipes, and breaker panels. He heard it as soon as he entered: a rhythmic clanging emanating from the pipes.

"Is that..."

"Yes, sir," the soldier said. "It's Morse code."

"Have you decoded it?"

The soldier nodded. "Two words repeating over and over: SAM. DEAL."

NBS STUDIOS BREACHED ON AIR

NEW YORK — A mob of protesters stormed NBS headquarters in Midtown minutes ago. While details of the beginnings of the event are scant at the moment, witnesses say several hundred angry protesters overpowered NYPD officers in front of the building, entered, and quickly subdued the private security guards inside before ascending to the floors housing NBS News studios using both elevators and stairways.

The subsequent events aired live, as the protesters stormed the studios and forcibly dragged newscasters off the sets. The broadcast went off the air briefly before being restored, by which time several of the attackers had taken the places of the ousted newscasters on set and begun ranting on camera about "the lying media."

Developing...

CHEYENNE MOUNTAIN

I SWITCHED the snow globe to the other hand and resumed tapping. Despite the alternation, both arms were exhausted from the overhead work. I tuned out the arm cramps by pondering what I was getting myself into. Until tying up and gagging General Harbuck, I'd been either acting under authorization or was a victim myself. Had I made a mistake? Should I have acquiesced to being locked up, then eventually turned over to the FBI as a fugitive for something I hadn't done? Pitt could have righted everything. Could he still? Should I go back to Harbuck and give myself up? Should I stop tapping on pipes and go find a phone, call Pitt, get him to extract me?

When I considered those options, a niggling in the back of my mind kept saying *no no no*. Pitt had gone dark on me, and could I trust him even when I did find him? Not necessarily. Pitt was a snake. Yeah, he'd always been a snake on my side, but a snake's still a snake.

Was my current plan of action any better? Would I end up on the run like a criminal? What would my daughter think? Who'd take care of Johnny if I disappeared? He was in good hands for the time being at the stables where I'd boarded him, but long term? I love that horse. And I still had to deal with the issue in the document I was still carrying in my pocket. No matter how many times I pulled it out and read it, it said the same thing. And now I was running out of time on it. My "time to act" window had arrived and would only last another day or two. I could hardly do that from jail.

After working through all these options, my decision came down to one thing. Hadn't Harrow done exactly what I'd done so many times around the world, getting the job done By Any Means? He'd gone way off the tracks to do so, but would any other approach have worked to expose those cockroaches? No. I was convinced Harrow was the good guy in this thing. I trusted him. More importantly, it was time to do what I'd always done to survive: Trust my own instincts. Listen to my Spidey sense. It said go back to COG CITY.

I decided to take a break for a couple minutes and descended the ladder. I was on the bottom rung when I heard a clanging on the pipes over my head. I listened, decoding the sequence in my head: S-T-A-N-D—B-Y.

Ten minutes later, I heard a muted version of the same grind I'd heard from the tunnel after Harrow re-blindfolded me and before he brought me up into the Amphitheater and left me here. I realized this was a point of no return with Harrow, as well. I was about to see the point of egress from the Cheyenne Mountain complex and the point of ingress into COG CITY. Once I was in again, there's no way he'd let me out with that knowledge.

The concrete floor vibrated, then started to move upward. I hopped off to the side, not wanting to be on the part that was rising. I saw that it was an entire section about fifty feet square, with the separation from the surrounding floor happening at what had looked like normal expansion cracks. The rising section looked to be six inches thick. I watched as the elevation continued and eventually stopped when the section was about ten feet above the surrounding floor. The bottom of the section was a massive steel plate supported by four steel columns near the corners that looked to be about a foot each in diameter. In the center was a row of hydraulic lift columns, their exposed steel shiny and damp with oil.

I looked down into the space beneath the false floor. Cool air drifted up from the space. A steel staircase had hinged down from the bottom of the floor, its foot resting on more concrete ten or twelve feet down. At the back of that space I could see a concrete stairway leading down in the direction of the tunnel that I knew led to COG CITY.

Footsteps now ascended that stairway, the footfalls quiet on the concrete. A few seconds later, two men came into view, General Harrow and a soldier in fatigues I'd seen in the "courtroom." They crossed the lower floor, looked up, spotted me. Harrow nodded to me and the two men climbed to where I was and stepped out from under the elevated floor. Both men's eyes flicked all around the space. Harrow had a sidearm, a Sig 9mm, in a hip holster. His companion held an M4 at the ready.

Harrow extended a hand and we shook. "Got your message," he said.

"The FBI's outside the mountain, waiting to take me into custody on bogus charges. Harbuck intended to turn me over to them when the mountain opened. I'd appreciate asylum from that until I can get it worked out."

"And what do I get in return?"

"What do you want?"

Harrow looked me in the eye for a long time, nibbling on his bottom lip. Finally he said, "The main thrust of our operation begins tomorrow and I'd love to have an operator like you on standby for any contingencies."

"What's the op?"

He shook his head. "You commit to doing what I ask tomorrow, and I'll fill you in completely. You'll be safe from the FBI with us until then."

"And after tomorrow?"

"One day at a time, Sam. One day at a time."

HOUSTON

SHEILA VASQUEZ PACED the dingy hotel room with the burner phone to her ear. She'd just dialed Sam's phone for the umpteenth time and it was ringing. She was so shocked when he answered that she almost dropped the phone.

SV: Sam?

SF: Sheila?

SV: Where are you? I've been trying to reach you forever!

SF: Long story. You go first.

SV: Holed up in a roach motel in H-town. I slipped away from the FBI when they were trashing the office.

SF: So you're on the run?

SV: Affirmative, but I've been working and I have some bad news.

SF: That should fit right in. What is it?

SV: Have you spoken with Pitt?

SF: No, he's gone dark on me. You?

SV: Same. Listen, I've reached out to almost everyone I know in the squad. They've all gone dark except one, a guy I dated for a while. I haven't seen him in a couple years but he claims the squad was shut completely down about a year ago. Says Pitt has been running his own operation without sanction, using money he stashed away from agency funds and old contacts he has around the government who owe him, or he has something on them, whatever. I think Pitt's on the run, too. And that means—

SF: —that you and I have been hung out to dry.

SV: Yeah.

SF: Damn, damn, damn. Why the hell would he do this? If there's no agency, why'd he have us looking for Sol?

SV: I don't know. I thought it was all on the level, Sam. I worked from home most of the time, talked to Pitt when I needed to, had no idea our outfit was defunct. My paychecks kept coming, so I figured everything was square. Sorry to break all this to you.

SF: Not your fault. Do you have a plan?

SV: No, and I'm scared shitless. What should I do?

SF: Let me see if there's anything I can do. I'll call you back at oh-two-hundred. I see this is a different number for you. Burner?

SV: Yeah.

SF: Good thinking, but now that you're talking to me on my regular phone, the bureau is probably headed your way. You need to change locations and pull the SIM card and battery from your phone. Power it back up at oh-one-fifty-nine.

SV: Okay, I will.

SF: Talk to you then.

DAY 11

01:03 Am Central

COG CITY

I ENDED the call with Sheila and slid my phone back into my pocket. My earlier qualms about her were gone. I was relieved that I hadn't made the tragic mistake of turning myself in and counting on Pitt to fix things. What in the world was he pulling? I stood and turned the new information over in my head and relief quickly turned to dread as I realized that even though I wasn't in jail at the moment, there would likely be no fixing things by Pitt whenever my time here was done. I was a fugitive. I pictured myself explaining to the FBI that I hadn't really done anything wrong, that I worked for a government agency so secret that no one knew it existed. Saw them laughing as they slammed the cell door.

With the phone call done, I walked back into Harrow's office. Sat down and told him what I'd just learned.

"Not surprised," he said. "I didn't know much about your outfit until I met Sol a couple years ago. With his help I managed to get hold of a few personnel files a while back, including yours. But as for Pitt?

He's been slinking around the shadows for a long time. I've met him. Never trusted him."

"I just can't figure what he's up to."

"Talk to Sol. See if he has any ideas."

"Good idea," I said. "Now how about you fill me in on tomorrow's operation?"

He did, and I realized my life was never going to be the same.

WHEN I FINISHED WITH HARROW, I went looking for Sol. Eventually found him in the diner drinking coffee. No one was working the place at that hour but he said it was always unlocked and stocked if anyone wanted to cook and serve themselves. I poured myself a cup and settled in at the counter beside Sol. I filled him in on the situation with the BAM squad and Pitt, as I had done with Harrow. Then I said, "Sol, you have any idea what that snake might be up to?"

He tipped his coffee cup, loosing a small puddle of coffee into the saucer. Picked up the saucer and slurped the coffee from its edge. I hadn't seen anyone do that since my grandfather when I was a kid. Finally, he said, "Hard to figure. He looked you up specifically to look for me?"

I nodded. "He had you on video abducting Acoma. Said it was too dangerous to have a former BAMmer running wild."

Sol chuckled. "Running wild, like a jungle animal?"

"That's about how he portrayed it."

He tipped and slurped again. "What makes more sense to me is that he found out about this operation and wanted to kill it. And he brought you to the mountain, didn't he?"

"Met me in town, introduced me to Harbuck, so not to the mountain proper, but..."

"He knows where you are," Sol said.

"Or at least where he last saw me. And knew I was here to look for you."

Sol nodded. Tipped. Slurped. Pursed his lips in thought. "That's not good. He can't get in here, not into the city, but I don't like the idea of him slithering around anywhere nearby. Especially right now. You have his phone number, right?"

"I do, but he's not answering."

"We don't want to talk to his ass, just find out where he is. Let's go."

WE WERE in a room I definitely hadn't seen during my earlier stay in COG CITY. It was a technofreak's dream, made me feel better just being there. Whereas everything else in "the city" looked old and dated, this subterranean chamber was a state-of-the-art command center. It made the swanky center Harbuck had shown me next door look quaint by comparison.

The room—more accurately, it was a rock-walled chamber—was filled with racks of servers, a long arc of computer workstations, and more video screens on the walls than I'd ever seen in one spot. Most of the workstations were manned, the people working quietly. The only sounds in the room were circulating air and the quiet tapping of keyboards.

Sol led me to an unused workstation on one end of the arc. "Have at it," he said.

I sat down, wiggled the mouse, and the screen came to life on a login prompt.

"Use my credentials," he said. "I rarely do. Tech's not my thing." He recited a username and password.

I entered them and a screen appeared stacked full of options on where to go next. I scanned them, my eyes no doubt growing wider the more I looked. I spotted one that said SIGINT-NSA and clicked it. My heart raced as I looked over the next menu of nerd-candy. I could sit here and play for a week if I were the creepy stalker type. I clicked PHONE LOCATE and a simple prompt appeared asking for a phone number. I input Pitt's cell phone number and clicked OK.

A map appeared, first at the United States level, then progressively zooming in until a red crosshair indicator came to rest on Colorado Springs. I found a big plus-sign and started clicking it, zooming in with ever more precision. When the map was at a level showing only a

couple city blocks on the screen, a message flashed that said
MAXIMUM PRECISION. I looked through the options on the right side
of the screen and found a list of overlay options. I clicked BUSINESSES,
and the names of restaurants and stores started populating the map.

Two seconds later, text appeared above the crosshair that said
MOUNTAIN SLUMBER HOTEL. I said, "Hello, Mr. Pitt."

DAY 11

01:51 Am Central

COG CITY

As part of our deal, Harrow had already assured me he would have my daughter picked up and brought in, along with Abby if she'd come willingly. They would both be told that I'd sent for them for their own safety. If Abby wouldn't come voluntarily, that would be unfortunate, but I'd made a decision not to fret over it. She was grown and could make her own decision. Just like she'd decided to leave me years earlier. Just like she'd decided to get my hopes up days earlier, only to shut that down. Ally's retrieval, however, was not optional. Ally was to be brought here, willing or not.

I made clear that her extraction was to be as non-traumatic as possible, and to increase the likelihood of that, I gave them the codeword that only she and I knew, which would let her know I had sent these guys.

I thought about calling them to let them know someone would be coming but that would lead to a flood of questions I couldn't answer.

Now I had to get Harrow to agree to let me bring Sheila inside. It was a tough sell but he eventually relented. Sol showed me a stash of burner phones kept on hand in COG CITY and I grabbed two of them. Since the FBI knew where I was and were waiting outside, I was hoping they weren't watching the jet. Pacing the sidewalk of Main Street while Sol waited on a street bench, I used one of the burners to dial the pilot. How the astronomical bill for the airplane and pilot was going to get paid if Pitt was in the wind, I had no idea and didn't really care. Pitt set all that up, not me.

The pilot answered and I said, "This is Sam. You still on standby here in Colorado Springs?"

"Yes, sir."

"How soon can you take off?"

"Fifteen minutes."

"Go to West Houston Airport near Katy, Texas. You'll be picking up a woman named Sheila Vasquez. She'll be waiting for you. Bring her back here."

"Roger that."

I thanked him and ended the call, then pulled the SIM card and battery from the burner. At straight-up two AM, I used the second burner to dial Sheila's burner.

She answered on the first ring. "Sam?"

"Sheila, hang up, kill the phone like you did before, and make your way to West Houston Airport near Katy. Our pilot's on the way to pick you up and bring you to me."

"Oh gosh, thank you, thank you."

"No problem. He should be there in under three hours, so be sure you're there and ready to go."

"Oh, I will be. Thank you so much, Sam."

"See you soon, bye." I ended the call and killed the phone. Walked back over to where Sol was relaxing on the bench. "I need to have a quick word with Harrow. Be back soon."

Sol gave me a thumbs-up.

I made my way to Harrow's office and knocked on the door.

"Come in."

Once inside, I closed the door and took a seat in front of Harrow's desk. "I have one more favor to ask." I pulled out the document I'd been carrying around in my pocket since the day Pitt barged into my life and handed it to him.

After he read it, he looked up. "Your time is short. Day after tomorrow."

I nodded.

"Bad timing for something like this, Sam, and that's the understatement of the century."

"Understood, but this is something I have to take care of. Can you help?"

He nibbled on his bottom lip, his thinking tell. After a minute he blew up a long breath and flapped the document in his hand. "Leave it with me. I'll handle it."

"Much appreciated," I said.

"It should be. And you dang well better be worth all this. I don't think I've ever gone this far out on a limb for someone who has yet to make a contribution. I'm trusting my instincts."

"Your instincts are solid," I said. I stood, shook his hand, and left.

After arriving back on Main Street, I found Sol still sitting on the bench. He said, "What say we go pay Bartholomew Pitt a visit?"

"How? The mountain's sealed." As soon as the words left my mouth, an image popped into my head of the ingress/egress tunnel that went not only toward the Cheyenne Mountain main facility, but also in the other direction. Alternate route. I should've figured that out long ago. There was no way all the people in COG CITY were surreptitiously coming and going through the main facility and the bulky secret access in the Amphitheater.

Sol grinned. "You figured it out, huh?"

I nodded.

"Come on," he said, standing up. "The general's cleared you for access to the main entrance."

We made our way down into and through the presidential suite, then into the tunnel. Boarded the little retro electric cart and headed west, away from COG CITY and in the opposite direction of the main Cheyenne Mountain facility. After a few minutes, we arrived in a mammoth space that doubled as a garage and a hangar. Like the other big spaces I'd encountered, the walls and ceiling were rock. To our right sat an assortment of vehicles, everything from Humvees to old Willys Jeeps, along with a few nondescript sedans and SUVs. The left side of the cave held three Black Hawks armed to the teeth.

"Let's grab some gear, just in case," Sol said. I followed him to a dark caged area behind the vehicles, where he entered a code that popped open the gate. We stepped into the space and lights flickered on.

"Oh, hell yes," I said, looking around at a fantasy of an armory.

Sol said, "Pick what you want."

After looking over the inventory of sidearms, I chose a Kimber 1911 .45, a suppressor, and a handful of extended magazines that were already topped off. I finished off the rig with a holster that had a loop on the side for the suppressor. Moving over to a rack full of optics, I grabbed a night-vision goggle and a compact pair of binoculars.

"I'm set," I said.

"Me too."

DAY 11

02:40 Am Central

COLORADO SPRINGS

AFTER LEAVING the mountain via a hidden exit that I can only describe as a real-life take on the Bat Cave, we drove to the Mountain Slumber Hotel and parked our SUV in a lot that ran along the front of the building. The place looked like a typical low-end tourist outfit. Motel, not hotel. Two story, rooms that opened directly to the outdoors. Some rustic trim thrown up on the thirty-year-old structure, an antler chandelier covered in cobwebs hanging in the small porte cochere.

I pulled a tablet from a small bag I'd brought with me and brought it to life. It gave me remote control of the workstation back in COG CITY that had the tracking info on it for Pitt's phone. Before leaving the futuristic tech center I'd started an NSA app running that would attempt to infiltrate the phone and provide me more detailed info from its innards. A badge now hovered above the phone number: ACCESS SUCCESSFUL. ADDITIONAL PRECISION NOW AVAILABLE.

After I touched the option for SATELLITE, an overlay showing the motel structure painted itself on top of the geographical map. I zoomed the map and this time it went all the way into a view of the motel that filled the screen. The little crosshair marker for Pitt's phone was now at the far right end of the motel on the back side. I handed the tablet to Sol and cranked the SUV. Drove left, through the porte cochere, and continued around the left side of the motel. Once we were on the back side, I drove slowly as I approached the far end. We got lucky.

There was only one vehicle anywhere near the area where Pitt's phone was supposed to be, and it was directly in front of the last room, backed into its parking space. Light glowed through curtains above an air-conditioning unit that extended onto the ground-floor balcony. I parked broadside to the sedan parked in front of the room, blocking it from leaving, then killed the engine.

With eyes darting frequently toward the room, we prepared, fitting the suppressors onto our weapons, verifying rounds in the chambers. We wouldn't need the night-vision goggles and left them on the back seat. It was also obvious that we wouldn't need the battering ram we'd brought. The eight-pound handheld sledgehammer would be plenty. I motioned for Sol to take it and he did.

We got out of the SUV and approached the door, me on the left, Sol on the right. I stayed back about six feet with the Kimber lined up for a headshot if need be. Sol stood with his back to the wall, between the door and the window. I nodded. With his sidearm in his left hand, he reached over with the sledgehammer in his right hand and rapped on the door with the handle of the hammer.

No response at the door. No indication of motion inside based on the backlit curtains over the window. He rapped again. Still nothing. One more time. Same result. We had the tools to pick the lock but that was too slow and gave the occupant of the room too much warning of our entry. The sledgehammer was the better option. I nodded again and Sol stepped to the door, facing it and standing off center to the left. I moved right, keeping my sights on where a head should appear if the door suddenly opened.

Using my left hand, I gave Sol a countdown with three fingers, then two. He drew the sledgehammer back. I closed my fist and he drove the steel head of the hammer into the door between the doorknob and the doorjamb. Wood cracked and the door moved a couple inches into the room. He dropped the hammer and I said, "Go!"

Sol moved in first, sweeping right. I was right on his tail, looking left, Kimber extended and ready. The room was empty. At the rear of the room through a four-foot opening was a bathroom vanity with a mirror over it. We moved side by side to that opening. To the right was the bathroom. We lowered our guns because we wouldn't be needing them. Bart Pitt was sitting on the toilet, pants around his ankles, head flopped back against the wall. Eyes open and staring at the ceiling. A purple hole in the middle of his forehead topped a thin trail of dried blood that stretched to the tip of his nose. Bartholomew Pitt was quite dead.

DAY 11

03:15 Am Central

COLORADO SPRINGS

AFTER I COLLECTED everything of Pitt's I could find in his room, notably including his phone, I drove us back to the mountain. I wanted to see how much of a presence the FBI had outside the Cheyenne Mountain entrance, so I took the long route back instead of going straight to the Bat Cave.

The entrance to the mountain was swarming with law enforcement. Red and blue strobes popped from so many cars, SUVs, and military-looking vehicles that the area looked to be in slow-motion like a strobed dance floor.

"This isn't about me," I said. "They've figured out the show was broadcast from here."

Sol nodded. "Concur."

"What's the chance they get into COG CITY?"

"Nil."

"You sure about that?"

He nodded again. "The tunnels have defensive measures, fail-safe doors that can be activated to seal off the city behind foot-thick slabs of iron."

"We should get back and be sure Harrow's aware of this," I said. "In case he wants to activate those fail-safes."

BACK INSIDE, we alerted Harrow to the commotion outside the mountain. He thanked us but said he already knew and would launch contingencies if warranted.

I went to my little room and tried to use my laptop to do a forensic download of Pitt's phone. It was locked and I didn't have the device with me that I needed to defeat the passcode. I went back down to the futuristic control center I'd visited earlier and logged into the same workstation that had shown us Pitt's location. After a bit of digging through the myriad tools available, I found an option that said CAPTURE DEVICE. A submenu offered choices of PHONE, COMPUTER, and OTHER. I chose PHONE and was met with a prompt asking for the phone number. I entered the number for Pitt's phone. The dialog responded with DEVICE LOCATED and a tiny icon of a ticking clock. Two minutes later, the dialog changed to DEVICE IDENTIFIED, SAMSUNG GALAXY 14, VERIZON, along with the serial number and IMEI for the phone. A new prompt asked me to CHOOSE ACQUISITION METHOD, with the available choices UFED, TAR, and LIVE MIRROR.

I selected UFED, the file format created by Cellebrite, the dominant tool in the forensic industry for forensic captures of phone data, which was installed on my laptop. The system never prompted for a passcode. A progress meter appeared, estimating time remaining at eighteen minutes. I looked at Pitt's phone. There was no sign that any activity was underway. While I was elated to get access to Pitt's locked phone, I was just as terrified by a tool that made it this easy for the government to suck everything out of a person's phone without so much as a hiccup. There's no way this system wasn't being abused to hell and back.

While I waited, I logged onto a public flight-tracking site and input the tail number of the private jet I'd sent for Sheila. It looked to be about an hour from landing and picking her up. After taking a restroom break and brewing a cup of coffee from a pod, I returned to the workstation. The acquisition of the phone data was complete. The system asked me where to save the UFED file and I pathed it to a flash drive I plugged into the workstation. With that in hand, I found an empty desk in a corner, fired up my laptop, and loaded up the data.

The first thing I checked was the date and time of the last user activity on the device, which was a call Pitt placed to a DC area code the previous day. I looked through the call log and saw that he had called this same number dozens of times over the past month. A web search for the phone number yielded nothing so I bounced back into the nifty NSA toolset and entered the number. Nothing. I was so surprised by this that I conducted the same search against numerous other numbers in his call log, as well as numbers from my own call history and a dozen or so random numbers. Every one of them yielded detailed information, including the owner of the phone account, carrier, cell tower data, and more. Only that one number was a strike. My Spidey senses tingled and I smiled as I formed a plan. Thirty minutes later, I clicked an icon that said RUN SCRIPT. Time to get some sleep.

WHITE HOUSE: STATE OF THE UNION SPEECH STILL ON FOR TONIGHT

WASHINGTON, DC - In a statement issued by the White House this morning, President Cartwright said "It is more urgent than ever that the people of the nation hear from their government in this troubling time. For that reason, I will deliver tonight's State of the Union speech as planned."

Reporters spoke with Vice President Sarah Houghton as she was leaving the White House. Miss Houghton, the first woman vice president and a former U.S. Navy SEAL, said the president told her the speech would be "extensively modified" to address the current crisis. When asked about her thoughts on the president's declaration of martial law, she declined to comment.

Tonight's speech will take place in the House of Representative chamber as usual, although the public galleries will be closed in reflection of the nationwide curfew that will be in effect at the time of the speech. Most members of congress have remained in town and are invited to attend, with security escorts to be provided them by a joint effort of the military, Secret Service, and Capital Police.

DAY 11

1:13 Pm Central

COG CITY

AFTER A FEW HOURS' sleep I'd taken Harrow's suggestion and spent the morning reading news articles, watching news highlights, and browsing social media on everything from political spats to the culture war to crime and foreign policy. The more I saw, the more I felt like an ass for becoming so detached from what was going on. For years, I had retreated into my own world where I worked my forensic cases, saw my daughter as often as I could, and spent the rest of the time in solitude with Johnny in woods and fields, tuning out the world. That was a mistake.

While I had my head up my butt, the country had been falling apart. I'm not a political creature, mainly because I have so little respect for politicians of any stripe. My experience is that most of them lie, cheat, and have only one real goal, that being to keep themselves in power. That said, my own personal beliefs and values lean heavily conservative. Common sense. Law and order. Freedom to practice my Christian faith as I see fit. Self-sufficiency. Traditional patriotism.

As I looked through social media, I had a tough time wrapping my head around the vitriolic hatred on display from the left side of the political and cultural spectrum. Any deviation from or disagreement with their long list of ever-shifting pet causes and favored groups was not just verboten, but demanded instant destruction. Over and over I saw threads in which innocuous comments resulted in warlike attacks on the "guilty" party. People were fired, blackballed, turned into social pariahs for the grave sin of expressing an opinion.

In a real mind boggle, this strict insistence on pure compliance with no dissent allowed was pure authoritarianism, yet those who espoused this ideology hurled invectives like "fascist!" and "Nazi!" at anyone who didn't toe the line. Black-clad, masked gangs of thugs who call themselves Antifa, or "anti-fascist," were living examples of a fascist mind-set but showed zero self-awareness. In cities controlled by the left, like the major metros of the West Coast, these lawless throngs apparently roamed the streets with impunity, violently descending on people who dared to wear the wrong clothing or who simply *looked* like they might not be thinking the right thing. Police in Seattle, Portland, and others seem to give them free rein, allowing them to block traffic on city streets, shut down interstates, and run wild in riots of destruction. How in actual hell was this going on in the United States of America?

Then there were the news media. Yes, I'd seen a taste of the bias exposed when Acoma was in the Hot Seat getting lit up every time he lied, but I had no clue how pervasive it was. Aside from a handful of alternative, relatively minor outlets, the entire industry had turned into one big far-left propaganda machine. Misdeeds by liberals and progressives were either ignored or dismissed as "conspiracy theories spread by angry conservatives." Scandals were declared "debunked" despite it being obvious that not an iota of investigation of the issues had ever been undertaken. Conversely, the slightest misstep by a conservative was trumpeted twenty-four hours a day with breathless gravitas and automatic assumption of guilt.

While I had committed to helping Harrow and would uphold my word, it was an understatement to say I had misgivings about what he was planning. The more I looked at the state of the nation, however, the more I came to believe that Harrow was right. There was only one way out.

DAY 11

7:35 Pm Eastern

THE WHITE HOUSE
WASHINGTON, DC

My life has afforded me a lot of unexpected situations but none to rival where I now found myself. Less than two weeks ago I'd been standing in my pasture. Contentedly so. Now I was walking into the Oval Office, where I found myself alone with the president of the United States. How did I get here?

President John Cartwright stood from behind the Resolute Desk, walked to me, and shook my hand. "Thank you for coming, Sam." He sat down on a sofa and gestured for me to do the same.

I did, and turned at an angle like he had so I could look him in the eye. "You're welcome, Mr. President."

"I've known Lucian Harrow for more than thirty years, and I've never seen anyone win him over as quickly as you did. How did you do that?"

"Can't say I have an answer for that, sir. I gave him my word and he accepted it."

"Did he make the right move?"

"I don't break my word. You should also know that, while I will carry out my mission tonight successfully or die trying, an assignment like this is completely outside my historical wheelhouse."

He looked me in the eye a good fifteen seconds without saying anything, then gave a curt nod. "Let's get to it."

I opened the small briefcase I'd carried in and extracted a document that contained a list of every Secret Service agent who would be around him tonight. Handed it to him. "Sir, look this over carefully. Is there anyone on there you *don't* trust without reservation?"

He took his time scanning the list. After three or four minutes, he pulled a pen from his pocket, checked three names on the list, and handed it back to me.

I looked it over. "Can you elaborate on why you chose these, starting with..." I looked down at the list. "Michael Perera?" My phone vibrated three staccato bursts in my pocket. I ignored it.

"We suspected he leaked information to the press, something he overheard during a meeting. Couldn't prove it, so we couldn't fire him or charge him, but he was booted off my primary detail. He's only on the list for tonight because we've basically called in everybody. Due to the situation."

I wrote LEAK beside Perera's name. "Leo McLaughlin?"

"Too buddied up to my predecessor, who has done everything he could to undermine me since he left this office and I walked in. Same story. Not on my primary detail but called in for tonight."

I wrote POLITICAL beside McLaughlin's name. "Timothy Alexander?"

"I have absolutely nothing to go on with him except my gut. The man has dead eyes, like a machine."

I nodded. "Nothing wrong with instinct. I rely on my Spidey senses all the time."

He chuckled. "Marvel fan, huh?"

"Indeed, sir." I drew a little Spiderman symbol alongside Alexander's name. "Anything else you want to tell me about anyone or anything?"

"I know Lucian has filled you in on what's going to happen tonight.

Just know that things could get unpredictable in a hurry. Nothing like this has ever happened in this country. Be ready."

"Count on it. Unless something critical draws me away, I'll never be more than ten feet from you, and don't worry, I'll stay out of the camera's view. Not my thing," I said with a smile.

He returned a tight smile. I reached into the briefcase, retrieved a black button the size of a half-dollar, handed it to him. I said, "Please put that in in one of your pants pockets, nothing else in there."

After looking it over, he rotated on the sofa enough to slip it into his right pocket.

I held up a similar device. Mine had a red button on it. I pushed it. When the disk in his pocket vibrated he jerked a bit and said, "Can't miss that."

"That's the idea. If you feel that, *immediately* get down and look to me for further instructions. Not your Secret Service. Me, because if I press this button, I see something they don't."

"Understood."

It hit me again that I was really sitting in the Oval Office, giving instructions to the most powerful man on Earth. How the hell do I get into such situations? I jerked my mind back on target. I said, "That's all I have." Then I remembered it wasn't all I had. "I hate to mention this but—"

He held up his left hand, palm facing me. Reached inside his suit jacket with the right, pulled out a folded piece of paper and handed it to me. I put it in the briefcase.

"Thank you, sir."

A light knock sounded on the door. The president said, "Come in."

The door opened and Secret Service agent Laura Drew, the head of Cartwright's primary detail, stuck her head in. I'd memorized all the agents' faces on the flight to DC but hers was easy since she was the only woman on the list for tonight. She said, "Time to go, Mr. President."

My phone buzzed my leg three times again. I ignored it again.

Cartwright turned to me and said, "Shall we?"

I nodded, closed my briefcase, and stood. Agent Drew was giving me the evil eye but before she could say anything Cartwright said,

"Laura, this is my friend Sam Flatt. He'll be joining me tonight as something of a special assistant. He has free rein and full authority."

Her face crinkled, her lips parted. "Sir, I—"

"Free rein. Full authority."

She closed her mouth and gave a curt nod. "Yes, sir."

He headed out of the office and I followed. As we passed Agent
Drew, her eyes met mine and they weren't friendly. I couldn't blame
her. These people live by rigorous routine and unflinching discipline.
At the last minute, a stranger had been thrown in on top of them.
When we crossed the threshold out of the office, she fell in behind us.
Two more agents materialized, speaking into their wrist mics and
leading our little procession.

It had been years since I'd been on any kind of official mission and
this one was the first ever of its kind. Doubts started creeping in, not
just about whether I should be assuming such a massive responsibility,
but also whether I was really going to partake in the events ahead. I
chased the doubts back, put them in a lockbox. It was almost
showtime.

DAY 11
6:50 Pm Central

COG CITY

GENERAL HARROW STRODE from workstation to workstation in COG CITY's high-tech control center, looking over shoulders, asking for status reports. The screens on the front wall of the center were all in action, bathing the dimly lit room in alternating flashes of color and shadow.

He stopped at a console labeled MILCOM, one of several new designations created for this unique operation. Dropped to a knee to be eye to eye with the young male soldier manning it. "Latest?"

"Active contact with all sectors, sir. All encrypted. Situational telemetry coming in from all. Reliable verbal links with all except one."

"Which one?" Harrow said.

"DC sector."

"What's the nature of the...lack of reliability?"

"Commanding officer not answering. Second-in-command keeps saying he's not available."

Harrow's face tightened, his lips drawing into a thin line. "Let me know the moment that changes."

"Yes, sir."

Harrow rose. Stopped next at MARLAW. Dropped to eye level. "How are the cities looking?"

A female soldier this time. "Largely compliant, sir. A few hot spots in the expected places. South side of Chicago. South Central LA. Memphis. Detroit. Baltimore."

"Gang nests."

The soldier nodded. "Affirmative, sir."

"Send those hot spots to MILCOM."

"Yes, sir."

Harrow returned to MILCOM. "Contact Chicago, LA, Memphis, and Detroit. I want our concentrations doubled in the hot spots you're getting from MARLAW. Tell them to pull personnel out of the quietest areas, probably the suburbs, to meet that need."

The soldier nodded.

Harrow stood, checked the time on a digital clock on the front wall, then walked to a workstation at the front of the room that was manned by Wilson. "Put the House chamber on the main display. Direct feed from the pool cameras."

"You got it," Wilson said as he clicked around his screen. Moments later, a live shot of the House of Representatives chamber filled the largest screen on the wall. "Audio?"

"Turn it up." Harrow then turned to the room and spoke loudly. "All monitoring personnel prepare. I want real-time updates of any anomalies on the wall as this develops."

Crisp acknowledgments of "yes, sir" sounded around the room. Harrow told Wilson, "Right third of the wall devoted to those updates."

Wilson nodded. "Ready to go."

The audio level of the House feed rose in the command center. No commentator blab, just the murmur of the room as hundreds of politicians ran their mouths among each other.

Harrow walked to his position at the front of the room and took a seat on a stool at a raised dais. Turned to face the front wall and its conglomeration of screens. "Not long now," he said to himself.

DAY 11

7:59 Pm Eastern

US CAPITOL
WASHINGTON, DC

OUR LITTLE CLUSTER stood in front of the massive wood doors, waiting. I was dressed in a suit just like the army of Secret Service agents deployed around us and around the chamber we were about to enter. I also wore one of their earpieces in my left ear, along with a wrist mic, that tied me into their comms. I'd hear everything the agents said among themselves and could talk back if necessary. The president was directly in front of me.

Through the doors I heard the traditional announcement booming from the audio system in the room ahead. "Ladies and gentlemen, the president of the United States!" The doors opened and the president stepped through.

My phone buzzed three times in my pocket, as it had every five minutes since I started my script running back in COG CITY, telling me that Pitt's phone was dialing the mystery number that even the NSA couldn't identify. After starting the script and getting a bit of sleep, I'd spent the entire time I was in COG CITY before leaving for DC walking around, mingling among everyone I could find in the facility, watching and listening for any sign that someone in the city was holding the mystery phone Pitt had been communicating with so much. I saw and heard nothing.

I'd also kept my eyes and ears open since arriving in DC, still coming up empty. The script had just moved into its second phase. I knew the president's speech would be the critical turning point in this thing and had set the script, starting at 8:00 PM DC time, to not only call the mystery phone every five minutes, but to send a text if the call wasn't answered: "URGENT! 911! CALL ME NOW!" Everything was duplicated to the phone in my pocket. If someone actually answered the mystery phone, I'd get five quick buzzes and be able to listen in to the answering phone via a tiny Bluetooth bud in my right ear. If the mystery user answered via text, seven buzzes and my phone would read the text into my right ear. If the mystery user didn't answer the call and didn't respond by text, the next text sent to them would be more emphatic, ratcheting up the tension and demand with each cycle.

Agent Laura Drew was right on the president's right hip, a foot behind him, as we moved into the room. Compared to the handful of State of the Union speeches I'd watched in the past, the room was subdued, the applause present but not uproarious. No cheering, whistling. The room was in a serious mood, just like the rest of the country.

The Secret Service chatter lit up, constant updates and check-ins as BONANZA moved into the room and started shaking hands with those lining the entry aisle as he made his way to the front of the room. Trusting that the Secret Service would spot and handle any external threats, I watched the Secret Service agents themselves, especially the ones identified to me by Cartwright in the Oval Office.

I spotted Perera dead ahead, waiting near the front of the aisle at the area where Cartwright would leave the aisle and make his way up onto the dais. I'd already seen McLaughlin and knew he was one of a pair of agents monitoring the corridor outside the chamber, the area we had just left. I couldn't see anything to our left or right, just the standing crowds of congresspeople. The trek up the aisle continued, the din gradually dying down the closer we got to the end of the aisle.

When we reached the front and the president started making his way around the left side and up onto the dais, the room grew quiet. The lead agent, Laura Drew, went right, as did Perera. I looked left as I followed the president and saw agents at the edge of the room, including Tim Alexander, the one Cartwright said had dead eyes. I now knew where all three of the agents of interest were. I was ten feet behind the president. When he reached the Speaker's podium, I stopped, staying just off the dais on the left side, which put me about fifteen feet to his right side, just out of view of the main camera that would stay on him during the speech. I liked the location because it also put me between Dead-Eye Alexander and the president. Drew positioned herself similarly on the right side of the dais.

Cartwright went into the standard opening, greeting the attendees in the chamber and his fellow Americans wherever they may be, blah yada yada. It was underway, and it was certain to be a speech never forgotten.

DAY 11

8:05 Pm Eastern

US CAPITOL
WASHINGTON, DC

PRESIDENT CARTWRIGHT WAS on target with Agent Alexander. The man had dead eyes, and more than once when I looked his way he had them locked on me. I gave it right back. Kept my head on a swivel as the president wrapped up his intro and motored into the real message. I noticed that there were no teleprompters; he was looking at paper on the podium. *Buzz-buzz-buzz* in my pocket.

"My fellow Americans, the conventional thing for me to say in this address is that 'the state of our union is *strong*.' That would be a lie tonight. The state of our union is *fractured*. The state of the United States is...*divided*."

Cartwright paused as a shock-murmur rippled through the room. I glanced out at the gaggle of congresscritters and saw bugged-out eyes and open mouths everywhere I looked. The murmur faded and he continued.

"We are beyond platitudes and sound bites. As the first president elected as an independent since George Washington, I came into this office with a sincere desire to bridge the chasm between left and right. I have worked day and night toward that goal. I have made good-faith efforts to work with both parties, to compromise, to find middle ground that would benefit all Americans. It breaks my heart to say that I have failed, but it gives me at least some personal solace to say that the failure was not of my making."

More murmur, although it died quicker this time.

"While both sides of the aisle," Cartwright said, pausing to gesture toward the divided room with both hands, "have shown plenty of intransigence, honesty compels me to say that the Republicans have made far more of an effort to cooperate.

"The Democrats, both those in this room and those across the country who join us electronically tonight, have turned into a mono-lithic force of obstruction, hell-bent on destroying anyone who disagrees with them on anything. Determined to stamp out not only policy differences, but even dissenting speech and, in some cases, even attempting to divine and punish 'wrong-think.' Today's left rejects the results of elections they lose. They protest endlessly, clogging our cities with lawless and, in too many instances, violent behavior toward their fellow Americans whom they perceive as less than human. There is a word for this behavior: fascism."

Applause and cheers erupted from the GOP section of the room, countered by boos from the Democrats, but the president quelled it as soon as it started by raising a hand for quiet. I checked left and right, checking on Agents Alexander and Perera. Both were scanning the room as they should have been.

"We've all seen last night's unconventional broadcast. Many have referred to it as barbaric, and that may be a fair criticism, but the results were of far greater concern to this nation than any suffering endured by the 'interviewees.' As that bizarre event unfolded, some-thing became clear that many of us have long suspected—known in our hearts. Our government is broken, rotten to the core. Our popula-tion is hopelessly divided, irrevocably so."

I'd never been in a place with a crowd of people that went as quiet as the chamber did at that moment. The shock and growing discomfort was palpable, charging the atmosphere of the room like static electricity. He turned so that he faced straight-on to the Democrat side of the room.

"The inflammatory rhetoric of the left has been used to stoke hatred among low-information and no-information voters. A disagreement over healthcare insurance is propagandized to those voters as 'evil conservatives trying to kill millions of Americans.' Law-abiding gun owners are deemed 'monsters who want schoolchildren to be murdered.' That we have come to a point when *anyone* out there would believe such reckless *idiocy* is proof that our education system has failed to generate adults with the slightest skill in critical thinking. Most of all, however, it proves that you"—he paused and stabbed a finger toward his audience—"lack even a modicum of honesty and integrity."

The cheering on the right and booing on the left started up again and Cartwright shouted into the mic, "*Stop*. All of you." Then he turned to face the Republicans and continued when the noise died. "Your own culpability in this situation is manifest. You could have fought back against this insanity long ago. Instead, you're cowards. You allowed your every move to be dictated by those who hate you. You claim to stand for certain values, while selling yourselves to the highest corporate bidders. Your constituents believe your promises and you betray them without a second thought.

"The bottom line? When it comes to DC politics, there may be a left wing and a right wing, but they're both attached to the same rotten bird, a vulture that feeds on the decaying carcass of the great American experiment in self-government."

When the president paused, the only sound in the room was air circulating through the HVAC system. The entire assembly of politicians was mortified. I heard my own pulse pounding in my ears as my senses absorbed the palpable tension that filled the space. Cartwright's face was red, mouth tight, eyes afire as he looked around the room.

He continued, "For the past year, a task force assembled by the Attorney General has conducted an extensive investigation into congressional corruption. That investigation bore filthy fruit. Of the four hundred thirty-five members of the House, one hundred twenty-two were implicated in schemes ranging from selling their votes outright, to sexual assaults covered up with taxpayer funds, to involvement in human trafficking, including children. In the Senate, thirty-six were implicated."

The room remained silent. Amid the silence, my Secret Service earpiece burst into excited chatter:

"All Oscar, all Oscar! Military approaching our perimeter at the front of the Capitol. Anybody know what the hell is going on?"

'Oscar' was the code for the presidential protection detail, the agents out front broadcasting to the entire group of men and women charged with protecting the president.

I recognized Laura Drew's voice and looked across to see her on the other side of the dais, speaking quietly into the mic on her wrist. "Military? What kind? Give me detail."

"APCs, at least a dozen. Hell, they're leaving the street, driving onto the grounds, looks like they're pulling—yeah, they're pulling right up to the steps. Advise!"

"Set the perimeter and maintain," Drew said.

The room outside my earpiece remained quiet. Then the president resumed. "After a year of study and consultation with trusted advisers and some of the top minds in our nation, I have come to one unavoidable conclusion. We cannot go on in our current state. A second civil war is inevitable. Rather than allowing that to occur and cause a grievous loss of life, I am implementing extreme measures."

DAY 11
7:10 Pm Central

COG CITY

HARROW STOOD at the front of the control room, hands on hips, watching the screen that relayed a live feed from the military team that had just deployed at the Capitol. As soldiers streamed from the APCs, the phalanx of Secret Service agents manning the perimeter walked to the bottom of the steps and spread out in a hopeless act of defiance. He saw a dozen or so uniformed guys—he couldn't tell if they were Uniformed Secret Service or Capitol Police—emerge from the building and join the suited agents.

He went to the MILCOM workstation. "Verbal link with the commander yet?"

"Still not responding to us, sir, but listen to this."

The soldier adjusted a knob and a speaker on his desk came to life. "Repeat, this is Colonel Daniel Harper. I am ordering the unit deployed to the US Capitol to immediately stand down and return to your previously ordered duties."

"Sonofabitch," Harrow said. He chewed his bottom lip for several seconds, ran a hand across his cropped hair. "Hook me up to the second in command. Lieutenant Colonel Adam Lindsay, right?"

The soldier nodded. "Yes, sir. Hold one." After a few moments, he removed his headset and handed it to Harrow.

Harrow said, "Lieutenant Colonel Lindsay?"

"Yes, sir."

"You are hereby promoted to Colonel and you are now in command of the Capitol operation. You are on scene there, am I right?"

"I am, sir."

"On my authority, I want MPs to locate and detain Colonel Harper. Then you are to execute your operation as previously ordered. Any questions?"

"No, sir."

"Carry on," Harrow said, pulling the headset off and handing it back to the soldier at the workstation.

DAY 11

8:10 Pm Eastern

US CAPITOL
WASHINGTON, DC

THE SECRET SERVICE earpiece was now a constant stream of excited chatter. Since I knew the plan and expected this, I got rid of the distraction by pulling the bud from my ear and letting it hang free on its translucent curly cord.

President Cartwright said, "As of this moment, I am temporarily suspending the Constitution." The chamber erupted in a cacophony of gasps, boos, and shouts. "Like hell! ... You can't do that! ... Have you lost your damn mind?"

Buzz-buzz-buzz. I looked to Agent Perera, then Dead-Eyes Alexander. Scanning the crowd as usual. Also obviously paying attention to what they were hearing in their earpieces. The din eventually morphed back into stunned silence as every eye turned back to the president.

"A military contingent is outside, securing this building. No one is allowed to leave. My Secret Service detail is hereby ordered to cooperate completely with the military commander in charge of the operation."

This stunned the room into silence.

"Out of the one hundred fifty-eight legislators who were implicated in the Attorney General's investigation, one hundred forty-one are here, according to entry records. You will all be arrested. Here. Now." Cartwright looked to his right and nodded to a woman I hadn't noticed before. She was seated in a chair against the wall, to my left. I recognized her as Attorney General Catherine White. She stood, climbed the steps to the dais, and walked to the podium, stopping immediately to the right of the president.

From an opening on the left side of the chamber, a procession of US Marshals emerged, at least twenty. They walked to the front of the room and fanned out in a line in front of the dais, looking out at the crowd.

The president stepped to his left and yielded the podium to AG White. She looked down at a sheet of paper on the platform of the podium and read off the first name. One of the marshals consulted a small tablet and pointed to a location in the area where senators were seated. Another marshal headed that way.

Buzz-buzz-buzz-buzz-buzz-buzz-buzz.

DAY 11

8:13 Pm Eastern

US CAPITOL
WASHINGTON, DC

THE PHONE in my pocket concluded its sequence of seven buzzes. Someone had just replied to the most recent auto-generated text from Pitt's phone. I scanned to my right. Dead-Eyes was diligently looking out at the audience. No phone. Checked out the rest of the agents, hell, checked out everybody on that side of the room. Turned to check the left. Laura Drew, the lead agent on President Cartwright's protection detail, had her phone in her hand. Looking at it. Thumb-typing on it. She gave a final touch and slipped it into a pocket. Immediately, the phone in my pocket buzzed again. Seven times. Good hell.

She was mirroring my position on the dais, me anchoring stage-right, her stage-left, scanning the crowd now that the phone was back in her pocket. The president watched as the marshal reached his quarry, a senator I didn't recognize. The marshal held out his hand, gestured for the senator to leave his seat and be escorted out. The senator's face was a caricature of surprise. I saw him mouth, "Me?" and point to himself. Then faux-indignance replaced surprise.

I looked back to Drew. No change. The AG was between me and Cartwright. No one between the president and Drew, whom he trusted implicitly or she wouldn't be the head of his detail. I heard a cry from the audience. Looked to see the senator's body locked in a rictus, thin wires running from his chest to the Taser the marshal held in his right hand. I supposed resisting arrest wouldn't be tolerated this evening.

Wanting to be positive I was right, I pulled the phone from my pocket and glanced at the screen, saw the exchange that had taken place between Pitt's phone and the mystery subject:

PITT PHONE: URGENT! 911! CALL ME NOW!
REPLY: who tf is this?????
PITT PHONE: CHANGE IN PLANS. CALL ME NOW.
REPLY: i'm working asshole. sotu.

NOTHING CONCRETE there to say it was Laura Drew, aside from the timing and my Spidey sense, which was screaming at me now. I slid the phone back into my right pocket and looked up to check on Drew. She was staring right into my eyes. Now all doubt was gone. She knew.

Life dropped into slow motion. Combat mode. I saw her hand moving toward her weapon, a shoulder-holstered Sig, probably standard issue .40 caliber. My right hand was already wrapping around the grip of the Kimber .45 on my right hip, my left hand diving into the left pocket of my trousers. Feeling the device there. Right hand retrieving the Kimber. Kimber clearing the holster. Left hand pressed the button in my pocket. Kimber at halfway point between holster and extension.

Drew's gun was no more than ten degrees below full extension for aim. I saw the president react as the buzzer in his pocket hit. My right thumb pressed down to disengage the Kimber's safety, felt the satisfying click of metal on metal as the lever hit home. Gun almost into position. Was the bitch really going to gun down the president of the

United States in the House of Representatives with the world watching?

Her gun, now fully extended, answered the question. I never heard the shot but I saw the muzzle flash just as Cartwright crouched to his knees and looked right, searching for me. My gun was up now. Drew's head filled my sights. I squeezed the trigger. Felt no recoil. Saw Drew's left eye disappear, replaced by a messy red hole where it had been.

Then I was climbing the steps. Moving toward the president. Six feet away. He was on his knees on the floor, a dog's pose. Two feet away. One foot. There. I reached down and grabbed his left triceps, yanked him into a low crouch, pulled him toward me and moved around him, putting myself between him and Drew. No need. Her body was on the floor, on her back, right eye open and staring up, her shooting days forever complete.

I turned back to Cartwright. "We have to go, sir! Now!"

President Cartwright was ahead of me, Secret Service agents seeming to materialize out of thin air, surrounding him and me. We made it to an exit corridor behind the dais.

He stopped, actively pushed back against the momentum being driven by me and the Secret Service swarm. "Stop!"

The swarm came to a halt.

He said, "We have to finish this. Tonight. With the nation watching and this particular crowd confined to this building."

One of the agents said, "Mr. President, we can't—"

"Tonight," Cartwright said. "Now. Go out there and restore order."

The agent drew a breath to respond, paused, exhaled, and nodded before scurrying away. Something occurred to me and I said, "Hey, wait a second."

He stopped and looked back at me.

"Go to Drew's body and get me her phone. All of them if there's more than one. In fact, bring me absolutely everything on her. Electronics, wallet, everything except her clothes."

The agent looked toward the president, who said, "Do it."

DAY 11

7:20 Pm Central

COG CITY

HARROW HAD WATCHED in disbelief as the scene played out on live TV, a senior Secret Service agent attempting to assassinate POTUS. Stopped not by the Secret Service, but by Sam Flatt, a guy with no experience in the realm. The guy Harrow himself had sent. The guy he had almost *not* sent. Thank God he had. His instincts about the man had been spot on.

He shelved his shock and adrenaline and went to the MILCOM desk. "Instruct Colonel Lindsay that no one is to leave the Capitol building."

"Yes, sir."

"And tell him to let me know when Colonel Harper is in custody."

Harrow walked back to the front of the room and crossed his arms as he stood watching the scenes at the Capitol. The Army had the outside sealed. Inside, the House chamber was still rowdy, bordering on chaotic. After a few minutes he went to MARLAW. "Status of those hot spots?"

"The added troops are calming things down, sir. Everywhere except Baltimore, that is. Still spread thin in the rough areas. Looting breaking out."

Harrow blew out a long, tired breath. That rat-infested hellhole would naturally be a thorn in his side. "Do we have more troops we can bring to bear?"

"Not without pulling from the Capitol."

"New orders. Looters are to be shot on sight."

The soldier's head jerked around. "Sir?"

"You heard me."

The soldier gave a quick nod and turned back to the desk.

Harrow went from station to station, monitoring developments, tweaking the deployments, occasionally returning to MILCOM to speak with his people in the field, people hand-chosen over several years and maneuvered into position. When he was satisfied that he could do no more at the moment, he picked up a phone and dialed his younger daughter. "Sadie, come to the ops center." He dropped the handset back into its cradle.

Five minutes later, she was there. Harrow said, "Is it ready?"

"Waiting on you, Dad."

"You're sure this is safe?"

Sadie nodded. "Positive."

"There's no chance of a launch, or some crossed wires that send the Russians or the Chinese into a panic?"

"They'll just lose control. Two minutes. Then I'll restore it. The message will be loud and clear that we have NORAD and we have the mountain, whenever we want to take them."

Harrow knew he was far beyond second-guessing. The point of no return had been irrevocably breached already, but this move still made him nervous. He stared at the screens on the wall without speaking. Sucked in a big breath. Nodded.

"Do it." He looked at his watch. "At nineteen-thirty. As soon as the two minutes are up, raise General Harbuck and route the call here."

She nodded and turned away, took off at a brisk walk. Stopped. Turned back.

"Dad?"

Harrow inclined his head, listening.

"I love you. And I'm proud of you."

FOUR MINUTES LATER, Harrow was sure he heard the alarms going off over in the mountain proper, even through the rock wall between here and there. He looked around. Nobody else seemed to be hearing anything. Maybe it was his imagination. He checked his watch.

Three and a half minutes after that, the phone on the console in front of him rang. He picked it up. "Marshall, we need to meet."

DAY 11

8:48 Pm Eastern

US CAPITOL
WASHINGTON, DC

THE HOUSE CHAMBER was once more in order. Full of scowls and sneering looks and flexing jaw muscles and pursed lips, but quiet. The marshals had finished their mass arrests, leaving the room not quite as packed as it had been before. The uniformed Capitol Police had cleared Drew's body. The brief wait for all this to transpire had provided time for the enormity of what I was doing to creep again to the forefront of my mind. Did I make the right choice? This was what, part revolution, part coup? The nation had made it 250 years without anything comparable except the Civil War. Was this step really necessary? Had I thrown in with the good guys or the bad?

I thought back to the sinister revelations of the cretins onstage in COG CITY the night before. The arrests here tonight, the legitimacy of which I had no reason to doubt. The propaganda of the media. The hatred and vitriol that filled social media. Most of all, I fell back to my Spidey sense. On that, I think I gave my instincts too much credit and guidance from God too little. I fervently hoped I'd chosen his side in this mess.

President Cartwright made his way up the steps onto the dais and back to the podium. Every eye in the room was on him. Well, almost. The Secret Service agents had tripled in number and they scanned the room with new intensity. I kept my eyes on them, moving from agent to agent.

Cartwright smiled. "Relax. She was after me, not you." The attempted humor fell flat, not so much as a chuckle when he paused, so he continued. "Anyone with an ounce of observational acumen realizes that our nation is now hopelessly divided. We have divided into two factions, conservatives and moderates on one side, and progressivism cum Marxism on the other.

"For simplicity, we'll stick with the red and blue color codes we've used to identify ourselves for the past several decades. Red wants a traditional America, the kind that thrived for two hundred years. Blue, as best I can tell, loathes everything about traditional America and seeks to 'fundamentally transform' it into some imagined socialist utopia."

He paused, looked around the room, met a lot of eyes.

"Those two visions are incompatible. Capitalism and socialism cannot coexist. Free markets and ever-increasing government control make terrible neighbors. Most of all, the melting pot that defined this nation for so long cannot mix and meld while an array of forces continually attempts to pigeonhole people into a series of hyphenated, balkanized communities.

"This conflict must end or a second civil war is inevitable. We cannot, *I* cannot, allow that to happen. For that reason, these two disparate factions of Americans are about to get a divorce."

The room broke into a new bout of chatter and murmur that continued until the president raised his hand for quiet. In my pocket, *buzz-buzz-buzz*, the script on Pitt's phone still doing its thing.

Cartwright resumed. "My fellow Americans, this process will be messy, complicated beyond measure, and easily the most difficult task our country has ever attempted to do. Be that as it may, we will do it.

We *must* do it, because the option is bloodshed that could cost the lives of millions.

"Tomorrow, our country will begin a process of division. Blue on the west. Red on the east." He looked past me to a female aide seated against the wall and nodded.

She looked no older than twenty-five. She stood from her chair, gathered up an easel and a rigid foam-board map that had to be eight feet wide, walked to the Speaker's well in front of the dais, and set up the exhibit. I only got a glimpse of it as she passed, but I saw that it had a thick red line running irregularly north to south, positioned so that it cut up through the west following existing state borders. It ran from the Mexican border on the south to the Canadian border on the north.

The president said, "Our blue friends will take the following states: California, Oregon, Washington, Nevada, Idaho, Arizona, and Utah. Red will take the rest. The border between the two will be fifty miles wide and will serve as a neutral zone, a buffer between two new nations."

He paused again and the room erupted in angry shouts aimed at the dais. One man rose from his seat in the area where senators were seated and started squeezing his way past those still seated. He looked up toward Cartwright and said, "I'm leaving. You've lost your fucking mind and your ass *will* be impeached tomorrow."

Cartwright sighed and nodded at one of the marshals, many of whom were still spread out along the front of the room between the dais and the crowd. The marshal walked right up to the front row of seats and pulled her Taser. She fired it over the heads of those in the front two rows and the twin electrified barbs embedded in the left cheek of the senator who was huffing his way out through his fellow legislators. He stopped, convulsed, and flopped over onto two female senators dressed in suffragette white. The marshal released the trigger on the weapon. Two of her male colleagues went to the senator, unceremoniously picked him up, and started dragging him through the crowd as they stood and tried to get out of the way. When they reached the aisle and turned toward the back of the room, the president continued his speech.

"I realize those in this room, not to mention those watching from home, may be alarmed by this evening's turn of events. I understand. I will also be candid and tell you that what we are about to undertake will be messy. There are myriad questions about how this division will play out in the areas of housing, property ownership, business operations, defense, and many more. Be that as it may, it is a necessary undertaking if we are to save lives and give both camps of our polarized nation an opportunity for self-government as they see fit.

"To that end, I will now lay out a rough framework of how this is going to proceed. First—"

A congressman I didn't recognize, seated with the Democrats on the House side, shouted, "You can't do this without Congress, without ratification, without a host of measures that will take years to implement!"

President Cartwright waited until he was sure the man was finished before continuing. "Under our broken system, this would *never* happen. The partisan rancor would continue until the violence in our streets that we're already seeing explodes into full-fledged war. So please understand this, Congressman Haire: This. Is. Happening. I have prepared for tonight. You are free to hate me for that. Free to label me a dictator or a despot. I expected that. Be that as it may, I will move forward.

"Here's how the first steps will play out."

COG CITY

HARROW WAS the only customer inside the little café when General Marshall Harbuck walked in. Harrow stood and extended his hand when Harbuck approached the table but Harbuck didn't take it. He didn't even sit. He stood, pointed a finger at Harrow, and said, "You'll spend the rest of your life in prison for this, Lucian. What in hell are you thinking?"

"No, Marshall. I won't. I now command the armed forces of the United States, by direct order of the president. Everything I've done has been authorized by him."

Harbuck's face crumpled into a look of disbelief. "That's insane. I don't believe it."

"Have you been watching the State of the Union?"

"I haven't had time for TV, but yeah, the news is spreading like crazy. I suppose you're behind the hack that took control of everything at nineteen-thirty?"

Harrow nodded. "Please, sit down. We've known each other a long time. Hear me out."

Harbuck yanked the chair opposite Harrow out from the table and dropped into it. "I'm listening. Explain the insanity of taking our nuclear forces offline for two minutes."

"Just a message that we control the mountain. Including NORAD."

Harbuck shook his head. "To what end?"

"Go online. Find the president's speech. Watch it from the beginning and you'll understand everything. I have the authority to command you or to replace you. I prefer the former." Harrow stood, pushed his chair back.

"That's it? You initiate mass sedition against your country and you tell me to go watch a damn video?"

"I'll be sending in someone to assume control of NORAD, no matter what. Don't make me replace you, too, Marshall. We're the good guys."

"You're a lunatic."

"One hour," Harrow said, and walked out of the café.

DAY 11

8:56 Pm Eastern

US CAPITOL
WASHINGTON, DC

AFTER THE MASS arrests and the forcible subduing and removal of the
defiant senator, the chamber had grown quiet and orderly. Anger and
puffery among the audience had yielded to trepidation.

Cartwright said, "These dramatic steps are not something I have
planned alone. I have the backing of our military. To that end, General
Lucian Harrow of the US Army is now the commander of the US
armed forces, supplanting the former Joint Chiefs. He will shortly
install leaders of his choosing for the Air Force, Navy, and Marines. I
say now to all members of our military, as your commander-in-chief,
you are hereby commanded to follow the orders of General Harrow
and his subordinates without question. Martial law, with its curfew,
will remain in effect until advised otherwise. As soon as we feel certain
an orderly transition is underway, restrictions will be eased."

The focus of the Secret Service agents amazed me. I assume most, if
not all, of them were hearing this stunning news for the first time. Not

to mention the fact that one of their own had just tried to assassinate their charge. Despite all that, they were pictures of diligent concentration as they endlessly scanned the crowd and entrances to the room.

The president said, "Congress is suspended."

His hand shot up, palm out, as soon as a new murmur started. The marshals looked to be ready to efficiently deal with any troublemakers. The chamber quieted.

"To the few of you who are honorable public servants, I apologize. To the rest of you, even though you have not yet been implicated in illegal activity, your days of selling out your constituents and selling yourself to the highest-bidding lobbyists are finished. Information packages regarding every one of you have already been prepared. These presentations will lay out your activities in simple fashion for your constituents back home, how much you've taken from which industries, how you've voted on legislation involving those industries. All trips and other perks you've been provided by those industries. These facts will be aired frequently on radio and TV outlets in your districts, and you will be there to answer to your former constituents, since all of you will be transported to your homes over the next few days."

At this, I had to fight the urge to pull my phone and snap photos of some of the faces in the crowd. Such was the wide-eyed fear blossoming across the chamber.

Cartwright said, "Supreme Court Justice Marcus Wilder has been working on a new, streamlined, and very basic legal code that will go into effect for the duration of the transition. While his service was not voluntary in the beginning, General Harrow tells me Justice Wilder has since embraced the duty of the task. This basic legal code will, of course, be based on the United States Constitution. It will cover both the red section, which will continue to be known as the United States, and the blue section, future name unknown, throughout the transition. By the time the transition ends, the blue country will have its own leaders in place and may name itself whatever it so desires.

"There will, however, be certain permanent, nonnegotiable limitations in place for the blue country that will be disclosed later. An information distribution system has already been developed. It will be available to all on the internet, and will also be continually transmitted and updated via the Emergency Broadcast System. This system will encompass all existing TV and radio stations, as well as periodic information transmissions to all cellular phones in the nation."

The president paused several seconds and looked out over those in attendance. When he continued, his voice had shifted from matter-of-fact to something I can only describe as wistful.

"I am truly sorry our nation has come to this. I will lead this transition, which we anticipate to take two years. At the end of that period, the United States will hold new elections. I will not be a candidate for office in those elections. Let us go forward in a spirit of life-saving change and make the best of the untenable hand which we have been dealt. May God bless the people of these United States of America. Good night."

DAY 12
7:15 Am Central

COG CITY

SHEILA WAS WAITING on Main Street when I arrived back in COG CITY from DC. She surprised me by grabbing me in a tight hug and saying, "Thank you for the rescue."

"Welcome. You know that Pitt's dead?"

"What?"

I nodded. "Yeah, Sol and I found him in his motel room yesterday, day before, whenever. Not getting any sleep and it's tough to keep up with days."

"You can tell me about it later. I figure you'd like to see your wife and daughter first?"

My heart skipped a beat. "She—they're here?"

"Yeah, I met them a little while ago. In the diner." She hooked a thumb toward the little café.

I thanked her and hurried over, opened the door and looked around. Saw Willie behind the counter. He saw me and a giant smile erupted. He pointed toward the right side of the room and I saw Abby and Ally sitting in a booth.

Abby was facing the front of the room and saw me first. Her hair was a mess and she wore no makeup. She was still beautiful and all my earlier irritation with her vanished. Then I saw her face color, eyes narrowing in that way that drew her eyebrows into an angry bunch with little space between them. Before I could say anything, she sprang from the booth. Walked toward me—no, *marched* at me—and as soon as she was in range, she slapped me across my left cheek and drew back her hand to do it again.

I caught her hand in midair. "Whoa, Abb. Chill."

"You sonofabitch! You had us *kidnapped!* Wha—"

"Mom, stop!"

We both looked at Ally as she eased up out of the booth.

She said, "Dad? What the crap?"

"Can we sit down?" I said. "There's a lot to explain."

Ally sat back down into the booth and slid over. I sat on the bench beside her. Abby stared at me, eyes still on fire, but eventually said, "Fine," and sat on the other side of the booth. The whole booth shook when she cranked up her angry leg-jiggle, arms crossed. Red splotches emerged on her neck and upper chest.

I looked up to see what Willie was thinking of all this. He pooched his lips out and gave his head a sympathy shake. I turned to Ally. "I had to keep you safe and I didn't have time to explain. I'm sorry for the way this happened."

"Safe from what?"

"Have you not seen what's happening? The president's speech last night?"

Abby said, "We haven't seen jack-squat, Sam. I was washing dishes and your daughter was doing homework when your storm troopers showed up."

I smiled. "White shell armor? Did they have blasters?"

Bad move.

"You think this is *funny?*" Abby said. They said they preferred I come with them but Ally was going either way. You, what, thought I'd let anyone take her without me?"

"No. I knew you'd come. I also knew it would be...smoother...for them to present you with a choice instead of an order. You don't respond well to the latter, you know?"

She said nothing. The leg jiggled harder.

"It will be easier to understand what's going on if you watch the president's speech from last night, but the short story is that a realignment of the country is underway."

"What's that even mean?" Ally said.

"The country is polarized beyond repair. Violence breaking out, escalating."

"Since we're not complete idiots, we did notice the martial law," Abby said.

I said, "The nation is going to split into two separate countries."

Both their eyes widened.

"Nevada will be in the 'new country.' Las Vegas itself is going to be in a special zone, a quasi-neutral area for the next couple of years. I was afraid widespread violence might break out. Couldn't take the chance of leaving you there. Here, you're safe."

"Two countries?" Ally said.

I nodded.

Abby said, "How long do you expect us to stay here?" She swept her hands in a grand gesture. "In this cave?"

"I hope no more than a few days, just long enough to see how things are shaking out in the wild. When we know it's calm, you guys can stay at my place."

Abby barked out a bitter little laugh. "I have a home, Sam. If this is your way to get me back, it won't—"

I slapped my hand on the tabletop. "Damn it, Abby, listen to me. This isn't about 'getting you back.' It's about keeping you *safe*. Literal battles could erupt out there between military units. Criminals will think they can run wild in the chaos until they're shown they're wrong. This is real. The western part of the country is being forcibly ejected from the United States. Do you get it?"

"And if we won't do what you say, if we decide to go home anyway?" she said.

I calmed myself, drew a deep breath through my nostrils, waited a few beats. I reached across the table and took her hands in mine. She didn't exactly participate in the gesture but she didn't pull away. I said, "I love you. Have since I first laid eyes on you. Do I wish we could make it work? Yes. A thousand times yes, but that may not be possible. Even if it's not, I want you and Ally to be safe until things calm down."

Buzz-buzz-buzz-buzz-buzz-buzz-buzz. After the assassination attempt in the House chamber, I'd sort of tuned out on ongoing vibrations in my pocket as the Pitt phone continued to run its script and dial the mystery phone that had belonged to the dirty Secret Service agent Laura Drew, but this was seven buzzes, not three. Someone had either sent a text to Pitt's phone or dialed it.

"You didn't answer my question," Abby said. "What happens if we decide to go anyway?"

The door to the diner burst open, the little shopkeeper's bell clanging like mad. I looked over and saw Sadie. She ran to where we were. Between breaths, she said, "Daddy needs you. Now."

"Give me thirty seconds," I said. She nodded and left. I turned back to face Abby. "I have to go. We'll finish this later." I motioned toward the counter with my chin. "Willie will tell you how to find Wilson and he'll set you up so you can watch the speech."

Abby yanked her hands away. "We're leaving."

I leaned closer and looked her in the eye. "You're grown," I said. "I won't stop you from leaving if you're that obstinate. But Ally is not. She's my daughter, she's a minor, and she's not going *anywhere* until I know it's safe. Believe that."

I turned to Ally, kissed her on the cheek. "Sorry about all this, sweetie. I'll be back as soon as I can."

DAY 12
7:27 Am Central

COG CITY

SADIE WAS WAITING outside the door. I said, "What's going on?"

She headed out at a jog and I followed. She said, "I don't know. Something about a phone call?"

My phone started vibrating in my pocket again. I didn't bother to count the pulses but I knew there would be seven.

We arrived at the command center out of breath. I saw Harrow standing beside the workstation I'd used to craft the script for Pitt's phone, the same workstation that gave me access to all the NSA magic.

As I approached he picked up Pitt's phone from the desk and held it at display. "Rang a few minutes ago. Incoming call from an unknown number. When we didn't answer, it received this text." He handed me the phone.

The text said: **time critical. moving to alternative plan.**

I sat down at the workstation. Pulled up the NSA tool I was using to track activity on Pitt's phone. As with the Laura Drew phone, the system provided no number, no IMEI, no other technical details on the phone on the other end of the exchange. There's no way the NSA system didn't *have* the info; it was simply blocking it from view. It had to be a government device. This time, however, it did show one critical data nugget: A location, displayed in a linkified latitude and longitude format. I clicked it.

A map appeared and quickly zoomed into the most famous address in the country, 1600 Pennsylvania Avenue, Washington, DC. The White House. Another dirty Secret Service agent? If so, POTUS was in danger. I clicked to zoom in tighter, not expecting it to work, but it did. How the hell was it achieving this level of precision? Some new ultra-granular system of micro-cells within the White House?

I kept zooming until the resolution maxed out. Goose flesh rippled across the back of my neck. The phone that had called Pitt's phone and then texted it moments later was in the Oval Office. I turned to Harrow. "Do you have a way to reach the president directly?"

"Assuming it's critical, yes."

"Start dialing."

He strode quickly to his little command podium at the front of the room and picked up the handset from its phone. Pushed a speed-dial button. Handed the phone to me.

After two rings, Cartwright answered. "Yes?"

"Mr. President, this is Sam Flatt. You're in immediate danger. Please listen carefully. Without giving anything away, tell me who's in the room with you right now."

After a moment, he said in a cheery voice, "That's great, darling. I'm so proud of you. I'm in a meeting with the vice president at the moment but it shouldn't be much longer. How about we have the kitchen whip up some breakfast?"

I heard him partially cover the phone and say, "Madison. She won an academic award." He was good. I said, "Just the vice president? No one else?"

"Sure, pancakes sound great."

"Have you seen him use a phone in the past few minutes?"

"Right. I won't be long and I'll text you when I'm heading up, okay?"

I pictured the vice president in my mind. Sarah Houghton.

Youngest VPOTUS in history. First female Navy SEAL in history? If not the first, close to it. A thoroughly dangerous woman. "I assume you have a button you can push for emergency assistance. Do that now and try to leave the phone open so I can listen in."

"Bye, Maddy. Text you soon."

I heard him put the handset back in its cradle. He'd engaged the speakerphone. I muted our phone's mic to eliminate the risk of giving away the ruse, then waited to hear the arrival of the suited cavalry.

DAY 12
8:30 Am Central

THE WHITE HOUSE

PRESIDENT CARTWRIGHT TOUCHED the button to activate the speaker-phone and set the handset back in its cradle. He was reaching for the panic button on the underside of the center drawer in the Resolute Desk when his vice president said, "Don't do it, John."

The woman seemed to have transported instantaneously from the sofa to where she now stood, right beside Cartwright, holding the point of a letter opener to the side of his neck. He pulled his hand back, laid both hands on the desk. She removed the blade from his neck but stayed within three feet of him.

Houghton said, "You didn't seriously think we'd allow you to go through with this idiocy, did you?"

"We?"

"The sane people in our government."

"Ah, right. The bureaucracy. The machine. Deep State. Whatever you want to call yourselves, it's all the same thing, a bunch of elected cretins teaming up with an unelected infestation. Keep the status quo in place. To hell with the people."

"Do you even hear yourself? You're shredding the Constitution and trying to literally rip the country apart, and you're throwing stones at someone else? Sorry, this isn't what I signed up for and I won't allow your tyranny."

Cartwright laughed. Laughed some more. Belly laughter. He wiped tears from his eyes. Here stood a woman defending the very system that had led the nation to the brink of civil war, calling him a tyrant. "Sarah, I accept that you believe yourself to be acting in good faith. You've served your country with such distinction, such bravery, that it would be wrong to do otherwise. But as I pointed out last night, this situation is past the point of no return."

"Bullshit. This isn't how we work. We solve problems at the ballot box, not with tanks and APCs in our own streets."

"How's the ballot box working out?" He leaned forward, placed his elbows on the desk, forearms extended, flat against the wood surface of the desk. Looked straight ahead. Watched her in his peripheral vision.

"Some states tried the secession thing a while back. Remember that?"

Cartwright screamed, "Screw you!" and slapped his left palm hard on the desk. Houghton flinched and actually took a step back. It was now or never. In one quick sequence he reached out with his right hand and grabbed a paperweight from the right side of his desk. An apple, made of solid glass.

As his fingers closed around the cool smooth surface he used his left hand against the desk and his feet on the floor to propel his chair back and to the left, putting a tiny bit of distance between himself and his erstwhile second. As the chair rolled, he drew back his right hand and threw the glass apple like a baseball. Not at Houghton, but at the door to the Oval Office.

It hit with a solid thud. A hot bolt of electric pain lanced his right shoulder. He screamed. Used his feet to wheel the chair further to the left of the desk. Looked at his shoulder to see blood coloring his white shirt. She'd stabbed him.

Now she held the letter opener in her right hand in an obvious combat stance, advancing on him. When she got within two feet he grabbed the arms of the chair and kicked out with both feet. He got a piece of her, enough to knock her back four or five feet, but she didn't go down and she'd also gotten a strike in on his left ankle. He was seriously outmatched.

Just as she lunged toward him again the door to the Oval Office burst open, framing two Secret Service agents, Leo McLaughlin and Dead-Eyes Alexander. Cartwright never heard the shot—had it been more than one?—but he saw a bloom on Houghton's right side, spreading on the white jacket she was wearing. The letter opener dropped from her hand as the hand moved to her side. She went down in slow motion, first to her knees, then a topple over onto her left side before she curled into something of a fetal position. She looked up at the president, her face furious, her teeth gritted to deal with the pain. "This isn't over."

The president looked to his left, to the Secret Service men. Smoke wisped from the barrel of Alexander's pistol. Maybe he'd judged the man poorly. McLaughlin said, "You okay, Mr. President?" and ran toward him while Alexander swept the rest of the room, gun at the ready. When McLaughlin was close enough to see the blood coming from the president's shoulder and ankle he shouted into the mic on his wrist, "Medic medic medic! BONANZA is hit!"

DAY 12

7:32 Am Central

COG CITY

IT WAS ALL GOING WRONG. Harrow and I listened on his speakerphone as the situation played out sixteen hundred miles away. After a round of verbal sparring between POTUS and VPOTUS, we'd heard a thud, followed by the president screaming. The entire command center had gone whisper-quiet, making the speakerphone easier to understand.

More commotion, an angry female grunt followed immediately by a small cry from President Cartwright. Now an angry female roar. Was that a door opening?

A BOOM caused the phone's tiny speaker to distort. A groan, followed by a muted *thud*. A voice: "You okay, Mr. President?" Moments later, the same voice, screaming, "Medic medic medic! BONANZA is hit!"

I punched off the mute button on the speakerphone and said, "What's the condition of the president?"

"Who is that?" It was the same voice we'd just heard. Secret Service. Couldn't tell which agent.

Harrow said, "This is General Lucian Harrow. Advise on the status of POTUS."

"Agents Leo McLaughlin and Tim Alexander on the scene, General. BONANZA—uh, POTUS—is bleeding from the shoulder and lower leg."

Then we clearly heard Cartwright's voice. "I'm fine, stabbed with a damned letter opener. You believe that?"

I leaned in and said *sotto voce* to Harrow. "General, if you want to keep him alive, you have one option. Bring him here."

Harrow locked eyes with me for two or three seconds, then said, "Mr. President, are you able to pick up the handset for a confidential conversation?"

The sound changed from the barrel acoustics of a speakerphone to the clarity of a handset. "What is it, Lucian?" Cartwright said.

"We need to evacuate you immediately, sir. How bad are your injuries?"

"Minor. Treatable on the go, I think. What do you have in mind?"

"I want to bring you here, sir. COG CITY. It's Sam's suggestion and I concur. I can absolutely keep you safe here but I'm not sure about anywhere else."

"Hold on." The conversation became muted as Cartwright lowered the handset and spoke to the men in the room with him. "Get my family down here. Right now. Tell Air Force One to prep for an immediate trip to Colorado. Spin up Marine One."

There was a moment of hesitation, but only a moment. "Yes, sir," a new voice said. "I'm on it."

I spoke quietly to Harrow again, after which he said, "Mr. President? One more thing. We need you to bring the vice president with you."

"Say again?"

"We need to interrogate her. Find out who else is involved."

"I see. Consider it done."

DAY 12

5:00 Pm Central

COG CITY

It had taken a while to break the ex-SEAL VPOTUS, but the Hot Seat did the trick on the fifth double-up of electric current. Once she caved, I knew everything she knew within a half-hour. Now it was time to break the news to POTUS and General Harrow. President Cartwright, Harrow, and I were gathered in the presidential quarters, the sixties-era furnishings and decor making it feel like I'd stepped through a time warp.

"Tell us what you learned," Cartwright said.

"Her subterfuge started long before your speech, sir. She had a source inside the operation who told her months ago what was on the horizon."

Cartwright said, "It had to be on your end, Lucian. No one knew on my end. Not even my wife. Hell, I wrote the speech myself. With pen and paper."

Harrow puffed his cheeks, blew out a long breath. "I kept it as tight as I could, but in lining up loyals in command structures, I had to tell them that *something* big might be coming, but I told no one the details outside—"

I held up my hand. Harrow stopped talking. "It was your son-in-law, General."

Harrow's mouth dropped, hung there, open. After a moment he recovered. "You think I'd let that idiot know *anything*? We compartmentalized the hell out of it."

I felt for the man but the situation demanded candor. "Pillow talk."

"Pam? You got this from the vice president?"

After a sad nod, I said, "Houghton didn't interface directly with Anthony and didn't know the full chain of communication that eventually terminated at her, but she knew he was screwing some young girl who works in the mountain, blabbed to her that his wife and her father were planning some kind of revolution, then somehow it made its way up the line into DC." I shrugged.

"Sonofabitch," Harrow said, and slapped the table.

Cartwright said, "And she chose an assassination scheme instead of a legal or political attack? Makes no sense."

"She tried. Lobbied your Cabinet to support her but she had no evidence beyond fourthhand hearsay and they all blew her off. She decided to take a more 'direct' route to seizing power from you."

"Who else was in it with her?"

"Directly, just Laura Drew, the head of your Secret Service detail. But Houghton says Drew was working with someone in the CIA. They had an assassin lined up for the speech but when you ordered such a dramatic increase in security last night, that fell apart. Drew decided to act herself."

Cartwright shook his head, then steepled his fingers and rested his chin on them. "Damn rotten CIA. Out of control. Have been for a long time."

Harrow said, "Despite the leak, we've been successful thus far. I'll handle my dolt of a son-in-law."

I said, "We have, but a rogue CIA is a huge problem going forward. We'll have to deal with that if the president is ever to be secure outside this mountain."

Both men nodded to that. Cartwright said, "Lucian, how are we doing with the military?"

"A handful of rank-and-file have gone AWOL, but not a significant percentage. Command-wise, we've had to replace two or three but I'm satisfied with where we are at the moment."

"How's Wilder coming with that legal code?"

"Says he'll have a rough draft tomorrow."

"Good." The president turned to me. "Sam, you've saved my life twice now. Not sure how to thank you for that, but know you have my gratitude. I hope you're willing to play a continuing role."

I didn't expect that, and once again the realization bloomed in my mind that I was really sitting here plotting with the president of the United States on what many would see as a strange revolution, an inside military coup of sorts. Many would see me as a traitor. I said, "You're welcome, Mr. President. As for the future, think about what you have in mind and we'll talk."

Cartwright stood. "I need a little sleep, gentlemen. Wake me if I'm needed." He walked off toward the presidential bedroom.

When he was out of the room, Harrow extended his hand and said, "Thank you, Sam. You're an honorable warrior." I shook his hand and nodded.

He said, "Oh, I handled the thing in California for you. In transit, be here tomorrow."

DAY 12
5:18 Pm Central

COG CITY

SHEILA WAS a wizard at research and I set her up at the command center workstation that had access to the NSA sleuthing tools. I also set up my laptop for her, plugged in the dongle for my forensic software that handled cell phones, and gave her a quick lesson on running it. I opened the brown paper bag that contained everything that had been removed from Laura Drew's body and pulled out the two phones, then pulled the phone from my pocket that I'd taken off the vice president. "Do acquisitions on all these first thing. Should be quick. I'll check back in a few."

I found Abby and Ally, asked if they'd like to have dinner with me in the diner. Ally said yes but Abby was still sulled up and declined. I had no time, energy, or inclination to argue with her. My daughter was scared but not hostile. We had a good talk over a splendid meal of roast beef, mashed potatoes, and some other goodies Willie had put together. I hugged her, kissed her on the cheek, and went back to the command center.

The data downloads from the Drew phones and the Houghton phone were complete. I pulled the IMEI numbers—electronic serial numbers of sorts for phones—for all three, gave them to Sheila, and told her to dig out everything the NSA had on them. Likewise for the different email addresses Drew and Houghton had used on the phones. All the devices had email content on them, but I was hoping the NSA system would find some that weren't on the phones.

With that research handed off, I started digging through the data from the phones. Within three minutes, I was staring dumbfounded at the screen. I tried to tell myself it couldn't be. But it was.

DAY 12
6:01 Pm Central

COG CITY

I found Harrow in his office and stepped inside without knocking. "We're compromised. Big time."

"How so?"

"Houghton's phone has everything about this place on it."

"I don't understand," Harrow said.

"Blueprints. IP addresses. Electrical. *Access control.* Our tunnel over to the main Cheyenne Mountain facility is no longer secret."

"How is that possible?"

"Don't know yet but it gets worse. They know POTUS is here."

"Who is *they,* Sam?"

"Again, don't know, but it's safe to assume they're not on our side."

Harrow pushed his chair back and stood. "We need to inform the president, then I want some more detail on this."

"If you don't mind handling that, I want to visit the esteemed vice president."

Harrow nodded. "Meet me in the command center in fifteen."

. . .

I WALKED into the jail and went straight to Houghton's cell. She was lying on her bunk, reading a sixty-year-old magazine. As soon as she saw me, she grinned. *Bitch.*

Then she rolled off the bunk and stood. Walked to the bars. Looked me in the eye and started laughing. "Your face! You really thought you were going to get good intel from me with your little shock chair? Silly boy." She threw her head back and cackled, looking crazy as a shit-house rat. She laughed so hard tears ran down her face. I watched and waited for her performance to run its course.

When she stopped the foolishness I said, "You're a badass. I'll give you that. I should've expected it from a SEAL. But the bullshit ends now. I'll be back and you're gonna tell me the truth."

"And why would I do that, you traitor?"

"I'm not the one who tried to kill the president."

"A *rogue* president who's pissing on the Constitution."

"Your view, not mine. I agree with him. The division is too far gone. Irreconcilable. This way, both sides get to have the kind of country they want. Hopefully peacefully, but you're not helping on that front."

She glanced at a clock on the wall in the office outside her cell. "Your time is about up, so why don't you go fuck yourself while you still can."

I had a bad feeling that she was telling the truth on timing.

CHEYENNE MOUNTAIN

GENERAL MARSHALL HARBUCK stood in the center of a circle of amber light cast by a floodlight high above in the Amphitheater. In front of him, eight US Marines, a Fleet Antiterrorism Security Team, commonly known by their acronym: FAST. Before Army Colonel Daniel Harper had been detained in DC for not following the orders of President Cartwright, he had secured the cooperation and loyalty of his USMC analog at the 1st FAST Company, stationed at the Norfolk naval base.

This was the only special-ops team Harbuck had been able to bring to bear, but he could not have asked for better. These men were highly trained in securing high-value targets and locations, their urban combat and close-quarter fighting skills unsurpassed.

Harbuck had given his entire adult life to the service of his country and he'd be damned if he would surrender it to a couple of madmen without a fight. He looked at the men awaiting his instructions. He dropped to a knee and unrolled a blueprint, flattened it on the concrete floor. Used his phone, wallet, and sidearm as weights to hold three of the big document's corners down, and stepped on the fourth corner with the toe of one boot.

He pointed to the blueprint and each Marine dropped to a knee for a better view. "We're here," he said, stabbing a finger onto the edge of the blueprint, just outside the border of the drawing at a point that showed a tunnel leading deeper into Cheyenne Mountain. "In five minutes, we'll open an access portal to this tunnel. With any luck, you'll have the element of surprise and have the facility secured before they know what hit them."

Harbuck moved his finger to another spot, what looked like an apartment with bold letters in the center that said 'PQ.' "Based on layouts we've examined of other continuity-of-government facilities, we're confident these are the presidential quarters. It's also your point of ingress. We have no idea if the president will be there, but it's imperative to capture him alive, so be careful. We want the man to stand trial, not be martyred and stir up a bunch of lunatics."

One of the Marines said, "What kind of resistance should we expect?"

Harbuck shook his head. "Wish I could tell you, son. I don't know."

Another Marine said, "But these are Americans, right? Our brothers and sisters?"

Harbuck nodded. Slowly. Sadness, not enthusiasm. "The rebels from Dixie were Americans, too, right up until they decided they wanted to be something else. That was more than a hundred fifty years ago, and we all know what happened, what it cost. Our goal is to end this now and prevent it from growing into something much worse.

"I know it goes against everything we believe, everything you've trained for, but here and now, you have no choice but to consider those inside this facility enemies. Minimize casualties if you can, but it's your duty to do what you must in order to secure the target. Your country is counting on you."

DAY 12

6:15 Pm Central

COG CITY

"I'll get to the bottom of the compromise but right now we don't have time," I said to General Harrow and President Cartwright. "I'm telling you we have an imminent problem."

"Why imminent?" Cartwright said.

"Drew's phone had the instructions for opening the 'gateway' into our tunnel, and it was the last thing accessed. That was *last night*, Mr. President. We're lucky they haven't already stormed this place."

Harrow looked at the president. "I concur. We have to prepare."

"What can you do?" Cartwright said.

"We can start with getting you out of here," I said. "The tunnel comes up right under our feet."

Cartwright nodded and stood. Harrow said, "Let's go to the command center. We'll need to protect it and you at all costs, so if need be that's where we'll make our stand."

Minutes later, we were in a small conference room adjacent to the command center. We'd pulled Sol into our confab. I turned to Harrow. "How many soldiers do we have?"

Harrow shook his head. "Not enough. We have a couple dozen between Army and Air Force, but look around." He swept his hand toward the windowed wall that looked out over the command center. "These people are techies, not fighters. We just didn't anticipate the need for a hard defense. Correction. *I* didn't anticipate it. All on me. I thought we were impervious in here."

"How many fighters *do* we have?" I said.

"Half-dozen," Sol said. "Plus me and you as equalizers." A tiny smile tugged at the corners of his mouth with that last addition and he winked at me.

Someone knocked on the glass door and Harrow motioned to come in. It was the soldier I'd seen manning the SIGINT desk, a fresh-faced girl who looked more kid than woman. She saw the president and froze. "Uh...I..."

Harrow said, "Out with it, soldier."

"We're picking up increased signals from next door, sir."

"What kind of signals?"

"Radio transmissions. Encrypted, so we don't know what it's about but it's directional and pretty close." She pointed in the direction of the main Cheyenne Mountain facility.

Sol and I stood simultaneously. I said, "General, we'll head to the tunnel. My suggestion would be to drag every fighter you have into action and set them up in pairs, staggered out along the path to this room. Lots of places to set up bottlenecks in these stairways and corridors. If someone gets past me and Sol, you'll have several points at which to stop them."

Harrow said, "I'm on it."

Sol and I headed out. The president said, "Good luck, gentlemen. We're all counting on you."

Swell.

DAY 12
6:23 Pm Central

CHEYENNE MOUNTAIN

HARBUCK LOOKED at the notes in his hand and flipped the circuit breakers off, then back on, in the indicated sequence. When the last one snapped back into the on position, he heard heavy machinery go into action along the rock wall that divided his facility from the target next door. He watched as a section of the concrete floor slowly rose. Unbelievable that this had been here sixtyish years and no one knew.

The FAST team made their final checks of weapons and gear, standing around the rising slab of concrete, peering down into the darkness as the gap between the slab and the surrounding floor grew. The motion stopped. Metal squealed as a steel ladder automatically slid down from the edge of the chasm, clanging when it was fully extended and came to rest on the bottom of the pit. It was time.

For the first time since he began planning this operation, Harbuck felt a quiver of nerves at the idea that he was sending men to forcibly seize the president of the United States. God forgive him if this thing went wrong. Maybe God forgive him if it went right.

COG-TO-CHEYENNE TUNNEL

"LIKE OLD TIMES, HUH, PARTNER?" Sol said in a whisper as we advanced through the tunnel in the golf-cart-on-rails, lights off, relying on our night-vision goggles. We'd dropped by the armory, the main one in COG CITY proper, not the one in the Bat Cave, and we were well-equipped. We were about halfway through the tunnel when we first picked up a bit of noise up ahead. I switched on a snazzy little directional mic that was mounted to my helmet and listened in my earbud. Turned to Sol and nodded. "This is it." All convo was now at a whisper.

Ten yards further on, I stopped the cart as I noticed something I hadn't seen in my previous trips through the tunnel. I pointed up to the ceiling.

Sol said, "Is that what I think it is?"

"Let's find out." I got out of the cart and looked up, the IR illuminator lighting up the view in my NVG like green daylight. I saw the bottom edge of a heavy steel door. It spanned the entire width of the tunnel, its edges resting in channels that ran from the ceiling to the floor, mounted to and into the rock walls. I looked at him. "Damn skippy."

I looked around for any kind of lever or crank that could be used to lower the door, which looked like it would qualify as a blast gate. I found none. Up in a corner beside the mechanism, however, I saw a hefty electric motor. Using the mic stuck to my throat that allowed me to communicate by sub-vocalizing, I radioed General Harrow. "Doom-Daddy, Uncle."

He responded immediately. "Copy, Uncle. Go ahead."

"This tunnel has at least one heavy barrier that deploys electrically," I said. I hoped there were more of them that we hadn't noticed. "No manual controls. Are you familiar?"

"Negative, Uncle. Researching."

"Roger roger. Advise when possible."

I dropped a tiny UV LED on the left side of the tunnel to mark the gate's location. It was coded to our NVGs and would only turn on if Sol or I were within fifty feet of it. I got back into the cart to continue forward.

DAY 12

6:25 Pm Central

CHEYENNE-TO-COG TUNNEL

THE LEADER of the FAST team, a twenty-four-year-old sergeant, looked back to be sure everyone was in the pit. They were. He flipped his NVG into place and signaled for the rest of the team to do likewise, then followed that up with hand-motion signals to move forward into the tunnel.

He hated underground bullshit of any kind. It always felt wrong, like being buried alive, and this one had an extra dose of ominous atmosphere about it as they moved into it, preparing to assault a location believed to be the HQ in which POTUS was holed up. His commander-in-chief; make that his *former* commander-in-chief. How in all hell did something like this happen in the USA? The sandbox? Sure. Some other third-world hovel of a country? Routine for those fuckers. But here, at home? It didn't seem possible, yet here he was, with orders to fire on fellow Americans if need be. Fucking nightmare, but the mission was what the mission was.

They proceeded carefully, watching for any sign of light or activity ahead. He rubbed his trigger finger on the trigger guard of his HK MP5 and felt with his thumb to verify his safety was in the FIRE position. He did it so much it had long ago morphed from a verification routine into a muscle-memory tick. He and one other member of the team carried the same submachine gun. Four carried M4 carbines. One was equipped with the M14 Designated Marksman Rifle (DMR) in case there was a need for longer-range coverage. The final man had an M249 light machine gun hanging on a strap. All wore holstered Beretta 9mm sidearms.

Once they moved out of the pit, he encountered a round steel platform with a pair of rails on it. Looked like it was built to rotate and point some kind of light-railed vehicle back in the other direction, its rails meeting up perfectly with a pair of rails disappearing into the tunnel ahead. Walking two abreast, he and his team moved past the platform into the tunnel that would lead them to what was supposed to be some old doomsday facility. He thought about the scenes at the end of *Terminator 3* and wondered if it would be anything like that. The third movie sucked ass compared to the first two, but he still loved it.

He rubbed the outside of the trigger guard. Caressed the safety. Hoped like a mother that he wouldn't have to actually fucking shoot at another American.

COG CITY

"QUICK," Harrow said to Sadie. "Find out if we have control over some kind of barrier in the tunnel." She sat at a workstation while he stood just behind and to her right. He could feel the tension in the command center, the air charged with concentration and nerves. His daughter's fingers danced on the keyboard. For the thousandth time, he questioned his decision to have involved both his girls in this operation. You could remind yourself all you liked that it was supposed to be just like being in charge of other personnel, all of whom had their own families, friends, or both who cared about them. But it wasn't. It just wasn't.

He looked down at Sadie's monitor as she cycled through screen after screen, some filled with arcane text, others showing graphics whipping by. She stopped on a screen that showed a skeletal mechanical drawing of what looked like a section of tunnel.

"Got it," she said.

Harrow leaned in for a closer look. The drawing depicted a thick door retracted into a channel in the ceiling of the tunnel. "Can we control it?"

"Working on that." She squinted at the screen. Scribbled something on a Post-it pad with a pencil. Lifted the little paper and stuck it to the bezel of her monitor and started plowing through screens again.

Hurry, Sadie, he thought. *Hurry.*

DAY 12
6:29 Pm Central

COG-TO-CHEYENNE TUNNEL

WE CONTINUED our slow drive forward on the tracks, the electric motor of the cart near silent, the dominant sounds consisting of our own breathing and the metallic whisper of small steel wheels on steel tracks. My senses were heightened, almost vibrating my mind as adrenaline continued to surge into my bloodstream. Battle. Fight-or-flight. The feel of being *alive,* so real and so maxed out.

Only this wasn't some mountain tunnel leading into some cave situated in some God-forsaken hemorrhoid of the earth. This was the homeland. My homeland. This wasn't supposed to happen. Not here. Then I thought about all the countries and empires that had come and gone through the ages. Knew that fighting men in those earlier times had experienced the same thoughts. The sudden shock of realization that what they thought was permanent and invincible was really fleeting, a blink in the chasm of time. Built by mankind. Brought down by mankind.

I glanced over at Sol. Had a *déjà vu* moment of us driving in some piece-of-shit car on a road that cut through a dust-filled land as we motored toward some dusty-ass village without a name. His face was a mask beneath his NVG, so fixed and devoid of emotion that it could've been a machine. I wondered if he felt the same tingly awareness of peaked senses that I did. Or did he coldly process his surroundings like a computer? The right moment to talk to him about that had never arrived. Wasn't arriving now.

Forward. A hundred yards past the newly discovered steel gate, we started setting our obstacles. If at all possible, we wanted to stop the incoming guys, not shoot them. We were on opposing sides at the moment but these were Americans, not depraved jihadis. The first trap was simple; we unspooled what felt like a mile of concertina wire and turned it into a jumbled mass of sharp points about twenty feet deep. It would at least slow them down.

Immediately on our side of the concertina field, we set canisters of tear gas that would deploy when the inbound guys triggered a tiny motion detector we planted along one wall. This gear was handy, tech-rich but simple. We had a good supply of the motion detectors and they could be paired to any of the defensive measures we put in place. They emitted no light-based beam that could be detected via natural eye or NVG and we were varying their placement to add a layer of unpredictability.

The thought niggling at the back of my mind was: *We can only delay them so long. Then what?* No time to dwell on that, so we kept working. We started setting up our final obstacle field just on the Cheyenne side of the gate and it was a doozy. I thought I could hear quiet movement in the distance of the tunnel now. We had to hurry.

DAY 12

6:38 Pm Central

COG CITY

"GOT IT!" Sadie said. Harrow looked over her shoulder as she entered lines of code in a window that looked to him like something from an eighties-era computer. "Call Sam, see if they can watch to see if it works when I enter the final command."

Harrow picked up a handheld radio from the desk. "Uncle, DoomDaddy."

Sam's voice came through the handheld. "Go ahead, DoomDaddy."

"Are you near the gate?"

"Roger that. Setting up the final obstacle field just beyond it."

"We may have a way to lower it. Need you to let us know whether or not it works."

"Standing by. Execute when ready."

Harrow looked to Sadie and nodded. *Please work.* Sadie hit the enter key.

Sam responded instantly, "Whoa whoa!"

"What's wrong? Is it working?"

"It is, but it's squealing and grating enough to wake up people in Denver. Hold fast."

DAY 12
6:39 Pm Central

COG-TO-CHEYENNE TUNNEL

THE GATE STARTED MOVING DOWN with a melee of sounds that the inbounds would surely hear if it kept going. We needed every scintilla of surprise we could manage. "Whoa whoa!" I said to Harrow on the radio.

"What's wrong? Is it working?"

"It is, but it's squealing and grating enough to wake people in Denver. Hold fast."

In a stroke of either luck or preparatory genius, we had brought a can of WD-40 along and used it on the wheels of the railed cart to make it as quiet as possible. I grabbed the can and doused the channels on the walls that the gate would ride down, then stuck its little straw nozzle into the button and aimed it up at every surface of the mechanism that I could reach.

I touched my throat mic. "Let's try that again, DoomDaddy." The gate started moving downward again. It wasn't quiet by any measure, but it was better. "We can live with that. Wait for my signal to finish closing it."

"Copy that. Standing by," Harrow said.

Sol and I put the last of our defensive measures in place and armed them, then stepped back onto the COG side of the gate. I pulled a small tablet from a pocket and powered it up. Launched the surveillance software. Verified that the cameras we'd hidden in the tunnel were transmitting. That done, I radioed Harrow and said, "DoomDaddy, drop the gate."

DAY 12

6:39 Pm Central

CHEYENNE-TO-COG TUNNEL

THE MARINE SERGEANT leading the FAST team squinted in his NVG as they crept forward in the tunnel, trying to make out what he was seeing ahead. The IR light projected ahead of them by the illuminators on their goggles was reflecting off something metallic and irregular. As they drew closer, it became obvious what it was. The cocksuckers had laid razor wire in their path.

He held up a fist and the team froze. He looked for the Marine who was carrying their breach tools. Found him. Motioned him forward. The sergeant whispered, "Get the cutters out and clear this bullshit." Checked his watch.

While the Marine cut the wire, two others collected the loose strands, coiled them as best they could, and moved them to the tunnel ground they had already covered. When they'd established a passable route through the center of the mess, the sergeant looked at his watch. Eight minutes. *Cocksuckers.*

He signaled for the team to resume their trek and they were

moving forward again. As soon as he and the man beside him moved past the end of the razor wire, he heard four small detonations. *POP-POP-POP-POP.* He recognized the sound immediately. *Motherfucking tear gas!* They were completely unprepared for it. No masks. The gas fogged the air and assaulted them. He looked for the canisters. Two in front of them. Two back at the far end of the wire field. The wicked shit was thick as soup.

His eyes were on fire. Lungs burning. He started coughing, gagging, trying to fight his reflexes. He looked behind him and saw the rest of the team in the same predicament. Someone retched. He said, "Fall back!"

The man on the opposite end of their formation, the Marine who had been bringing up the rear, stumbled and fell into the tangle of razor wire to his right. The sergeant heard him say "*Shit!*" in a hiss. He'd fallen face-first into the wire, all the way to prone, his legs blocking the center aisle they'd cut through the wire. The next man in line tripped over the legs. They were all flipping their goggles up, trying to get at their eyes in vain attempts to find relief by rubbing them. In addition to being blinded by the gas, they now operated in pure darkness.

The sergeant heard another curse, then another, as more men got tangled in the wire. This was a clusterfuck in the first degree. At that moment, he didn't feel the hesitance he'd felt earlier with regard to attacking fellow Americans. If he could get at the cocksuckers right now, he'd kick their asses proper.

DAY 12
6:48 Pm Central

COG-TO-CHEYENNE TUNNEL

WE STOOD on the COG side of the gate with our NVGs flipped up and watched the slab of steel as it slid down in its channels. As its bottom edge grew closer, I saw that it had a pair of notches that would fit over the rails on which the cart rode. When it was perhaps a foot above the floor of the tunnel, a nub affixed to the channel on the right wall tripped a small lever on the edge of the gate and something folded down from the backside of the gate with a *clunk.*

I knelt and pointed a red-light penlight at it. It was a seal that looked to be made out of the same type of material as fire hoses. In fact, it looked a lot like a fire hose except for the rail-notches that matched those on the gate itself. When the gate hit bottom, the seal flattened out along the floor of the tunnel and around the rails.

Leaning close to Sol, I said, "Let's see if we can find any kind of locking mechanism." It only took a minute to realize there was none. I touched my throat mic. "DoomDaddy, Uncle. You guys see any way to lock the gate from your end?"

"Affirmative, Uncle. Is the gate in place? You men on our side of it?"

"Roger that. Make it so."

A mechanical sound began immediately above our heads. We looked up, trying to see what was happening but the mechanism was obviously nestled into a space in the rock ceiling of the tunnel, hidden from sight. After about fifteen seconds of grinding and squealing, a couple loud metallic *clanks* sounded with enough force that we felt the impact on the narrow crossties beneath our feet.

"Should be secure," Harrow's voice said in my earbud.

"Looks that way, DoomDaddy. Can you check the feeds on the cameras we planted?"

"Hold one." A minute passed. Then two. Three. Finally, Harrow said, "Negative on the cameras, Uncle."

I started to insist they double-check a list of settings, then stopped myself as I stared at the heavy steel gate in front of us. "Roger," I said. "It's the gate, a blessing and a curse. Unexpected serious obstacle for our invaders, but it's blocking our wireless cameras and leaving us blind for the other side."

Without warning, I heard a subdued *POP-POP-POP-POP* from the other side of the gate. Sol winked at me and said, "Our guests have reached our accommodations."

DAY 12

7:10 Pm Central

CHEYENNE-TO-COG TUNNEL

THE FAST TEAM sergeant looked around at his team. They'd retreated a hundred yards and waited for the gas to clear. The men looked like hell with their swollen-rimmed bloodshot eyes and splotched faces, but he judged them fit to resume their advance. He circled a finger in the air and the unit headed forward again.

When they reached the point of their previous forward progress, he held a fist in the air. There was something else ahead and he decided a clear look at it was worth the risk of light. After flipping up his NVG, he touched a rubberized pad on the grip of his MP5, switching on a tactical LED flashlight mounted beneath the barrel. He played the bright beam of light slowly across what lay ahead.

He felt certain they'd tripped some kind of motion sensor that had activated the tear gas. After killing the flashlight, he flipped his NVG back down, slid a tiny switch on the side of the NVG to activate a mode that would show light from nearly any spectrum known to man, and pulled a small aerosol can from his belt. He sprayed it generously, creating a mist that should reveal the presence of any kind of laser beam or other light emission that was creating an invisible field for them to trip. He saw nothing. Switched back to visible light and instructed his men to do likewise.

What lay ahead looked like the end of the road; a pile of garbage bags ran the width of the tunnel. Beyond the pile, which was four or five feet high, was a rusty steel wall. He retrieved and unrolled a laminated map of the tunnel, studied it for a moment. Pointed at the metal wall beyond the garbage. "That's not supposed to be there. Let's move that shit and see what we can tell about it."

Four men from the center of group moved up. The sergeant and his fellow point-man watched, while their two-man rear guard kept an eye on their six. The four slung their rifles and spread out to move the mass of garbage bags out of the way. When the first man touched a garbage bag, the sergeant heard a tight _whooooosh_ sound from the pile. He only had time to think _Cocksuckers!_ before the four canisters hidden in the garbage pile did their job.

The canisters used their charges of compressed air to fire like little cannons, each one delivering a cylindrical projectile four inches in diameter and eight in length. As soon as a projectile cleared the barrel of the cannon, it did its own work via a small mechanical apparatus at its core that expanded the tightly packed cylinder into a flat round net that spanned eight feet.

The cannons, tripped by a simple ribbon laid out beneath the supposed bags of garbage to detect the slightest change in pressure along its length, were set to fire in a fast sequential order. The first one was aimed to deliver its bitch of a net about twenty feet out. The second, fifteen feet. Third, ten. Fourth, five. The result was a series of four black nets dropping onto the team within two seconds.

Although the sergeant and his men had actually trained with nets similar to these, along with host of other bullshit non-lethal weaponry, he'd never encountered ones like these. Hell, he didn't even know ones like these existed. The moment a net fell over something, a circuit switched off the trickle of battery power running throughout the structure of the net. When that current was removed, the fine wire woven throughout the net reverted to its non-powered state and collapsed the net in on whatever it had snared.

In this case, the nets had caught seven of his eight men. The one that dropped nearest to the garbage bags fell across him and the man next to him, then instantly cinched itself around them, drawing them tightly together. He thought about vacuum-packed meat as the two of them toppled forward and landed hard on the rock floor. Neither of them could move as they lay there tangled together. The sergeant yelled, "Anybody still free?"

One voice answered. "Me, sir!"

"Double-time back and get somebody down here to get us out of this bullshit!"

DAY 12
7:22 Pm Central

CHEYENNE MOUNTAIN

HARBUCK LOOKED over the edge of the pit as the Marine climbed the ladder. When he reached the top, the Marine said between breaths, "Sir, we require assistance."

"Explain."

"Some kind of nets. Everyone else trapped in them. Never seen anything like them, sir."

Harbuck bowed his head. Massaged his temples with his index fingers. *Damn you, Sam. I know you're behind this. I feel you down there.* He looked back at the Marine and nodded. "We'll get someone down there." He then raised a radio to his lips and keyed the transmit button. "Team two, you have formidable adversaries inside. Be vigilant. Execute."

DAY 12

7:23 Pm Central

COG-TO-CHEYENNE TUNNEL

WE'D BEEN COOLING our heels for a few minutes, frequently pressing our ears to the massive steel gate in an effort to hear what was going on beyond it. We heard nothing for quite a while, but faintly picked up the commotion that told us our inbounds had encountered the net cannons.

In my ear, Harrow said, "Uncle, how much faith do you have in the gate?"

I glanced over at Sol, who shrugged. I said, "It'll take them some time to get out of the final countermeasures. Once that's done, unless they have some way to electrically raise it, they're not coming through the gate for a long while. Looks to be six inches of solid steel." I heard Harrow talking to someone off-radio.

He said, "I'm told they can't raise it."

"How do we know that? Remember, they have all our blueprints and other resources from the compromise."

Sadie's voice in my ear: "Even if they find the routine to control the gate, it won't matter. I set a password on it that they're not gonna crack this century."

I said, "If that's accurate, I think we're secure from this route for hours at a minimum."

Harrow was back. "Good, because the cameras at the alternate entrance show what looks like a FAST Marine team sniffing around outside it."

"That makes no sense," I said. "Nothing about the Bat Cave was in the blueprints, right?"

"Bat Cave?"

"Nickname I—"

"Never mind," Harrow said. "Correct. The tunnel that leads to that facility is on the original blueprints but it dead-ends inside the mountain. My contractors opened the final hundred feet of the tunnel and built the facility, the *Bat Cave*. I intentionally destroyed any documentation of it. Doesn't matter now. Get your asses over there."

DAY 12
7:37 Pm Central

ALTERNATE ENTRANCE, AKA BAT CAVE

I LOOKED at the surveillance feeds Harrow had routed to our tactical tablets. "Eight-man team," I said to Sol, my voice echoing around the large space of the Bat Cave. "Wonder if that's what came at us from the other direction?"

He shrugged. "They haven't found the entrance."

"Is there a way to open it from the outside?" I said, thinking about the way Sol had opened it using a military-looking remote control unit when we came back in from our trip a night or two ago. In our night approach, I hadn't been able to see the door at all until it started lowering. Its camouflage made it look like just another part of the grassy slope out there.

"There's a crank that will lower it, but it's well hidden. I doubt they'll find it."

"What's the construction of the door?"

Sol shook his head. "Pretty much a standard hangar door, sheet metal behind the false front."

"Something they can cut through easily enough," I said.

"Yeah."

We had initially responded in the other end of the tunnel in the heat of the moment. We'd gotten lucky when we found the blast door to drop in place. Now here we were at the other end. I chewed my lower lip while I thought through the situation. I touched my throat mic. "DoomDaddy, Uncle."

"Copy, Uncle," Harrow said in my ear.

"General, it's only a matter of time until they find the door and force their way in. We can play the countermeasure game inside the tunnel again, but there's no blast door to lower on this end of things. We can slow them down but eventually they'll get through our tricks. What are the rules of engagement once that happens? Do you really want us to start shooting US Marines?"

No answer.

"DoomDaddy?"

"Hold one."

I waited. A couple minutes later, Harrow was back. "Sit tight, Uncle. I'm on the way."

NBS NEWS STUDIOS
NEW YORK CITY

BRYCE ZACKER, president of NBS News, stood looking out the glass wall of his 65th-floor office that looked out over Midtown Manhattan. Behind him, the speakerphone on his desk chattered: "Look, Bryce, I'm doing all I can. You did see what happened last night, right?"

"Senator, my give-a-fuck tank is on dead empty. I don't give one shit what you're going through. I've donated enough to your bullshit campaigns to own your ass for the rest of your life, not to mention how my network has protected you more times than I can count. You get this fixed or I'll see to it that your career is *over.*"

The senior senator from New York went silent for a moment, then in a low, calm voice, said, "My *career* is already over. You know the one good thing about that? I don't have to put up with pompous douchebags like you anymore. Goodbye, Bryce."

The phone went dead. Zacker turned, walked the twenty feet from the window to his desk, which was made of some burled rainforest wood he couldn't remember the name of, and picked up the phone. He yanked its cord loose, then hurled it as hard as he could at the man-sized fireplace on the far wall. It fell short and came to rest leaning against the head of his bearskin rug, the mouth of the beast fixed open like it was charging him.

If he could just get the network back on the air, he and his colleagues at the other networks could go a long way toward correcting this fucking disaster. They'd been shaping the public mind for a very long time and they could do it again, but this bullshit state of emergency rendered that impossible. Neither he nor anybody else could broadcast a damned thing as long as that asshole Cartwright kept the news system commandeered with his emergency-powers bull-shit. They'd been locked out of the airwaves, cable, satellites, hell, even their online sites. All of them were running that bullshit Emergency Broadcast System junk twenty-four hours a day. Somebody needed to take that fucker completely off the board before he ruined everything Zacker had spent fifty years building.

Unfortunately, he didn't have any presidential assassins in his contact list. He did, however, still have his personal Twitter account. With a fuckload of followers, too. Yes indeed, he did.

DAY 12
7:55 Pm Central

CHEYENNE MOUNTAIN

HARBUCK KEYED the handheld radio and brought it to his mouth again. "Say again, Team Two?"

"I repeat, the door is opening, and it's nothing we've done."

DAY 12

7:56 Pm Central

ALTERNATE ENTRANCE TO COG CITY, AKA BAT CAVE

I WAITED as the big hangar door crept up, its bottom flipping outward while its top tilted and slid back inside the Bat Cave. I looked to President Cartwright one more time and said, "You sure about this, sir?"

He placed a hand on my shoulder, squeezed, and nodded his head. "It's the only way to nip this activity in the bud. You come with me," he said.

I nodded and we started walking. Wilson stood at the right side of the door, one of the high-end cameras from "the show" held on his shoulder. The rising door had already created a space of about ten feet between its bottom edge and the floor. Outside, a winter sun was settling into the western sky in a blazing portrait of a thousand shades of pink and orange.

Twenty feet beyond the door, eight Marines stood abreast, weapons raised. We kept walking. As the Marines recognized the president, they began looking back and forth between him and the Marine who stood slightly forward of the other seven. I wore my Kimber sidearm and an

M4 carbine on a sling but my hands were empty. I hoped like hell the president knew what he was doing.

When we were within six feet of the obvious leader of the team of Marines, the president stopped and I did likewise. He locked eyes with the leader and said, "What's your name, Marine?"

The Marine snapped into a more upright posture but didn't lower his weapon. "Sergeant Crumpton, sir. Bob Crumpton."

"Is this how you greet your commander-in-chief, Sergeant Crumpton?" Cartwright swept his hand across in a gesture encompassing the entire team of Marines. Their faces were filled with nerves. All of them, and despite the coolness of the late, late afternoon, several were visibly sweating, fidgeting.

Crumpton said, "I, well, sir, I've been informed by my superiors that you are no longer the commander-in-chief."

"Which superiors, Marine?" Cartwright's voice was strong, loud.

"Colonel Harper, sir, and General Harbuck." In contrast to the president, the sergeant's voice was dwindling in confidence.

The president stepped forward, to within a foot of the sergeant. When he spoke again, he sounded like the gunny sergeant I knew he had once been before transitioning into special ops. "And tell me, *Sergeant* Crumpton, which one of those is your commander-in-chief? Is it Colonel Harper?"

Two of the other Marines actually took a step backward, eyes wide. I saw a sheen of sweat beading on Crumpton's forehead. "No, sir."

"I can't hear you, Marine!"

"Sir, no sir!"

"Then it must be General Harbuck who's your commander-in-chief now, right?"

"Sir, no sir!"

"Since the vice president is in custody for attempting to assassinate me, perhaps you view the senile, alcoholic Speaker of the House as your commander-in-chief?"

"Sir, no sir!"

"Then by all means, Sergeant, I want you to tell me right this second, who the hell *is* your commander-in-chief?"

Crumpton's Adam's apple bobbed. Once. Twice. His lips parted, then closed. Finally, he went ramrod straight and snapped off a perfect salute. "You are, sir!"

8:08 Pm Central

COG CITY

ONCE THE PRESIDENT's pow-wow with the Marines played out and we'd moved back inside COG CITY, I reminded Harrow and the president that I still needed to brief them on what I'd learned from VP Houghton during my enhanced interrogation. The president said he needed thirty minutes to make some urgent calls before the briefing, so I left Sol standing guard outside the presidential quarters and headed to the command center to check Sheila's progress researching the data on the phones I'd given her.

When she saw me enter the room, she stood and excitedly gestured me over. When I got to her workstation, she said, "Your forensic app crashed, started giving me a 'no dongle found' error. Good news is, I'd already exported the histories from all three phones into a spreadsheet. Look what I found." She pointed to her screen and I leaned in to look as she started explaining the connections she'd found between Secret Service Agent Laura Drew's "mystery phone" and the VP's phone. She couldn't have known that I already knew of their connection, so I let her continue rather than dampen her enthusiasm.

"Good work," I said. "Anything deeper turn up with the NSA tools?"

"Not really. Hey, you mind if I take a break? I'm hungry."

"No problem."

She grabbed her purse and headed out. I dropped into the vacated seat at the workstation. Looked over to my laptop where the forensic app still showed its dongle error. I removed the dongle, which is just a USB stick that looks like a flash drive but is really a license that you need in order to run a protected app. Then I cleared the error message and closed the app. Re-launched it. Same error. I pulled the dongle again, looked at it. It had a hairline crack in the plastic. Odd.

I reached under the workstation and grabbed my laptop bag. Unzipped its outer pocket and retrieved my spare dongle. It was expensive to maintain two licenses to the absurdly priced software but I'd had a case a couple months ago in which I needed to process a pile of phones in a hurry and the job had justified the expense of the second dongle. I'd let one of the dongles expire when it was time to renew the license.

After plugging in the spare, I ran the software and again and it opened without issue. I waited for it to load the most recent dataset and eventually its screen populated with the three phones. I clicked over to the TIMELINE screen and browsed to the past few days. Scrolled through the list, correlating activity in my mind as I watched the screen. I saw an entry and stopped scrolling. Looked closer. Leaned to the right and looked at the same date and time on the spreadsheet Sheila had left open on the workstation. Scrolled some more. Cross-checked another entry.

I rolled my chair to the right, squaring up in front of the workstation again. Minimized the spreadsheet and loaded the browser with the NSA tools. Looked back over to my laptop for a number. Entered that number into the NSA system. Started the search. Watched the results populate the screen. Scrolled through them. Leaned back. Chewed my bottom lip, processed what I was seeing. Scrolled up to another date and time of interest. Wheeled left to my laptop. Pulled up the same date and time.

Clicked through to another NSA screen. Entered a name. Scrolled through the results. Entered another and looked through those results. Did some more names. Lather. Rinse. Repeat.

Then I jumped up and left the room at a run.

DAY 12

9:15 Pm Eastern

TWITTER
GLOBAL

1/3 What's going on in our country is unconstitutional! This "president" has no right to do these things and must be stopped!

2/3 I hereby call on the PEOPLE to rise up and stop this tyrant! Do you really think the members of our armed services support this? NO! Do you think they will shoot you for standing up? NO!

3/3 As the president of NBS News, I will lead the charge in taking this country back! Meet me at 43rd and Broadway tomorrow and noon! Spread the word!

AFTER COMPOSING HIS TWITTER THREAD, Zacker felt better. Much better. He was a leader, after all. Tomorrow the world would begin to understand that. He closed his laptop, pulled his cell phone from his pocket, and stood at the window looking out over his city while he started calling employees, asking—better, telling—no, demanding—that they be at tomorrow's protest.

When he'd called all his top people and instructed them to call all their people, he slid his phone back into his pocket, gazed out at the world's most magnificent city, and said, "Shit's about to get *real*, assholes."

DAY 12

8:33 Pm Central

COG CITY

As I RAN, the pieces of the puzzle continued to slide across the board and click into place. All of them, everything that had eluded me from the very beginning. I took the stairs down to the presidential quarters three steps at a time, the steel steps and frame vibrating and echoing in the concrete chamber. When I finally reached the bottom, I burst into the complex, sprinted through the "courtroom/TV set" where the "televised trial" had taken place, then slammed the door open to the residence.

When I stepped through the door, I almost tripped over Sol on the floor. He lay on his back, eyes open and glassy, a pool of blood spreading beneath his head. He was conscious, but barely. An ugly purple hole with scorching around the edges pierced his left cheek. An inch higher and it would've hit his brain. *Damn it!* His gun was nowhere near him.

General Harrow was getting up from the floor, a gash at the top of his forehead streaming blood down his face. He wobbled and fell back onto his butt, reached up to his head, drew his hand down and looked at the blood there with glazed, confused eyes.

Sheila was six feet away from him, holding a snow globe smeared with blood. The globe contained a kitschy bust of JFK. Behind her, on the other side of what passed for the Resolute Desk in this place, VP Houghton stood behind President Cartwright, a gun in her left hand held against his left temple.

"You two girls have been very bad," I said. "Took me a while, but I figured it out." I pointed at Sheila. "You screwed up by damaging the dongle. I had a spare. And you screwed up even worse by letting her out of her cell." I pointed at the VP.

Sheila shrugged.

"I quickly spotted the differences between what the forensic app showed and what you had in your spreadsheet. The moment I saw it, I knew you were the mole, had been the mole all along."

She shrugged again. I said, "Then I ran *your* phone number through the NSA tools. Saw that it wasn't your mother you were talking to in the restaurant that night in New York. You were talking to Pitt. Had been talking to him all along, keeping him updated on all the details.

"At first that made no sense. We were all on the same team, or so I thought. And hell, Sheila, *you're* the one who told me Pitt was really acting alone, that BAM had been officially shut down. Why decide to tell me once the shit hit the fan?"

"I didn't know," she said. "I worked for him in the same little office I always had. Thought it was the same thing. When I found out that he was, well, rogue, and the FBI had gotten involved, I decided you deserved to know. I didn't want you going to jail because of something my dad had you doing."

I mulled that over, then shifted gears. "Back to tonight's discoveries. Instead of running just phone numbers through NSA, I started running names. That's when it *really* started coming together for me."

I kept talking, walking slowly toward Sheila as I raised my voice, became more animated. "Imagine my surprise when I saw that Pitt's real name, something I'd never had occasion to look for, happened to match your maiden name: Pittman."

JERRY HATCHETT

She drew a deep breath at that. I was six feet from her. "Pitt was your father. Guess who else had that same maiden name?"

That big breath Sheila had taken came out in a deflating sigh. Houghton said, "That's close enough, Flatt." I glanced at her and saw her press the barrel of her gun harder into POTUS's temple. He looked stoic, especially for a man who'd been targeted by his VP not once, but two times in as many days.

I stopped moving. Looked momentarily to my right, saw that Harrow's eyes were clearing. Looked back to Sheila. "Yeah. I know. Know why Pitt wanted me to focus on the kidnappings and not the attacks on the media. It's because the two of you were behind the media attacks. It was your sister who was killed by the Antifa goons in Portland two years ago. Not just her, but her child, hell, even her dog.

"And the media covered for the pieces of shit who do things like that, whose fellow pieces of shit have been wreaking havoc around the country for years. It pissed you and your father off, but poor Bruce Berringer, your brother-in-law, it *devastated* him, didn't it? Destroyed the man's life to lose his entire family like that. So one of you went to him, told him you'd supply him with the cash, the training, to get payback on the media. Which one was it?"

Sheila said, very quietly, "Dad."

I nodded. "Was Bruce supposed to kill himself? In that suicide bombing of the Portland newspaper."

She shook her head, tears streaming down her face now.

"That's what I figured. He was already a destroyed man. Found out that killing didn't make him feel better. It just finished *him* off and he couldn't take it anymore."

"I don't know," she said.

Houghton's head jerked to her left. I glanced right and saw Harrow pushing himself up off the floor, then falling back into an ass-ugly wingback chair that sat nearby. Houghton's eyes turned back to me. Sheila's chin was on her chest, her shoulders shaking in little jerks.

I turned my attention to Houghton. Pointed a finger. "You," I said, "are just a run-of-the-mill politician now. You wanted the power of the presidency."

"There's *nothing* run-of-the-mill about me, Flatt. I went through BUDS. All the way. Did you? I fought for my country. Did you?"

"As a matter of fact," I said, "I've done things for my country you can't possibly imagine, but that's irrelevant. Doesn't matter what you *were*. It matters what you *are*, which is just one more power-hungry DC cockroach. It was supposed to be clean, wasn't it? You'd have some CIA goon kill POTUS and you'd move into the West Wing. But his speech"—I pointed at Cartwright—"caught you flat-footed."

"What I don't know is how you recruited Laura Drew to try to kill him. A Secret Service agent who'd risen to the pinnacle of the organization, the head of the presidential protection detail. How'd you pull that off? Get someone like her to sacrifice herself? Some kind of leverage? Threaten her family? What was it?"

Houghton said, "Fuck you."

"Whatever," I said. "Doesn't matter how. It failed when I dropped her right there on the dais in front of the world." Then I started laughing and pointing at her.

"What the hell is wrong with you?" Houghton said.

"You—" I bent over in laughter. Turned a half-step to the right as I raised back up. "—thought you were going to what—kill the president of the United Damn States *in the Oval Office* and get away with it?" More laughing. Watching Harrow slip forward in the chair through my peripheral vision. I made another slight rotation to my right as I straightened up, keeping my head turned toward Houghton.

"I wasn't there to kill him, you dumb-ass. I was there to make him see reason. You fucked that up. Scared him on the phone. He attacked me and I responded. Instinct."

"Riiiight," I said. "You have some kind of leverage on him, too? Some gift from the CIA? Something special to make him 'see reason'?"

"One more time," she said. "Fuck you. The good part? No one will ever know what happened in *this room*."

I ignored her. Turned back to Sheila. "Why in the world would you help her by ratting us out, sending those plans to Harbuck? Don't forget that I rescued *you* from Houston."

Sheila shook her head. "Jesus, Sam. Can't you see how crazy all this is? Splitting the country? I did what Dad asked me to do."

I didn't expect that. "When did you talk to your father?"

"Called him from Houston with a burner. After you told me the jet was on the way to pick me up."

"And he knew about the plan, the speech?"

Sheila nodded. "Had the plans to this place. Sent them to me. Told me to use the burner and send them to Harbuck. Said you'd gone rogue, were joining a coup."

Two moles. That didn't fit but it could wait. My peripheral vision told me Harrow was ready. Feet slipped back a little under the chair, heels up, poised on the balls of his feet, his hands gripping the front of the arms on the wingback.

Time to play my hole card. I said to Houghton, "Just one more question: Why'd you have Pitt killed? That crusty old intel guy know too much? What was it?"

Sheila's head whipped toward Houghton. "What?!"

I gave the tiniest nod and Harrow sprang from the chair. As Houghton pivoted the gun toward him, I pulled the Kimber from my right hip. Brought it up, her rotating head in my sights the moment my gun was extended. The .45 ACP round hit her at an oblique angle just behind the edge of her right eye. Her gun fired at the same moment.

Harrow was falling, but my first instinct was to protect POTUS. I've seen weird things happen with people who should be dead. I ran at the desk, leapt, cleared it and hit Cartwright in an ESPN-highlight-worthy tackle. Houghton lay crumpled on the floor right beside us, the gun she'd obviously taken off Sol still in her open hand.

"Uh, you mind getting off me, Sam?" the president said, his voice muffled with my chest on top of his head.

"Sorry," I said, standing up. I walked to Sheila, who was now sobbing. Took the snow globe from her hand, chucked it across the room, then went to Harrow. I yanked the radio from where it was clipped onto his belt, keyed the transmit button, and shouted, "Medic in the presidential quarters! Now!"

As I waited for them to arrive, I stood there in the adrenalized high of successful action. Successful *violence.* My mind wandered back to what Pitt had said on the day he dragged me into this thing: *It's who you are, Sam. You'll have to admit that someday.* Was this that day?

DAY 13
9:05 Am Central

COG CITY

AFTER I WOKE UP, showered, shaved, and ate breakfast, I found General Harrow, his right arm in a sling, talking to the president in the command center while they watched the video wall.

The president stuck his hand out and I shook it. "Thank you," he said. "Again."

I nodded. "You're welcome, sir."

"You're an extraordinary man, Sam."

I shrugged, no response coming to mind.

He said, "I want you on my team."

"Sorry," I said. "I think this will do it for me and presidential protection. I'm pushing forty, need something a little quieter."

"You misunderstand. I don't want you as protection, at least not physical protection."

"Then what?" I said.

"I'm creating a Department of Technology. New Cabinet position. I want you to run it. Sort of a C-T-O for the country."

"Mr. President, with all due respect, you hardly know me. I—"

"You've been saving my life for days, and I took the liberty of looking up your work history since you left the—well, whatever you left that you were doing for the country." He winked. "You're a tech wizard. Let's put *that* to work, for the country."

"I'm honored that you asked. And I'll think about it."

"Good enough, but don't take too long."

I gestured up at the video wall. "How're things going?"

"Absolute mess," he said, and slapped me on the back. "As we expected. Lots to straighten out, but it will be worth it in the end. By the way, there's a New York asshole named Zacker, runs NBS News. Planning some march up in the city today, noon Eastern."

"Okay?" I said, wondering what that had to do with me.

He hooked a thumb back toward the NSA workstation. "You mind taking a look, see if there's anything we can use to persuade him to tone it down?"

I drew a breath to unload on him for asking such a thing, but thought better of it. Instead, I said, "Something you should know, Mr. President."

"What's that?"

"*If* I were to take the job, and I'm not saying I will, but *if* I did, one of the first things I'd do would be to dismantle the ability to spy on our own citizens. Completely. What would you say to that?"

Now he looked like he was about to blast me, but he likewise held off and instead broke into a smile. "If you were TechSec, that would be your decision."

"Would I have your word on that?"

He extended his hand. "You would."

I shook it.

He said, "I guess your answer is no on Zacker? It really is for the good of the country to quell these little tantrums as best we can while we put out bigger fires. Temporarily. We're not going to run a police state. We're just at a critical moment."

"I won't use the NSA tool to spy on him, but I'll respond to him. You a poker player?"

"Love the game," he said.

TWITTER
GLOBAL

1/3 Mr. Zacker, you don't know me but I'm part of the team that put on the broadcast a couple nights ago.

2/3 If you thought Rob Acoma's on-air confessions were rough for your network, you should hear what he had to say about YOU off-camera.

3/3 You do what you feel is best at noon. I'll do what I think is best after that. Have a great day. BTW, FAKE NEWS sucks and its days are numbered.

DAY 13
11:40 Pm Central

COG CITY

AFTER HANGING out in the command center long enough to see that no march or rally ever materialized in New York, I turned to General Harrow. "Give me ten minutes to get there, then come on over to the diner?"

He nodded. I said, "Thank you again for handling this for me."

"My pleasure, Sam." He squeezed my shoulder. "Good luck."

With that, I left.

TEN MINUTES LATER, I was in what had become my favorite booth at the COG CITY DINER, Ally to my right, Abby across the booth. The scowl on Abby's face had softened a bit, but she was still far from being a happy camper, and I had a feeling it was about to get worse.

My heart raced and my pulse pounded in my ears. The little shop-keeper's bell on the front door tinkled and the racing and pounding worsened. I turned and watched General Harrow enter with a teenage boy in tow. We had met for the first time earlier that morning.

They walked to the booth. I stood, placed my arm around the kid, looked first at Abby, then Ally. "Ally, I'd like you to meet Eric Estevez, your brother."

Both Abby's and Ally's eyes were the size of half-dollars. Mouths hung open. Eric looked down at his feet and I noticed he was chewing his bottom lip.

This time I kept my eyes locked on Abby. I said, "It's a long story and I'll explain all of it later." I moved back just enough to be behind Eric and silently mouthed to the booth, "Please."

Ally looked at Eric and said, "Hey." Then she patted the vinyl of the booth seat I'd just vacated. "Come on." He looked up at me and I nodded. He slowly sat down in the booth.

I moved to Abby's side. She scooted over and I sat down beside her. Underneath the table, she pinched my thigh so hard I almost yelped. But I didn't. I smiled at my daughter, then at my son. Looked toward the counter. "Hey Willie, reckon we can get something to eat over here?"

EPILOGUE

THREE DAYS LATER

Noon Central

MONTGOMERY COUNTY, TX

I ENDED the call with Sol and slipped the phone back into my pocket. He had gotten lucky, miraculously so. The bullet punched through his cheek, the bottom of his sinus chamber, then exited the back of the neck, all without hitting anything vital. His surgery had gone well and he was already back in action. He said he was calling from some off-the-grid cabin buried in the Rockies. Sat phone. Wanted to know if it was well and truly untrackable. Given the particular model he had, I told him yes.

Someone in the background kept moaning, or maybe trying to say something. When I asked Sol about it, he only said, "Cockroach. Big one."

I let that go, but I'd heard from Harrow that Robert Hecht had mysteriously vanished from his locked cell. Damn shame.

Abby and Ally had come back to the farm with Eric and me when we left COG CITY. I told them the truth about how I'd fathered a son while married. It was embarrassing to say these things in front of my daughter, but I thought she was old enough to take it and deserved the truth. Most of it, anyway. All my BAM Squad work wasn't overseas. I'd done an undercover stint in which I spent a weekend at a cartel boss's mansion in Mexico, setting up what he believed to be a lucrative new partnership for US distribution of his wares. For Ally's sake, I described it as a special undercover assignment I did for the DEA, which was a little true. The DEA did provide all the intel we needed for the op, but they had nothing to do with the fact that I killed the cartel boss at the end of the weekend and put his head on top of a tiki-torch pole beside his absurd swimming pool. (I didn't share this in front of Ally. Duh.)

From the moment I arrived, a gorgeous young woman in her early twenties had latched onto me. Her name was America Estevez. I politely told her I was married and not interested. She told me she was a gift to me while I was there. Said if I shunned her, her boss would assume she'd done something wrong and punish her. She pointed out one of the servant girls scurrying around who had a scar from the bottom of her left eye down to her lip. It was obvious she'd been a knockout before that happened. I asked if that was what had happened to the scarred girl. America said yes. Begged me to play along. I did, but it was only supposed to be for show.

Except when I got to my room to go to bed my first night there, America was there. In a sexy nightie. She walked up, put her arms around me. I whispered, "I'll play the game around the house but I can't do this."

She whispered back, "Cameras in here. He always watches, likes it. Please. You see what he will do to me."

So I did it. Not to cheat, but to save a young woman from a terrible fate.

Abby exploded. "Oh, I'm sure it was quite the chore for you, but you're such a man of duty, right, Sam?"

"I've just told you the unvarnished truth, Abby. I'm not proud of it, but that's what happened. I'm sorry it happened, but it did. And it's not Eric's fault."

"How long have you known?"

"Couple weeks. I got a document from ICE. He'd shown up at the border and applied for asylum. They run DNA tests now, you know? When his was processed, it matched him to me as a son."

"How'd they have your DNA?"

The truth was that my DNA was on file so my remains could be identified if need be. "Government employee," I said, hoping she'd take the hint that, aside from the undercover job I'd just described, Ally knew nothing of my true job for the government. And didn't need to.

"Oh yeah," she said.

"Anyway, I got bogged down in this case and General Harrow helped me out by sending someone to bring Eric to me. And that's that."

Abby stormed off from the conversation and I didn't try to stop her. I was tired of explaining myself to her. Tired of hanging on hoping we'd put things back together. And just plain old tired from a couple rough weeks.

I still tried to get her to stay until things settled down, but she bolted back to Vegas in a huff. Wanted Ally to go with her. I said no and, to my surprise, so did Ally.

I WALKED out to the barn, where Ally and Eric were bathing Johnny. He had his head held high, his eyes closed in bliss as they scrubbed. When I arrived, he snuffled, bowed his head, and touched his forehead to mine. I said, "I love you too, buddy."

My phone rang. I pulled it from my pocket and looked at the screen for the caller ID. It said WHITE HOUSE 911.

THE END

A WORD TO MY READERS

THANKS so much for reading *Boiling Point!* I owe the many fans of Sam Flatt an apology for taking this long to deliver the second installment in this series. I'm sorry, and it won't happen again. I'm making a commitment to you to deliver new books on a far more timely basis.

IF YOU ENJOYED IT, would you please take the time to leave a rating and review on Amazon or other bookstores and book communities? It means so much. Nothing drives the success of a book in today's environment more than you, the reader, leaving reviews and spreading the word online and in person. Word of mouth is quite literally the lifeblood for authors who don't have mega-dollar marketing budgets behind their work. In the age of the internet and social media, it's *you* who holds the key to my success. Anything you can do to spread the word will be eternally appreciated!

CLICK HERE TO LEAVE A REVIEW ON AMAZON
SUBSCRIBE TO MY NEWSLETTER HERE

Thanks!
Jerry

LET'S CONNECT!

I love staying in touch with readers, exchanging emails and Facebook posts, and generally getting to know each other. Please subscribe to my newsletter to get this ball rolling, then connect with me on social media!

- Subscribe to my non-spammy newsletter
- Like my Facebook page and let's talk
- Follow me on BookBub
- Follow me on Amazon
- Follow me on Goodreads

ALSO BY JERRY HATCHETT

Pawnbroker

Seven Unholy Days

Unallocated Space

Projectionist

www.ingramcontent.com/pod-product-compliance
Lightning Source LLC
Chambersburg PA
CBHW020459260626
47156CB00006B/1793